*Lomita For Ever*

# *Lomita For Ever*

Trevor Eve

This edition first published in 2019

Unbound
6th Floor Mutual House, 70 Conduit Street, London W1S 2GF
www.unbound.com


'How It Seems to Me' by Ursula K Le Guin is reproduced by kind permission of the Estate of Ursula K Le Guin.

ISBN (eBook): 978-1-78965-042-6
ISBN (Paperback): 978-1-78965-041-9

Cover design by Mecob

Printed in Great Britain by CPI Group (UK)

*For Sharon*

# Super Patrons

David Baillie
Stephen Bruce
Adrian Eden
Terence Flanagan
Judith M. Galloway
Dan Kieran
Ewan Lawrie
John Mitchinson
Justin Pollard

*How It Seems To Me*

In the vast abyss before time, self
is not, and soul commingles
with mist, and rock, and light. In time,
soul brings the misty self to be.
Then slow time hardens self to stone
while ever lightening the soul,
till soul can loose its hold of self
and both are free and can return
to vastness and dissolve in light,
the long light after time.

– Ursula K. Le Guin

# *Chapter One*

'So, I think things started to go a little wrong in the womb.'

Everett Millen whispered to himself while staring. Staring at his mother, whose whiteness was turning pink in her swimming costume; a little tight, the fat escaping the restrictions of the one piece bought for a different body.

This was a rare visit to his mother's home. She was asleep, well, more passed out, after lunch, on a yellow garden recliner. The plastic strands were wound round and round in a basket weave to form a springy web. He could see the build-up of sweat where skin met plastic. He went inside to fetch a towel. At least to protect her from the sun.

His mother had always called him Ever.

He has been known forever as Ever.

# *Chapter Two*

He drove out of Palm Springs on Interstate 10.

Hot and dry like a purring cat hanging around his neck: stifling. He liked the heat, but he was allergic to cats. So there was a dissonance between this image and his comfort.

The gas station man, who was of South Asian descent, felt the necessity to inform him, with a natural courtesy, of the correct 'pay first' procedure at American pumps.

Ever knew this anyway, but in a descent of brain fog he was happy, for that brief moment, to have the burden of thought and decision removed from his mind.

Paid and full, the car drove west on the freeway towards the large sprawling mass of human life; organised, but in the way a child might spread building blocks from the centre outwards until the boredom hit and the blocks were just kicked and piled, not really in any order, just piled, without enthusiasm, while waiting for tea.

This was his lot, so get on with it and be positive because, Hindu-style, if you do it well, you might not have to come back.

He let the heat wrap him until the mountains gave way to the alien invasion of the wind turbines, then rolled up the windows and air-conditioned himself. No alien air for him today; besides, he needed to get rid of the cat.

The outlet stores of Cabazon were now behind him, thirty minutes out of the desert; the white gloss shopping bag sat on the passenger seat, the neat folds of his purchase collapsed into a crumple. For the next part of the journey he relished the thought of the suits he had just bought at irresistable knock-down prices. So, mentally dressed in Armani and Gucci, he drove off the interstate and entered the sprawl. He was getting sorted, that would bring some calm, a sliver at least. But he wasn't carrying, yet.

Packing heat, that is.

A gun, that is.

The LA basin was waiting with its lid on; the sun had done its damage to the nitrogens, creating ozone, resulting in the photochemical smog. Eyes burn from PAN – no God of the wild, but peroxyacyl nitrates; breathing becomes harder, buildings form pollutants on their surface; the people spew out their dolly mixture of emotions and, well, everyone wants your blood, and when all the blood is gone, the soul is easy pickings. The Angels have to work hard in their city recovering all those lost souls.

One hundred and ten miles, north-west a bit, towards the middle section, where the wealth increases and the buildings change and the time invested in the environment becomes apparent.

Ever was driving into Beverly Hills. No e at the end of Bev-erl-y. One of the first things he'd learnt about American culture. That, and always be positive, and if someone asks you how you are, don't tell them beyond great. Never say how shitty you really feel.

In Palm Springs, Ever had stayed in a room at The Willows Hotel that had once been inhabited by Albert Einstein, and it was there that he put the proposal to himself.

The connection within his brain that received the proposal interpreted it as a solution, and it seemed less than odd. It seemed completely and refreshingly understandable. He knew why it was, he knew why he was there.

Ever considered himself English, though born in America and ambitious in the very general sense of the word, with a desire, through that ambition, to accomplish whatever he set his mind to. But, to achieve this particular ambition, he just needed to be lifted out by the bored child that had piled the blocks; picked up by the neck and saved. Saved to carry out his purpose.

Out of the sprawl, that to him was everywhere.

Physically, but mostly mentally for him, it was a mass of a mess that seemed, every day, to cover more of him and make the possibility of ever coming up for air more inconceivable. This was obviously the way to do it. That's what he told himself anyway. He was getting a little older now, and quite honestly just pure pissed off at the way nobody seemed to listen.

Energy equals mass, was as far as he could get, in the context of Einstein, but it seemed that the two words had a correlation to what was needed: one to get out of the other. Logic, the last resort of the intellect, the defence system that breaks down all that the imagination can construct. Fuck it, he thought, why not? What else was he going to do? Wait like everybody else? For how long? Until you die, of course, like the people in the sprawl.

No, Einstein was right. Energy equals mass times double chaos.

Sleeping in a hotel spiritually inhabited by Einstein from

days past had had an effect. An inhabitance. A takeover. Mini though it might be.

He had made his decision.

The car pulled into the short drive.

The eighty-year-old baronial studded gates slowly opened on an uneven path and he drove into the underground parking lot. He sat, and sat, contemplating what he had agreed with himself to do. The jazz station 88.1 fuzzed its clarity, as the signal struggled for life under the soil. He had unplugged his own music and now Miles Davis had finally died, God bless him, giving way to an unenthusiastic Frank Sinatra, singing 'What a Swell Party This Is' – a Palm Springs resident whose boredom sometimes leapt out of his singing, killing the desire to listen. He would have done it. He did do it. Sold his soul, or more precisely, sacrificed his soul. Maybe that's what left his singing – maybe his soul just disappeared into the cool desert night; then he would drive back to LA for another fix, replenish his soul and start to sing with genius again.

The plates on the rental were registered to the state of Utah, with a background of the Delicate Arch rock formation. This had instilled in Ever the feeling of being a pioneer, even though he picked the car up in LA. The Wild West plates were now feeling calm, no more wind blasting them up the highway. His shadow crossed the insects, dead on the headlights, as they blinked off on the time delay.

He paused, turned and patted the car before leaving, as if it were a horse.

Dark would bring his doubt, when he had no relation to the rest of the world, nothing to distract him, just surrounded by the black, pushing itself into his clothes and then covering his skin. Dark: he was now getting dark. But he would rise. Rise out of it all, and that was the important thing. Keep on track.

The flight of stairs up to the ground level brought his first awareness of noise: the metal opener inserted in the lock. Unusual, but eminently simple and successful, it allowed him access to the courtyard, then four steps to the Spanish apartment. He opened the door and the faded heat of the day seemed a memory clinging to the curtains across the window. Backpack and white gloss shopping bag were placed inside the door. Lamplight only, a 'no' to the overhead option. Then his eyes fell on his intention. The paper bag containing the medical marijuana that would now take him out of the anxiety state, delaying the paranoia, at least until the morning light when he could handle it a little better. Not a lot better, but somehow the options in life became more apparent, more optimistic, in the day. At least other people seemed to be getting on with it, so there was a hope. A possibility that it was all possible.

His life had become, at this point, a Q&A, with himself and whoever was around to listen.

To satisfy the need, his need. It was real what had happened. It was true. That much was known. What was it in him that drove him to ask the questions all the time, why couldn't he get on with it?

Like everybody else?

But how many other people had decided to do what he was going to do?

Not many, he supposed.

But then it was because he had never felt human, never felt the need to construct like the rest, always waiting for the thing to happen that would take him out of life's systematisation, the process that he was going through.

Life was going to be different for him, from now on, that's what he wanted, why else had he come? And if it wasn't going to be different then he would make it different by his own devices. His own determination. His own action. That defines it: an action, the ability to do an act.

Here he was, living in his own cinematic experience but holding an objective viewer's eye on all his activity. Ever had done this since he was a child, though he didn't know then that everybody else didn't do it; now it was the only way he could turn his life around.

Enter the movie from the left, walk straight in and become him. Grasp the role.

He would welcome the sight of himself in this as yet unwritten movie. At least he hoped he would, and he was prepared, if needed, to involve himself in other people's lives uninvited.

Not to harm but to engage, to connect.

He must watch, observe, and make himself invaluable to this end.

To change his life through another.

A parasitic involvement: an osmotic method of dependency.

Because he had always needed help: this time was no different.

Just a new script.

# *Chapter Three*

Rodeo Drive.

It runs perfectly in whichever way you choose to look at it. No soul, a monument to consumerism, the church for shoppers and watchers. He walked up and down believing himself to be the troubled looking for the troubled with a feeling that he could be the salvation.

Who would he salvage?

It would be a pay-off, a trade for what he had decided. Save one, drop one, like in knitting.

He took a break, a rest if you like, from the long, meandering trek from his apartment along Fountain down onto Santa Monica Boulevard then into the world of the artificial, and cooled himself in the public parking car hotel, two free hours, that eased off Rodeo and cosseted the shiny metal rooms in which the pampered drove themselves around. And there he would have a little smoke. A little of the medical to give himself the cloudy belief that he was doing good.

Sitting next to a 1995 burgundy Jeep Wagoneer, he looked at the plastic wood and thought what a beautifully unnecessary concept of design the car was. Plastic wooden panels to convince no one, so that it existed as a falsehood from the start, in fact, was pleased with itself as a fake. The perfect car for Los Angeles, but the colour was wrong. Burgundy, a solid block, lacking in excitement, a complete non-thriller as a tone. Dulled by the sun, which had varied the intensity of colour in patches that were infinitesimally scratched by the endless washing that is demanded by the LA car; it looked outdated, not oozing enough class to pull off old age, to become a classic.

Then came one, and then another female form, lifted by scalpel-inflicted pulls of skin and muscle to defy the downward drag of the concrete gravity. An attempt to reach perfection, to rise to the heavens where they might exist on the goddess plane, to breathe the rarified air of the beautiful.

One was carrying a Bijan bag, yellow with squiggly script; the knowledge that everything was expensive in the store gave the bag an arrogance to hold its own despite its lack of taste. Another sky-ward-lifted face, carrying three large Barney's black bags; cheaper, maybe, maybe not, but the choice of car proved disappointing. A Lexus. A pale blue Lexus. A colour he had hated going back to the beginning of time. His time, anyway.

A dullness that was smashed.

By a loud Spanish voice, propelling itself into a cell phone with an anger that seemed to have no effect on the old lady she was pushing in a wheelchair towards a large black Suburban that beeped as the lights flashed at the button command of the now-shouting Mexican.

The old lady was left by the side of the car as the phone argument continued, sitting calmly in the wheelchair. A black raven was obscuring her face; the large, black, wraparound glasses that could be for blindness, or just sun terror. They seemed heavy for her delicacy.

He watched, taking a long inhalation on the medical; the wheelchair woman turned, and the look betrayed an assessment that put blindness out of the question. She continued to stare through the Spanish shouts, a smile stretched across the tight landscape with lips that wore red; he envisioned the red oozing into the tiny ravines that ran top and bottom of the chasm. He smiled back, he felt, very slowly, time between them paused, until the play button was pressed by the Mexican, the film started again and the wheelchair was pushed to the back of the car.

The old lady stood now, not looking, and, slowly supporting herself along the side of the car, walked to the right side and rested, while the Mexican listened intently on the cell phone, manipulating the wheelchair into the cavern that had opened up at the back of the black mass of metal. The look came back his way, but the smile had gone; now she just stood staring, and he felt he was waiting in the dock.

Go on then pass the judgement, I am not going anywhere. Really I am not.

The door slammed shut on the other side of the car. No engine started but the immersion in the phone call had obliterated the existence of the waiting lady.

Now, without thinking, he got up and walked towards the stare.

He was entering the film, walking in as an extra.

But he appeared to have lines.

'Can I help you?'

'You're British.'

'Yes, well, English actually.'

'Oh my.'

She said, lingering in the moment.

'Manita will help me in a minute. Do not concern yourself. She has a family issue.'

The offer of information seemed unnecessary and excessive to a stranger.

He didn't wait, but opened the door.

'*Un momento por favor.*'

Came from the driver's side. Not abusive, but firm. Followed by the translation:

'Please, if you don't mind, just a minute.'

He'd got the message first time.

'Manita will come, it's OK. Thank you.'

He returned the large black block into its hole. As the lady had made no effort to climb into the car, he assumed she wanted to allow the phone call its own privacy.

He walked away with the nod of his head, repeating the pattern three times, a nod, then a nod, then another nod, and returned to his position by the Jeep Wagoneer. Pulling hard on the medical as he hunkered down. And she stood, still not looking in his direction. He felt such a sadness for her and a sense of disappointment in the behaviour of the Mexican woman. Money can't buy you love. Money can buy you a big black hearse to be driven around in. What's the difference, alive or dead? Dead or alive.

The driver's side opened to release the sound of Mexican music carrying a relentless joviality as the carer came round to help the patient patient into the car.

She sat first, then her legs were helped and swung to line up with her body. A clear two actions. Doors slammed, the engine started. Not an exciting sound, just a massive sound of solid power. Spreading across the concrete like a sheet. American: like the continent.

The car reversed, the window on the passenger side lowered and the black glasses spoke.

'Can I return the favour?'

Ever had a look of blankness on his face at the question. Had he heard? Yes, he was just not expecting any further acknowledgement of his presence.

'Is this your final destination?'

The humour was evident in her tone.

'No, just a stop on the way.'

'To?'

Again the blank look, which he now understood to be a wave of stoned face.

'Would you like a ride?'

'Thank you.'

Came the unthought-out reply. There seemed no other. He got up from down, and moved towards the black mass. He dropped the smoke and stood, giving her an opportunity for closer appraisal, a chance to change her mind. He wasn't pushing, he didn't want to. She must have approved of the viewing, which he extended, now, without facing her, his foot taking its time to flatten the roach into the concrete.

'Please. Hop in.'

What were her eyes like? And where would he say he was going?

In that order came the thoughts. Occupying his brain to deny a valid and assessed response to her invitation. Those thoughts and the overwhelming desire to hold her in his arms.

With love, and maybe the slightest little bit of lust.

And maybe the result of the marijuana.

The sprinklers on the grass and the magnolia leaves had left a glisten.

That the sun toyed with in its own time. The black mass car pulled into the drive of the large 1950s ranch house on North Oakhurst Drive. One of the few that had not been demolished and turned into a mansion bulging out of the restriction of the perimeter that limited its expanse, like fat surrounded by a belt.

The wood was freshly painted grey, the Mexican was now questioning the old lady about asking the man for tea, and he presumed, as the second part was in Spanish, that maybe there was a stronger opinion about letting him into the car in the first place. The voice dominant, over the now-reduced volume of the music. The explanation was returned in English, from the old lady, that he was from England and that is what they liked at this time of the afternoon. They had sat in silence, apart from the invitation; the lack of questioning struck his chemically calmed brain as just a little strange. He inhaled the smell of leather and the strong scent coming from the passenger. Chanel No 5.

The same scent his mother used to wear.

Not too disturbing.

Well, a bit.

'Help me. Your arm, please. Manita will put the car in the garage.'

Garage came out old American, the same stress on both syllables – English inflection. The rest was American, with just the faintest rounding of the r at the end of car.

Manita drove the black mass back down the driveway to what he assumed was the garage at the side of the house, on Elevado, and disappeared from view. But the journey continued in his head to satisfy his imagination; he wondered just how cross Manita really was.

The big brown front door opened into a big brown panelled hallway, that opened without restriction on to a big brown panelled room, with the garden and pool beyond. All this was seen in one panoramic sweep of eye. The two enormous sofas were covered in white, a soft white linen; save for two standard lamps and a baby grand piano in black, that was all the room was wearing.

He thought that if anyone really played the piano in a room this size they would have a Steinway Concert Grand. The full nine feet. There were no paintings on the panels and no pictures.

He still hadn't seen her eyes but, as he turned, her right arm lifted from his to the black glasses; they obeyed gravity, slipping from her grasp, and she fumbled them to the brown wooden floor. He still couldn't see her eyes, her head having travelled towards the fallen pair.

'I'll get them.'

Seeing him bend to pick them up, she did too, without the noise that often accompanies the old and movement; both heads raised at the same time, then he saw her eyes and she looked into his.

'Thank you.'

Came from below her eyes and they were blue. A dark blue, the whites still clear and strong, despite the age that burdened her.

'Shall we have our tea now?'

'Thank you. Please.'

Politesse times two; the wrong way round. A door slammed in another space beyond them. Manita returning from the garage access at the back of the house.

'Manita. Tea please, if you don't mind.'

A surprising strength carried the voice into the place beyond. The bolero jacket and skirt Chanel-ed its way onto the sofa and he sat opposite, feeling full of manners and convention. He was placed in her life; so far there had been no effort and no need for lying.

He was in his outlet Armani, quite the gentle man, a gentleman.

# *Chapter Four*

The little boy spent most of his time on his own.

Well, he had parents, and there were the neighbours: Spasha and Roy, from Greece, who seemed often more present in his life than his parents.

He was nine years old and small for his age.

The reason for the neighbour-focus probably stemmed from his mother being slammed against the headboard, the blood crawling down her face. This was a solitary incident that for some reason never coloured the feelings he had for his father and never brought a sympathy for his mother. Even at that age he felt clear about this emotion. But also because they became a safe refuge, Spasha and Roy that is, after he was accused, he was convinced, wrongly, of arson.

He liked to dig holes, big holes at the top of the garden which backed on to a wheat field. It was midsummer and hot. The reason for the holes was so that he could put the old tent that his father had, and his father had had before him, in a faded heavy green canvas, a simple classic pointed tent like a slice of cake the other way up and not very long, and peg it down to surround the dug out earth. It was just long enough to lie down in. The hole, which was like a trench in the ground, meant that Ever, being short for his age, could almost stand when at the apex of the tent.

When darkness descended, he could be found at the bottom of the garden, lighting a fire; he would have a potato ready to throw into the ashes to cook and then he could feel like a man living in the wilderness, a survivor, in the rough outback of the suburban Midlands. The fire produced, as it does, sparks, and the wind, as it does, found one, or may have been two, of these unsuspecting embers, the little bits of burning wood, and the swirling wind, with its deceptive knowledge, carried them towards the wheat field just feet away, through the pieces of upright wood posts, at two-foot intervals, connected by wire that constituted the fence.

It was dry, very dry, being midsummer. Within minutes a fire had started and he stared at the fire; it began to snake its way through the wheat. His first appreciation, beyond the flames, the colour of the flames, was the crackling noise and then the wafts of heat, carried towards him on the swirl that also carried the smell, the rich, depth of dark smell. And the black smoke that hung, blocking the moon in the sky.

The world had changed in minutes, transformed in all physical aspects, into a display of beauty, but it had caused destruction. There he realised the opposites, that both had a wonder, the purity of the golden wheat field blowing without concern and then the fire that had changed its life, killed its future. Stopped it from existing in the form it was intended to in life. No longer in the image of creation but in the image of destruction. Why were both so truly wonderful? It made him warm and he felt protected.

Then he realised the fire was devouring, spreading across this field, he could hear shouts from the other side of the fence. He still didn't feel he had done anything wrong, as he felt he was able to deny to himself that it was his fault, and then the sound of fire engines could be heard, they were driving up the field, up the hill from the neighbour's side which was the last house in the row. Two fire engines.

He thought he should move, make an effort; their hoses powered water over what was now a field of black; not golden anymore. Killing his orange night. He stood up to watch. Eventually, with barely anything left of the wheat field, acres of blackness now, the fire was brought under control. And then he remembers being questioned, first by the firemen, then a furious farmer appeared, then the police, and everybody was looking at him and asking him questions and then, and then, and then, oh God, why? He was accused of starting the fire.

He stood there looking and listening to this anger directed towards him. The shouting. He denied it because he genuinely believed he hadn't – started the fire, that is. He didn't have to go through the effort of lying, he could make no connection between the fire and himself. He was left with his mother, now screaming at him; his father wasn't there. But his own fire, outside his tent, was there, smouldering, evidence, undeniable.

He was so small.

The police said they would return. He looked at his fire, that was now almost out, and could see that his potato was almost ruined, burnt to a hard, black lump. He ran, he ran to the neighbours on the other side who were also now returning to their house after the commotion. To Spasha and Roy, who made him baked beans on toast, put bits of bacon in it, and tinned tomatoes. This was something he had never tasted with baked beans before. Bacon and tomatoes. He loved it. So loved it. And they weren't cross with him and he sat with them, knowing that when he went home his mother would hit him with a wooden spoon.

But the lasting memory of that evening was the baked beans, with bacon and tomato.

And his burnt potato.

And the beauty of it all.

## *Chapter Five*

The United States of America has a Cancer.

Or rather a Moon Child birth sign, as the association with a terminal disease is not the connection a positivity-obsessed nation likes to make. July 4th – its birthday.

Astrologically, the vibrations of Palm Springs were perfectly tuned to his. But as both the world and Ever appear to vibrate at 7.83 Hz this was not conclusive reasoning.

Perhaps, then, his return to Palm Springs was encouraged by the frequency of UFO sightings in the area, and Ever's desire to have a symbiotic relationship with the alien travellers. It had been tried, not in Palm Springs, but tried. He had lain naked outside for a night, save for a T-shirt inscribed with lipstick-red writing – FREE SPERM HERE – a descending vertical arrow pointing to his genitalia. This event was not conducted without the ingestion of mind-altering chemicals. No sperm, however, was taken to consummate Ever's dream, the creation of the HUMIEN race. This only gave conviction to his belief that they didn't want his sperm because he was actually one of them. They had already placed him on earth. He was the experiment.

The word to define this new race had caused him some concern. Humanalien. The combination could have gone towards hum-anal-ien. But the prospect of a race of anals always brought him back to HUMIEN. He was young.

There are some things in life you have to take control over.

It was astrologically determined that he should be there.

The events that were to happen there were the predictions of his psychic.

His therapist should have been told, and, thank God, his doctor wasn't needed.

Yet.

The four horsemen – Astrologist, Psychic, Therapist, Doctor – the dependent Ever needed these four in the absence of human closeness in the life that was left to him, to do his depending and avoid his own personal apocalypse.

This convergence of energy, linked to the ever-flexible plasticity of the brain, seemed to give him comfort, made it feel appropriate when approached, sitting down for brunch in the Parker hotel. A brunch that had replaced his inability to play a round of golf in memory of his father. He had stood on the first tee. Had addressed the ball. And had dropped a tear and left.

The first beat – his psychic's prediction proved correct: the approach of a girl with intent. A sexual intent.

The name to beware of was Tracy. This Tracy was supposed to have HIV.

And at the same time, this eventuality, this person called Tracy, would change his life.

Well presumably if you contracted HIV your life would be changed. That was Ever's interpretation anyway.

'I saw you from over there.'

Not difficult – his comment, unvoiced, uncharacteristically judgemental.

'I thought I would come over and say hello.'

'Hello.'

Was his spontaneously feeble reply.

'Anne.'

She spoke with a lilt and a tilt of her head and a smile.

This second beat, though, brought relief. He thought no more about it when the name was offered. Anne. An Anne, an antidote – a wonder, but a bit of an anticlimax.

With an enjoyment, he felt the concern crawl through the sludge to the back of his mind and extinguish.

Fuck it, who could go wrong with an Anne, and she looked fine, well fine-ish, if a little high on the acne scale, covered in thick make-up, concealing bumps as opposed to white-headed, pus-filled spots. Bumps were un-poppable and in the long term, far more devastating to the face that housed them. Hard immovable mounds – cystic. Ever was dermatologically skimming the surface.

'Hi Anne. Ever. My name is Ever.'

'I will love you, Ever, forever.'

Anne didn't miss a beat.

Ever, in perfect syncopation, replied,

'That's what my mother said.'

'But you didn't fuck your mother.'

Silence was the only response. Not a calculated response, but a genuinely shocked, silent one.

'Did you?'

She said having interpreted the silence from her perspective.

And then, when he still couldn't summon up a reply, she just started laughing.

And so did he, muttering a distracted and distant,

'No.'

A syllable amidst the exhalation of tone-filled breath.

It really made him question the question himself.

But he made the decision, acne or not, that a fuck would not be out of the question.

# *Chapter Six*

Ever had done a turnaround in the womb.

Or rather his soul had.

This is what he always felt.

You choose the parents that are going to nurture you into the world. Hoping you have a better time than the last time around – or you may feel you have some lessons to learn. Always appeared a dodgy reason, that did, because even spirits must be wanting to give themselves a break when they come back again. Make an easy choice. Who wants to buy into pain and suffering?

Anyway, for him, he realised this halfway through the pregnancy, and removed his soul from the process. The earthly arguments that he was witnessing from the comfort of the womb became too much and the idea of entering this world with his soul, to this parentage, was bleak.

Then what happened to the foetus, the baby, soulless? Who was born then? Did he return or did another soul come down and hitch a ride? Who was the sickly boy, gasping for breath, clinging to his mother? Was he really just waiting for the soul to return and take pity and fill him with spirit? Is that why he was always at the point of death from his lungs? The lungs the source of grief; the physical manifestation of grief. Asthma, bronchitis, pneumonia; these were Ever's defining character points. A boy defined by illness. Expressing everything through illness. Painfully shy, as his soul hadn't arrived to fill him with passion and purpose.

Yet.

He was waiting, for his human being-ness to be completed. He was a vessel with no rudder; the only things that could fulfil him and fill him were animal desires, food and sensual base feeling. A reptilian brain. He was a bit like a dog. Responding to the senses, heat, cold, smell, noise. He explored the immediacy of his environment without judgement. The judgement that the presence of an old soul can give, that had-been-here-before, déjà vu; so his knowledge was acquired in the absence of experience.

But when would the soul or new soul, or indeed any old soul, come back?

No, it was him. He thought it was him. He had to think it was him. Because he could never know if it wasn't him because he could never have the realisation of it not being him because he would never have the concept of realising if it wasn't.

It had to be him.

Take him or leave him.

He took it. Him.

Yes. It was his soul, it had come back and he should just lump it.

The Angels had done their work.

# *Chapter Seven*

Tea arrived with attitude and broke the silence that had allowed them both to sit.

Sit there as if. Sit there as if they had sat many afternoons before, contemplating the stagnancy of the leaves in the pool that moved with the gentle breeze, not with the mechanical consequence of filtration.

Birds of paradise lined the perimeter of the pool and looked like they should be appreciated as an exotic plant, but somehow betrayed an ordinariness, like a tourist standing out of place in the wrong clothing.

The yellow-y orange-y and the blue-y purple-y. Just the wrong colours, the wrong hue. Ever was big on hue. Somehow, nature had taken a little break, had a little moment of taste relapse.

'Milk? Sugar? No, you can't have sugar, no one should.'

She took away the need for a response.

He was consoled, he didn't want sweetening anyway, but revelled imperceptibly in the control that he interpreted as care. It was nice to be cared for. To be thought about. Considered. He just hoped she would give him milk.

No names had been exchanged and he wondered whether he

should ask the question. Her shape was thin, and her skin had witnessed hours of sun in an era when people loved it, without guilt. Her hair swept back, clean and grey but thick for someone who must be seventy? Eighty? Had he any idea at all?

Her dress rolled over her thighs and he could see the underneath of her right leg in its motion of crossing lightly over the left. It was wrinkled with the pressure of leg on leg.

Her precision at pouring betrayed the ritual of someone conditioned by solitude, giving every moment purpose and elegance. The ritual of the day; he wondered if, at six o'clock, there would be a drink poured with the same attention to the physical movement of hands and arms and a sweeping of the air that moved with pleasure out of the way, sensing this effortless lift of cup to lip and lip back to saucer, which was held in the left hand as the right did the sweep.

Not work, just rhythm. Grace.

'Tell me.'

Broke his trance.

'Why are you here?'

'You invited me.'

'But why accept, have you nothing to do?'

This completely stopped him. He had a lot to do, but why had he accepted? It was pertinent as a question.

Her legs uncrossed, and he felt the embarrassment of looking at them as they did so. Something that women must take so much for granted. But this one watched his watching, and he awkwardly slurped his tea, attempting to convince that was what he was intending to do while his gaze was fixed. Post movement she sat still with the confidence of someone who was used to being observed.

He thought that she was really quite beautiful. Wrinkled and thin, but really quite. Her question had still received no reply.

'I suppose I am not very happy really.'

She said without any emotion at all. After a contemplative silence, that appeared to concern neither of them.

He had rented the apartment on Havenhurst Drive.

In West Hollywood for one month; it should be ample time, he thought, to carry out what he needed to do. What he felt committed to do. The only thing at thirty that he felt able to do now; knowing that he would never get away with it, but incapable of doing anything else. It was like an inertia, set in concrete.

Thirty years on earth and a realisation that in fact he didn't really have quite the same lust.

At least in quality and quantity anymore, this hit him like a missed sit.

Gosh oh God, that which drove him now didn't even get him standing.

He was however stood and looking at himself in the bathroom mirror, embedded in the Spanish tiles in this rented slice of Mexican architecture, expecting a sense of lack of recognition. If the feeling had changed, will the response to the image change? It was still him but the purpose for any of his physicality didn't seem to be there.

His hands moved objectively over his face, as if the face had no feeling.

Why were they needed, the mouth, the eyes, all of it? The breakdown of these component parts was becoming unnecessary.

They didn't have a function if he didn't have a function.

So that was an interesting way to face the next years of his life.

Different at least with these dulled animal desires.

His shoulders dropped as his hands left his face; he slumped and felt like his tongue looked. He promised himself to stop analysing the lingual papillae, with the bacteria and debris that was lodged on their fungiform crags.

He knew it all from the very beginning – the soul bit.

How do you live a life without a soul, because it had never come back? Or had it? How would he know if he had a soul if he'd never had a soul?

'Stop, please stop.'

This he voiced, head hanging down, staring at the basin, relieved that he had nothing to throw up.

His hands threw water at his face.

'Stop.'

This was not a birth and mother issue.

No, get to the present.

He stood there, inhaled a big one, a chest full of air, now bearing the medals of victory in this mental skirmish.

Ever had fended off the dawn attack, well not dawn, but he had fended.

The change that has brought about this ascension into a higher dimension of sensibility is a tragedy. No longer a reptile. No longer requiring to be succoured and satisfied; life seemed to present another distinct emotion.

The feeling of loss.

And pain.

His father had died, and he loved his father and he always thought and felt that his father loved him. But could his father really have loved him, when he had removed himself from his son's life without even saying so much as why or goodbye?

But if it wasn't his father's fault; a pause in his thought – was death a blame issue?

The toilet flush escorted him out of the bathroom.

He had thought of nothing else since his father's life had ended.

Appearing as an accident but in an emotional condition that could have implied purpose.

A finished man with nothing that he could construct to live for, and Ever had witnessed the demise, the whole decay of a soul. A putrid decay. A vibrant, happy functioning soul that had wound down to death. No one really can understand what happens to a man when purpose is taken away, when all that you have focused on is no longer allowed to happen. When people tell you that you can't do what you want to do, what you know how to do; you are forced to a stop, and look at a wall and go blank. Switched off. They have switched you off; they did it, they stopped the joy. They decided – the human race that is.

One man, he had broken it down to one man.

Although it was probably more than one, but somehow one was enough to carry out the retribution.

He saw it as more than revenge, it was a statement for all lives that had been controlled, affected by other people because they didn't care.

A big thing of his, this caring.

When it comes down to the final moment does anyone give the slightest squidge of shit? He believed the man didn't, and so he was going to make him care – or rather make sure that he would never have the option not to care again. A son was going to sacrifice himself for his father to show that somebody, somewhere, did care.

And it was not even an effort.

He sat having tea in the brown room.

He so wanted to tell this physical dignity poised in front of him what he was going to do, but knew he wouldn't, so instead these words came out.

'I am so sorry, has your husband died?'

'Sweet boy. I was married once, twice actually, but long gone.'

And then he caught sight of her finger that was not bearing the restriction of a ring. A manacle of possession. Her hands brown and shining, as the cream of years nourished the wrinkles in a battle that would be forever lost.

She raised her slightness to her feet with a greater agility than he had perceived before, she said she needed to rest, and it was so nice to meet him.

They walked, slowly, to the front door across the brown polished floor, she had taken his arm for support again, the daylight from the garden was now dimming, they entered the lobby, equally brown; the windows, blinded by white linen curtains, stood either side of the door that anticipated its opening as it had previously witnessed their arrival.

The sounds of a tray being removed behind them betrayed the presence of Manita, quick to clear the slightest obstruction to the order of her life and return the cups, saucers, milk and unused sugar to a kitchen that he could only imagine.

Was it, too, brown?

Or 1950s Los Angeles beige, with a tint of the dreaded green, as if dullness was needed to compensate for the endless sun that now seemed a little less endless in the face of a changing climate.

'My name is Lomita Nairn.'

And her hand hung in the space between them.

He touched her skin, satin or silk, confused in that second as to which was softer, then his name syllabled out of his mouth. Two of them.

'Ever.'

She remained impassive, demanding explanation by her stare.

'Short for Everett. I will love you Ever, forever, my mother used to say, so...'

She smiled and said,

'Come again. We'll have dinner. Maybe. That is if you would like. Or – do you prefer to watch a motion picture?'

'I don't mind.'

Intrigued by the formality of the words – motion picture.

'I sometimes watch old ones in the evening. Dinner is optional.'

'Yours?'

Responded Ever, with a smile and the consciousness of flattery.

'No. Good heavens, no, one I made, not really, but... that is all.'

The 'but' held for a longer moment than a moment and he sensed it, the feeling of something that hadn't been done for a long time. That sense of nothing in the in-between time when something should have happened. But hadn't. And didn't. And Lomita, in that indeterminate time, did not know why she had proffered the mention of a motion picture. Of the one film. She was frozen with the mistake.

'I would be delighted.'

Not sure as he said it why he would be or what about, but he decided he wanted to see her again and talk. Yes, next time talk, not stare. The smell was there again. The perfume and just the cleanliness. The organisation of it all, as a person.

'Goodbye Lomita, if I may call you that, or Miss Nairn.'

'Lomita is fine.'

She said and he thanked her for the tea.

The pause stood for a time.

And then.
And then.

He walked down the circular driveway.

The short distance to the road, he turned right onto Elevado and then left up Doheny. Up the hill to Sunset, passing the almost concealed and decaying precision of an early Frank Lloyd Wright construction, with the singular intention of buying a bottle of tequila at Gil Turner's on the corner.

He hoped, and had concern, that she would have made the journey back across the big brown room with safety, Manita escorting her for a rest on her bed. A large bed he imagined. A California King he supposed, without any evidence to support his supposition; he thought of her fragility in the expanse of bedding.

On his walk east down Sunset, a brown bag in his hand enclosing a bottle of Patrón Silver, he realised the only way he could get in touch with her again was by knocking on her door at North Oakhurst Drive. No attempt at the exchange of numbers had been made.

He felt strangely pure passing the bars and clubs, preparing for the night's energy, the comedy clubs and the bookstore and the sadness of Tower records with nothing left to sell. And Book Soup on the other side that was still selling, books that is.

He felt he had been in the aura of a spiritual being like a monk, or more appropriately a nun. Although nuns didn't always have that quality of calm and oneness with the universe. Where did that thought come from? How many nuns and monks had he met?

But he had been washed and wanted to bathe in her again and be blessed by her and sit at her feet and tell her all the things he could never tell and sleep in her bed and be read to and she would put out the light and she would kiss him goodnight.

Lomita Nairn was worth a Google. No, she deserved more than that.

She deserved to be happy.

# *Chapter Eight*

The tequila bottled had supplied half its contents.

To the man disappointed that Lomita Nairn had produced nothing from the Google god. Nor had any variation of what he presumed to be Nairn. Narne, Naryn, Nerne, any number of other fucking ways to spell the name.

He rolled his second joint and looked at the stars, the French windows of the apartment opened onto the courtyard that housed two other similar abodes, now both shuttered against the dying heat; the sound of muffled voices and air conditioners wrapped around his ears, his eyes looked to the stars and the moon and he closed them, the chair rocked on its bent bamboo rails and he felt sad and started to cry. Quietly cry, this was not unusual, as crying seemed to wash him clean, an internal shower that he enjoyed, and he cherished the privacy of that emotion. One that he never needed to share with anyone, a solitary experience that left him feeling calm and, well, just calm, and of course alone.

He missed his father and he hoped that his father wasn't missing him. That he had found a peace that, earthbound, he never had.

He fell asleep, still rocking gently in the chair with the warmth holding him in its arms.

He had last seen his father in New York six months ago.

When his father was supposedly meeting a gallery owner, to organise an exhibition, even though he didn't have any paintings – yet. It was just for a weekend. Ever paid for them both to stay at the Bowery Hotel; away from home, eating, drinking and having fun, his father seemed to be putting on a face that was brave, at least; he seemed OK, frustrated maybe with his life, but essentially OK, and in many respects in a better place than Ever himself.

Although he never did meet the gallery owner.

But Ever did carry blame, it was an issue, towards himself, he should have come out earlier, when he had sensed the change, the attitude, the feeling, the enthusiasm disappear from his father. He could hear it in his voice, read it in his emails, but he was so consumed with his own turmoil in his brain that son never came to see father.

The person he loved the most. And his father would never have burdened him with any kind of painful truth.

And now.

Now.

What?

Lomita Nairn had eaten her dinner.

A grilled chicken breast lightly coated with olive oil and some green beans, haricots vert, the same dinner she ate, when at home, every night. Well, there was the occasional variation. On a tray, on a California King size bed, lying on the top of the bedding, on a lilac satin eiderdown, faded but the stitched squares still carried a plumpness that comforted her delicate limbs.

The television would normally be supplying sound but now displayed itself in silence. She thought about Ever. She was not a sleeper. That luxury had long left her, two or three hours a night was the only peace she was given from her mind, and the continual reassessment of her life.

Her life of seventy-six years. Born 9 July, early 1940s. That was all she would admit to. She didn't want to think about being a child again. A time when she thought and planned everything, believed that it was all going to be all right. She didn't want to relive that.

She took a zolpidem and a shot of whisky. The particular whisky she liked was a single malt, called Oban, the taste of which she demanded to linger in her mouth, and she swirled it, making sure it accessed every particle of tissue. It comforted her, and she prayed to drift off, dreamless, for just a few hours.

The whisky and sleeping pill numbing, just ever so slightly, her thoughts. So she would be unable to connect with disappointment and her dreams would no longer, if she was unfortunate enough to have them, house the hope of great things to come.

Ever rocked in the roll of the chair, concentrating his mind in an attempt to determine whether he had been asleep or not. He tried to remember a dream; in a trickle of treacle his thoughts came back.

The act of focusing on life had for Ever's father more than occasionally defeated him.

The condition that age and a battering bring with them; it is known as the stoop.

A bending forward from the hips as if driving through a

heavy gale, with shuffle steps. That coupled with a thickening around the middle, a general filling out of all the finer points of youth, as if the sculptor had got bored and given up the defining process, given up the chipping away to sustain angular perfection.

Then it turns, it turns through age, backwards, the artist no longer attempting the perfect ideal. There is no time left. Not sufficient time. The backwards process of age has taken the perfection away and then spends those remaining years defiling it. Life is a forward process and then a destruction. This backwards process, a reversal, an obscuring, makes youth seem like a gift that should never have been given, or at least ever cherished; an anger sets in, even though we know that nothing can challenge the process.

This was the process his father had been submitted to, the physicality of defeat.

The mystery of human frailty, this error, passes us by in our moments of trying to survive, but is unavoidable in the end.

Why is it, then, challenged by some? Ever was in a half-dream, now, revisiting the face-lifts in the Rodeo public parking. Image after image came to him. Why then do some call in the sculptor, the surgeon, to attempt to carve the stone back, back to its perfection, when they know the stone has worn. When no sharpness can now be attained, no accuracy of line; it is brittle and its smoothing produces a flatness of definition, no detail of personality.

It has lost its ability to present its original image.

The artist, the sculptor, just looks untalented, unskilled. And the model looks like a very bad piece of work, something that should have been binned in the studio.

Ever's mind was swimming in the waves of tequila, and drowning in 10 mg of Ambien.

But they were all in the same frame. The face-lifted women

and the failing, the disintegration of the artist. It was the same. Old and fighting. Just different canvases.

Is this the position that Ever's father found himself in, then, on that day when it all seemed to go black?

The unskilled artist binning his work, the attempt to retrieve his past abilities had vanished as he stood bent with his aged stoop. The past glory in crumbled and brittle collapse. Now in this old man's life there seemed to be no hope after what was dished out by the God, the Source of the Universe, the provider: the unfolding of events in a misconceived and over-ambitious life.

A life that had no handbrake, only an accelerator, a throttle, it was jammed and going in the wrong direction. Stop the race, it's a life that needs no victory. God. Please. But no one listened to the torment and the pleading.

Aren't there too many screaming, pleading people, all screaming and pleading at the same time? All the noise. All the chaos. Seven billion screams.

And so, the father crashed, so to speak, let go of the grip on his own life. The fatal final autonomous disintegration – all the worry over.

He would never be made any younger.

His canvas could bring no joy anymore.

Ever would be forever bereft.

# *Chapter Nine*

Lomita Nairn lay on the crisp white cotton sheet, having thrown off her lilac quilt. There remained almost no indentation as she turned her body till her legs were dangling over the bed. She reached for the Oban and pulled at the stopper. How much longer will these hands be able to prise the plastic-topped cork out of the bottle, with a twist-requiring grip? It was something that would end one day. She sat up, excited by the decision to have another sip of the Oban. The drowsiness had not taken over with the pill, her brain was still telling her things she did not want to hear. She would change that and think about what she wanted to think about until her peace came.

These nights developed in thought but she would always try to force them back to something happy, sometimes to Bobby Layne.

She finished the sip with a cracking smile.

Her town in the 1950s, Pittsburgh, was hell with the lid off.

The steel industry produced the dense fog of pollution that had clouded the city, creating a darkness of apocalyptic gloom. Lomita had grown up with the demoralising legend of the 'valuable man' escaping the city for New York or Los Angeles because he could no longer face life in the grime. Running away: and the concept of a new life would grow from this seed planted in her brain.

She plumped her pillows and lay back with the memory of playing outside and running around, simple enough but the air was filthy from the coal-burning steel works. There was a wheeze in the chest, a sting in the eye, and that smell in the air. Still, the pollution that caused the infamous midday dullness very slowly gave way to brighter days as natural gas was pumped in to provide energy. Buildings were being sand-blasted to remove the grime. The transformation had started.

A second chance. Everything deserves that, she thought. And everyone.

Duquesne, just outside city limits, was where they moved to, so that her father had easier access to the factory. That was his world. Work and steel.

Then the dark-haired, doughnut-cheeked image came to her. Standing on the podium at her school. Glasses, slow talking, extremely shy, instantly forgettable, yet she never forgot.

'If you want go, go out and get it. Find a light and follow.'

Spoken in a monotone without the enthusiasm that the words implied.

He had only got to New York at this stage, drawing shoes for the manufacturer Israel Miller, but he had escaped. He was free. And he had brought with him some of his work that had been in an exhibition in New York. He had made it, broken away. His name was Andrew Warhola. He had attended her school, Schenley High School, and was now returning to speak as part of the 'Everything Is Possible – Just try' programme.

Then just a few years later he burst into prominence and covered his birthplace in glory. Although Heinz and its 57 varieties and the Steelers had been doing that for nearly half a century.

She did meet Andrew Warhola after the talk, along with a whole crowd of girls keen to be in the presence of someone who had escaped. He would soon morph into the silk-screen printing, flaxen-bewigged Andy Warhol and truly do Pittsburgh proud.

'Drawing shoes.'

Lomita voiced to the room, still amazed at how people start and blossom, and wondering what kind of shoes Warhol would have produced had he continued.

This reflection made her sad, not about the missed career of a shoe designer, but about the idea of being allowed to blossom.

She took another sip, and then followed it with an inhalation of the malt aroma.

Two people, same place, with dreams of changing their lives.

But it hadn't ended that well for him, for Andy, he was dead. Fifty-eight. Luck, that's what you need.

Luck, her foulest four-letter word.

Her best friend at the time, Betsy, was moved away, along with hundreds of other impoverished families, to make way for redevelopment. The new city.

Lomita felt a guilt when she became aware that she was going to benefit from the removal of less fortunate people like Betsy. But this development enabled her to leave school and find employment at the newly built Carlton Hotel on Bigelow Boulevard.

It was either that or the Henry, both completed in the mid-fifties, but the Carlton won her over because she had read about the hotel of the same name in the South of France, in the magazines she scanned as quickly as she could at the news stand before the paper vendor complained about her lack of purchase.

She had seen pictures of the elegance of the film festival in

Cannes, and she would close her eyes standing on the sidewalk. She, for that brief moment, became one of those women in a silk taffeta gown with curled hair, bobbing in the gentleness of the breeze while the cameras popped and people shouted for her to turn this way and that, and thank her for being her. Just for being her.

And anyway the name Henry reminded her of a spotty boy with a stomach problem who sat next to her on the bus on the way back from school, so there was really no contest; that, and the hour bus ride from Duquesne posed easier access as its drop-off point was on the corner of Grand Avenue, a two-minute walk from her place of work. Her decision was made – the Carlton Hotel.

It was the gem in a city that was witnessing wealth and sophistication. The molten steel solidifying into money.

Her employment was as a chambermaid and this, she felt, rather like an air stewardess, carried a new-style status, enabling contact with that amazing thing for the provincial dweller, the sophisticated out-of-towner.

There was, for her, one memorable visitor to the hotel, who had come from Los Angeles to watch the newly-merged Dons and Rams play the Pittsburgh Steelers; the Steelers won that game 27–26 in the last three minutes. Saved by an eighty-yard touchdown pass from the Steelers' quarterback Bobby Layne.

And here we are, revelled Lomita. A gentle fist pump and the barely audible cry:

'Bobby!'

The result, though still precisely recalled all these years later, had no real interest for Lomita; it was all about Bobby Layne, who she had a crush on – from a distance – a crushingly heavy one. Her first sense of weakness in the knees, pining and obsession. She had learnt all his statistics and scores just in case she ever met him. She got nervous in anticipation of the meeting and imagined the panic that would lead her to vomit forth all these facts just to show her interest in him and the game.

She now felt a laughing sigh of relief, and an amazement that she still remembered some of those useless facts.

Other than that, that particular game just meant she had to pull a double shift: the hotel was filled to capacity.

Until.

The biggest until of her life, well almost.

Bobby Layne standing waiting for the elevator on the second floor. Lomita was pushing her trolley towards the elevator and this 6' 4", thick-haired blond, parted on the right, blue eyes, turned towards her and actually spoke.

'Good evening to you my dear.'

Lomita was now laughing out loud in her room and felt like she felt then, consumed in a fit of giggles. That was all she could do then and all she was doing now.

She couldn't speak, he too started laughing as he walked into the elevator with a –

'Bye now.'

She blurted,

'I like you.'

I like you, she thought, what a strange thing to say. But she said it to Bobby, a man she never knew. Bobby's spell had been passed to her. When she arrived in room 412 for a turndown the Memorable Guest said,

'Go ahead – I'm just leaving.'

Then at the door he turned to her and said,

'With your beauty,'

He paused, took a breath and started again.

Lomita closed her eyes, clutching her heavy crystal tumbler, recalled the following words that became like an anthem for her.

'With that ethereal beauty you should be in motion pictures, and if you are ever in the City of Angels, contact me.'

Bobby Layne had made this happen.

This was her dream.

She never forgot the word he used to qualify her beauty – ethereal – she had to make a special trip to the library to find out the meaning. No one she worked with knew what it meant either.

Lomita looked over at the cushion on the other side of the expanse of bed. The word 'Ethereal' was embroidered on it. Bold, flowing script, in red and green, with dashes of gold thread.

She still has the card that he gave her to this day.

Although she feels very differently about it now than she did then. Then, it represented a passport, a ticket, an escape from what she felt was grime and gloom.

Her childhood was coloured grey, she had been in a black and white movie; she always wanted it to be in Technicolor.

Her father would come back every day from the factory with the dirt on his face outlining where his goggles had been. He was grey, the eye protectors leaving a whiteness around his eyes like the area had never seen the sun. Clean and softer, almost baby-like, where the rest was cracked and lined. A mark and facial signature that was always there to her eye, however much he washed – she was embarrassed now at how much she made him wash. Wash and wash. So as not to give away, on their walks down the street to the newly opened department store, just to look around at all the expensive goods under one roof, never to buy, that he was a labourer. Just a welder.

She wanted him to be so much more. Something, at any rate, just a little bit special. He deserved it.

He welded metal beds for the military. His target was a hundred beds a day; his task was legs to frame; he prided himself that he never fell short.

But the work was hot, dull and dark; his spirit was as molten as the joints he welded hour after hour. An industrial boom time for the post-war economy, but the souls doing the work were only comforted by the food in their stomachs, and the football and the hockey and of course the baseball. Their brains were slowly softening, the steel taking all the strength.

'The spirit is pouring out of us, dying on the factory floor.'

It was the most poetic thing she had ever heard her father say.

When her father's health started to deteriorate, his increasing days off brought no pay and that is when she was forced to find work. She was only sixteen, and had never in any case been considered academic, but she knew that her physical perfection and charm gave her a charisma that made people see her as a little bit special. She had been voted Most Beautiful Girl in her school, a surprise which had led her to enter beauty competitions – pageants – making her own clothes, having watched her mother for hours, moving the materials through the jackhammering needle of the electric machine.

She eventually won the title of Miss Pittsburgh 1959, having won the Rib and Reef Beauty Challenge at the restaurant in town that provided her and her father with all the food they could eat as a victory prize.

But it was the Miss Pittsburgh title that killed her friendship with Joan Happenstance, who came second. It ended a lifetime relationship, albeit a short lifetime, that Lomita had cherished.

With the sweet comes the sting.

It's lonely at the top.

This final triumph earned her father many free beers in the local bars, their choice not his: he never bragged about his daughter. He was a quiet man, a phased-out man. A man committed to a path for which he acknowledged there was no choice.

The card that she had been given two years earlier lay on top of the cupboard in her bedroom next to a framed picture of her mother sitting proudly behind her Singer sewing machine.

Her mother had done alterations and tailoring for a pittance. The idea of recreating that life was terrifying to Lomita. It made her shiver now at the thought of it, but she hoped she had never made her parents feel they weren't good enough.

She didn't want to change dirty sheets in hotel bedrooms anymore, she wanted to fulfil her dream of being on the silver screen. She had no knowledge of what to do if she was ever put on the silver screen, but that did not deter her.

Her mother had taken her own life when Lomita was eleven years old.

She didn't want to stay with that memory, she wanted to go back to thoughts of Bobby and ethereal beauty.

But there it was for Lomita, clear as day in her mind, the Singer sewing machine, the only thing she owned; her mother left it for her, with a little note.

*I hope you never need to use it.*

To leave her father had been a trauma and she could only do it by telling him she would be gone for a short time and that she had booked a return ticket. With the money saved she took the Greyhound bus across country and arrived in Los Angeles in 1960, barely eighteen years old, with the calling card secured in her bag. A handbag, and a suitcase made from reconstituted cardboard, contained all that she owned in the world. All except the Singer sewing machine, which remained proudly on top of the cupboard in her bedroom in Duquesne.

She had, with the guilt of a lie, purchased a one-way ticket; the journey had taken the best part of three days.

Lomita returned her bedroom to darkness and laid her head on the pillow, realising her neck was still holding its weight. In forcing herself to relax the image of her standing at the bus station at 6th and Los Angeles Avenue came to mind.

She shed a tear at what she thought then.

The dream starts here.

She had felt, at the bus stop, like Claudette Colbert in *It Happened One Night*.

And, one night, it would.

One day.

# *Chapter Ten*

Ever woke as the sun was coming up.

A fly woke alongside him and darted from skin point to skin point, telling him to wake and supply some food. Or maybe it was just being annoying, but he liked to think everything had a purpose. Even a lonely fly. It was the perfect personal alarm clock.

His mind, he had moved inside to empty his bladder and hopefully relieve his liver of the Patrón, focused on his purpose for being in this city.

He chugged down half a litre of Fiji water as the shower started its slow journey from cold to hot. He stepped under the stream and then turned it to full cold for his daily two minutes. The one relief of warm climates like LA was that the cold never got really cold. A November shower in England was an exhilarating freeze that filled him with resentment until it was over and then he felt exonerated of all guilt. A hair shirt puritan, good for a few drinks at any rate. Through pain comes redemption.

He was building up to it. The visit. The day he would dress in his Cabazon Gucci outlet suit, shirt, no tie, to find the offices of the man who had prevented his father from achieving any success in the last seven years of his life.

An artistic drought for him that took away all that he lived for, stopped his breath from feeding his body, soul, blood and just every cell that needed the life-force to supply the charge that put creation in his hands and fire in his spirit.

A slow and cruel stifling of life.

For money.

For someone else's uncaring, that word again, and unthought-out confiscation of talent. He was going to pay; when was not clearly set in Ever's mind. But the surety of action was. Today was the start of that action. But that thought paled in the light of the practicalities that he must first tackle to put the reeling world into some kind of shape before he would take it apart.

With, he thought, a pleasure.

After the brunch in the Parker Hotel in Palm Springs.

Anne, without very much more conversation, took him to her room and they had sex. That is really the only way to describe it. It was practical and seemed to serve as a physical relief, more on her side, really, than his.

The reveal of the complexion on her face, as skin massaged skin, proved sufficiently disturbing for Ever that he was forced to close his eyes to enable climax.

Her bumps, when the make-up was smudged off, swelled a bright red with a sense of fury at being on her face: he thought they must have been uncomfortable for her as his kisses moved from mouth to cheek and quickly back to mouth. The lingering on the face did not encourage him to lick or taste her skin to take the dew of salty sweat that had started its production from the glands as her motion and energy increased.

Her muscle tone was soft, the skin smooth on the body, but the muscle felt to the touch as if no exercise had flowed through its tissue allowing them just the slightest bit of tension to enable upright posture to be possible. She was, he supposed, really quite weak or he imagined if that was his own musculature, that he would feel weak. Incapable.

The aftermath of the coupling produced an increase in conversation, and during the what do you do and where are you from, a question that seems to obsess the pioneer DNA that carries the genetic instructions swirling in the American, his mind returned to earlier times.

He pondered, or more than pondered, he was profoundly moved, by the fact that this was the first intercourse he had had since his separation. He took in the updated 1930s sensation of the room, with its strange bedspread that now lay crumpled on the end of the bed. Striped, in what he understood to be candlewick, alternating with a smooth cotton in three-inch, he guessed, intervals. Chocolate brown, the candlewick, and cream, the cotton, a stark jolt in the dominantly white room. A terrace, potted with dwarf palmetto palms neighbouring the chairs, now received the fade of the sun, which shrouded the mountains in the distance, giving the feeling of space and an endless freedom. And luxury. Organisation and detail that spoke luxury, and allowed one to bask in that which takes effort and time.

Which is what you pay for.

At least what she was paying for.

The separation had been a long drawn-out event.

He presumed they usually were, when the truth of his marital partnership and the reality of the birth father of his son, who was now almost three, became apparent.

They had been married for twelve months when she became pregnant. His delight and enthusiasm for the whole process was unquestioned and being conventional, a reaction, he always thought, to the lack of organisation in his parents' life; he desired it and believed it to be the correct thing to do. Marriage and the creation of a family. He felt it would consolidate what was proving to be increasingly difficult.

The marriage, although he was convinced he was in love, lacked a closeness. It was as if his wife did not understand the concept of love anymore, of caring, or indeed of being a mother, so his relationship with his boy, Jacob, became consuming in a way that was both paternal and maternal. He wondered, on an almost permanent basis, why she ever married him in the first place, even though at the time it seemed inevitably perfect, but the cruel blow of angry truth was revealed on a Wednesday night as he was bathing Jacob – his customary way to spend an evening after he had prepared his food – when father and son played together for half an hour before the first little signs of grumpiness intimated the start of bedtime tiredness. He always looked forward to telling Jacob a little story, and hoped that in return Jacob looked forward to those moments as much.

It was then, towelling Jacob dry with the happy sounds uttering from his mouth, forming the words in the relentlessly adorable way that makes each one a gem, that his wife, after a day of yet more friction, opened the door of the bathroom and in the tradition of continuing a row that he assumed was over, told him that he was not the baby's father.

The moment froze; his love, he was aware, did not change towards his son for the slightest of seconds, his disbelief at her words was solid in conviction, and his first reaction was that she was just trying to say the thing that she knew would hurt him the most.

He continued the towelling-down, picked up his son and carried him to what he considered to be the safety of the boy's bedroom. He wanted him to hear no more, anxiety was spreading across the little boy's face as his concern for his mother's now increasing rage became clear. Her concern for Jacob was non-existent. She followed Ever into the room with a force and determination that disturbed.

'You think I'm fucking with you, don't you? That it's not the truth, but it is. It fucking is. I'm telling you.'

It seemed to be an anger growing out of her own guilt.

Jacob started to cry, probably not out of understanding but just from the tone of his mother's voice. Ever didn't have a response, save a quiet:

'I'm going to read Jacob a story, you can stay if you like but, please, he needs to be calm before he goes to sleep.'

'Fuck you!'

Came the reply and the door shut firmly, with a positive close, but not, he noticed, a slam. The temper was worn out and he thought the words had been calculated to punish and cause a temporary pain. Which of course they did.

He couldn't now remember what had brought this extreme revelation to the proceedings save that it was about the usual why didn't she carry on doing her job, it would bring her some satisfaction, and her consistent response of why should she. She'd married him, he was a successful lawyer, why the fuck did she need to work. It was her choice and she didn't want to do it anymore.

Because, love-of-my-life-wife, if you don't want to work, then maybe when I get back in the evenings and I'm tired, as much as I love doing all the domestic things, just once, just fucking once, it would be great if a meal was cooked or Jacob had been bathed, so I could, you know, relax.

But he never put voice to those thoughts, he wouldn't, he couldn't, not quite like that. Close to it, but no, when he did, when he had spoken out, it was with just a little more fucking tact, for God's sake.

It made no difference.

He was tired of it all, in his own way, but had never considered the end of the marriage, let alone the thought that he might hear those words.

Not the cruellest words he could hear.

He continued with the bedtime process, told Jacob his story. A story that was not from a book but one that continued over the months to pour effortlessly out of his head, about Billy and Pete and Rosie, the redheaded beauty who joined the two boys in their endless adventures and who they both adored, and Mr Magee who always got them out of trouble. Jacob's little sobs had quieted now, and his eyes started to close as Ever reflected on the possibility of the truth having been spoken.

His eyes too closed, lying next to the bundle that he loved more than anything. And he wondered behind his closed eyes why the idea of divorce never came into his mind.

The repeated question started with:

'Hey, where the fuck have you gone?'

Rising to a shout—

'Hey! Hey!'

Then the discussion of occupation and intentions in life continued and the not always inevitable exchange of contact information was begun.

'So, email is always the easiest way to get hold of me,'

She was saying, but he was not fully in her world.

'And the address is A Tracy, that's A – T – R – A – C – Y @—'

He stopped her right there with a white-faced exhalation that contained the word:

'What?'

Somewhere during the last ounce of pouring out breath.

'Tracy.'

She said.

'My name is Anne Tracy, why so dumb-shit shocked? Simple enough name.'

Ever said nothing and did a lot. Like getting dressed, no polite 'sorry', or 'have to go'. Just a silence that left Anne Tracy with a look of bewildered sadness and a feeling of being revolting.

'What the fuck – what the—?'

'I am going. Have to go. Go.'

And the door was his only aim and he shot straight through it, down the stairs to the parking lot, drove for ten minutes till he pulled up at the start of El Paseo, and wound down the window.

Thought he was going to vomit and then opened the door.

And did.

He felt at that moment that his luck with women was not the strongest card in his pack.

The psychic had said not to sleep with a girl who would want to sleep with him by the name of Tracy, as she carried HIV, and this person would change his life. He had this mantra in his head. She also predicted that he would find a solitary card – the Ace of Hearts.

He had left the psychic's apartment, a block to the east of Park Lane in London, he was walking along and saw on the pavement a playing card – the Ace of Hearts – just lying face up, he picked it up, his hand shook a little. So, she talked sense: this authenticated her prediction, in his mind at any rate. Hence his dedication to the mantra – just make sure then you don't fuck a Tracy. Make sure you make sure you don't fuck a Tracy.

He just had.

He just had.

But he didn't know if she had HIV.

His second thought was to drive back and ask her, his first thought was to get drunk. How could he ask her, and if she had, would she say? And if she said she had, would he want to hear it? And if she said she was on medication, that her viral load was undetectable, what would he do then?

Better to live in a state of his familiar disbelieving denial.

It wouldn't necessarily mean that he could get it, that he would die. Not with modern antiretrovirals.

Did it?

What did the psychic say?

That he would get it. No, that she had it. Change his life. Oh God. That was all. All? Of course – he could get checked. What is the percentage chance?

No, stop it, get drunk.

Forget.

He drove back to his hotel and with the spirit of Einstein, started the process that leads to drunkenness. Made the resolve in the light of the possibility of looming death to avenge his father and fell asleep. The next morning, he checked out of the hotel, and also made the decision to get himself checked after the dreaded incubation period that the virus required to take hold.

Three weeks, he researched, was the time frame.

He started the drive back to Los Angeles.

His reason for the journey to Palm Springs on his arrival in California, apart from astrological advice, had been to play a round of golf at the Monterey Country Club in Palm Desert in honour and memory of his father. The round of golf that had never got beyond that first tear-soaked tee. They had played there from when Ever was an eight-year-old and they were the moments he treasured the most. His father taught him everything he knew about the game, Ever was a scratch player by the time he was sixteen. He was saddened that he hadn't managed to fulfil the tribute.

But it was not to be, and now he was pulling into the gas station to be aided by the friendly South Asian man before the drive back to the business end of his journey.

And Interstate 10.

# *Chapter Eleven*

Ever had been born in Los Angeles.

Well Santa Monica to be precise, at St John's Hospital. His life was a yo-yo, a peripatetic existence, back and forth to Los Angeles and the shocking gloom of the West Midlands. This depended on the whim of his father and the mental state of his mother.

His father was born in the Midlands and had a small house there, that looked like the original design for a Barratt Home. An easy construction to replicate, like the typical child's drawing, front door in the middle, windows up and down either side, and a garage, for the emerging popularity of the car in the 1950s, on the side.

Ever always thought it was out of proportion, that there was too much space for the car. He worked it out one day, pacing, and was disturbed to realise that the car had more room than he did to sleep.

Ever's father had been left the house by his father, and as an artist he was grateful, to have a base, at least.

A free base.

His mother and father separated when he was fourteen, his mother taking the house in England where he followed, for his education, leaving his father in Los Angeles, and Ever then made the frequent trips, typical of the child of divorce, back and forth. It was not a bad way, Ever soon realised, to spend your teenage years.

So his walk into Beverly Hills that morning was to go past the doctor's office on Bedford Drive, three blocks west of Rodeo, with the intention not of going in, but just to be comforted by the knowledge of its presence. A doctor who had known him all his life and who he knew in three weeks he was going to need. He received that comfort, seeing the name of the practice on the board displaying the occupants of 420 Bedford Drive.

But this fresh day, with Lomita and a hangover in his head, brought about a journey to a different venue.

To the lawyer's office on Ventura Boulevard in the San Fernando Valley.

An easy car ride, it was just off Highway 101, and after travelling a block past the exit he was pulling up in the parking lot looking for a shaft of shade in which to park his Utah-plated rental. A good deal he had crafted through Hotwire on a new-model Land Rover Discovery, so he felt he was moving around this familiar, but nonetheless foreign country in a little haven of the old country. He had picked it up at the Sixt rental company on La Cienega.

'It came in from Utah. That's got to be seven hundred miles I guess. Salt Lake City. Never been myself.'

The rental man spoke with deliberation and pride. Either in the achievement of the car or his country. It was his country, of course, thought Ever. This is America after all. It was a pride in his country.

Ever just saw it as a lucky escape from Salt Lake City, a place where it was hard to get a drink, so he didn't much care for it, and neither, he was sure, did the car; its main concern was to be put in some shade. A tree was all there was but the sun would move and he knew he would return to an oven. An English oven, built in Liverpool, and owned by India.

The elevator released him on the third floor. He had spruced himself up and put on the grey suit jacket that he had neatly hung on the little hook supplied by the rear seat grab handle.

Ron Riley Associates, Attorney at Law, the plaque said, printed on plastic. He thought that it needed the gravitas of brass.

Ever was standing in front of a blank-faced receptionist, one he'd never seen there before, she was listening with a vagueness that seemed to place her elsewhere, he was in the process of spelling his name. A man he had known his whole life arrived to interrupt at double LL. This man who had named his son Everett. Not out of any kind of admiration for Ever as a person, he was only two at the time, but just because he liked the name. Everett.

They gave each other that tentative hug that familiar males do, although the Americans have a greater reticence towards male intimacy than the Europeans, where a kiss is sometimes offered to the cheek. So, a little bit awkward, but meant with a genuine warmth, he then offered Everett his condolences at the tragic circumstances of his father's death.

Ron looked, of course, older; his eyes betrayed the look of a man who had spent the last thirty-five years staring at paperwork and the computer's arrival had in no way dimmed the strain that produced a shade of grey around their sockets.

The death had happened two weeks ago.

The burial had taken place after a perfunctory police investigation.

His father was found, having apparently been bending down to mend a leaking pipe that had continued to leak. He was found two days later floating in the flow of water that had now alerted neighbours as it seeped out of the house and down the path.

He was bloated and unrecognisable, still holding the spanner in his hand, having suffered a heart attack.

His heart had broken.

His life reduced to nothing.

The leaking pipe remaining untended, bleeding its purpose away. His talent had finally been drowned. The police ruled out any suggestion of foul play, the scene seemed to reveal its own clarity, and their immediate decision presupposed laziness rather than any sense of conviction, or indeed much interest on their part.

Paperwork is such a curse. Ain't it?

Ever organised the funeral from England with the express intention of not being there himself. He was, he realised, having booked his flight, actually incapable of being there. He had no desire to witness the funeral parlour's attempt at making the body presentable and cried the whole day long while the funeral took place 6,000 miles away.

His heart ached, the relentless implanted pain of an increasing agony, and he longed for his father to be alive. To be alive as he remembered him, before disillusionment scuppered his take on life. His father's two friends, one, his old canvas maker from Culver City, and the other, his drinking partner from Chez Jay's on Ocean Avenue, and of course dear Ron and surprisingly Everett, his namesake, were the only ones in attendance. So, an Everett was there, not with the same intense emotional connection but with a physical presence and a name that matched. After the ceremony at the Larson Family Crematorium on Broadway in Santa Monica his ashes were scattered off the Santa Monica Pier in memory of his hazy, drunken walks from Chez Jay's on his way home to Chautauqua Boulevard that led down to the ocean. The surfer's shack he ended up in, one of the few on that road, was at the bottom end of the hill, so he could still hear the sound of the ocean that rolled with him to sleep at night.

Ever could not go through so much pain again in so short a time.

It had been confirmed only three months earlier, after a DNA test.

His son was indeed not his.

And the tragedy was, he supposed, that he never really questioned that his wife shouldn't have custody of the child; in the absence of divorce proceedings, he hadn't even contested it, he still felt that he was his baby boy.

She was living in their marital home, but he knew, in his heart he knew, but denied himself the cerebral acknowledgement, who the father of the child was.

His love did not diminish in the slightest, but he felt a pain in his guts all the time knowing that the boy would grow up calling that man father and he would, he presumed, be known as Uncle Ever.

A remote, but ever-loving figure, in the distance of his growing boy's life.

He missed him with the pain of an absent limb.

Ron presented Ever with the documentation, his father's accounts and assets which according to the will were transferring to him. He signed with a sadness for his father, knowing that the business end of his life had amounted, in the final tally, to nothing.

'I hope I see you again. I mean, please keep in touch.'

A surprising expression of sentiment from Ron, but this time he avoided the embrace with an extended hand.

The further lack of successful cards in the pack of females that were dealt to Ever came in the form of his mother. She also failed to make an appearance at her ex-husband's funeral.

She was a wonderful, fun-loving, gin-drinking party animal, who Ever adored and indeed she adored him, but she had never really understood the concept of being a mother. A party she understood, emotion she understood, when it related and connected to her, and those emotions were like a roller coaster, up and down, and without the benefit of medication, understandable in the absence of a professional diagnosis; she was tossed about like a boat on an ever-changing sea and you never knew what ocean you were going to be sailing on. The happy, becalmed, or the viciously white-capped, aggrieved, and sadly churning waters.

Life, she had determined for herself, had not treated her well.

She was in psychological terms a narcissist. Through and through. Indeed, if a conversation did not interest her, in that it wasn't about her, she would, without compunction, tell the person to shut up. Pure and simple, and in a way, honestly direct.

Ever had an admiration for her, as you never knew where you were with her, her unpredictability meant that you also did. She was like the sea. Just be careful. Check the weather report. Or better still the shipping forecast.

Ever loved the shipping forecast.

Viking, Tyne, Dogger, Fisher, German Bight.

What were all those places?

But didn't it sound importantly international?

# *Chapter Twelve*

This was the day for the visit.

Reluctant as he was to make it, to a gallery in the newly developed downtown district where one named Ingmar Lorken had his Frank Gehry-designed art temple.

The man, he knew, would not be there, and if he was, Ever would not have known what to do.

Ever hadn't seen the man for twelve years, since the time when he was a collector, well, a buyer, of his father's work. The man who finally would give this wonderful artist the recognition he deserved. Those were his words at the time. Their clichéd cloyingness ran cold in repetition, summoning up the memory of his father's enthusiasm at receiving a massive cheque for having sold all his work; purchased by Mr Lorken himself. Ever's father had been given the promise of an exhibition housed in the yet-to-be-completed gallery.

Ingmar Lorkenau, Austrian father, Swedish mother.

Ingmar himself removed the 'au' from his name. Easier life, spelling-wise, in the new-found land of America, and the numerological conclusion of the remaining twelve letters added up to three. The trinity in the Torah, body, soul, and spirit. Believe it or not.

Elohim made man composed in his image, and it had worked for Mr Lorken.

He was doing very well indeed.

Ever stood outside the metal curved signature of Gehry's three-dimensional piece.

He was sad at the thought that it never happened for his father. The exhibition did happen, not there, but in an inauspicious place off Venice Boulevard by Ocean Avenue, unpublicised, with the works remaining unsold.

With the advance cheque, he tried to buy all his work back, but Mr Lorken refused, deciding to hedge his bets on the possibility that one day Ever's father's work would be of value. But that was the destruct button, and further attempts at creation were met with increasing dissatisfaction of nuclear proportion.

He became destructive towards his work and depression led to breakdown and breakdown to an inability to paint anything at all. The money ran out, the ability to soften Mr Lorken's resolve went with it, and death was the ultimate release. The fallout cloud had spilt its pollution.

The destruction of his father, albeit not self-inflicted, was as a result of losing ten years of his work to the depths of a warehouse. This was the thing that consumed Ever more than his own life, and he too lost motivation to do anything, and became obsessed with the futility of it all.

The lack of point.

Of purpose.

A nihilism.

John Everett Millen was an abstract expressionist in his later years, having started life as a figurative portrait painter, painting to commission with diminishing enthusiasm. His later work, though, had an energy and physicality that poured emotion onto the canvas. It was visceral, massive, a true joy to witness, to watch, for hours, day after day, always seeing the fresh and finding the spirit anew each time. He was a talent, with the value of Roman coinage.

At least that was Ever's opinion.

And what did Ever know?

To purchase the gun.

It was a handgun he wanted; Ever was going to require a California driving licence, which he had always kept up, a copy of his residential lease and, as he was born in the US, he had the passport as well, should it be needed. Although strangely the valid driving licence was the more official requirement. The supposal being that if you were capable of driving a car you would be capable of firing a weapon. Interesting correlation. He could get the FSC, the firearm safety certificate, at the LA Gun Store for twenty-five dollars with a brief written test and practical proof of his ability to use and understand the weapon.

He wanted a SilencerCo Maxim 9, a 9 mm gun with an integral silencer that looked like something out of *Blade Runner* and used Glock magazines, so ammunition was easy to source, therefore hard to trace to a specific weapon; accurate at short range, and although he didn't have a plan, he knew he didn't want to make a noise.

A phone call to the store confirmed they carried that particular weapon. He gave no further information and asked for none, beyond the fact they had four in stock.

The gun would cost him about $1,450, and the store he'd called was in Van Nuys on Cohasset Street, and Kate, his friend on Waze, would be able to take him straight there. Kate was wonderful; he imagined her to be dark-haired and efficiently attractive, a great companion, and many a conversation had been struck up between the two of them, particularly when Ever thought he knew best. He very rarely did, but he liked the challenge.

The day for the purchase was not decided but at least he was fully prepared. The one decision he had made was to make a return visit to see Lomita Nairn.

He would do that before purchasing his firearm. He did not know why that was his choice, but it was.

It was five o'clock and he guessed Lomita would have had tea.

Possibly sitting outside under the shade on the terrace, as the late afternoon presented a warmth that had not much decreased since noon.

This time he was driving; his Discovery pulled up outside the house and rested on the brow of the semicircular drive that summited its gentle incline.

He felt a little presumptuous and was not without a coating of sweat under his arms that he felt stick to his shirt, grateful it was navy blue.

The car was doing its ticking, creaking, cool down. He walked up the three shallow steps, formed by red brick in herringbone pattern, and stood in front of the large brown door.

He turned around, watched a hummingbird with wings a blur fly off the bougainvillea on his step-noise arrival and his casting shadow.

There was a dulled brass button that was, he hoped, a working bell and without allowing nerves to alter his intention, he offered the middle finger of his right hand to the rounded and smoothed surface. He pressed and heard nothing, so pressed again, the same absence of noise, so thought he should wait.

And wait he did.

He assumed that the bell didn't work. He was preparing to knock or leave, he wasn't quite sure which action to take, but in that moment of pondering, the door opened and Manita stood with an unsurprising absence of expression but with a greeting of,

'Hello' –

that carried a degree of pleasantry.

'Is Miss Nairn in? I mean available to see me. That is if she wants to see…'

Before he could finish his meandering explanation, which by the fact he was standing at the door, made his intention obvious, Manita disappeared and in the action of turning around, closed the door. Safety of course, he thought, she wouldn't leave it open while checking.

Don't lose confidence. Of course, totally understandable, and before his jumbling thoughts were allowed completion, Lomita Nairn opened the door and was standing before him.

Backlit from the low lantern sun that hung at the back of her garden and invaded through the large window.

She looked like an exercise in perspective.

And dramatic.

They both smiled.

His followed hers, which had been there as she was opening the door. But she was first. He consoled himself, she must have been the first to smile.

'Hello. I sincerely hope you don't mind me calling around unannounced, it's just I had no way of announcing. I mean—'

'Not at all. Please come in. It is truly lovely to see you. And thank God tea is over and it's time for a drink. Give me ten minutes, I will change and you can do something for me…'

A pause.

'…that I would dearly love.'

'Of course, I would be delighted.'

There was no pause before his reply.

'Take me out for a goddam cocktail. Somewhere glamorous and it's on me. I'll be back.'

Not what he expected, but his mind was already doing a tour of potential sophisticated cocktail establishments. He didn't want to let her down on choices, he wanted to be the initiator, the all-knowing male. He wanted to be in command of the situation. He wanted to be in control of this element, at least, of his life.

He presumed he could sit down in the big brown room but didn't: the cushions were immaculate and perfectly plumped, having received attention, he guessed, from Manita. His nervous observations, this time, which he just did to occupy his thoughts, revealed there were no books in the room. No television and nothing as far as he could see that supplied music, except the piano. He had got that far in his assessment when the door to the left of the room opened and there stood Lomita.

She was wearing a black trouser suit with the material on the legs flowing softly; they were wide, like a forties shape, the jacket nipped to the waist, her hair up, and with the turn of her head he could see it was in a French pleat, beloved of his mother.

She wore only, as far as he could tell, the red lipstick, although the shade was gentler in tone, and didn't form such a contrast to the delicacy of her face. She did, he thought, look so elegant, and light, and floating as she walked tentatively towards him, on shoes with only the slightest of a heel.

'The Polo Lounge, haven't been there in twenty years.'

The decision was taken from him already, with the realisation: I am not in control. I am out of control. He now was aware, as he opened the car door for her, momentarily releasing her arm from his, that a cream blouse nestled around her neck underneath the tightness of her jacket. And indeed, she did have the gentlest suggestion of blue eye shadow on her upper lid, bringing out the fierce blue of her eyes. The dropping sun hit them and made her tense the muscles around them, ever so slightly, in defence.

He drove.

She spoke.

'I can only walk short distances without a wheelchair, it's nothing serious, just my hip. But with a man I can hold his arm, it's just that with Manita I feel wrong, clutching on to her. But with you, I don't mind, if you don't mind me clutching, and if we walk slowly I'm fine. I should have the surgery, but the doctor is worried my heart wouldn't take it. Why my heart shouldn't take it I don't know, I feel strong, but I have a murmur or something. Oh God, too boring, I refuse to talk about my health. It is so not the thing to do, to talk about one's health, everyone has a something-or-other and to be quite honest who wants to hear it? Just get on with it all. Don't you think? And my past, I don't want to talk about that either, just want to go on, keep going on, although I will tell you my husband died thirty years ago and I used to come here, you know, to the Polo Lounge, with him. I went a bit after he died, with my bridge friends, for a while, but then I stopped playing, so I guess it must be about twenty years or so since I've been here. That house on the right, that is now a monstrosity, that used to be owned by some man from the Middle East, years ago that is, and when they wouldn't give him the planning permission he wanted, he didn't build a thing, just put statues of naked women all along the front and painted them with pubic hair. Hilarious don't you think? I never knew him but kind of liked him for that, made me laugh every time I passed, all gone now. He sold it. But hey. You just seem like the right one to take me. I hope you don't mind cos I didn't really give you a choice but actually if you do mind I don't really want to hear it. So please don't mind, I have to tell you I'm excited and thrilled that you came round, I was hoping you would. I don't see that many people now, really, I don't know why. That is all right, it is really all right with me, I don't know why, just, I suppose, I don't know, I get into my own head and somehow... you know. Oh well, tonight is just the perfect evening and it has been quite a boring day so... My goodness, here we are already. Don't forget to give me your arm wherever we go, look on me as something that will fall over if you don't hold it upright.'

With that the valet opened her door, there they were on their own red carpet walking up the entrance, the green and white striped awning running above them, into the Beverly Hills Hotel, past reception; granted a courteous nod from all three men behind the desk, but not the woman, who was buried in her computer, approaching the hostess on the right at her little, but all-important desk, to the entrance of the Polo Lounge.

Ever felt a sense of guilt going into this establishment, owned by the Sultan of Brunei, who, in his small, oil-rich kingdom, had imposed strict Sharia law, calling for the stoning of gays and lesbians, and understandably had received a boycott from the liberal Hollywood community.

Not that Ever was a member of the liberal Hollywood community, but he believed that anyone should be entitled to live how they want, hell, isn't life hard enough?

Presumably the Sultan had deep enough pockets to withstand the boycott and probably couldn't care less.

He hadn't changed his laws anyway, in the end, but Ever's concern at that moment was not for the Sultan, but Lomita, who he assumed was unaware of the situation.

There certainly was no need to have made a reservation and the first thing Lomita said was,

'Why is it so empty?'

It seemed the explanation was going to be unavoidably forthcoming. The discussion of sexual behaviour seemed to close down her interest, her eyes no longer focused on his, and although he sensed a disapproval of the persecution of people with alternative sexual orientation, her concern wandered and she studied, with an over-forced intent, the cocktail menu. Something that a person familiar with the process of cocktail hour would not need to do.

It puzzled him, and he stored it, in some part of his brain, as to why this sophisticate would not wish to engage in one of the topics of the time. In response to his monologue she just said,

'Let's drink.'

The waiter arrived at the booth they had been escorted to, greeting them with the customary,

'Welcome to the Beverly Hills Hotel.'

Although at that moment Ever questioned whether he wanted to be welcomed, felt that he was being congratulated on joining a union of fascists.

They both sat on the inside-iest bit of the booth, close to each other. Close so that he noticed the closeness. Lomita ordered first, with the command of a seasoned drinker.

'Grey Goose martini, up with a twist. Dry.'

He ordered the same.

Her choice of a French vodka, with a comparatively recent commercial explosion onto the market, was the second noticeable and memory-banking thought for the evening. He would have expected the eighties favourite, Stoli.

But she was right there with the times. Right there in so many ways, smelling as she had, on both occasions, when proximity allowed, as this did, of Chanel and order; she exuded a sense of perfection, right down to her appreciation of the little details of the things of life. Something he so admired, and was determined to force into his life.

An adoption of a style.

Ever's monologue about the Sultan had brought a silence to the proceedings which he regretted. The martinis arrived, the waiter with a real expertise had waited for this pause in the conversation to bring their drinks, and they requested a little more time to decide on the food. Ever's need to impart his knowledge, to give himself a confidence by informing people of things they didn't seem to know, was, he had always felt, a compulsive weakness.

Don't give it all away, just let it dribble out.

In impressive

and unexpected moments of wow.

And then you can

wow.

Then it works.

'It's not that in any way I support anybody or any regime as horrible as this one that you are talking about, it's just I find that if you cut those kind of people out of life, I mean certainly in my life, then really very little ever happens. Do you think all those Russians who own your football clubs, or soccer, or whatever you call it. Do you think their money is in any way honest, do you not think they've inflicted atrocities on human beings to get where they are?'

She took a large mouthful of the martini before continuing.

'Banks, for Christ's sake, hedge funders betting on the futures markets, crippling economies, shorting on food supplies, copper, gold. I am sorry to be supporting this shithead, but I want to eat. What do you want? I'm having the Caesar salad, what do you want?'

Ever was a little taken back, filled with a surprise at her

knowledge, even though it suffered from a few inexactitudes clouded by emotion; he was reluctant to get into the specifics and defence of any of her general argument in detail, but she had more than a goddam point.

He wondered if he had made any mention of his job and found the coincidence of the subject a little disconcerting. He tried to move his thought on, so as not to hold up the evening, but got stuck in this reflection, for a second or two. Money is usually made by people capable of a ruthlessness towards both their own sensibilities and other people's. They are made of different stuff, able to put themselves through a stress pattern that would finish the sensitive; his work as a lawyer in a hedge fund company, overseeing the legality of acquisition contracts, had indeed revealed many an asset bought and stripped and resold, and people, thousands of people, losing their jobs, all for the benefit of already unbelievably wealthy clients.

His pondering had run its course.

'I will have...'

A slight pause followed, as if something monumental was about to be said.

'I will have the Wagyu burger and some fries. Medium rare.'

Was the summation that followed the pause and he had nothing to say to her attack or defence, whichever way you took it. She looked around for the waiter who was no more than six feet away and asked Ever with the most charming deference,

'Would you mind ordering, my sweet? And I would adore another martini.'

She poured another mouthful down her ruche-bloused throat.

He was now in the authoritative position of commanding both food and drink and concluded the order with two requests of his own.

'A glass of cabernet, I would be happy if you would make the choice. Full bodied but soft, rounded, please.'

He felt he was describing a physical desire, so moved on.

'And some San Pellegrino, if sparkling water is your preference?'

'Fine, my sweet, I won't be drinking too much water, but the bubbles are fun. Thank you. Oh and—'

She called the waiter back.

'The dressing on the side, please. Thank you.'

She turned back to Ever.

'You see in my life, and I have already promised not to talk about the past – but in my experience the shit people have both saved me and destroyed me.'

Ever somehow felt that to ask for qualification on that topic was inappropriate, so he stored it as the third point in his memory bank. She continued.

'I came here, to LA, I mean, in 1960. My God what a time ago, and in all life, I mean, it depends on who you meet first, or who you know, as to how it all pans out for you. I mean, you come here and get picked up by Billy Wilder or whoever it is now, I don't know.'

He expected her to say Spielberg but that was too obvious for her.

'By—'

She continued.

'Darren Aronofsky or a Tarantino and your life path is immediately on an exciting and positive track. You meet some exploitative little scumbag who wants to fuck you, please excuse my language, it's the martini, and make some cash out of you and the next thing you know you're in glamour magazines wearing very little, with a nice enough place to live, admittedly, but your track is pretty much set from there. And let me tell you, my sweet, it may have some pearls on the way and may put some diamonds on your fingers, but you are heading on the track downhill. Full speed, well, depending on how long you hold out physically. You know, not strength-wise but looks-wise. You are, wherever you are, a commodity, a tube of toothpaste, you just hope they keep liking your flavour.'

Ever decided that it was again inappropriate to ask her to elaborate on this topic and instead allowed his mind to rest on the two things that had occurred to him while she was talking.

Firstly that 'my sweet' seemed to be her term of endearment and he hoped it wasn't a general one she used for everyone, that it was reserved for him alone; the other was that when she started talking she liked to carry on. She got fired up and didn't stop. He reflected on both these observations and regarded them as qualities that he liked. As he prepared to slice the burger in half he considered asking for ketchup and mayonnaise, but they arrived as the request was on his lips.

And he toasted her for the second time that evening with a glass of his Grgich Hills cabernet.

'Here's to—'

Before he could finish, she interrupted, or rather completed, the toast with,

'Health.'

A definitive and unquestionable affirmation of the most important thing in the world.

'Health, my sweet.'

She reiterated. She seemed to eat small mouthfuls of her salad, pouring on globule amounts of the creamy dressing, a dollop at a time, and pushing the chicken to the side of the plate. Essentially she was eating iceberg lettuce, but at a cost.

Polo Lounge cost.

But the martini was taking a hit.

It was her decision that the time had come to leave; she

opened her purse and pushed a bunch of notes into his hand, hidden from view, under the table.

'The check I think, don't you? When you're ready, otherwise I'll be forced to have another martini and then that Sultan is going to get it in the neck.'

She gave a gentle laugh; he realised it was the first time he had heard the guttural sound come up from the depth of her throat. Somehow, it had always stayed on the surface. He thought that if it was louder it could be a really expansive, joyous, infectious laugh. A laugh of pure fun, of not caring, of freedom. He thought he loved it. He knew he loved it. She was a person who most definitely knew how to have a good time.

And he, at that moment, wanted to be the one to share those good times. He found himself laughing too, he turned and thanked her for the most deliciously entertaining evening. He thought of the times in life he had said those words; he felt a pure satisfaction that tonight he really meant them.

They departed down the red carpet, he had the three points locked in his memory bank, unsure why they were there or what relevance they had, and anyway the points had been wined and dined.

They'd be gone in the morning.

As they opened the big brown door she asked if he would be kind enough to escort her to her room.

They walked, as was the established custom; she grasped his arm and at the door of the bedroom, she said, in an inconsequential way,

'Please hold me tight as you say goodnight, my sweet.'

He did, whispering the word in her ear as a definite two.

'Good.'

Pause.

'Night.'

They held their closeness for what seemed a time, a long

time; he took in the feel of hair against his cheek and his hands remained politely just below her shoulders. He allowed himself the luxury of breathing in her exquisite air and was captured by the closeness in a halo of light that glowed around them, it seemed as a protection from anything the world might throw at them.

A glow.

Then they moved apart with a momentary look into each other's eyes, as if acknowledging the aura they had created. He walked to the door that would take him, rather light-headed, to his waiting warm and murmuring car.

A car that would transport him hopefully to his destination. Lomita was saying, thank you and goodnight, he sensed her warm smile, knew she was still looking at him during his traverse across the room, he didn't turn around, he couldn't, but closed the front door, and climbing into his car his hand went to his erection.

Just an adjustment.

He had had an erection while he held her, was she aware and had the thank you, which he sensed was spoken with a smile, been an acknowledgement of the fact? The fact of the erection, his mind fixed on that being the only possibility or, the thought poleaxed him, was it just plain embarrassing?

He drove with the desire to masturbate the fantasy of Lomita out of his brain.

He drove, and he would be home soon, masturbating. Lust returning.

Lomita Nairn.

He had pressed his body into hers and felt his penis hard against the hardness of her right hip, just as the bone gives way to the flesh. He could feel the fragility now, and felt that he could have snapped her in two. He wondered what she was wearing underneath the feel of the chiffon trouser material. Silk or cotton. Something with delicacy, he didn't sense the unevenness that lace lends to skin. She didn't seem to move, he didn't know if it was his imagination, but hadn't she pressed in harder and did she not shift her body ever so slightly to receive his hardness closer to her abdomen?

Closer.

He wanted to be inside her. Who would ever have thought? Think. Present or past. Lomita Nairn.

They had agreed to meet the day after the next day, which, one guesses, in sober language is two days' time.

## *Chapter Thirteen*

The firing range.

Did not require ear defenders with the Maxim 9, as there was truly very little noise. But they hung around his neck and he fired the first two shots with them, then the tall, bulky bearded man with dead eyes had suggested he take them off.

'You see, barely any sound at all.'

Well, there still was, Ever thought, for him at least, a hell of a sound, just less than the normal.

Now came the technological lecture.

'The suppressor assembly at the front of the pistol uses a series of baffles and expansion chambers to allow the propellant gases to expand, decelerate, and cool; this reduces the velocity and noise made by the gases as they leave the barrel. That's why you get that sound, it's the block baffles structure, cumbersome, I think, for me, I don't like it, but it takes down that bang. So less bang more buck.'

This made the bearded man laugh, at least.

Ever understood the words but was baffled – the choice of word made Ever chuckle to himself. First one then the other, one laugh apiece.

'It will just be good for my ears, you know, less noise on a firing range, and well you know, and hunting.'

'You'd have to be one hell of a shot to hunt anything with that unless it was right in front of you, big, and not moving.'

He laughed again, his eyes stayed the same. Ever didn't know if he had convinced.

'Well, she's going to take a lot more work to get her. Fingerprints and photo ID, the manufacturers are trying to make it easier, but we can't co-operate just yet, so you're not going to be able to walk out of here today with her, it could take you months.'

It came out as a real slur of a: 'takeya'.

'Months?'

Ever hoped he hadn't shown too much desperation.

'The ATF, the governing, regulating body, whatever the fuck you want to call them, I call them assholes, make our fucking life hell, excuse me, it has to verify all purchases and that takes some time.'

'Who are they?'

'Alcohol, tobacco, firearms, and explosives, strange mixture of stuff, but they can all kill you. I guess. So, there you go.'

He laughed again.

'You want something now, that you can walk out of here with, with the basic tests and verification, and you want 9 mm?'

Ever supposed this was a question and grunted.

'Uh uh.'

It sounded knowledgeable and manly.

'You can't do better than a Glock 17. Police just went back to them. Packs a noise though. Cheaper, at around $550. You want to give her a go?'

This time the ear protectors were a necessity and it was with a sense of disappointment that he said,

'I'll take this one then.'

The only consolation was that Ever was relieved he had hit the target. Then came the inevitable 'where you from originally?' Ever was surprised the question had taken so long.

'LA and then moved to England, for a while.'

Was his customary reply to all comers.

'Don't need to know what you want her for, but she's nice isn't she?'

Except the isn't she came out as 'inshe', and he assumed the man with dead eyes was talking about the gun.

'Yes, very nice.'

But Ever had nothing to compare it to, except a .177 air rifle he had attempted to kill a sparrow with when he was eleven years old. He hit the sparrow, but it didn't die, so he had, in a panic, got a shovel and bashed it until it was dead. That was the unpleasant part, the bashing, not the firing.

So that was him and guns.

'She's great.'

He felt an idiot feminising the weapon.

'I'll take it.'

'Magazine maximum is ten, State law. Want a box of twenty-five or fifty of the 9 mm babies?'

Now infantilising, but this was a question.

'Just twenty-five is fine, thank you.'

He certainly defied convention by refusing to say 'I will take her'. It just didn't seem right. But he supposed if it is seen, as some perceive, as a penis extension, it could work. He then had to take the written FSC, and produce documents to prove in the thinnest context, his sanity and existence, and soon he would be walking out into the Van Nuys sunlight with a gun capable of killing.

But not quietly.

'Get caught carrying in this state, it's a felony. Well, put it like this, you'll have a long and expensive old time trying to prove otherwise, if you're with me. So don't fuck around.'

A little strong, hold on there, cowboy, thought Ever.

'Straight home, self-defence on property, unless you want to drive to Texas and have some fun.'

He was laughing, Ever imagined, at the idea of either just having fun in Texas with a gun, or the idea of Ever being in Texas with a gun. It didn't matter which. No fun was going to be had with this baby. A purely practical purchase. Then the thank yous and the pleasure doing business with you sir, another strange American tradition.

Obviously the military carried over into the civilian. But why not just drop it?

He was walking into that sunlight.

Back in his car, he switched on Waze, he had missed Kate, and found himself relating the events at the LA Gun Store, and told her to be nice now, I'm carrying.

'I don't want no trouble from you.'

He was tempted with this change in personality to add the word 'Bitch'.

But he wasn't sure if she was getting the joke.

So he gave up and just said,

'Get me home, Kate. Make it quick or else.'

He was packing heat now.

It had been an exercise in physical necessity.

On his return from Lomita. His balls were killing him, and he needed the ejaculation to bring him the gradual delight of diminishing pain, so that thought and sanity could return to the once-horny male.

He poured some post-ejaculation Patrón Silver, adopted his porch-equivalent position, to stare at the stars and once again be defeated by his lack of knowledge of the universe, wondering repetitively why he'd never learnt or remembered what goes round what or how many light years away the stars were, and the fact that they had already burnt out when we were still able to see them.

Is that why stars on earth are called stars – not because they shine but because they are already on the way to burning out the moment they start to burn with a light that gets them noticed?

They, that are sacrificed on our earth, for our pleasure. Reward them while we want them and then just let them burn out. They will always be replaced, grains of sand and all that, they keep coming.

They always will.

His thoughts went then with an agony of mind to Jacob. He decided to FaceTime.

He wondered what they would be doing, whether it was a good time or not, which he couldn't work out, the time difference was defeating him, would she mind, whatever time it was anyway, oh Jesus: who cared, another tequila and he most certainly wouldn't.

The picture eventually came to life on his phone.

Just as he was giving up hope.

It was his wife, she was still his wife, he was surprised in the moment of seeing her face that she had answered his call.

'Hi.'

Was her calm response to what was a greater invasion than just the regular old phone call.

'How is everything? How's Jacob? Is he there, can I see him?'

'He's here, Jacob baby it's—'

There was a long, long, gap of brain time thought and then,

'It's Ever.'

The word, his name in that context, stabbed him, like the cliché, straight through the heart. Not Dad.

'What am I called now?'

The tequila said.

'Oh God, I don't know, babes.'

Oh, how he hated that word, 'babes'.

'Just let me see Jacob please, on the phone, please.'

A scuffle, off camera, and he was looking at his adorable, yes, he would still say it, with pride, son.

'Hi, my darling.'

The words came out of Jacob's mouth that produced a spontaneous inhaled grab from Ever.

'Dada! Dada! Mama, Dada.'

'How are you my baby?'

'Dada... Billy and Pete where are they? Dada are they not good? Are they dead?'

He was puzzled at Jacob's understanding of the word 'dead' and wondered in that moment if that's what his mother had told Jacob about his own absence.

'I love you so much, they are fine my darling, just on a little holiday with Mr Magee and Rosie, they'll be back.'

He didn't know when.

But then in typical child fashion, boredom came over Jacob and he started to mumble goodbyes, going now mama, why has the television, the word taking eight syllables, gone quiet and he was gone.

'Thank you.'

Ever said.

'That's OK, next time just use the audio, I look like shit. It's early.'

'OK.'

'Bye.'

And then another.

'Bye.'

Spoken at the same time, they were gone and that was done.

He and the tequila had done it. Once again, the internal shower washed him clean. He wondered what was happening to his life.

What was he doing and going to do.

With all that to live for.

And Lomita Nairn.

# *Chapter Fourteen*

'Good morning.'

He said, still three feet away, approaching the solitary female.

'I wanted to inquire about an artist whose work I couldn't find on your website, and wondered if you knew of him, or had carried any of his work. Which I believe you did at one time.'

Ever was speaking, a bit ramblingly, to a rather exquisitely tasteful woman of about thirty-five, who was sitting behind a Calacatta marble desk with a backdrop of Carrara marble that covered an expanse of wall that must have emptied an Italian quarry. She removed the black frames with clear glass from the bridge of her nose, they could have been tortoiseshell, and asked, understandably, for the name and period of the artist. She was English but in her correct, aloof and professional manner made no comment on his compatriotism.

'Contemporary?'

She posed as she posed.

'His name is John Everett Millen.'

He said the three words with an obvious pride, and a sense of emotion in the back of his throat that thickened his saliva.

Ever felt he needed to up his game with this opponent.

'I can look on our database to see if we have ever had any of his work, but…'

She halted, and started up again, having gathered her thoughts in a reflective beat.

'If he is not currently for sale on our website it is unlikely. Is that M-i-double-l?'

'Yes.'

Confirmed Ever.

'E-n, or I-n?'

'E.'

Came the reply.

A time.

'No, he is not listed. Let me check the off-sale stock list. Sorry, this is quite a slow process, as I have to access it by warehouse location and there are a quite a few. Please take a seat.'

And she pointed to another Carrara quarry section, where black leather sofas that had been responsible for the death of a few cows were resting, waiting to dwarf the occupant.

'Many thanks.'

'Please read our catalogue of the current exhibitions, we have three at the moment including a magnificent Koons retrospective, some of his earliest work from the seventies.'

'Many thanks.'

He repeated, but he had no interest in the catalogue.

'And if you would like tea?'

She continued with an admirable efficiency and attentiveness considering he was just a man off the street.

'Or coffee, or water, Jules will be delighted to help you.'

Jules was revealed behind him as he turned around. Jules looked out of place not being on the pages of *Vogue*, black dressed in black, she stood out against the perfect backdrop, seeming physically overqualified to bring the cup of espresso that was ordered.

'No sugar, thank you.'

He had walked into this inner sanctuary through two enormous glass doors that closed as if hermetically sealed, keeping the noise of the regular gallery visitors as a mime show in the background. He had assumed he was in the right place. Reasonable assumption now.

Jules presented, the only word for it, a white treat of a tray that emphasised the brilliant blue, yellow and red of the tiny Talavera cup, the only alarm of colour in the space, the cup set in an off-centre saucer, with the steam from the coffee still rising. He anticipated its deliciousness, but was desperately thinking what to say to Miss England if she found his father's work. It surprised him that he had arrived with no plan, which made him think, only briefly, that he was hoping nothing would be found. That he could go home. Ditch it all. The coffee was piping hot and just as his mouth was beginning to accept the heat after much blowing, he heard the clip of exceedingly high heels, that clean, sharp clip allowing the minimum contact with the floor. He looked up to see the pencil-tight skirt belonging to Miss England standing in front of him.

'May I?'

She sat next to him, equally enveloped by the sofa, but experienced enough to just occupy the edge, and showed him a printout of the detailed inventory of forty-seven pieces of work, all listed by title, works by John Everett Millen, that had been housed in a warehouse in San Bernadino.

Ever felt his breath stop, and his heartbeat became irregular, then faster for the briefest of time.

Tachycardic.

These were the works that had cost his father his life. Their titles, their names documented in black and white. Ever was transfixed.

'Did you want to purchase?'

Broke the silence.

He did not know what to say. Could she hear his heart thumping?

'Their value is, I mean are, what are they selling for?'

'I have no idea – they have been on our inventory for so long, with only one inquiry...'

The last word she pronounced in an American accent. Starting with the liquid you write with.

'...that I would have to consult with our marketing director, or it may even be a question for Mr Lorken himself. But twenty-seven of the original forty-seven have in fact been sold... eight years ago. To the one purchaser, prices not indicated here, but I may be able access them as a guide, for my eyes only, so to speak, to assess valuation relevant to the remaining pieces.'

The first thought from Ever was the ARR – the Artist's Resale Right – why was his father not informed? It would have been a percentage on a decreasing scale as the paintings achieved a higher price, so the financial reward might not have been life-saving, but apart from the income generated, it would have given him a confidence that people actually wanted his work. That was the major factor. Being wanted. This was a shit thing to hear.

A fucking bitch shit, fucking thing to goddam fucking hear.

It wasn't Miss England's fault but, by God, he looked at her in a different light.

At this moment he would have liked to have punished her in a way he would not have the courage to voice, but he enjoyed the private thought.

'Can I take your details, if that is your interest, and we can get back to you? Or perhaps you would like to view? We can have them transported to our private gallery here, but I would need some bank references, some validation, as we can only cover the expense if we're confident that it's a serioius request.'

My God, Ever thought, in the quietest part of his brain that wasn't affected by his heartbeat.

First thought.

What happened to the fucking money, bitch. Cunt, was the first word that came to mind, but he was mildly embarrassed at the strength of that and it received an instant dismissal.

Then a touch of calm approached his brain, oh, that was nice, like a river flowing through his bones. Then – my God, me, who am I? I have no way of convincing anyone of my validity. But he wanted to see those works, those paintings, displayed, hung even just once, in this gallery. And the next words that spurted from his coffee-laced mouth were, improbably:

'I represent Lomita Nairn, she is a collector and remembers admiring his work many years ago.'

'Fine.'

Replied Miss England.

'If you give me your contact information, I will report back to her and we can go from there. That would be no problem, Mr…?'

The question hung in the air. Who was he?

'Mr Jacob.'

Good, valuably Jewish: like his son – came out.

'I am Mr Jacob, and obviously for privacy reasons Miss Nairn would prefer to make the initial contact.'

'Of course, completely understand, and thank you for your interest. If you wouldn't mind coming with me back to my desk, we can catalogue the necessary information. You might also…'

She continued, on the walk.

'Like to inform Miss Nairn – or Mrs?'

'No, no Miss.'

'Well, Miss Nairn, of our Basquiat exhibition, which opens in ten days. I would be delighted to extend an opening night invitation to you both; Mr Lorken will most definitely be in attendance and I am sure would be most interested in discussing Miss Nairn's collection.'

And finally, to his relief, he was sweating,

'It has been a pleasure to meet you, Mr Jacob. My name is Peony Money-Root. With a hyphen, as you will see on my card.'

He was ready now.

'May I ask you a question, Miss Money-Root?'

He felt a little stupid calling her by such a name considering what her ancestry must have done to warrant it. But the surname was at least easier to negotiate than the first name.

'Would the artist not have been entitled to some percentage of the sale of his paintings under the Artist's Resale Right agreement?'

He had her now, he thought, the bitch would be struggling now, then his dominant world dropped a score and ten and he realised how stupid he had been. As he had been gaining in confidence, it suddenly occurred to him that why would he know, or care, whether any monies had been paid or not. When he was just an innocent representative of a collector. He knew his father hadn't received a cent. Ron Riley had confirmed it.

Fortunately, he was dealing with Miss Money-Root, who didn't know the meaning of the word perspire, or being caught out, and fortunately, he guessed, analysis was not her strength, or indeed her need. Specialist knowledge, good in her own field, enter a different game and flat on her face she was likely to fall.

'Indeed he would, Mr Jacob, had the works been sold in the

UK, or Australia, or even Mexico. But not in the United States – that policy is not in operation here. And, although I shouldn't really tell you, the collector whose name sits alongside these purchases is in fact a United States resident and the deal was done on US soil. We operate a policy of discretion on all our sales.'

My fucking God, she got me, he thought. Ever had well and truly been full-faced, cream-bunned got. Ever thought, she's not a bitch, just really damn good at her job.

'Thank you.'

He uttered with a respect that had sprung faster than a wasp's sting; he felt differently towards her.

But the knowing would have been nice, wouldn't it, be honest, that wouldn't have taken much, just a note. The being wanted would have been much appreciated by his father, he thought, but looking at Miss Money-Root, not being wanted was something she had never experienced. She knew nothing about it, only as a concept and, in that form, it had probably never even crossed her mind.

Spoilt was the word he had been struggling for, through all those derogatory adjectives.

Just plain privileged.

But that was a fuck of a thing to be in its own right.

Cunt.

Ever was breathless, collected the relevant paperwork and receipt of information and walked across the floor, of yet more Italian quarry extraction, in what seemed to be the noisiest, loneliest and most endless walk. Intimidating came to mind. He was totally intimidated. My God, he needed a smoke. His father had sold paintings and he never knew. It could be put no simpler.

It was a sin.

Fuck to the death the cunt that lives as Mr Lorken.

# *Chapter Fifteen*

Ever's grandfather was Grant Everett Millen.

Ever had never questioned why the name Everett had been passed down through the generations, as if just a harmless connection, a consistency, a continuity. But it carried with it the association of where the name has lived and been for the men in the family.

Ever's grandfather was born in a lunatic asylum in 1900 in Staffordshire, St Edward's in Cheddleton, an austere Victorian pile of a building, housing the primitive treatments inflicted on the so-termed mentally insane.

His grandfather's mother wasn't insane, neither was his grandfather's father, he was working as the caretaker in this asylum. Their home address on their son's birth certificate was Asylum Cottages, hardly communicating, Ever had always thought, a qualifying charm to the word cottage.

Was it there, for the twelve years that his grandfather grew up as a child, that the seed of insanity was planted and nurtured by his grandfather, unaware, and passed on in a latent genetic form to his son, John Everett Millen, who then started to show the signs of mental disturbance, and then these seeds grew in the semen, his semen, forming the DNA that was passed on to Ever in innocence having been absorbed through environment? Mental imbalance starting as environmental and ending up as internal and naturalised – nature's process. Who knows if the grandmother had intercourse with any of the inmates and a male microchimerism effect took place, harbouring the DNA from her sexual partners and passing on mental imbalance.

It had definitely found its way in as a consistent gene.

Ever had not taken his own mental condition into account, in terms of not allowing it to determine, initially, his life – not that he was completely crazy or anything, at least that was what he thought in his more positive moments.

Ever was now thirty.

He had had a complete crash into the wall three years previously and had since been on what doctors like to describe as a long-term low dosage of antidepressants.

A 25 mg tablet split in half, finally settling on Lustral as his pill of choice, after a disastrous experience on Prozac. Lustral was the UK brand or in the US it was called Zoloft, but they both contained the same compound – sertraline.

A selective serotonin reuptake inhibitor, more familiarly known as an SSRI. Ever knew that in treatment of the brain, it had the sophistication and equivalence of using a sledgehammer, but doctors love prescribing it, it gets you out of their office and back on to some kind of road to recovery, and anyway they know very little about what goes on in the brain. Like faces, brains are all different, but all are treated the same. And they are able, the doctors, to pat themselves on their pinstriped backs and console themselves that the SSRI is supposed to be a major advancement on the earlier model, the tricyclic antidepressant, like amitriptyline, which Ever had also been put on at one point, and which he likened to LSD, an even earlier attempt at hammering the brain into some kind of submission to enter an alternative world.

Ever loved these, the Amys, as he called them, and kept them for purely recreational purposes – for when you just didn't want to think of anything at all.

Just float, with a little shake in the hands, being, as far as he could see, and there was no one to tell him otherwise, the only downside.

Whether the brain ever truly gets any of these chemicals out of its smudge mass is questionable, but it's not a very long life one has, and on the basis that everyone has something, maybe they're not too bothered.

They being medical folk, who we seem to trust with a stupidity that always struck Ever as profound. Just numb the fucker, minimise his neurotic options and stop him moaning. No one can cope with the depressed moaning of a manic depressive, a bipolar, a chronic depressive, a general anxiety-ridden human.

Take your pick, and those are the mild ones.

Options, that's what you want.

Ever had tried every day in his attempt to cut down on his dosage, he didn't want to be drug-dependent, not pharmaceutically drug-dependent, at any rate, but it didn't work, and his inertia and anxiety became so intense it was impossible for him to do his work.

It had all started out of the blue, with an uncontrollable bout of crying, extraordinary fear that everything was going to go wrong in his life. And he ended up being taken by his wife to a pinstripe and sat in the corner of this psychiatrist's office, or consulting room, as they like to call them, lying in a heap, in a heap of tears, on the floor in the corner, with this man pronouncing in a way that he has since found all doctors, psychiatrists, and psychologists, even psychoanalysts, to have, pronouncing with a coldness and detachment and a pomposity that they assume must be helpful to either themselves or to the poor beast of a patient, in that it keeps the objectivity in place, but it is shit. Because all that comes across is a feeling of, that word again, not fucking caring.

Caring being the word, not fucking.

Nothing seemed anything other than black.

No road out, they put him in an institution and filled him with a mind-numbing drug, thioridazine, now banned because it has a habit of causing slow, repetitive, purposeless, involuntary movements on a permanent basis. It was banned in 2005, so technically he should never have been given it, they probably had some left over, but what a one to be put on – that, Valium and sertraline all at the same time.

But the first drug they used, for its sedation properties, was trazodone, which is an antidepressant of the SARI class, a serotonin antagonist and reuptake inhibitor, a hypnotic, delivering a sleep-inducing and antidepressant effect. It makes it difficult to stand, as dizziness is a major side effect, but the one thing that does stand up, with a 1 in 6,000 chance, is your penis – the rare side effect of priapism.

So there was Ever, the odds against him, with a permanent erection that delivered no pleasure, unable to be relieved by ejaculation, ultimately supplying nothing but pain. Desire, strangely, was not aligned to the physical condition. There was no desire to penetrate. So that medication was eliminated; this is why they must have dug out the thioridazine, which just numbs you and droops you into an entirely different condition. Numb nuts.

Maybe should have gone for the ECT.

With this pharmaceutical inside him he was unable to feel body parts and had no sense of having any genitalia.

Then came the decision as to whether to actually have electroconvulsive therapy, ECT, administered under general anaesthetic, as small electric currents are passed through the brain with the intention of triggering a small seizure.

It was not surprising it was considered an option as the cocktail he was on had produced a zombie, visited only once by his wife, and as far as he felt, he could and would be left there to rot.

He could not take in, or analyse, any of the updates he was being given; how can you give information to a brain crash? Not that it was his decision to make, of course, no, by this time you are considered to be a fucking nutcase, but the cold woman, who made him feel cold, temperature-wise, who he remembered was dressed not in a white coat, as he would have expected, but in a clean-cut, two-piece suit in beige, a skirt and jacket; she looked executive, not medical. She was the, or at any rate, his, overseeing psychiatrist in the hospital, and she and his next of kin – in this case his wife, atypical, as she was not prone to bouts of great caring anymore – were to be the decision-makers.

The combination of these two women, he remembered, filled him with a terror that in his state of ever-growing anxiety he found hard to deal with.

The decision was taken.

There was to be no electroconvulsive therapy at the moment, while they waited to see what happened when the drugs took hold, as apart from the numbing, the medical shit has to permeate the pathways and channels of your brain and that takes a few weeks.

It was vetoed, in spite of the cold, beige besuited woman saying that it would be the most effective and quickest treatment to get him back on the road to recovery, and Ever was there in the room, but you must remember he was considered a nutter, so no acknowledgement of his presence from the moment he entered was ever proffered.

He was institutionalised for four weeks; his workplace was initially told it was a bad case of flu, but with thanks to his doctor, who he also considered to be a friend, it had developed into a more serious and credible-sounding debilitating condition called pericarditis, which did not carry the same scary prejudice that clings to those with mental conditions. But it has the seriousness of being an inflammation of the lining of the heart.

Good one, eh?

Any questioning relating to his absence was effectively dealt with.

No further questions asked; just sympathy pouring forth.

So you see, Ever did not have the best medical history to buy a gun.

Yet as it was never recorded on his medical files and took place in England, he was in the clear.

God help the world he was wandering through.

But it was understandable that his thoughts of suicide were often and intense. The psychiatrist who has the power to fry the brain of another human being, claiming to understand the channels that run in this glutinous mass of grey and smelly blancmange that is the brain, is in Ever's mind an absurdity, but it is, of course, questionable whether his mind is capable of that assessment.

It was for the avoidance of the ECT, the major thing, that Ever bore an enormous gratitude towards his wife. His brain did not get cooked by the cold impersonality of the beige woman, who he remembers amidst the confusion and breakdown of the connections, the failure of the synapses to allow the neurotransmitters to dump their serotonin and dopamine into the synapse gap thus producing, through their connectivity, the process that is known as logical and positive thought.

For three weeks with these drugs, with escorted walks around the grounds, in his down time, in his room, he could only face the banality of morning television, the simpler it was, the better, and when it was over he would draw.

The same drawing, time after time.

Of a house, a driveway, and a garage.

That garage, bigger than his bedroom.

He never thought he would be the same person again.

Ever was staring at the In-N-Out Burger drive-thru entrance.

Twenty-seven.

The number or the eventuality of that number wouldn't leave, would go nowhere but with him.

Clung to him twenty and seven.

Two.

Seven.

It was there – twenty-seven paintings sold.

That was good, wasn't it?

His father never knew. Would that have helped him? He never knew – the twenty-seven.

Two and seven is nine. The trinity of trinities.

That was good, wasn't it? He was an artist who sold. Someone wanted him.

Dad!

Ever screamed, silent, in the car.

Dad, can you hear? You were wanted 27272727272727272727. I love you. Twenty-seven times you were loved. Weren't you?

Where are they?

The magnificent twenty-seven. Where are they, those

twenty-seven paintings? Are they glorious or miserable now? Wherever they are.

Who's watching them now?

The horns of the cars behind, honking, unaware that a man had frozen. A man had stopped his life, or rather his life had just stopped.

It was involuntary.

It was not his choice. There was a man, a boy really, with an electronic order pad who was at first suggesting he make an order or move on and drive out, then telling him to order or move out, and the suggestion in his tone was that the next command would be quite simply, get the fuck out of here if you're not going to order, but Ever, hearing, yes, and grasping the order of the words but not comprehending, could not move.

A security man arrived and ordered him out of the car; he stepped out without objection, with the customary, 'I hope you have no objection, sir, but I am obliged to remove your car from this property as you are causing a hold up and contravening...'

The rest drifted into a significance he cared not for and there was no complaint from Ever as he was handed back the keys to his car, which now stood on the roadside, securely off In-N-Out Burger property, and he was no longer receiving abuse from the waiting customers. He was given a free bottle of water, and with,

'You take care now.'

From the security man, Ever climbed back in his car and just sat there.

Blank, wondering whether his soul had ever really come back into him as a foetus and what was he doing leaving his wife, taking four weeks annual leave in one go, buying a gun, lying to an art gallery and including a woman he barely knew in a deception involving a collection of artwork, justifiably but heartlessly bought by a gallery owner.

Who he hated.

His thoughts, however, were not in that sequential order but came darting in a jumble of words and in varying intensity, with worry being the dominant emotion.

What had he done?

Who was he?

Was he about to break again?

He had taken himself off his pills six months ago, because he felt he could cope and because he had lost all sexual desire, something that he felt drove his wife away, well, further away than she already was, she was never too close.

And the frames of the film had started to miss.

There were bits that jumped, he missed the continuity from moment to moment. A jump like a turn of the head, then the head was back without the completed movement having happened in his brain, without the time experience that made it a continuous movement.

That had happened again, while he was considering going for the full burger and fries at the In-N-Out.

The frames leapt, he didn't feel like him. He didn't know who he felt like because he had no term of reference to feel like anyone else. But it was another person, another feeling, the feeling that he could do things that he wouldn't want to tell anybody else about, through shame.

Shame, that was it, it was a shame to be him at that time.

He felt the overwhelming sadness and fear that he would lose control and be back, back in an institution with all that he wanted to achieve gone.

It wasn't that he wanted to live long anyway, just live to make a little mark.

To live and to feel love and tell people he loved them, really loved them, he thought, and that he was not full of anything bad.

He wasn't bad.

He just didn't feel too good.

Ever sat in the car and reflected with the warmth of wanting to love his wife.

Clarissa.

That was her name, he had allowed it to come into his brain for the first time. He had written her off. He had always felt that her decision to have a child with another man, with Adam the violinist, was an act of abandonment, and, he supposed, cruelty. But she had taken him through his breakdown, helped him, and what if, through his developing sexual incapacity, she had decided to have the child with another man and was never going to tell him and they would have grown up as a happy family unit? What if it was done with love, out of love?

He had driven her away, she had never offered to leave, she was happy to remain, she just had at times found his behaviour intolerable, but then if he was insane, imbalanced, whatever they wanted to classify it as, and as far as she or anybody else knew, that was going to be it, forever, maybe she understandably wanted a child, and maybe this was her way of showering them with a love.

As the thoughts were formulating in a brain operating at a low level of intensity that would have been on a control button at a point on the scale of two out of ten, even he was aware that there were a lot of what ifs, and buts, and suppositions. A family who had never got close to this perception of love in their relationship, and he had just reacted in a primal way. A first base reaction. Aware that she could have been steps ahead, what if, in another way, she had got it all sussed, what if she wanted him still, with Jacob?

Was it him who was incapable of realising it, of sensing the love between them? Had he got it so very upside down and back to front?

A man who had misunderstood a situation.

Rare.

But would she return to the man who had given her the child? All his loving, his kindness seemed to disappear out of the window that he now wound down for air. Cracked, to allow the stream of hot evening air, full of toxic fumes as a million cars travelled home from where they'd come eight hours earlier, to fill his lungs and oxygenate his brain.

His poor brain.

He sometimes felt so sorry for his brain and wondered if he was responsible for it all going wrong or whether it was a progression of the predisposed genetic condition that could've been inherited, now that he was focusing, from either side of the family.

Because there was his mother. God bless her, but she was still around and suffering from what she wouldn't get diagnosis or treatment for. Ever remained convinced she was bipolar and a narcissist. She just claimed life's unhappiness and drank her way through. The result, either way, was just disinterest.

And either way tomorrow was Lomita Nairn day, and at that moment he wanted her to hear his words of love.

And only her.

To be the first one, with this moment of illumination. Would the lights stay on? Should he tell her he was mental? He felt a pang of hunger, but didn't have the courage to rejoin the In-N-Out Burger line.

# *Chapter Sixteen*

Sushi.

Simple, no car drive-thru involved, hopefully no line of any kind, and a straightforward process of ordering, and sake. God bless sake, but he didn't bless the sake drinker. At least not in the morning.

He drove then, slowly, very slowly to a little sushi bar in Beverly Hills, Shiki on Canon Drive.

It was empty. Fine. It often was, not a good advertisement but he found the food to be delicious.

He always sat at the counter in a sushi bar, he supposed in memory of his father, who first introduced him to the food. When his father first came to Los Angeles in 1980, having decided to change completely his style of painting, and life, coming, like so many before him, for the light. He had stayed at the Chateau Marmont Hotel, in the days before there was a restaurant in the evening, and he would go around the corner to a ramshackle building known as the Imperial Gardens – now a nightclub that was forever changing ownership, but was currently painted a hideous shade of pink, and called, he supposed appropriately, Pink Taco.

There, in the old days, his father would sit at the bar and

the food would arrive without ordering, then at the end of the night he and the chef, with whom he had struck up this silent rapport, would relocate to another room; it was a building of many rooms, closed off by dusty old curtains, and no one ever asked what went on behind some of the curtains. It was owned and run by an unsmiling old Japanese lady, with, one imagined, a ruthless control, and there they would sit with a bottle of vodka and play, at the now old-fashioned Pac-Man tables, getting pleasantly inebriated or totally trashed depending on mood and who was winning.

So Ever always sat at the bar and tried, not always successfully, to create a relationship with the chef, to get suggestions of the delicacies of the day. A sushi bar is the one place that lends itself to eating alone. You have no self-consciousness about being Billy-no-mates, it just feels a perfectly natural thing to do. He felt at home. Comfortable.

The counter at Shiki was always, for some reason, a bit greasy, and he wondered why they didn't give it the same scrubbing attention they gave the preparation surface, just the other side of the glass.

At the same time as ordering jalapeño yellowtail sashimi with ponzu sauce, and halibut sashimi, and some cooked yellowtail collar, he ordered, of course, a large Asahi beer, and some sake. Fashion has changed, it used to be always served hot, but now as the appreciation of the finer sakes has increased, cold is the order of the fashion aware. Ever didn't count himself as one of those, and ordered it hot.

He also asked for a pen and paper.

If you pour the sake in the beer it is a faster high, but tonight he wanted to stay calm and sober. He was grateful for the calm, that the terror had decreased, that he could see and feel and sense, in his way, his concept of what he knew to be normal. The food was being prepared, something he always enjoyed, like a theatrical experience, to watch, having ordered the two dishes from the chef, the drinks and collar, being a hot dish, from the waitress. That was the tradition, although his collar order was passed immediately to the chef. Who cooked it in a little Belling-type electric grill. Simple, basic, but produces nectar. He was feeling a little more himself now, a little more of the soul he recognised was returning to his body. And after the first intake of beer, having asked the waitress if she wouldn't mind pouring his sake, which of course she understood, it was considered bad luck to pour your own, at least he was told that once and had stuck to it, he ordered a beer for the chef and started to write.

*Dear Lomita,*

*I came to Los Angeles with the singular intention of sorting out my father's estate. He died nearly four weeks ago. I met you and had no intention of looking for any kind of liaison with anyone, it just happened, and I feel we like each other. I certainly do. And very much look forward to seeing you again tomorrow or today depending on when you read this. But I have a lot of explaining to do about my life and what has happened in it so far. Albeit it has been a short one, which I intend to do, the explaining I mean. To you, as our relationship develops, and I sincerely hope it will. But I have a confession to make. I went to see the gallery that bought my father's entire collection of work ten years ago and said I wished to view it. They informed me that some of the paintings had been sold (something, sadly, my father never knew). They said that the remaining collection was warehoused out of town and before they could hang it for a viewing, understandably they would require references in terms of financial credibility in light of potential purchase. I couldn't give my name as I am the son (for reasons that I can explain later) and secondly, I can in no way satisfy any kind of financial investigation. Although I have no idea what the price of purchase of these works would be, and only really just wanted to see them, I know what the gallery paid (will also go through that later). Here comes the embarrassing bit. I gave your name, in terms of you being the interested party as the collector and that I was acting for you. If you don't want to see me tomorrow when I come round at six o'clock just send Manita to the door, tell me to go away and I will completely understand. The gallery has no info on you as I said you would be responsible for contacting them directly, so we can forget the whole thing. If you want. Please forgive me. I have had a bit of a bad day today in other ways and would be happy to explain that too, which might throw some light on my behaviour. If I don't see you again (and I so don't want that to be the case, even if it's only to apologise for what I have done and then you can kick me out) it has been a privilege and an honour to meet someone so garlanded in beauty, intelligence, and finesse as you. Thank you for your company.*

*With love, I think,*

*Ever.*

*p.s. Sorry if this is garbled and confusing I am drinking a little sake. Sorry.*

*x*

He thought long and hard about putting the kiss at the bottom, but did so because the length of the thought process took him through another order of both the beer and the sake, so by that time, he needed to summon the discipline for just the one kiss.

He asked for the bill, the check, and also if they had an envelope.

They brought the first request, understandably, but failed on the second so he asked for another piece of paper and fashioned it into an envelope-y kind of thing, a memory from school days, wrote the name Lomita on the front, realising he still wasn't sure of the spelling of Nairn, especially after the beers, and didn't want to get it wrong, securing the letter inside. Done. Good evening's work. He hoped. Not that he was wishing to exploit her at all, but he felt genuinely stupid for what he had done and would be happy to continue their relationship whether she could help or not.

Who knows, she might be broke too, although something in her manner seemed to suggest an ease with money, at least either past or present.

He guessed he would soon find out.

As he got up to leave, four girls rushed in and shouted across the restaurant, oblivious to whoever was in there, which as it happened, was only him.

'Food to go, we've come to pick up our food.'

Almost in a chorus, the last word food had the extended vowels that put it into a singing context; they were obviously regulars as the waitress smiled and no names were asked for in exchange. No one seemed to take offence at what Ever perceived as a rudeness, so if the staff didn't, why should he? They looked at him as if he was sizing them up, which he wasn't, and they blocked the exit, being pack cool. He politely said,

'Excuse me please.'

That seemed cue enough to prompt the mockery that only the hunting pack have the courage to engage in.

'Oh, he's British, a Brit, oh, an English man.'

In the worst take on an English accent possible. Two were apple pie, pure blonde Americans and two were of mixed ethnicity, with an extract of Middle Eastern blood, that gave an even skin tone and smoothness of colour lending a natural and un-made-up glamour to their faces. All about sixteen or seventeen, products of the rich and living their own reality show. Ever smiled, they moved aside, as he hit the sidewalk, there was a white convertible BMW, with another girl sitting at the wheel as the car's engine revved and then was put silently to rest.

'What are you looking at?'

She shark bit him; to be honest he was looking at the car which was of greater interest to him than she was, although he didn't have the heart to tell her, he didn't want to disappoint, guessing that she must have felt super-attractive and confident behind the wheel, he smiled again and crossed the road into the public parking, where he had left his car.

As he drove out onto Canon Drive all the girls were climbing into their car with their takeout order. He wound his window down for air, the heckling started again on recognition, and he thought how unacceptable it would be now, if it was the other way round. They screeched the wheels on the road, like he used to when he first got a car, demonstrating their dominance in the most masculine of ways, screaming out of the window as they drove off.

He waved and found the reversal quite an interesting experience.

His only silent comeback was that they weren't as attractive as they thought they were.

On his drive home, he passed by 633 North Oakhurst Drive.

He dropped the letter through the letter box, which was, he had observed, in the door and not the traditional mailbox at the bottom of the driveway.

He had crept quietly, not wanting to go through any explanations now, and walked back to his car which he had left round the corner on Elevado. A Beverly Hills police car drove by, the toughest police force in America, they say, in possibly the most respectable neighbourhood in America, at least the only city without a slum area. They slowed down at the unusual sight of a walking human, and having wound down their window, observed that Ever had a respectable car to get into; they accelerated and looked for other riotous trouble.

A quiet night was probably ahead.

Opening those gates at the entrance to Havenhurst.

He secreted his car underground. The first thing he did on entering the darkness was to go to the supply of logs in the corner of the room, to the left of the fireplace, and look at the hiding place.

The hollowed-out log, two from the bottom, where he had secured the Glock 17. It was there. Comfort. He took it with him, up the one flight to the one bedroom that was housed upstairs, and in true movie style, put it underneath his pillow, safety off. Why? He wasn't sure, but it made him feel secure and at least no one else was going to get it.

No tequila, the stars would go on burning without him.

For one night at least.

They would manage.

He very rarely slept the sleep of the innocent, and tonight he felt the need to resort to one of the sleeping pills his doctor had given him, with the instruction not to make a habit of it.

That was six years ago, and he had made a habit of it; with the help of his friendly pharmacist he had downed a considerable number in his time. Zimovane, one of the Z group of drugs, a non-benzodiazepine. Zolpidem is another member of the grey cell killing Z family, more common in the US, where it goes under the trade name

Ambien. Now they, Ambien, they are special, they take your brain away for a while and what they do with it you can never remember. But tonight it is a Zimovane, the medical name for this hypnotic agent is zopiclone, a fuzzy-brain maker, that did not always work but he limited himself to a maximum of 15 mg a night, never more, twice the recommended maximum dose. He took less if he could, you felt shit in the morning. The claim was that they were a contributor to something or other, dementia, that's it; the one to look forward to if you can remember.

Those medical folk again.

There was no hope, then.

It, at least, staved off the dream he had had since childhood, which always felt like he was not asleep but fully awake, and hovering above his bed was a large, pale blue hand, there comes his dislike of the colour, swollen as if someone had blown it up like a washing-up glove. Pale blue, there it was, without any explanation as to why, or any indication of any action that it might take, but it was always frightening, even as an adult he found it frightening, it woke him from what already felt like a woken state and he found himself now disorientated with a genuine feeling of terror. Panic. A panic that it hadn't gone because the waking state brought no relief as he had had no concept of having been asleep. He was just there. He supposed it was because it always seemed to have the intention of taking him away, where to, he never knew, and, to be fair to the swollen pale blue hand, it never had. In thirty years. But he supposed there was always a first time. One night.

This was a sleepless night, even with the drugs; his thoughts were of Clarissa, Jacob and Lomita precisely in that order. The time spent on each was not consistent with the order, the pain was greater with some than others and the love also carried a variation in intensity. But, as always with Ever's brain, the choice was not really his.

He lay there being played with by his brain and wondered why his brain had these times of acting with complete independence.

# *Chapter Seventeen*

Ever felt he needed to be more anonymous.

He thought that he should trade in his rather stand-out rental and purchase an old car.

Or at least purchase an old car and keep the rental, if Lomita was still going to be in his life. He could buy a car, he had a ten-day period to transfer the title, but could give a false name, never do the transfer and then the car would be untraceable to him. He had in his mind a thing that he wanted to do, that would carry too much shame to tell anyone, even to acknowledge to himself. And he needed the shame car to be able to do that thing and then he could just be rid of it. Drive it to a waste patch in Koreatown or the like, and with no record of ownership coming back to him, he would be able to just dump it. And with it hopefully the shame and the guilt.

But probably never that, with his brain, they would both stay with him.

He just hadn't worked out whether what he had decided to do would make him feel better about his father. He was worried about the state of his brain, he could feel the anxiety and the pressure and the dark; that feeling of doing the extreme without caring about consequence.

As was once said of him at school by his housemaster.

This boy has no moral compass. How the housemaster knew at the age of fifteen had always been a mystery to Ever. But in his own way, though not a bad person, Ever understood what he meant; he had no stop buttons, no censorship for when he wanted to do something. He put his head down and did it. Consequences later. He remembered the time when he had to change his modus, whether conscious or not. He was still small for his age, with constant bouts of illness, and was bullied endlessly – then during one episode of being beaten up by the same lumpen idiot, he decided to pick up a broom and swing it wildly round and round, screaming that he had gone completely insane. Making contact with the broom on the side of the bully's head, severely damaging his eye socket, something he was not proud of. But from that moment he was known as a crazy guy, the boys started to leave him alone; one or two more manic screaming fits were needed, at certain times, to solidify this new persona, and it proved to be a successful self-protection process.

This crazy guy persona, at school in England, got him promoted from the Fourth XV at rugby to the First XV as he employed this same degree of mania on the pitch, and that too proved to be a success. Head down and go.

Reputation seemed to be all.

An interesting concept that had stayed with him all his life. But as his life progressed, he wondered whether the put-on mania was in fact not put on, but the start of a mental change that would begin to haunt him and that he couldn't control.

Anyway here he was, having a bit of a struggle in life, going upstream while it felt the current was getting stronger and forcing him back.

But what was it that was pushing him on?

Why was he doing this? Had he forgotten?

He thought he wanted to kill Ingmar Lorken.

No, he knew.

He returned to the Lorken gallery.

Downtown, with the hope of seeing the man himself, not to speak to, but to find out where and what he did during the day. Ever didn't valet park, he just sat in the car and waited. He saw no one but made the decision that he would do this every day until he saw Mr Lorken and could get the pattern of this man's life.

Let's see what Lomita has to say.

Hopefully not fuck off, get out of my life.

There was an obvious trepidation. Almost a sweat-inducing panic, as once again he extended his digit to exact the pressure, thinking, strangely, given the circumstances, that Manita should polish the brass bell button.

He waited and heard no footsteps; unsurprising as the door was opened by a person in a wheelchair.

It was Lomita, looking tired, but with a smile, that smile, and he cried, with relief. Released it all on to the herringbone-pattern red brick step.

She said nothing, letting him expunge his pain, and the air around joyously responded to her wave, encouraging him inside. She wheeled herself across the brown floor, this time to waiting double doors, that were open, on the right of the big brown room. It was the dining room.

Places were set for two, adjacent to each other. She wheeled her chair to the head of the table, with her back to the garden, and he was afforded the seat on her left, offering a view of the recently manicured lawn that gave its pristineness away not only by its physical immaculacy but by the smell of fresh cut grass that always made Ever think of cricket. And incongruously, at that moment he thought of his 101 not out, made when he was fourteen.

And then she spoke.

'Unfortunately, I was still awake when your letter came through the door, and I had, I suppose as a result of that, a bad night.'

That was not, Ever thought, a good start.

'But I'm not about to reprimand you, or anything, you are a grown-up, I am presuming anyway, otherwise where do we possibly begin. But you used my name. My name.'

The last two words were repeated with greater force.

'And that is not a name that I throw around in any context. Let me give you a brief history of myself, my sweet.'

That phrase again.

'I think I should make something clear about myself.'

This took him completely by surprise; he was convinced the opposite would happen, that that exact proposal would be directed towards him, demanding an explanation from him.

'I...'

She continued.

'Was married to a man I thought, or rather took to be a lawyer, which indeed he was, but that was not all he was. He was Robert, or in fact Roberto dePirizone, that means nothing to you, but he was known as the boss, he was Italian, here in Los Angeles, in the very early sixties. So, use your imagination. I came here, and had, in pursuing my dream, my dream to be an actress, contacted a man who had given me his card years previously, when I was working in the Carlton Hotel in Pittsburgh. My home town. He had told me, and indeed did tell me when I arrived, that he could get me into motion pictures. I never, through a set of circumstances that I am not ready to go into, never did make a motion picture as such. But I made a lot of money, that is the point I am getting to: that is the answer to the question that you are sitting there wanting to ask me, that you were so concerned with that you dropped a note through my door at eleven-thirty at night.'

Her tone was increasing in volume, backed up with a suggestion, or maybe more than a suggestion, as she went on, of anger.

'And let me tell you, just because we have had dinner and you got an erection when holding me, gives you no claim to my name. Although it is my maiden name, and no one connects me with my past, which was—'

She halted.

'No, I am not going to explain all that to you now. Yes, in answer to your selfish concern, my financial status if checked by some pretentious gallery, would be more than adequate for whatever it is you want to do. And that brings me to the question. What do you want to do, my sweet? What is the little mess you have found yourself in? Are you wanting me to buy these paintings, or just for me to appear to be impressive enough for them to hang them for a private view? And be honest with me. I don't know you, I like you, but those are two very different things. And knowledge clarifies a situation far more than liking someone. So, tell me about your little mess.'

Ever was incapable of saying a word and wanted to leave, but his hatred of people leaving tense situations instead of resolving them insisted his body remain in the chair. He looked out at the garden and got lost momentarily in the colours, now that the sun was dropping behind the trees making them golden. The threat of darkness was starting, it was always a threat, and he realised his life was indeed a little mess. How could he tell her what he really wanted to do, which he probably was not mentally stable enough to be able to explain with a logic that would convince or substantiate itself. He was defeated. She, presumably, sensed his defeat and continued –

'We are eating food from Mr Chow's, they are delivering. Squab with lettuce and spare ribs, followed by duck and pancakes. We will drink a sauvignon blanc from Australia, Margaret River, I prefer it from there, the grape has a more mineral quality, as long as it's ice, ice cold. And you like San Pellegrino don't you? So that too.'

He nodded and with effort spoke.

'Thank you. I could tell you, but you know, Lomita, I think I am wrong, and there probably is little point, so maybe if you don't mind we can eat and then I should take my leave.'

'As you wish, but I hope you like spare ribs, I ordered them because men always seem to like them and I hate them.'

Men always like them, lodged. He knew so little about her and had, in a rather patronising way, because she was old and seemed frail, overlooked the fact that she had lived a life, had her own disasters, and joys, and tragedies; he felt like his mother. Just looking at everything from his point of view, his perspective and, yes, he did suppose that his intention, however much he shrouded it in the vagueness of liking her, was to quite simply use her.

'I think I wanted to use you.'

He didn't think he had said it but he had.

'You wouldn't be the first.'

And that laugh gurgled in the back of her throat again, it forced a smile that he tried to resist forming across his face, and he too made the sound of the first suggestion of laughter.

The doorbell rang, at what he assumed was the tradesmen's entrance; he could hear the distant exchange of words indicating that the food had arrived.

And sure enough, after what seemed minutes sitting in silence, a tray arrived carrying the wine and San Pellegrino and a bucket of ice, obviously to back up the need for the sauvignon to be at its particular ice-cold temperature. But it would weaken its mineral strength, the ice, he thought, staring at the silver bucket, seeing a convex face stare back. His reflection was surprised by his concern. Manita left the room, without attempting to pour anything, returning with the ribs and squab and lettuce. Lomita was in mid flow.

'...and people pouring my wine in restaurants, and the water, is my absolute hate. I get so annoyed, I drink at my own pace, they don't feed me for God's sake, I don't eat at their pace, so why in God's name do they demand I drink at their pace. Moneymaker that's all. The ribs are all for you. Did I tell you I hate them?'

'You did.'

The first words he seemed to have said in a while, they sounded flat, but in no way did he wish to appear ungrateful or rude.

'I am in a little pain so have taken a Vicodin, which I love – it makes me go a little trippy.'

The word 'trippy', which initially seemed out of place coming from her mouth, on reflection seemed appropriate as this was a girl who had grown up in the hippy era. A sixties, Aquarius, flowers-in-her-hair girl.

'I have...'

She went on. There was no stopping her, he didn't intend to try.

'A pharmaceutical treasure chest, all brought back from Mexico, where I have a house. I love Mexico. Manita and I are always down there, I much prefer it to here. Don't you want this plum sauce on your lettuce with your squab?'

Not really sure what squab was anyway, or the way to eat

it, he spooned some of the sauce onto the lettuce. It seemed a very simple dish for a restaurant to bother with, and he got no tips from her as to what to do, she had pushed the squab to one side and was doing her usual, well it was only his second experience of her eating habits, but he was familiar with her thing of picking at a lettuce leaf. It tasted like chicken and he took a knife and fork to the whole thing, in the absence of any alternative being proposed, desperate to move on to the spare ribs. The things that all men loved.

'You mentioned though, that you sometimes watch a movie after dinner, and I assumed, I'm not sure why, it would have been one of yours.'

He instinctively thought he should attempt to crawl out of the hole.

'Well I am sure, sorry, because of your looks. I'm sorry, I don't mean to appear, sorry, I can't think of the word.'

'You haven't quite regained your composure, have you my sweet? Wrap it.'

'Sorry?'

'The squab, wrap the lettuce around it.'

He obeyed.

'Did I say one of mine or just a motion picture?'

'You said… I'm not sure.'

He said in deference; still crawling out of the hole.

'I thought you did?'

He doubted now.

'That's what has stayed in my mind at any rate.'

'My, I must have had a weak and trusting moment both at the same time. Not much chance of that. At least let's get on a clearer footing as to what it is you want, and in a way who the fuck you are, other than that you are in my house, eating, and you have to be nearly fifty years younger than me. It is a little disconcerting, also because sex is not something I go in for.'

A strange expression, go in for, he thought, as if it was a sport that you had to choose at school. He saw sex as just something that you wanted or didn't and had never considered it to be an add-on option. An option to take up or not.

'How old are you anyway?'

'Thirty, nearly thirty-one.'

'Oh, that makes a big difference.'

A rare moment of sarcasm.

'The ribs are delicious.'

Relieved that he had something that consumed him fully, hands, mouth, and napkin. The works. Fully occupied and he didn't feel the embarrassment of having to make conversation.

'Married, are you?'

She asked dispassionately.

Now forking a small amount of the squab onto the lettuce and wrapping it into a roll, the plum sauce having lined the lettuce. So that's how it's done; he felt a moment of stupidity, but small by comparison to how stupid he had felt for most of the evening.

'Yes, but separated, the child turned out not to be mine. Not that it affects my love for him. He's called Jacob, he's two, nearly three really.'

Why is everything a 'nearly' thought Ever.

'Well it's not the love, just the sense of connection I suppose, well, incorrectly perhaps, really, the sense of ownership, and I know, before you correct me, you don't own your kids.'

'I wouldn't know.'

She interrupted.

'I don't have any. And your father, what about him?'

'The person I have loved more than anything in the world.'

He could see the invitation to carry on in her look.

'I watched him destroy himself slowly over a period of years. His creativity was, I suppose, his life, the thing that motored him, and it just left him. Disappointment and pain, well an agony, just took him.'

The invitation remained.

'It happened after this man bought all his work and then did nothing with them, you know, the paintings. He just warehoused them, waiting to see if he ever broke. You know, became something.'

'I know.'

She interrupted the invitation, with a mild annoyance.

'I understand what you are saying.'

'It took away his will.'

Ever continued.

'I think in a way watching his heart break broke mine. My brain anyway, well that's not entirely true, and, well, this will probably get me kicked out of the house, but I have had a lot of mental problems, well, issues, and I don't blame him or anything, but I have been filled with a desire, a real burn, to correct what I thought, what I think, is wrong.'

'Why are you blaming someone who paid good money for his work and afforded him some kind of lifestyle, I am assuming, anyway?'

Ever had often tortured his way around this one; he didn't have to think to reply.

'It was the fact that nothing sold.'

Ever paused, looking at the ice in his glass, it was in the last throes of its usefulness. The ice was melting. It must be so relieved, he thought, its job was nearly done, flowing into a liquid peace. Lomita was wating for his eyes to raise. When they did it took Ever no time for his pain to return.

'Well...'

He started with little confidence knowing that he was going to be exposed in his argument.

'I thought, as he did, that nothing had sold but then I found out that over half of the paintings sold eight years ago.'

'Well that's…'

'No hear me out, sorry, please.'

'Of course.'

'Thank you. Somehow that makes it all worse. Because he never knew, that's the point, he never got any money, which apparently he wasn't entitled to… anyway…'

Ever swirled the glass to break down the last fractures of ice. There was a gentle tinkle from the glass.

'So that is almost worse to me, that is just cruel.'

'Why?'

'Not telling him anything basically, so he was none the wiser.'

'But is that what stopped him painting?'

'He lost his belief, yes, his confidence in his talent.'

'Carmen Herrera is in her hundreds and still painting and she didn't get her first show till she was in her fifties or sixties; she just gets up and does it every day. That is belief, that is belief in self. Not affected by outside forces, by approbation.'

'So?'

'So maybe you're blaming the wrong man.'

This sat like a lit, unexploded firework; no one sure whether to go near it again.

There would have been time to cook potatoes in the bonfire.

'Jesus, I'm sorry,'

Ever acknowledged the hiatus.

'I really am, I'd only just found this out, about the sale, you know, when…'

'When you roped me in on all this.'

Lomita's statement was a flatline of emotion. The confusion and contortion were disconcerting, he was evidently sponge-ing up all the pain.

'How much?'

'What?'

'How much did they sell for?'

'They have no legal requirement to tell me, apparently. Discretion was the word used.'

'Obviously.'

'But promises were made that were broken and that to me seems wrong. Anyway what I'm saying is that, what happened to those paintings is what finished him. Sold, warehoused or whatever. The way he was treated. It broke him. Maybe I am fucked up, I don't know, I am confused, I know, but I think that it will, in some way, bring him a peace.'

Lomita said nothing, not asking the question, waiting for the mop up of pain to stop.

'Then I can pray to him at night and tell him it's all OK.'

This created another silence in the room.

'Then he can rest.'

Lomita didn't want any more silence.

'Well, obviously, there is "discretion" because if the paintings went for a lot of money or very little they wouldn't want the sale price to have any effect either way if they were taken to auction. They'd want a clear shot, I guess. It seems logical to me. The less people know is always better. But it is possible they have stagnated since the purchase eight years ago, you know, the value just got stuck.'

'How do you know?'

'How do I know or how do I know?'

Ever nodded, not sure at what.

'Because as much as I tried to ignore the business practices that went on around me in my previous life, I picked up a little.'

Lomita smiled tantalizingly.

'So I'll ask you again: are you blaming the wrong man?'

Ever's food energy had dissipated, he sat back in his chair, in a slight slump, and downed the last of his ice-melt wine.

Please don't question me don't make me confused I came here clear don't change my course don't belittle me with your knowledge it is all irrelevant I know what happened to my father you don't don't bring your objective uncaring analysis into my life. That was what he wanted to say. He didn't, those thoughts were subsumed into the words:

'I think I should go, I don't feel too good, I am sorry to be an eat-and-runner. I was wrong, I leap to situations in my mind and take them to places they haven't gone to in other people's. I imagine people are feeling the same as me and that they – I am sorry. I am so sorry, I was wrong.'

He stopped abruptly, finished with his attempt at explanation.

'I have got the thing for you. Diazepam or lorazepam, both big downers, though highly addictive, so you can only have 5 mg.'

'I don't mind.'

Ever said, without pause for thought, fondly familiar with downers.

'Whichever.'

She wheeled herself away from the table, just as Manita came in with the duck.

'Don't worry, Manita, carry on, I am coming right back.'

This, Ever had eaten before; the meat was shredded off the bone, he knew to plum sauce the pancake and put a little cucumber and spring onion and then the duck. He was relieved to have that knowledge and knew it would be delicious. But first he poured himself another large glass of the white, dropped a slightly melted cluster of iceberg cubes into the glass and drank. And drank. What was he doing? The silence of the wheels on the polished floor could be heard as a smooth absence and she returned with a little purple pill. A half.

'Diazepam, you'll feel calmer in half an hour, don't worry about mixing it with alcohol, it's not going to hurt you, you just shouldn't drive. But you can stay here.'

Ever went quiet, groin quiet, at least.

In acknowledgement of the obviosity of the male, Lomita quickly followed –

'I have an en-suite guest bedroom, of course. You are more than welcome.'

She smiled an 'end to all that' smile.

'So basically what, after you have viewed these paintings, which I presume you have seen before anyway, do you want to do with them?'

A very good point, as Ever could not tell her what his real desire was, even he considered it to be tinged, to say the least, with an imbalance. A lack of sane proportion to the act committed.

'Buy them? Own them? What, tell the guy he's a schmuck? I can guarantee he already knows that. Anybody with money knows that deep down, that's why they've got the money, to cover it up. That's why they worked so hard in the first place, and if they didn't work hard and it just came to them, well—'

She let the 'well' hang, as the conclusion to her statement didn't demand a voice. It was obvious.

He was preparing his second pancake, with the air velveting over him, the wine giving him a glow, feeling a little connection to the soul that he liked to connect with, but rarely did. She popped a bigger pill of a question.

'You are not contemplating revenge, are you?'

'What do you mean?'

He knew full well she knew.

'On him, what's his name again?'

'I never told you. Ingmar Lorken.'

'Oh my, yes, we've all heard of him.'

'I don't think so, not revenge.'

He lied, with no conviction at all.

She seemed to ignore this unconvincing denial.

'What would you do? Hurt him? His family? He already feels totally unimportant – that's why he collects things that are important.'

The collector's psychological profile. And then with the laugh, really coming from deep in her throat.

'Or do you want to kill him? Complete his collection.'

They both were laughing, that was his spontaneous reaction to her infectious noise. And for the first time the dinner relaxed, she poured more wine for herself, then stood for the first time that evening. In her stand she groaned.

'My God, pain is a curse. Just getting a little cramp.'

She walked slowly around the table. She was dressed in a long silk dressing gown of a wild pattern of flowers and birds. Dramatic. Ever thought that it was probably Hermès; that was the most expensive brand that came to mind.

'Do you like it, my gown?'

She did a little, delicate and slow twirl.

'Pucci, fabulous eh? Made for me in 1969. I look after things, you see. Beautiful isn't it?'

It was. She completed her walk around the table, she came around behind him, rested her hands on his shoulders, lowered her head towards his, then draped her body like a shawl across his back and said, very quietly,

'Do we like each other, truly? Do we trust each other, truly? I don't do that easily and if you're thinking about revenge, my sweet, I can tell you some things about revenge that may make you change your mind. That is, if your mind has both the capability and capacity to receive the information.'

She smiled with affection. He was unable to see it, but sensed the warmth in the moment.

'I just don't know if we have reached any kind of point that I can tell you. I don't tell anyone. So why you? Except I rarely like people. And I like you.'

Ever was at his most immobile and silent. He could feel her breath, smell the wine and that perfume, that smell of hers that he had never smelt on anyone before. She kissed his cheek and moved back into her wheelchair.

'My film, Christ, I said that to you, what was I on? My film. No, my sweet, we are not going to watch that.'

The singular indicated more than just the existence of a solitary film in her life; she had picked out the word as if it were a mouldy fruit in a bowl.

Ever was so confused by signals that were all different – one minute, please hold me as you say goodnight, next no interest in sex. Why did she let him be there? Had he been able to force his way in because of physical attraction? At first he'd thought she had a lonely miserable life, but now she appeared to be a sophisticated woman of the world. What did she want with him? Why ask him back for tea if it wasn't a physical attraction, no that really is too stupid – too male. But what was he doing expecting her to help him, what could he offer in return? He supposed, no, he thought he knew, that it would be sex, but what was he doing implicating this woman in what he was intending to do, which was, essentially, murder in the first degree? Was he blaming the wrong man?

He quietly out of the silence spoke.

'I feel tired but I am OK to drive.'

'Are you sure?'

Was all that came from her, and on thanking her for dinner, he got up and walked to the door. She made no attempt to salvage whatever situation they were in, just said with a calm voice.

'Drive carefully, my sweet.'

He closed the door, got into his car and felt his soul leave him.

He was on his own again, lost with a crazy idea that obsessed him and a life he didn't really want. His default position. His only gratitude at that moment was extended towards Lomita, who had the kindness to feed him and entertain him after he sent her a stupid, childish, drunken letter asking her to do what? God, please damn it all. He drove off very slowly, feeling heavy with the pill and wine. Disappointed in himself again, and feeling like the crazy boy who had to swing the broom. For what, Ever, why do you do what you do? Why do you want to?

Twenty-seven times he wanted to swing the broom.

It didn't make a difference, the twenty-seven, he didn't want it to, it had made no difference to his father.

# *Chapter Eighteen*

The time was coming for him to be checked by the doctor.

And he had forgotten to mention the Basquiat exhibition. Not that he gave a shit, but he did, he just wanted to meet Ingmar Lorken.

He admired the turmoil that had been the short life of Jean-Michel Basquiat.

He turned right onto Sunset.

His slow concentrated crawl seemed to attract the attention of a woman who, at the lights, indicated to him that she would like a ride. Having felt his soul float away, so now more convinced of his lack of moral compass, he paid attention; she looked drunk, drugged, just out of it on some substance, he decided no, then she walked to his car and tried the door. That thing that happens to those sensing the adventure happened, he unlocked the door and she climbed in.

'Just down Sunset if you can. If you would. Thanks. Do you mind if I smoke?'

He had said nothing. And was not going to object to her smoking; you don't pick up a girl and then impose the moral etiquette of no smoking.

'Fine.'

He muttered.

'How far you going?'

He thought of a cross street.

'Highland.'

'Thanks guy, I'm Mari.'

'Hi.'

He said, not offering a name.

'Do you want me to blow you for the ride, and maybe a few bucks?'

He gave this serious consideration.

At the next lights he looked at her long and hard. Why not being his first thought.

The roots had been growing out so long they could no longer be called roots. She was about thirty-five. User of something hard. Smelt of perfume, strongly. Wore leggings. Tight top, small breasts, all covered with a fake leopard-print coat. Thin face, not unappealing, not much make-up. Teeth, there at least, if not pearly. Eyes – dark. Ethnicity – Caucasian. He could see no reason why not.

'Sure, how much?'

'Twenty, take me to Cahuenga and you can fuck me if you want. Another twenty.'

Oh Christ it was getting worse.

'No, a blow job is fine.'

'OK, when we get to Cahuenga.'

'Sure. OK.'

They continued with her talking about her music, how her boyfriend was not supporting her and that she couldn't get any gigs anymore. She rounded off,

'Life is going pretty good otherwise though, you know, nothing to complain about.'

My God, thought Ever, how positive is that. Sitting in a car offering to blow a stranger. And life was pretty good. It's strange how strangers can get down to something as basic as sex without any circumnavigation when they want to. Yet in a relationship it becomes a major issue. They had reached Cahuenga.

'Just pull down the street. Take a right.'

'OK.'

'Got the twenty?'

'Sure.'

She went to unzip his pants and leant over to grab his cock. He wasn't sure if he was going to get hard, already feeling there wasn't too much that was sexy about this.

Then she vomited all over his lap.

Christ.

That was one thing that he could not cope with.

Vomit.

He thought of Clarissa and how he could never deal with Jacob being sick. It made him feel embarrassed at this predicament. As if they could see him. He grabbed the keys from the car and leapt out, screaming.

'Get out! Get out!'

She was wiping her mouth, insisting she was really sorry.

'I know a place you can clean up.'

She was saying.

'Just near here.'

He went around to her side and helped her out. The stench was making him retch. He dumped her on the side of the road. She put up no resistance and just tried to light another cigarette. He gave her a twenty-dollar bill anyway, U-turned and drove back to Havenhurst, retching the whole way, windows down, sticking his head out of the window. The car would never lose this smell.

He cleaned as much as he could off the car, most of it had been deposited on his lap, and as quick as each retch allowed him he ran into the apartment, started the stream from the shower and got in, clothes and all.

What is it about him that brings out the worst in people?

When he has good intentions in the first place?

If you can call stopping for a blow job being a good intention. He wasn't really going to do it, it was just out of interest, come on, no punishment now, no guilt. Please. His brain persisted in its independence. Everything he deals with goes to bad. It wasn't a bad idea to get a blow job. But then vomit. Christ.

Clarissa, Jacob, his father, his mother, Lomita. A hooker. Even with a hooker, he drew a negative outcome in her life. Ever, come on. Did he produce the positive anywhere? He stripped off in the shower, trampling his clothes on the tiles. And decided to bag them in the morning to take them straight to the cleaners. He took a comforting pharmaceutical aid. The introduction of the Z family to the wine and diazepam seemed to do the trick.

Better than the trick that had just been turned.

# *Chapter Nineteen*

The next day found him driving early to the Lorken gallery again.

Having dropped off his clothes at Holloway cleaners, to spend, he decided, as much time as it took, just sitting outside in his car, waiting for the man. He could smell the stale vomit in the air, windows down and disinfectant sprayed on the seats, hers and his, to cover the splatter. But still – could he smell that smell? Breathe in. Yes it was there, was it less now? Now though surely, another breath, less, was it, no, still there? Well, now his imagination was engaged and so he could just be summoning up the smell. Now he would never know. Once that kicked in.

He presumed, or was it assumed, no there was evidence, that this man would make some kind of an appearance at some point in the day.

That was his determined, main occupation of the day. But his preoccupation was, should he ask Lomita? And how could he ask Lomita to the private view of the Basquiat exhibition?

Ever was truly appreciative, well, a fan, of Jean-Michel Basquiat's work. *Philistines* being one of his favourites, and *Fishing* had to be up there, looking like it was stripped of all goodness and raw to the world. Took him to his cheese-grater experiences. His skin scraped raw, all nerve ends exposed; the vulnerable pain in mental collapse.

The exhibition promised to be the largest collection of his works gathered in one gallery in the last twenty years, with all the celebrity collectors donating to the exhibition. It should be, at least, an event.

Ever had always felt he understood the substance of what went into Basquiat's work. It represented a mania and disturbance of the norm that he empathised with, also Basquiat had a mother who spent a lot of time in mental institutions, obvious really. Heroin was not a shared experience though, Ever thought, but that's a detail. An act away.

It was all in Ever's head, in his own imagination, the connection, but that is what it all is in life anyway. Isn't it? Yes, for sure. Perception, how you perceive things, from whichever stance you want, or decide to take. Basquiat was all done by the time he was twenty-seven, another member of the 27 Club.

Ever paused deep, deep down inside.

Twenty-seven. Jesus Christ. Twenty-seven. His father was a twenty-seven. A member of the club in his own way. Unique version. All, all of them twenty-seven.

27 27 27.

Stop saying. Stop seeing. Breathe. All he could see inked on the retina focused by the cornea was twenty-seven. The number twenty-seven.

His hand smacked his face, stinging his cheek. He focused on the sting.

It fuzzed the image, it brought him back out of his mind's eye.

It was Basquiat's talent, of course, yes, he wanted to see what he had never seen before, the majority of his catalogue in one place, live in the painted flesh. It was not a disingenuous whimsy.

This made him compare and reflect on his father's work; it worried him.

That maybe after all the agony, the taking on of the pain, that his father was not a crippled and halted genius. Maybe he just wasn't a genius. Ever couldn't bear the weight of that. Ever had always felt that he himself amounted to very little, that his father had become the giant, the adored one in his life, the idolised one. He had wished as he was growing up that he had his father's reckless abandonment and, well, just that lightbulb illumination quality.

He didn't know if he would be accompanied to the Basquiat by his meal ticket, and yes, he was now clear and honest to himself about the use of Lomita, as that's what she was. His ticket. And she knew. What a silly man, that was the right word, silly, a small and insignificant description of something, what a silly man to think that his whatever, his appeal, could cajole someone into doing what he wanted. What he wanted for his own ends without anything in it for her. Horrible arrogance. He felt a bad person, something he never considered himself to be. Driven by neurotic compulsions, yes, but not intentionally bad. But maybe he should come out of the insane closet and admit what his intentions really were.

Dammit, but he did like the woman and that in itself had a degree of abnormality about it. Did it, though?

I mean is that wrong?

Is it taking advantage?

Is it cruel?

At that moment, what Ever recognised as a Rolls-Royce Dawn Drophead coupé pulled up, with the top down.

A majestic swoosh of a car. In electric blue, not the colour he would have chosen, with a pale tan upholstery, but in whatever specification, it was a beautiful car. But shouldn't the car be allowed to do the work, not the colour? You don't need both, unless you do, and that in itself is worrying. A dream on four wheels, the maximum that can be achieved out of a 120-year-old concept: the motor car.

It was him. Short, well shortish, with dark, dyed hair and a suit and shirt in a more sombre tone of grey, at least not competing with the car, covered his fattening frame, as he valet-parked with an obsequiousness from the attendants giving away his importance.

He was walking into a building that bore his name.

What must that feel like, Ever wondered, to have that money, that power, that control over your life, with no one to tell you there was nothing you couldn't do, and still get such a bad hair dye job?

It was all going to stop for Mr Lorken though. It gave Ever a feeling of power greater than Mr Lorken could ever feel, it disturbed him in a way that made him realise his wish was from a head space that had mixed itself into a distorted mode. He felt in the second, and it only lasted for that second, that he needed help, and then, worryingly, it was gone. Which is the true sign of madness, really being able to deny its existence and justifying the extremity of one's actions without the concept or awareness of a conscience.

His mind scanned to Lomita. He thought of her remark about revenge, his good soul clicked in for that split atom second and he wanted to talk to her, ask her what she meant. Advice, that was a positive sign, and maybe a way back. A way back into her life.

An excuse at least, to see her again.

He got out of his car, having been the second in line to valet, after the electricity of blue had rendered all else into insignificance, and followed Mr Lorken into the gallery. When he walked in, the man was nowhere to be seen. Had he gone into an office? A private escape. But then a glimpse of the grey passed by the entrance to where men were working, painting the walls of an empty space. Preparation, he presumed, for Jean-Michel Basquiat. He deserved a fresh coat of paint. He had come to discuss the hanging of the paintings, that would be his function in the process, that would be his control over the event. It would all, of course, be decided by him. Everything was, of course. Who lived. Who died. He was God. He was Ingmar Lorken.

Would he be, soon, an historical figure, confined to the history books of great benefactors perpetuating the belief that it was all done for the greater good of the world. So that the world could share.

Egomania, thought Ever, pure ego-fucking-mania.

The security guards, two of them, crossed the area in an informal march at the entrance to the space that housed the one they perceived to be the great man. They would obviously prevent any communication between Ever and Mr Lorken. However it was not their intervention that presented the obstacle, as Ever's phone rang, a rare event in itself.

It was Clarissa.

It was a time when Jacob would be asleep and he answered the call, dismissing his instinct, which was to not.

'Hello.'

They both said, at the same time, a time delay and a sort of distort corrupted the purity of what should be simple, having put men on the moon nearly fifty years ago.

'How's Jacob? Is everything all right? Where are you? Are you at home, or where?'

'I am at home, Ever.'

She stated with a formality, the obvious suggestion in her voice being that any alternative accommodation had now proved unsatisfactory.

'I am at our home. I assume that is all right with you.'

'Fine, of course. Fine.'

What else was he going to say?

'When are you back? I thought you would be back soon. Jacob misses you. He still calls you Dada. He doesn't understand anything else. You are his father in his mind, Ever, and the other guy—'

She didn't bring herself to the point of name.

'He doesn't really seem to be too bothered either way.'

Clarissa was Jewish, hence the name Jacob. Culturally, not in any religiously orthodox way. But it was still a conscious, constant awareness of custom and certain holidays that were observed. Ever liked that, he felt his wishy-washy, non-committal, I-suppose-I-am-Church-of-England religious, if you could even call it that, commitment was a little sad and certainly ineffectual. So he welcomed a commitment to something, and Judaism didn't seem half bad. His grandfather's wife had been Jewish, so, in his head, it carried the continuity of skipped generations.

'I miss him too, and you.'

He said the latter as an afterthought, which she seemed to pick up, judging by her lack of response.

'Well, when are you coming home? And what are we going to do when you do? You have to be back in what, just over two weeks?'

'Yes.'

He replied vaguely, as a return, at this point, seemed remote and so incredibly distant.

'About that. I guess I'll come home, and well, see how we go. Is that what you want?'

'Well, you are responsible for Jacob.'

'Wait.'

He said, a spontaneous and instantly regretted interjection.

'Am I? Am I really? After all you said, in fact, and the, and the—'

It was difficult to form into a word. But he did.

'Betrayal.'

'I didn't call you to go into all that on the phone. I just wanted to see how you are doing and whether we have any kind of future, you know, plan. It's not unreasonable to ask. I have responsibilities too, we both do.'

'Do I? I thought you removed those responsibilities from my life. That seemed to be your intention at least.'

'I'm going now, Ever.'

That was so typical of Clarissa, at the point of actually talking about some serious shit, she would pull out. Discussion, calm discussion, was not for her. Emotional argument was her thing.

'I miss you OK, that's it, let me know what you're doing.'

'OK.'

And then after a long 6,000-mile pause, that seemed to travel every mile, Clarissa said, without much enthusiasm,

'I guess I love you, Ever.'

'OK.'

He said.

And the phone call ended with the words.

'Give my love to Jacob.'

He wasn't sure if she caught them or not.

He retired the phone to the inside pocket of his jacket, aware that the radio waves, even though a form of non-ionising radiation, might be causing his heart a problem. He stood and thought, I have a child, why in God's name isn't he truly mine? Then thought again, about its magnitude in this, his endless chain of emotion.

And then thought again that maybe he was thinking too much.

Again.

No sign now of Mr Lorken.

Should he go and see Miss Money-Root? But then he had no information to give her.

He sauntered to the door, not something he did very often – saunter – and was passed, thinking about Jacob, by a well-built man, carrying a bit of extra. He realised the truth of his size as he saw him closer – he wasn't so short – pulling out a ticket, about to collect his car from the valet.

Ever followed fast, desperately searching his pockets for his ticket; in the panic, of course, he couldn't find it.

A twenty-dollar bill was flashed as the Rolls, which had not been moved anywhere, was opened and the keys were handed to Mr Lorken.

How long would it take them to pull his own car from the bowels of wherever the hell they had taken it? He gave the valet the found and crumpled ticket and a ten-dollar bill, but didn't want to lose Mr Lorken. He wanted to track him.

He dropped his phone under the swish of blue, or at least pretended to. He addressed the driver of the Rolls who had just fired the engine into purr mode.

'Can you hold on a second, sir. I've just – it's my phone – under your wheel.'

Ever instinctively adopted his American-accented voice. The one he had developed when he stayed with his father and wanted to blend in, until he realised the power of the English accent with Californian girls. In this instant he felt achievement and pride in his new persona; in the next second, he felt Australian.

'Not a problem. Not a problem.'

These were the first words he had heard this man utter. What prophetically wrong words they were because he was everything that was the problem.

'Nice car to have your phone crushed by though.'

Came the limp reply from Ever, still holding his head facing the gutter. Another moment of sleuthing pride – the unseen face. He had made contact with his target, it was a weird and damaging feeling. Somehow the man now had a personality, was a reality to him and not just a figure of hatred and bitter resentment. He was now actually a person who he bitterly hated and resented.

'Thank you for waiting.'

Ever said, as he fluked the phone into his hand. Turning away and with his back to the car he lobbed across a nonchalant—

'Enjoy.'

And with that, the effortless movement of three tons eased itself from the roadside; just as Ever's car pulled up and the keys were handed to him, dangling with a disdain between finger and thumb. The smell hit thick – windows down. He could follow his man.

Out of downtown, the journey went onto the 10 and the Rolls turned off at La Cienega.

Was he going home?

Ever hoped. In the crawl that had been the freeway he had no difficulty in following this car: It stood out clearly and it was indeed a pleasure to watch its movement scoop up the road in almost silent procession.

The destination was appearing to be Beverly Hills. Ever was

not carrying his gun, the Glock 17, the end to the anguish of his father's life that lived in Ever even after his father's death. It all seemed so easy in these moments when his soul had left him.

Kill the cunt.

That was all his mind could construct. And what was wrong with that? Nothing, Ever, he told himself. Nothing. The smell of sick sank into the back of his nose and seemed appropriate.

La Cienega took him left on Burton Way and onto Little Santa Monica, a right up Crescent, two four-way stops, one at Carmelita, the other on Elevado: was he nearly a neighbour of Lomita's?

He then crossed Sunset to the north and headed for North Crescent Drive.

Gates opened as Ever stayed way back, concerned at the possible awareness and paranoia that a man of such wealth might have of being followed, although he had never been directly behind, always keeping cars between them and moving lanes on the freeway. But now he stopped. Pulled up, engine off, just able on the curve of the road, to see the massive gates open, as the electric blue car Rollered its way inside to the cool, Ever imagined, of a large probably temperature controlled garage, and a rest.

Ever did not feel good.

He must have sat in his car for what seemed an hour. Oblivious to the street cleaners and the passing cars.

He'd grown accustomed to the smell.

It had started, he was going.

And it was not in a good direction.

Ever returned to Havenhurst.

He could sense the hyper anxiety crawling over his body, his nerve endings were raw, the cheese grater had been taken to his skin, exposed all the nerves to the cold whisper of air that hit them and caused pain, an anxious pain that could only get worse. There was never any thought that recovery might happen, only the consuming knowledge that it was going to get worse, cause more vulnerability and fear. Hope of any outcome that would help, that might be positive, just went into the ether, into the rising air, leaving him in the lower gloom where the air had no sustenance, where breathing didn't really work, it didn't refresh, it didn't nurture, it merely allowed the lungs to take in a supply that stopped you dying. Although many times Ever had tried to hold his breath, to stop the process of breathing, hold his breath until – always the word until – as it carried a future. Filled with a misery and a depression that he could feel building from the roots that his feet took comfort from in the ground, he knew he was in trouble. Knew he was in for a bad time, knew that he needed help, he was taken over by the bad thoughts and wanted just to bury his head in shame, to protect himself from his mind, his actions and not go through what he felt was inevitable.

Twenty-seven.

He wanted to be medicated, he wanted to be put somewhere where he could become useless, and not have destruction in his head. He wanted it all, and it would go to black and blank. He wanted to sit in a chair and stare, and do nothing. Not eat, not sleep, just do nothing, because he would have no choice to do anything, it all left him, oozing out of his body, his hope, his feelings of love, of being loved, of wanting to see people, of wanting to hear noise, he wanted done with it, he wanted it all to stop, but he knew and it brought him great sadness that he didn't have the courage to make it all stop. His energy had gone, he was weak, his brain had no focus, his name was slipping from his mind, his feelings were going from his body, he didn't want to be clean, he wanted to smell, he wanted nothing good that life might have had to offer because it wasn't for him. Life wasn't for him, it was for all the other people who knew how to live it, who knew how to construct it, who had normal responses to situations, to people, people who understood what you were meant to do, who had reaction to conversation, to humour, that wanted food, that wanted to live. He didn't, he had closed down and he sat in the chair and managed all he could manage. He managed to urinate, to urinate in the toilet, and that was an achievement, and close the curtains and turn the day into night. The night and day had no difference, there was no need for light, it did nothing, he was dark and his eyes couldn't recognise light, and his mind couldn't feel light, he was heavy and it had all gone. That is what it feels like, that is where he would be now until, until, who knows, until the until happens, and that you would never know until it did. Ever sat and sat and sat. And that was that.

# *Chapter Twenty*

Two men ripped the dress off the woman with the bobbed hair and revealed a red bra and french knickers in a matching tone.

There were no words, she was thrown onto the bed having been backhanded across the face, and the lipstick on her face was smudged like blood across her cheeks where she had received the mouths of these two men.

Her underwear was taken off as she was turned onto her stomach and the penis of the dark-haired man was pulled from his pants.

Hard and desperate to find its hole.

She was pulled to her knees and her anus took the fingers of the other man while the cock entered her from behind, first pummelling her vagina for what seemed an agonising period of minutes and then pulled out as the man who was not inside her rammed his cock into her mouth; she gagged and then took it, as if weak and numbed into submission; the inevitable extra thrust on removal from the vagina caused a visible cry of pain, although no sound could be heard as her anus took the cock.

The man convulsed as his load entered her.

The other man pulled his cock from her mouth; as she collapsed onto the bed his sperm was forced onto her face and he rubbed it all over her face and then pissed on her slumped body.

She was out cold and both men, you could see, thought they had done a good job.

The woman on the bed didn't move, but the woman in the room did and turned on the lights and switched off the projector.

That was her movie.

One fifteen-minute stag movie as they were called and shown in private clubs. And that, at the time, 1964, was about as hardcore as they got. Lomita sat in the dimmed light, and she sat and sat.

She had not watched the movie for many years, but now looked at it barely recognising that it was her. Her objectivity allowed her to remember the circumstances with a clarity that she had been unable to face for most of her years.

She wanted it to help Ever. She could recognise a track that he was on that would eventually destroy the life that he already felt was destroyed, but my God he knew nothing, he was a child with a distortion, he knew nothing, she felt that she could make him know something and make him understand that life is full of consequences. Life is one giant consequence and she would like him to know that, but she didn't know if she would ever see him again. Maybe it was all too late and he had already done that which would determine his life: maybe she was wasting her time because maybe he didn't care.

At this particular moment he most certainly didn't care, he could barely care to piss in the designated place for pissing.

It was just that Lomita had lived with people who took revenge, who believed in that code, and they were the most miserable people she had ever known. In her entire life. You cannot go through life righting wrongs, especially ones that you aren't even sure are wrongs in the first place. She was familiar with the distort. She wanted to tell him how life can go wrong through maladjusted intention. She wanted to help him because she had nobody else.

Nobody else in her life.

And he was tangible, and she liked him.

Ever had spent three days sitting and drinking water and not washing and needed help.

In a week he would have to go to the doctor but couldn't go like this, they would snap him up and throw away the key. He could only think of Lomita and got out of his chair and in the boxer shorts he was wearing, found some chinos and pulled them on over his stinking body; with the T-shirt that he had been wearing, found some flip-flops, the keys to the car, his phone, and his way to the garage. He drove as slowly and conscientiously as he could.

To North Oakhurst Drive, hoping and praying that Lomita would be there but he would just sit there, anyway, until she became aware of him. He pulled up, the now familiar driveway, on reaching its gentle rise pushed the horn on his car, once, and waited. Manita appeared at the door and he did nothing, he couldn't move. The front door had been left open, he was staring at it, hoping with a quiet prayer. The next thing he knew Lomita and Manita were helping him into the house to the previously unseen guest bedroom with bathroom en suite. They lay him on the bed. He was crying the whole time. Lomita went to her pharmaceutical trove. She came back with 20 mg of diazepam and encouraging small sips of water she helped him swallow the dose, carefully returning his head to the pillow; she then pulled up a chair, the way people do with sick people in a bed. She just looked at him and held his hand, his crying very slowly diminished to silence, but the tears continued to run down his face. And the tears she was witnessing in his life she could feel in her own and more than ever she wanted this man to be saved from himself. Revenge for what had happened to her didn't help: nor would it help his father.

After all he was already dead.

The work had been done, the city had sucked his blood and let's hope the Angels had saved his soul.

Ever's physicality had been something of a surprise to Lomita. Initially. A pleasure, but he was almost unnecessarily handsome.

A well-built specimen, he was 6' 2" and weighed about 180 lbs; being only thirty, well, nearly thirty-one, he was very muscular, in a wiry way, his hair was dark, cut short as the curl annoyed him when it grew long.

And he was handsome.

Very.

As he lay there, Lomita was aware of the effort she had been forced to expend in helping Manita, who did most of the work, in getting him to the bed. She felt exhausted and would have liked to enjoy the comfort of lying by his side. She looked at him, his eyes were now closing as a result of the benzodiazepine; she wondered what it was that brought people to this city that destroyed more than it created.

For her, it was clearly an ambition to be an actress, a conviction that she would be one of them, the goddesses, the ones that had reached for the moon and held on. For Ever, his ambition was to fulfil an intention in a more altruistic way, to make something of his father in his own mind after his death. To give him a memory that his thwarted ambition, his failure had never allowed. Ever wanted to place him on a pedestal of worth. To make the sacrifice: to make him great.

A selfless act by a son, but then this son was not of sane mind, by his own admission. He had lived in the shadow of his father, and was obsessed with the agony of his father not becoming the man he was convinced he should have been.

Her situation was different, she was the wronged party, the woman not recognised for her talent, but abused; with a husband who adored her and had tried to give her life a quality that it might not have deserved. A dream that might have had no right to have been dreamt. Built on stuff of nothing.

Maybe they both had no talent.

Maybe the people who do make it in this City of Angels have talent and the Angels fly with them, guard them, look after them, and keep them from wrong. For a while anyway.

But maybe those that come here and shouldn't have are punished. Severely.

Lomita listened to his breathing: anxious, irregular intakes.

What was she going to do with him, shatter his dream and minimise his father's talent, attempt to show that maybe he was just ordinary, and revenge would change nothing.

Lomita stood to ease her cramp; she was dealing with her own thoughts about herself. She knew nothing about Ever's father or the quality of his work. She just knew that in her own mind and to the world she had been turned into a piece of trash. Nothing could have changed that. Nothing ever has.

Is that what happened in the City of Angels, why were they all here? Why didn't they all leave the place that housed the most horrible people on the planet and some of the most talented?

Not that the two qualities are necessarily mutually exclusive. Is it that they couldn't face the fact that they weren't all really talented, wonderful human beings, so they stayed, to feel part of swimming in the same pool, although they were at the wrong end?

The shallow one.

Lomita made the decision to see Ever's father's work.

She could calm him with her medications but he needed nutrition and caring to get back to being able to feel of value to himself again.

She sent Manita to Whole Foods, down the road on Crescent Drive, to buy more food, as they normally had a supply of salad and very little else. She wanted a chicken to roast, then to make a soup with the carcass, feed him the nutrients that the bones supplied – it would be easy for him to keep down.

Ever, through his haze, was obsessed, he kept mouthing, an involuntary mouthing, almost unaware of the presence of Lomita, that he had left his gun. He was worried about his gun. He needed to go and get his gun.

'Jesus Christ', thought Lomita, not one to normally blaspheme, swear yes, but not blaspheme. She was witnessing the stark reality of this man's mental derangement, that he was intending to commit what had been suggested in a vague and laughed-about way over dinner. His intentions towards Mr Lorken were not just fluff blown into the wind.

'I can go and get the gun for you, put your mind at rest, give you peace of mind that your gun is safe and you can relax. Feel able then to do what you want.'

She had no idea if this was what you should or were meant to say in these circumstances, but she knew that if he told her where the gun was she could, at least, keep it from him.

'No.'

Was his reply.

'You can't do that. No, I will do that.'

She said nothing; she didn't know what to say.

She left the room to make him some sweet tea, while she waited for Manita.

Manita had worked for Lomita since before the death of Lomita's second husband, over twenty-five years ago; her daughters had been educated by Lomita. One was now a nurse and the other ran a beauty spa. They were close, the boss and the housekeeper, they had the unspoken understanding of time; from Manita, as a single parent, there was an immense gratitude.

But Manita did have a furious temper, usually directed at her daughters for what she perceived to be their stupidity in the realm of relationships; that was understood by them both to be a fact of life, and it was tolerated by Lomita.

Lomita came back with a tea with two sugars, the sweetening ban broken, to her the substance was poison; but there was damage that needed to be repaired in the blood. The production of some glucose to give the system, the brain, quite literally some food for thought.

Ever took the cup as he sat himself up against the pillows and she realised that the next thing needed was a bath; the smell of stale wafted across her space.

'I am going to run a bath for you. Are you up for that? Are you OK with that? With me here?'

No response came.

It occurred to her that she had nothing for him to wear in bed, except for a pink robe that would be small but covering. Manita would wash what he was wearing on her return.

Then alongside the last sips of tea, there was a muttering.

'A bath would be good. Thank you. A good idea.'

Ever smiled for the first time, through the grey of his face, realising that he must indeed smell. Lomita was glad he had only laid on the top of the bed: the sheets would be clean for him to get into. She went to the bathroom and the sound of water could be heard, promising its soothing warmth, flooding into the bath.

Her head turned around the door, leaning with both hands for support.

'I can help you if you don't mind.'

'I don't mind,'

Came his reply.

'I would appreciate it.'

She moved to help. They walked across the thick grey of the wool carpet to the marble of the bathroom and he started, without embarrassment, to take off his clothes.

He felt the temperature of the thundering bath and without acknowledgment of her presence, removed his boxer shorts and climbed into the bath.

She knelt by the side of the bath; was relieved and felt a feeling of joy at the trust he had showed. She didn't shy away from taking in his body, its muscle tone, the scarcity of hair covering his chest, the thickness of hair on his legs and the circumcision of his penis. A body part that had brought her minimal pleasure in her life, as her second husband, to her knowledge at the time of marriage, and to her relief, was a homosexual. They had married as he was looking after her business affairs; he had made an unbelievably good job of it, they were close, and the companionship suited them both. There was a great sense of loss when he died, although he had had a male lover for the last two years of their five-year marriage. He was handsome enough and was an effectively entertaining escort.

Ever lay in the water, soothed, with his eyes closed. Lomita savoured him, she wanted to be held by him, held in a way that she hadn't experienced for many, many years; there was a brief moment for her, of love. He was completely oblivious, unaware that he was responsible for engendering that feeling.

She turned on the hand shower that sat on top of the brass

taps. Without any words spoken in asking or answer she picked up the shampoo, she moved his head back and started to wash his hair, massaging it with an enjoyment. She had never experienced this feeling before, she had never washed a man's hair before in her life. She felt an excitement of privilege in her body, and wanted: just wanted the physicality of it all. The touch, the feeling of excitement as her hands caressed his head, it felt so new. For him, he was immersed in the world of the practical, she made no effort to change the feelings she knew he didn't have in this moment in his being. He submerged his body under the water, soaped himself all over and felt like a baby boy. He felt cosy.

Lomita stood up slowly, as the effort of the day became more evident in her limbs. She presented in front of him, like a matador to a bull, a towel that he stepped into, he walked two steps closer and took her in his arms, held her tight making her blouse wet through, she enjoyed the change in temperature that her body felt, she didn't mind the wetness; they held each other and he whispered,

'Thank you Lomita, thank you.'

Into her ear that was closer than the breath's express from his mouth. They, after a time separated, they both felt the need, for different reasons, to rest; with neither of them saying a word – they had the unspoken oneness of function – they walked back out of the bathroom and both lay, not touching, on the bed, drifting into a sleep that had the comfort of familiarity and pleasure. And the closing of their eyes brought them together in the mutual darkness of that sleep.

A gentle knock at the door and Manita entered carrying a tray with the steam rising from the soup.

They had been asleep for over two hours and Manita

expressed no surprise, nor any judgement, in seeing their positions on the bed, which unbeknown to her had remained unmoved from their initial fall into sleep.

Lomita opened her eyes first, moved to take the tray from Manita and sit at the side of the bed, ready to feed her patient as he began to stir from his drugged slumber.

'Would you like anything, Miss L?'

Questioned Manita.

'Not just yet.'

Lomita's focus was on getting some of the soup into Ever's shrunken, presumably, twisted stomach. Manita, unasked, gathered his clothes from bedroom and bathroom for the wash.

'Here, I'll feed you.'

Lomita offered.

Manita closed the door behind her.

Ever ate without saying a word. The cheese grater scraped across his nerve endings, Lomita blew on the spoon of chicken and vegetable soup, that slightest breath made him wince in pain. The cooling waft of air sounded to him like a gale, he became disorientated by the magnitude of the sensations; he felt small and vulnerable in a giant world.

'Thank you.'

His swallow allowed. With a tenderness and gentleness of movement, her hand cupped under the spoon guarding against a spill, she returned the spoon to his lips and he thought, no one has ever done this before in my life. Well at least not since I was a child and not with this care, certainly not my mother. Two virginal experiences in the space of a matter of hours had happened to two people, both unaware of the contribution made to the souls of each other.

'Why are you doing this for me?'

He eventually summoned the energy to ask, the soup caressing the raw lining of his guts.

'Who are you? Why do you want to help me? You know nothing about me, do you?'

Lomita shifted in her chair with the intent to gain more comfort for the words to come.

'It is to do with being broken and the need to be mended, which I recognise in you.'

She said in a matter-of-fact way.

'Maybe if you want a bare-bones answer that is why I am doing this. As I think I told you when we first met, I get unhappy and this makes me happy, my sweet. It's selfish.'

She smiled.

'Give me a good reason as to why I shouldn't, anyway, as a compassionate human being.'

The throat murmured again. Her laugh on the point of arrival.

'I came here and wanted to fulfil my dreams like everybody who comes here. But you want to change the course of history. To make something out of someone else's shattered dreams. I don't think that is possible.'

She changed her thought.

'I don't think that has any basis in sanity and reality.'

'My father you are talking about? Why not? He was ruined.'

'Was he? Was he really? When I came here, I can't remember if I told you, I went to see a man who had given me his card, back in Pittsburgh, my home town, when I was sixteen, you know, to get me into motion pictures, and I got photographs done. Head shots, as they call them for audition purposes. And they did get me auditions, but no work. No work resulted from me schlepping around town, except I got to know my way around. I got nothing in the world I dreamt of being in, the world of motion pictures. And I became what was known as a glamour model. I had to earn money, and gradually the movies were slipping further from my grasp. I got taken to clubs and asked to strip, which I never did. The Whisky was the club I remember the most. Not the A Go Go, that was later. And there I met a man, Roberto dePirizone.

'You did tell me this.'

'Did I? I must be getting old. How embarrassing. It's the Vicodin.'

'But go on, it's OK.'

Ever said, rather distantly, as the third spoon of soup was fed into his mouth.

'The boss of the Cosa Nostra in Los Angeles. The mob.'

'I get it. I remember, you have told me this.'

'Well it'll take repetition, believe me. I was—'

She said, holding the spoon, steadily, in mid-air between bowl and mouth.

'A gangster's moll.'

That laugh, again, started in the back of her throat: she was amused at this description of herself.

'And I had a certain profile, I was exceedingly beautiful, although I say so myself.'

Ever needed no effort of imagination to support the belief.

'Then I got a screen test for a movie, at least that is what I thought it was going to be, and I was excited to have something on film that I could show people. I didn't tell you this bit?'

'No,'

Ever, uncertain himself.

'You know, something to show people what I could do. I arrived and was given something, a coffee or whatever to drink, but they had drugged it. What followed was the lowest point in my life. It was a stag movie, fifteen minutes long, and those kinds of movies were only allowed to be shown in private clubs. I had the thought once, I think, and I don't know why, of showing it to you, but I watched it again recently and realised it was an impossible idea. Out of the question.'

She had returned the half-full bowl of soup to the tray that rested on the bed between them.

'I was living at the time at the Hacienda Hotel and that cost, not a lot, but it cost. So I was desperate to work. But in this, which was not a screen test, I was raped by two men. And that is all I can tell you. The point of what I am saying is that Roberto heard about this and paid money for the film, well that's what he said, anyway, and I have it in my possession to this day, the one copy. But what I am talking about, is the revenge, the attempt to change my status, to eradicate what was the truth in my case. That I had no talent. And I am getting to that.'

Ever had started to speak, he wasn't sure what he was a going to say but felt the moment demanded a comment and was relieved when she said,

'Let me finish.'

And then, after a brief pause, acknowledging the abruptness of her command, a please followed.

'He had a saviour complex, I imagine, and asked me to marry him. My only condition was already dealt with, that he get hold of the film, you know, buy it or whatever. I was relieved at the time to be rescued, as that is what it felt like. I was by now, in my mind at least, just a whore. The next part I did not want to happen.'

Lomita again shifted in her chair, this time more to alleviate her doubt at continuing.

'He had the legs of the producer and the director and the cameraman smashed to splinters with baseball bats and the two actors were shot. Killed. Those three men spent the rest of their lives in a state of terror in wheelchairs. Did I feel better? Did it make things any better? Was my talent or status altered?'

'Are you trying to tell me my father has no talent?'

Ever presented this with no aggression, but with an empathy to her story, and strangely an ironic smile.

Lomita didn't take it negatively, but she took a calming breath to regain any composure that might have been lost by Ever's question.

'No, I have no idea if he does or not.'

She put herself back on the tracks.

'I have had this feeling only once before in my life, do you have any idea what it is like to be with someone who has done that kind of thing, in your name, in your name, for you, does it help? No, it causes a pain, a disturbance that kills something, deadens your soul, it is unbearable to be around someone who is capable of doing that. Would your father want to be around you if you took revenge like that for him? When you are in the presence of that, that degree of imbalance, of mania, disturbance, don't you understand, anybody of sane and sensitive mind cannot be around that kind of person. You become helpless in that situation, you do not want to be in the presence of that person, because that person, by going there and doing that, even if, like you, it's just in their mind, they're still corrupted, it becomes impossible to be with that person.'

Lomita twisted in her seat, stretched a little, exhaled and shook her head at the memory.

'I feel drawn to you in the way I was drawn to Roberto and it scares me to think that it happened once and could happen again. What does that say about me? I then could not love him because of what he did, I couldn't help, I had no power, but now I can and do and then we can remain in each others' lives.'

She stopped and shook her head again, this time momentarily embarrassed at what she had just said.

'If not with me,'

Another pause.

'You can at least remain in someone's life, your wife, your child, otherwise you can't, don't you understand? You remove yourself from the possibility of being loved by decency, by decent human beings. I don't want that for you; please, never never, don't let it happen, not twice in my life, this time I can help, I can have control. I beg you.'

During her increase in passion her voice had not risen in volume and she could see that Ever was drifting now in and out of a sleep. She threw in the words now as a ball tossed to a disinterested dog.

'Oh God, I am, first off, not trying to tell you anything, just everything, really.'

The emphasis was on the word, trying.

'I am saying that actions do not change the internal mechanism of a person, of a feeling. When they are done like that, for them. It doesn't alter the outcome. The reality. They are merely actions, but they are performed with a consequence.'

She didn't know whether to continue or not.

'I am listening,'

Ever sensed her dispirit.

'We had only been married six months, Roberto and me. Would you like more soup?'

'Thanks, I'll do it if I want more. You talk.'

Ever didn't move, he was struggling through his drowsiness to stay awake. It was like driving a car in the rain at night: forcing his eyes to stay open and losing the fight.

'It was after six months of marriage, when Roberto raped his underboss's wife. I am not in any way condoning his action, but you can imagine sex was not a favourite pastime of mine. But you see I was not capable of being with him; he had done it all for me, done it, but it was an act of cruel insanity and who wants to be with that, that is what you live with. Nothing else, you are alone for all time if you do that.'

She decided to lighten her story as she was most definitely losing him to sleep and introversion.

'My name in the film, by the way, my credit, if you could call it that, was the name Sunny Rose Ray, funny eh? No sun was shining that day or ever again for Sunny Rose Ray. Are you with my story?'

There was no reply. She continued regardless. Sunny Rose Ray, the name, had dropped him off into, maybe, a happy doze. No rain now at least.

'Anyways the underboss, Diego Vialli, as a result of the rape, shot his wife and then himself. After that my husband, God I can't believe I called him that, I've erased that connection for so long, strange feeling, anyway his leadership of the mob was questioned, they had lost confidence in him, and the police got hold of him and for two years they had him in court for everything they could think of, but in the end, in 1970, the only thing they managed to pin on him was that he was an illegal immigrant and he was deported back to Italy.'

Lomita was now surveying the room while talking, as if she might never see it again. With a disbelief, probably, that she had come this far.

'He had enormous difficulty, as you can imagine, getting any of his money out of the US and during the trials we were transporting the money, can you believe it, all of it in about eighteen trips to our house in Palm Springs. He buried it in a vault that he and my second husband-to-be – he was the accountant – had built underneath the terrace. When Roberto got back to Italy, obviously with the intention of returning eventually, to claim the money, he was shot by Vialli's family. And yes, you've guessed it.'

Ever was fading from exhaustion and showed no reaction to the statement. He was not capable of taking in any more. He was asleep.

'I was left with all that money. Twenty million dollars. Which was why I remarried.'

Lomita looked into the middle distance and with the option of stopping, carried on, talking to herself.

'The accountant, it was a perfect political partnership, with his knowledge we cleaned the money through venture capital investments, start-ups, property and offshore investments, mainly in the Cayman Islands – it became virtually impossible to trace it back to me. We were clever, weren't we? We most certainly were.'

The last remark was addressed not to Ever, but to her second dead husband, with a smile and an affection.

Ever was not responding now, he was in the first stages of a deep sleep. Lomita got up to plump the pillows; to bed him down for the night. Talking, while perfecting the lie of the bed.

'My favourite house being in Mexico. I adore Mexico. We must go sometime. But the law didn't leave me alone, I spent two million of those dollars defending myself in the courts. Can you believe this? Eventually they found four-fifths of an ounce of marijuana in my underwear drawer – I had never smoked the stuff in my life.'

She knew she had lost him completely now, the diazepam as well as being a relaxant is an anti-anxiety pill; she could see the tension drifting off his face like a passing cloud over the sun, revealing the brightness after the period of gloom.

'The mob were after me, and the IRS, and eventually I owned up to three and a half million dollars. I just threw my hands in the air and said that was all I had, all I knew about.'

She had known he wasn't listening but this was for her: she realised she had never recounted this story, and it gave her a sense of catharsis. She continued. It felt like an invitation to talk. To talk to herself. It gave her a sense of pride that she had survived.

'Their real anger, from the authorities towards me, I think, was because I had fraternised with Jack Ruby who shot Lee Harvey Oswald and you know who he shot. They thought I knew something about it all. I didn't. I was sentenced to fifteen years in jail, in the Louisiana Correctional Institute for Women, for some strange reason, the location I mean. My lawyers continued to fight my cause and eventually proved the drug was planted. That and the fact that the police had no warrant to enter my home got me cleared. But I spent two years in prison. Two years. Can you imagine that, two years?'

She was now almost enjoying addressing an unconscious audience. It was her reflection and consideration of her own life. She had no self-pity, just triumph.

'But when I came out I was a lot wealthier than when I went in. They never checked the house in Palm Springs as it was owned by an offshore company and untraceable to me, anyways my husband had been working away on our investments. A criminal bond, if you like, bound by marriage. Clever, eh? In the end, I felt I had won, achieved something, after the depths of shit I had swum in.'

As if to bring her story to a close in her own mind, at least, she summed up with –

'So you see Ever…'

That was the first time she had called him by his name.

'I had quite a time of it.'

There was a long silence, Ever's closed eyes made her realise that she had probably lost him even earlier than she thought, and she wondered if in fact he would remember anything at all by morning.

Then out of the blue as if he had been with the whole

process, in the true state of a manic depressive anxiety crash, his egocentricity produced words.

'I must go to the doctor.'

She thought she had done some good, imagining his desire to visit a doctor to be the result of a responsible decision to deal with his own mental state. She wasn't aware of his real reason, that it was about the time for his test – his STI test.

Maybe he was aware, in his half-dream, of his desire to return to the land of the male again. And that had turned into concern still active through sleep.

Along with the gun. That and the Basquiat exhibition.

'Will you come with me? Please. To the Basquiat exhibition?'

She realised her life story had held no significance for Ever, in this mode of self-centredness that had dragged him out of his sleep; but she wondered if it might implant itself at a later date.

It was dark now. She suggested he rest. He asked if he could have one of those calmers, as he called them. On her return with the medication, feeling truly like a nurse, she asked if he wanted her to turn off the light.

'The main light, yes please, but I would like to leave the bedside one on. If that's OK?'

Thinking of the pale blue swollen hand.

Before she closed the door, although his eyes were closed, she said,

'I'll come, but you'll have to wheel me around, I can't walk around an exhibition. And we'll have to have an agreement. I'll tell you tomorrow. I'm tired.'

The agreement was not something she was sure how to propose.

She stood outside the closed door and now felt disappointed that she had told her story, she should have known his brain was in no state to take it in, or even remotely comprehend what she was trying to get across. But on moving slowly away, across the big brown room, her feeling changed: that is why she'd told her story, because he wasn't listening. She didn't want anyone to know, really. Maybe bits had sunk in, she conceded, walking into the kitchen, now fully comfortable in her reasoning. Manita had left her a piece of the roast chicken and some salad. She poured herself a large glass of sauvignon, the one from Australia, and reflected on whether she was being Mother Teresa and doing this for herself, not curing, just enjoying the process.

She was relieved to see Manita had retrieved his Land Rover Discovery key, attached to the Sixt rental tag, from his chinos, and also his phone. She put both in a drawer and before she went to bed, she made sure all the alarms were on.

She didn't want her patient escaping. She didn't think she would bother to propose the agreement.

No point.

# *Chapter Twenty-one*

'He is not yours, I'm telling you. Why don't you fucking believe me? How many times? I am sorry, of course I am, how does apologising change anything? But don't you understand in your fucked-up brain?'

He always felt that recurring accusation was a cruel blow too.

'I wanted a child, I wanted us to have a child. Together, but, well you know, fuck it, stop looking at me like that.'

'But how are you so convinced he is not my child?'

This is what he never wanted to hear, and it was at this point, at this question, that he usually woke in a sweat. And, on cue, Ever awoke, and was indeed covered in a thin coat of sweat; heaviest over his chest, where he could feel the sheet was also wet.

He sat up not knowing for a while where he was, in that moment of disconnect that sleep gives you when it stops, before the realisation of life kicks in. Something Ever rarely wanted to kick in, his life, although the dream that woke him was as bad as life. It was life.

He sat up in bed and looked around for the clock, which was on the other side of the bed, standing digitally red on its own bedside table. He didn't really need to look at the time, it would be five minutes past four: it always was, and 4.05 turned to 4.06 while he was confirming what he already knew. A waste of a head-turn, except it also revealed the television remote that he hoped would control the flat screen on the wall opposite the bed. And turn its darkness into light.

In a very short time he had figured out how to turn it on; everybody's television seemed to have a different process, but this was simple, as the power button illuminated itself when the remote was moved from its resting place, he pressed it and that seemed to produce an almost immediate picture, but no sound, which he didn't want anyway; it revealed itself to be a shopping channel.

Had the previous occupant really watched a shopping channel?

A shopping channel, the perfect visual delight for the brain that can take nothing in, although that is exactly what they wanted you to do. Take it all in. A woman was massaging another woman's neck with a cream, obviously claiming it worked tightening wonders, and he watched expecting the miracle to happen as his dream came back to him in the form of waking reality. Clarissa and Jacob, the son wasn't his, playing around in his mind like the nightmare of hearing a stupid song that you can't clear from whichever part of your brain is insisting on keeping it going and going, till you have to try really hard to think of another annoying song to replace it with, and then the two songs compete. One jealous of the other's dominance. Or was that just his brain? For Ever it was usually Kate Bush and 'Wuthering Heights'. As a kid he remembered his mother playing it on repeat. Or was it Withering? He moved off the subject quickly, in case his brain put the disc on the turntable. Oh God, he could hear her, wailing. Focus on the television. There was a woman presenting a large jar of cream to the camera with the price on the left-hand side of the screen dropping every thirty or so seconds. Would they eventually give it away? The Jacob dream had started to have same repetitiveness as the pale blue swollen hand and to be honest he would rather have that waking, sleeping nightmare.

Clarissa he had met while swimming.

And he saw her every Saturday for weeks at the Porchester baths before they actually spoke, which wasn't at the baths, but around the corner at Planet Organic, squeezing avocados, and he realised she was there, next to him, also testing the avocados for ripeness. So they spoke, unsurprisingly, about avocados, then they decided to sit there and have a coffee; then that progressed. The following week they had lunch and then he recalled their first official date.

He was still sweating and wondered if he had a fever, as he wiped the sweat with the sheet and returned to his thoughts of Clarissa, going through them as if repetitive thought would eventually give him a greater insight into what had happened. Of course it never did. There was only one reality, one truth, and he knew it. But it helped him to see his part in the process. Although he knew it was an exercise that he did and he always came to the same conclusion. That it was his fault, his brain again.

They went to eat Indian at the Malabar restaurant at the back of the now closed Coronet Cinema in Notting Hill. That was their first official, evening date. He smiled recalling that they ate so much food and drank so much beer he had to take a piss twice on the walk back to Oxford Gardens where she lived; then Clarissa was also forced to piss. So by the time they reached her flat the intimacy barrier already seemed to be broken. Her flatmate was away and they stayed in bed the whole of the next day, being a Sunday; the physical attraction that they had both felt proved to be unquenchable. They made love and never left each other's arms for twenty-four hours. She had no embarrassment or shyness about her body, about the pleasure it gave and could receive. And he felt, he remembered, a little embarrassment at first about this physical freedom.

She had a degree in psychology, from Birmingham University, and was now finishing a PhD in addiction counselling. She always talked freely about her previous sexual encounters, something he didn't want to hear, and her first love, a musician, a classical musician: a violinist and, more stuff he never wanted to hear about, the violinist's deterioration through addiction. Heroin. So it appeared obvious as to why she pursued the line of work she was in.

The woman had now moved on to a cream that took away dark circles under the eyes, and he could see the difference immediately as they just banged a load more light on her when the cream had been applied. She looked like a blank. No lines, just a couple of eyes that could barely stay open through the glare of light, staring out of a bright, white face.

Clarissa never wore make-up, she was from Liverpool with a strong and determined accent. Kirkby, to be exact, which she always described as a shithole that every year got shittier. That's town planning for you.

The woman's neck, however, looked no different, even with the searchlight on her face. He was now looking at her, feeling annoyed, and wondered if anyone else was watching this.

Their parents never met, because of his mother's complete obliviousness to any world, thought or emotion that wasn't about her, and his father was living in Los Angeles, and, Ever thought at the time, doing fine: painting. No, please don't go there, don't punish me with that guilt pain as well…

He was talking to his grey cells, which rarely listened to his instructions, which was why he was trying to occupy half of them with face-tightening creams, and now, lo and behold, the application of a mascara that must have some special quality, but he didn't know what, he couldn't hear anything.

Neither of his parents came to the wedding, but Clarissa's did, committed Liverpudlians both, to Liverpool FC and the city and stony broke, had been all their lives and now lived on their state pensions. With a little help from him and Clarissa after the marriage, gladly given, like for holidays and attempts at improving their flat. Which, bless them, didn't bother them either way. After years of living where they did, their environment, the quality of it, lost significance in their lives. Clarissa moved into his mews house in Bayswater and started counselling at a residential rehabilitation centre in Hammersmith, Hope4. Their lives couldn't be more different; he earned a lot more money than her and didn't help people other than those who had more than enough money anyway; she helped people who were basically fucked.

The mascara, he gathered, was waterproof, so how the hell did you get it off? Cream, his semi-focused brain eventually settled on. Cream. Sure enough, one eye was receiving water, the other removal cream. The wet cloth didn't make the slightest smudge on her face, but her eyes looked sore, and he wondered how much she was being paid for this.

What he was doing now, not sleeping, had been his problem since he was eight, but it was Clarissa who tried to wean him off the sleeping pills that he took with a recklessness that in her mind classified him as an addict; his mood changes and depression and wall-staring she diagnosed as a chronic sleep disorder, the result of a lifetime, a short one, of pharmaceutical abuse.

It was after the first really bad crash that his doctor put him on his first round of antidepressants. The brain-frame mashers. Prozac. They made everything worse, probably because he carried on with the sleeping pills, refused to quit wine in the evenings, and the more-than-occasional cocktail, and the benders every now and then. He never told his doctor about his intake of substances. Why should he? Hell no, don't be ridiculous, he wasn't an alcoholic.

Clarissa, he could tell, lost a certain admiration that he supposed, well hoped, she had had for him once, maybe, although his work as a lawyer for a hedge fund company, analysing and guaranteeing the legality of certain acquisitions, she had despised from the start. What was legal, she would say, about buying assets, companies, stripping them of everything, people losing jobs, restructuring and selling on. And making more money in the process than the entire wealth of many countries. He had no defence: most of the time his brain could only take in what he had to do at work. The consequence, the conscience aspect of it, he forced himself to ignore. He was becoming increasingly distant, his mind would skip, and his focus would blur, on just about everything but the thing that paid his bills. The money.

Ah, now the woman was stripped of all the creams, and mascara; the lights were dimmed, to make her look worse. Ever thought she looked better. Fresh and definitely younger. Was she the same woman?

He wasn't very good with faces, Clarissa often accused him of having face blindness, which she called – oh what was it? She used the technical term. He couldn't recall it right now, as he was questioning whether it was the same woman.

After a few months on his medication, he lost all desire for doing anything, hated his work and talked to his father on the phone every day, to get advice, help, anything really; he didn't know what to do, but he could no longer turn to Clarissa, who more and more frequently would go to see her parents at weekends. The violinist, Adam, was playing with the Liverpool Philharmonic. But he didn't know that at the time. Then the big crash happened. The one when they put him inside.

Prosopagnosia, that is what it is, the word for face blindness, that is what Clarissa called it. He was thrilled at his ability to recall the word. And repeated it out loud to the television.

'Prosopagnosia I have you see, so I don't know who the hell you are.'

He had to stop the Prozac as all he could think of was killing himself, had a brief return to wanting Clarissa and for a short time he felt she liked him again, but then. Then out of the blue it all went black. The wall came down in front of him, he couldn't see round it, and it all went black. It was when he came out of the mental institution that she gave him the news that she was pregnant, and he wept with relief that they would now have a child to bond them. But the pregnancy changed Clarissa and he put it down to hormones, like men do, it's simpler that way. That and periods. It excuses them from thinking that there is any contribution they can make that might be of value.

They were now selling a cleaning substance, that cleaned everything from grease on stoves, to cars, to windows, without the need for water, just pollute yourself with this killer chemical. What did it clean out of your lungs?

And instead of growing closer, they grew further apart, after Jacob was born; Clarissa seemed to lose interest in her job, which she quit, and in her relationship with him. Post-natal depression, it was put down to. She was competing with him in the brain stakes. No contest. Ever, although still taking the pills, found himself doing everything with Jacob, and somehow it made up for the soulless immorality, yes, he had started to feel that now, of his work. She looked after Jacob in the day, but was more than happy to do nothing the minute Ever returned from work. And then came The Black Wednesday. His own personal Black Wednesday.

The price on the left-hand side was not dropping so rapidly for the cleaning product, as there were only ten, seven, two. All gone. Clean out of cleaner. Ever felt he should have got some, felt a pang of disappointment that he had missed the opportunity.

Ever wanted to speak to Clarissa and Jacob.

In a moment of intense isolation and fear that they would be lost forever and that he would never see them again, or he would fail to recognise their faces. A completely irrational thought but what if his face blindness, whatever the fuck it was called, he'd forgotten the name again, what if it worsened into a permanent state? He looked for his phone on the bedside table and then with the dawn coming up he could see the detail of the room forming like a polaroid coming to life and searched for his trousers, pants as they called them. He was in pants country. He could find nothing. The sweating returned, they had robbed him, stolen, taken his belongings, he had no contact with the world, he saw the phone by his bed, the landline, and tried to dial Clarissa's number but couldn't make it through: some idiot voice telling him that his call could not be completed as dialled. Was it an incorrect number? She offered him the option of trying again and he did try again. And then the panic truly set in. He leapt off the bed and stormed out of his room.

The man stood in the centre of the big brown room.

The Los Angeles dawn was taking the cold desert night away and warming the air with the first glow of sun, drying the damp that covers the world outside; he stood naked in the room. Cold, both from temperature drop and anger. He was screaming, screaming about his phone and how they had stolen it from him, and he was trapped, and his voice was developing the break of sadness that now joined the anger.

It was the ictal phase of a seizure.

His body movements were contorted, he was biting hard on his tongue, blinking rapidly, his eyes moving upwards, his body, the parts of his body, felt alien to him and appeared to have a different shape and structure; he was observing them as though they were not his limbs, he was intensely pale, unable to swallow the saliva build-up in his mouth that poured out like he was spewing water, and he had an intense feeling of embarrassment. Yes, embarrassment.

Two women emerged from separate ends of the big brown room, both in dressing gowns of different quality, one was silk, in a dark shade of blue, and skimmed the floor; the other was a pink robe made from towelling that hovered unevenly over the knees of the wearer. Knees that had been heavily knelt on in their life. Both women were standing in silence as the screaming and now sobbing was reducing the man to crumple his body down towards the polished floor; the exhaustion of his emotion made the sounds decrease in volume, now the crying was the dominant force, replacing the anger, the repetition of *why have you done this to me* becoming the main accusation. An accusation directed at these two women but without the need to move towards them or even look at them. He felt colder and started to shake at first, a shiver, then uncontrollably, a full-blown shaking, a kind of paroxysm that took over and his crying was now a whimper and his whys turned to *please, you mustn't do this to me, please*, and then even those words started to peter out into *my boy, my baby boy*, and by this time he was curled on the floor, trying to make himself into the tiniest ball of human that he could possibly become; the words stopped and the sobbing decreased and he pissed himself all over the floor and that brought a silence, he remained shivering and wet in his own urine. The two women were still stood, the blood had gone from their faces, and their look was of both a horror and a sympathy and Lomita was crying.

Manita disappeared and came back with a blanket and some cloth and went towards the now inert Ever and wrapped him in the blanket. He was aware of its soft warmth but could feel even in his moment of isolated epileptic seizure that it must be cashmere, his skin crawled; he let the dark beige blanket fall to the floor. Manita started to mop the urine with the cloth, a cloth that was wholly inadequate for the job. Lomita was stock still and the crying was silent now, tears making tracks down her cheeks forming their own decision about destination, where they would end up, how far they would travel.

He was now in a postictal phase.

Becalmed. This was the tableau that could be seen from above by God and from the left and right and centre by the human element. Ever broke the silence and said,

'Sorry.'

Lomita came forward, with all the strength that her pained body could muster she helped him to his feet, they walked into her bedroom, the urine dripped off his body, she took him to her shower and turned it on, he walked into the storm of water, she followed him in to offer support in spite of her fragility, her robe was immediately darkened by the stream of water.

Her tiny frame held him, the water washed them both as one, and made their understanding of each other be as one.

His erection returned for her and he lifted her around his waist, her robe parted and without a willingness or a resistance from her, he entered her, and she cried and cried. Neither of them moved a muscle.

The water was washing away the sins of the world; they had both been more sinned against than sinning.

He came inside Lomita.

## *Chapter Twenty-two*

Emotional exhaustion had taken them into a morning sleep.

That they were now awaking from, the positions of their bodies were the same as the last time they lay together, side by side, adopting their own independence, yet grateful for the proximity. He lay flat out on his back. When they came to, she just said, matter-of-factly,

'When exactly is the Basquiat exhibition? And when would you like to view your father's work?'

He could say very little, except,

'Two days' time and as soon as. Thank you.'

And then,

'When did I tell you about it?'

Her story would take a retelling.

She stood from the bed and felt his sperm dried and sticky.

It had trickled from her vagina onto the inside of her right thigh and a memory returned. This was only the second time she could remember being filled with semen. The first time, so overpowering in its horror, took away any potential joy this might have held.

She went into the bathroom but before wiping between her

legs with a wetted towel, immersed her fingers into herself and smelt them; the smell produced no sensation in her; she then tasted her fingers and an intensity of memory returned.

The taste.

This was such an emotional experience for her that again an objectivity kicked in, a cut-out button, and turned the act into an almost solely practical event. Clean and protect. She walked calmly out of the bedroom to the kitchen, with an announcement regarding food that received a response in the negative from him.

He was unaware she had been crying; she had found it difficult to be entirely practical. She had wanted his sperm, it had been taken with love, for the first time.

She would have wanted it, she couldn't imagine how much, if the time had been right.

Another time: out of place with this one.

He needed to go about the duty of communicating with Miss Money-Root.

And Lomita's thoughts for the day needed to go through the process of being centered on making sure he was sufficiently relaxed and medicated with the diazepam. He was still sweating. Their life now had a mutual intention, to get him on his way back to recovery – his fitness. There on a chair in the corner of the bedroom were his neatly folded and ironed clothes; placed with purpose by Manita. Top of the pile – his cell phone.

The horror that struck him halfway through constructing the email to Miss Money-Root was that he had made love to Lomita.

Unprotected.

And he did not know the status of his condition. That, in

addition to everything else, was something he couldn't even contemplate coping with, so made no attempt.

He had had an epileptic fit. It was slowly dawning; he had commited those to history, to his childhood.

But his main concern was the exposure of this condition to two innocent people. His embarrassment at incrementally revealing who he really was.

He called to make an appointment with his doctor, Dr Aran Anand.

An American Sikh doctor, whose entire staff were dressed in white, himself included; they wore white turbans and were all part of an ashram. Any offspring they had were all sent back to India to be educated at a boarding school there, so they rarely saw their children. But they were dedicated to the cause of helping the community of Los Angeles, at least the wealthy part of that community, in a place they considered had the best and the worst the world could offer. A fair description, Ever had always thought, of the city.

Heaven and hell.

He carried so much guilt that it was difficult for him to stave off the anxiety it produced; he was in a turmoil as to whether he should tell Dr Aran the whole story of his anxiety and depression, which had never been treated by him, or just deal with the STI scenario.

Anyway he booked an appointment for tomorrow morning at eleven. They were always so pleased to see him, he was always fitted in. He had, after all, been a patient since he was a child.

The two things that dominated his thoughts at the moment, that were at the forefront of that grey smudge of his, were to get his gun and buy a car.

He had decided to conceal the real reasons for both these actions from Lomita. Because, from his perspective, both appeared to have an understandable logic as to why he should carry them out.

His thoughts to himself in the moment – the rental on the car was running out, and was too expensive, so a cheap car fulfilled the need; collect the gun, because it was irresponsible to leave a weapon unsecured in an apartment that could easily be broken into? Was that too feeble as an excuse? The first one he knew he could pull off. Was he feeling unwell? Was the sweating in the night a result of the dream, or was he in fact ill?

The facts, then the worry – his brain on the anxiety train again: what if all the carriages crashed into one another? A pile-up.

Then there was Lomita. It had been a natural, spontaneous act which he loved. Loved her for it. Loved her. Wanted to stay with her. Wanted to be comforted by her. They had awoken for food, but he had no appetite, no sensation of hunger, no sensation of anything physical. Eggs were suggested, she was going to eat two poached eggs: he wasn't, he had declined the offer, when Lomita had left the room.

He was left alone, alone in her room, was he accepted, was this expected to be the norm?

He didn't want this, he didn't want to repeat what he had done. It was done; he felt it never needed to be done again. He wanted to phone Clarissa and speak to Jacob. He wanted the life he had constructed, not be an intruder in the construct of someone else's life, he didn't want to be a part of a life he had not created, not built, not laid the foundations for.

He was entering at the end of her life: his life was at the beginning. He was feeling panic again, rise up through and into his bowels, then his stomach, then his throat, and then his mouth turned sour: these problems he could stop creating for himself. For all those around him.

He felt like being sick, he walked calmly, as calmly as he

could, to the bathroom, knowing on his arrival he would put his head over the toilet bowl, with control, and throw up. He was right. He swilled his mouth out and sucked at the tube of toothpaste in the absence of his toothbrush. He didn't feel he had reached the toothbrush sharing stage.

Clarissa and Jacob wouldn't leave him, would they?

He returned and sat tentatively on the edge of the bed, feeling he had no right to get back into the bed. Her bed. He felt his intentions had changed: there was forward movement.

He checked out the internet as he sat.

Without the full weight of ownership, on the bed – for cars. Autotrader. Maximum price $2,000, saloon, mileage irrelevant. He looked for cars exclusively in Chinatown and Koreatown. Anonymity he thought, both of car and place. He had never had any connection to that area of LA.

I don't know, a fucking Nissan, Toyota, Honda, that would do it, a car with no memorable appeal at all. An instantly forgettable one, what kind of car was it? Oh, I don't remember. What colour? Oh, kind of beige, browny, kind of colour. Maybe a four-door or two-door? I don't know. You just couldn't remember anything about it? Nothing specific, no, not really.

That's what he wanted. A kind of ordinary sponge-pudding-cake of a car.

He looked on Autotrader, put in the 90012 zip code for Chinatown, the price, under $2,000.

The third car that came up was perfection: a used Honda Accord EX V6 sedan in a dull, faded, red colour with 176,000 miles on the clock. Price – $1,900. A dull, sun-worn red, reminiscent of the insignificant burgundy Wagoneer he had seen the day he met Lomita. Private owner.

Perfect, but he had to email the seller to get the number. Not so perfect, he wanted no record of this sale, he was going to give a false name on taking all the paperwork, he was convinced with the right seller that money could buy blindness and disinterest; he was not going to fill in the paperwork before he did what he had to do; that gave him ten days.

He was going to have to open up a new email account, which would take minutes, Joe Smith or the like. He started the process.

It took six minutes.

He appeared in the kitchen, minutes later.

Lomita was eating her eggs: he declined, again, the offer of any food. Not a word was spoken after his refusal, he felt a mild embarrassment in the company of Manita, but she seemed to carry no censoriousness of any kind. He was grateful for that and thanked her for the attention she had given to his clothes. On the walk back across the big brown room he returned to the guest bedroom. Even his mother had given him the guest bedroom, he had guest bedroom knowledge; he decided he must terminate his lease – on his apartment – although, where would he go afterwards? He couldn't face the thought of there being an after, as that would change everything, it was only the fact that the before had some sort of positivity; the after carried something that he didn't know – he didn't know how he would feel about not knowing, how he would feel, or how he would cope. It would be the biggest unknown ever, and he wasn't very good at dealing with what was, what was the known, let alone the unknown.

A massive unknown space, the only thing that existed would be the completion of his obsession; he would have carried out his task. So maybe keep the lease and let it run its course. One more week, pay up till then, and move his stuff out when he wanted. Otherwise all the convenient closures at once might lead to a connection. The only connection that he could think of, that could lead back to him, would be the gun, but it was a Glock – with Glock ammunition – so to trace it back to him would be an endless million-million-fold task.

Forget that.

Don't think, don't add that to the list.

He was getting no response on his FaceTime audio from Clarissa and didn't try again.

He wasn't perhaps in the most coherent frame of mind to speak to them. But what did he do now, in the immediate future, in the absolute happening now, in Lomita's house? How did he get out, was he well enough or would he sink back into the deep?

His questions were answered by Lomita in her wheelchair, knocking on his door and without waiting for a response, opening it and asking if he had organised what she had asked regarding the gallery.

He nodded the confirmation, and then she dictated the next action. That they should go to his apartment, he was not going alone, she insisted on that, to get his gun, and he should come back here and stay until he had had a few days after his doctor's visit so his recovery could be monitored. She of course was still under the belief it was a visit to deal with his emotional condition. That was information: this was a surprise.

'I feel, and I have given it thought, so hear me out, that you should not consider it your position now to sleep in my room. If that is OK with you. I really need some time to deal, if that's the right way of putting it, with what has happened. This is not a negative response, it's just a request for a lull in the middle of this storm.'

'That sounds fine with me,'

Ever said, completing her speech without a pause. Relieved but he didn't expect her to be the one to voice it.

'F-i-ne.'

There was a suggestion of disappointment that there was no objection. The 'i' was stretched in reflection.

'Give me thirty minutes and we'll go. Good?'

He nodded and she did a U-turn: a slick, well-practised manoeuvre.

She was, in her understanding of the situation, way ahead of him. I guess, thought Ever, she is mature.

But he always seemed to have to wait for her.

Both Lomita and Manita appeared to have agreed not to let Ever out of their sight. They now sat in the same configuration as when they had first met on their drive in the black Suburban. It turned left down the slope into the underground parking off Bedford Drive and instead of valet parking, as was custom, Lomita stayed in the car, but like a guardian angel, or maybe just a guardian, Manita followed him to the third floor and into the lobby of the doctor's office, where they both sat. After the joys of reunion with two familiar faces, he was then called in, by a younger face he didn't recognise.

The man dedicated to curing humanity of its ills greeted him with the usual hug.

He competed with Lomita on the fragility scale. Super thin, with a long beard, as full of energy as always.

'Well, what is it Ever? How are your folks?'

He broke the news of his father's death, accidental, about which Dr Aran was profoundly shocked and saddened. It was his father, not his mother, he had known. At least the best.

'I need an STI test, the full works; I slept with someone and they were ill, I don't know, stupid, I know, but I want an HIV test as well.'

'Well, options: I can send you to a clinic for an oral swab test, the quickest result to see if antibodies have developed, proteins that the body makes against the virus, not testing for the virus itself. But it can take three to twelve weeks for those antibodies to develop, so I should probably do your bloods and send them to the lab. I would have to do that as a follow-up anyway. Or I can do a combination test, looking for antibodies and antigens. They can test for everything but the blood HIV test is a little more reliable. But the best is the NAT test, nucleic acid testing, actually looking for the presence of the virus in the blood. What is the timeframe? I mean when did intercourse take place?'

Dr Aran always spoke with the confidence of someone giving a lecture, in a thin voice, with many downward strokes of his beard, and although he always offered options for any scenario, Ever always knew he would make his own choice.

'Three weeks ago.'

'OK. Repeated?'

No judgement at all, one of the amazing things about doctors. They deal with life and death, and the imparting of the good and bad to patients all the time, with a consistent equilibrium.

'No, just once.'

'A thousand to one. If luck lies in the bed with you.'

If luck goes with the fuck, Ever reinterpreted silently.

Dr Aran's was an unusual response. Ever smiled at the attempt, though, to lighten the situation.

'That is possibly just enough time for an initial test. I think we'll go with the NAT test. The most expensive, and the results will take a few days. I can give you a finger prick test right now, but you will still need a follow-up. So, no, I think pointless, and unnecessarily concerning, and revealing ultimately nothing conclusive, so—'

He was talking to himself, really, not Ever. As usual. But with consideration.

'And after the NAT test you will need a follow-up after six weeks, for complete accuracy. And then again in six months.'

'Six months?'

'To be absolutely sure. Yes. But in the meantime, you can be on the alert for what is usually described as the worst ever flu-type symptoms. Sore throat, swollen glands, sweating etc. The body's initial immune reaction to the virus, and then a dormant period.'

Ever had a weak moment.

And with that, Dr Aran put both his hands to the side of Ever's neck to feel his glands and took a temperature check.

'But I haven't seen you for—'

He checked his records.

'My goodness, Ever, nearly three years, so I'm going to give you a full medical. Temperature normal. But your pulse is high. What are you taking, medication-wise?'

'Nothing.'

Lied Ever.

He always did, lie that is.

'But I always get checked by my doctor in London, you know.'

Ever volunteered with a vague lack of concern.

'But he's not me, and they miss things there, they don't check like I do.'

There was a humour in Dr Aran's reply. And a finality.

The process of blood extraction was started by the nurse who had escorted him in; she had been taking notes in the corner, practised in invisibility.

'I'll be right back.'

The bloods were done; as the nurse left with the vials and her notes as to what to do with them, Dr Aran returned and asked Ever to drop his pants for the digital rectal examination.

'Even in one so young.'

Was Dr Aran's comment.

Lube, a finger and a wipe-down.

'Small and smooth, fine. All done.'

And the nurse, as if on cue, returned for the muscle testing, arm extension, press down, to check for the supplements that he might need.

'What have you been doing Ever?'

He placed various bottles of supplements on his body, one after the other, and muscle tested him with each one to detect possible depletion in his organs, thus finding the relevant supplement that might revitalise his system.

'Your adrenals are shot.'

That is usually the case, to be fair, Ever thought.

'But your heart is racing here, stress levels are high. Wait, I'm going to give you the finger prick test just to see where we are.'

The nurse went for the necessary equipment.

'The bloods will follow up, but we may get some sort of indication. It should normally be after at least four weeks, but we can see if your antibodies are active against a virus. It'll take twenty minutes for the result, so I suggest you have some acupuncture here with Dr Sheema.'

Ever also knew her well and that it would be a pleasant enough, if not this time an entirely relaxing, waiting experience. He always came out with a load of herbs and vitamins, sold on site by another white turban-wearing Sikh woman, Lola, who had also known him since he was a child. Remarkably she was still working there. They were pretty much all faces he remembered, apart from the nurse in the room, who had escorted him in, the prettiest face and the youngest face he had ever seen there.

'Good. Don't worry, I'm sure you'll be fine, and if not, I can deal with it.'

And with that the doctor was off, light-footed, even in his clogs, with a stroke of the beard, hand drawn from chin downwards to the end, being the typically final gesture on his departure.

The needles were mainly placed around the meridians to promote relaxation; she always seemed to have a way with the four-way pulse procedure of knowing what was needed. He was drifting into a doze when a hand squeezed his arm, the thin wrist carried a gold IWC Schaffhausen watch.

'No antibody action, I think you're going to be fine, I'll be in touch with the bloods and take it easy on yourself. God bless.'

Done and dusted, thought Ever, all he had to do now was pray. He paid under the watchful, but he had to admit, caring eye of Manita. He wanted to hug Lomita with a relief that she wouldn't be able to share.

Thank you, thank you, he kept saying to himself in the elevator to P2, the parking level housing the Suburban.

'What did he give you?'

The first question that was fired at him as he opened the big black shining hunk of door.

'Nothing. He told me to take it easier on myself, and I had some acupuncture, which was great. And these supplements'

Showing, with a child-like enthusiasm, his white paper bag.

'Did you tell him you were consuming diazepam to calm yourself?'

'Yes.'

He lied for the second time in an hour.

'He said that was OK, I told him they were prescribed by my doctor in the UK. No more than ten milligrams a day for three weeks maximum, after that if my anxiety state is still high, to return and, anyway, I'm glad I went. Thank you for taking me.'

'We're not done yet, my sweet, your apartment.'

Ever was feeling lame.

They drove, this odd combination of people, to Havenhurst, and pulled up outside, not down in the underground, as from the sidewalk there would only be three steps for Lomita to negotiate. Yes, she was coming in, there appeared to be no choice.

The apartment was dark and cool. Curtains drawn, everything as he had left it, their effort over the years of fighting the sun from invading the cool had caused them to fade from the green to an insipid version. Patches where the sun was less ruthless gave a hint of the original colour. It was more successful as a colour with the fade, in fact. Nature at work again.

There was a smell of trash that needed to be emptied and he noticed the apartment had the same brown flooring as Lomita's house. Without the shine, it was wood minus effort. An equation which equalled no Manita.

Lomita didn't comment on his accommodation, probably realising his lack of commitment to it, and therefore that it didn't demand an attempt at a consoling appreciation.

He went to the logs, left of the fireplace, and sure enough, the second one from the bottom of the pile, hollowed out during an entire stoned evening with a Swiss Army knife that he always carried, still contained the Glock 17. Lomita asked to look at it and handled it with a surprising authority.

Ever being the only witness to her ease and efficiency.

She interpreted his look, understanding his observation.

'You don't think I was married to Roberto without understanding how to use a gun, do you? Seriously? For my own protection, of course, but he taught me, it was an absolute necessity.'

And then as an afterthought.

'Or perhaps you missed that bit?'

'What bit?'

'Of my life story.'

She said with more than a suggestion of mockery.

'No, I was with that bit, I admit I was a bit drifty. But I was there for that.'

And then as if he sensed her doubt he reconfirmed.

'No, I remember that bit well. How could I not?'

'A Beretta 70 he gave me, carried eight rounds in the magazine, and it was a close-range gun. But, hey, I figured any self-defence was going to be at close range. Don't you think?'

A question Ever had never been asked to consider before. Though he nodded, as if an expert.

'This is a cumbersome gun though, heavy. Pack a punch. Where's your ammunition?'

He didn't respond quickly enough for her.

'Surely you didn't just buy enough for the mag? That would have been stupid, and suspicious. A giveaway that you just wanted to kill someone. One person. No, always buy a stack. You know, convincing them it's for the range, or hunting. That it has an ongoing usage.'

He was mesmerised by her language for weaponry: the basic and innate understanding of the code – the code of guns.

But he was stuck on the fact that murder of a person had been casually dropped into the conversation for the first time, there had been a specific, unequivocal mention. He didn't know how to reply.

'No, I bought a box of twenty-five rounds.'

A pause, waiting for further potential criticism of his action.

'It's a 9 mm.'

'I know,'

She said incongruously.

'Police use them. So, get the ammo.'

The ammo, as she called it, was under the bed, upstairs; like a shamed dog with its ears back he went to retrieve it.

On his way up, he turned to her.

'I'm paid up for another week and then I'm out of here, so if it is OK with you, can I bring my stuff? You know, clear everything out. I only have a couple of bags.'

'Oh, so I can house a murderer you mean?'

The laugh came from the back of her throat.

'That's right.'

Ever said, trying to lighten the tone.

'It wouldn't be the first time.'

She said for the second time.

The laugh grew and lived with the words she spoke.

He attempted to continue the joke element of the situation.

'A man on the run.'

But the stare and the pause suggested he had failed. The joke seemed to have been put to one side. Run its very short course.

'I hope we don't get to that, my sweet, with my help, I hope we don't get to that.'

That carried a finality that he made no attempt to question.

She moved outside and sat by a table with two chairs that nestled in the courtyard, her legs were aching; she took in the Spanish architecture of the Mi Casa – the name in blue lettering on a patterned Mexican tile in the wall – the atmosphere of the place, with its little 1930s Hollywood separate apartment buildings; she wondered if, in her time, she had come here and sat with friends, all hopeful of turning their lives into the magic of silver.

Each little casita housed one or two bedrooms. She got up and walked around; her legs were still aching, maybe a little stroll would help. If the people were of like mind, the intimacy of the community could be comforting, she thought. She went back to her time at the Hacienda; before her life had lost its sheen, and the shine was still there to be polished.

Ever came down with a suitcase and a soft bag in under ten minutes. He was travelling with the lightness of a feather.

'Ready?'

He nodded his response, then realised he needed to put the trash out so that the smell didn't build up. He packed up the trash bag and deposited it down the chute which took it to the underground parking and the garbage bins. He had bought no provisions to speak of, he decided to leave the nearly empty bottle of Patrón Silver, with a gratitude to its consumed contents and to the universe that had shared it with him.

Those stars.

He closed up the apartment and opened the front door, by which Lomita was already leaning, turned the lock and dropped the key back inside. He would inform the caretaker in a week of the fact. He was gone, starting his journey towards invisibility.

On the way back, he requested a stop at the Holloway cleaners, not really out of the way, and then his guardians drove him back to Oakhurst Drive. Manita, as usual, had no attitude, or comment to make, as she opened the tailgate where he had deposited his luggage.

Ever's life had taken a turn that was not only unexpected but had now implicated people. This was never his intention – yes it was – he remembered his desire to meet someone that day, that day an eternity ago in the public parking, for what, for support, did he know he was going to crash emotionally? Lomita had acknowledged, clearly, her awareness of his situation. But time was running out; his mind could never rest on the outcome – how could it?

It would change everything in his life forever.

His phone bird-chirped with the arrival of two emails, one from Miss Money-Root, who being the true professional, was dealing with the minion not the money; mind you, she had no choice. He had opened a special email account for her as well. She sent an electronic invitation, for two, named, at 6.30pm for the preview opening of the Jean-Michel Basquiat exhibition. The other was from a Bruce Wong. Perfect on both counts. Bruce Wong's communication contained his phone number and a thanks for making contact and a please call to arrange inspection. Bruce Wong sounded perfect.

A strangeness hit him on his return to Lomita's house.

He had lost his independence but gained some sort of trust. He was now a house guest with a difference – one with a gun. He unloaded his bags into his room and acknowledged the need to reply to his two communications. He unpacked his suitcase, then took the plastic off the dry-cleaned suit, hanging it up, not bothering to transfer it from its wire hanger. He looked at it on the rail: he hated wire hangers. He withheld his number and dialled Bruce.

'Hi. My name is Joe, Joe Smith,'

He repeated, as much to convince himself as Mr Wong,

'I sent you an email about the car you have for sale.'

'Hi, thank you for getting back to me. This is me, Bruce. When you want to come and see?'

Ever suffered a momentary loss of breath, he needed to take a gasp to restart the process, it was the realisation that he was continuing on this path. A path, certainly not to glory, but to completion and the defence of a life lost.

Details taken, he was calming himself when his bit of peace was broken.

'Miss L is resting, do you want anything to eat?'

Asked Manita, following the door knock and entry.

'No thank you, I'm fine, really, but would you mind telling Lomita that tomorrow's exhibition, which she knows about, is quite a formal affair. She might like some advanced warning. Notice, you know, in terms of what she was going to wear.'

Why he was carrying on explaining to the woman who ran Lomita's life suddenly struck him as ridiculous, but it didn't stop him. It was polite, guilt, overkill.

'Sure.'

Door closed.

Shopping channel? No, he denied himself the agonising pleasure.

Why was Lomita allowing all this to continue? The saviour, everybody wants to be a saviour. He felt tired by his day's endeavours; lay down, hot and feeling weak, and closed his eyes. He had the dream of the pale blue hand and woke from the already-awake sleep in a sweat.

## *Chapter Twenty-three*

The Same Old Shit was about to get under way.

From SAMO to the biggest exhibition in town.

The valet parking had quadrupled in size and the lines were endless. Fortunately for Ever and Lomita, Manita was driving them in the black Suburban and was able to drop off, wait, and find her own space, in her own time.

Ever helped Lomita, resplendent Lomita, out of the car and waited while Manita extracted the wheelchair from the black mass. While standing, Lomita's impact was evident and able to be fully appreciated.

She was adorned in a flowing black A-line dress, pintucked at the waist, which caressed her black velvet low-heeled shoes, just avoiding the floor, with rhinestones covering the body and the full flow of the skirt. Her hair was pulled into a chignon, she wore a white orchid pinned to the fabric at her shoulder, her make-up was minimal, a necklace of white gold with a pear drop diamond circled her neck, with earrings to match. A ring of equal diamond size adorned her finger. She was, by any standards, and there were some standards there, absolutely unquestionably beautiful, delicate, with the effortless quality of the unashamedly rich.

She floated through as Ever pushed her along in the wheelchair, which diminished none of her magnificence, and showed his e-ticket to one of the many security guards. They joined a gaggle of famous faces, many of whom had been early purchasers of Basquiat's work before the record was set by Yusaku Maezawa, the Japanese billionaire, who set an auction record of $57.3 million for one of the artist's series of ten 'Untitled' works, then the following year broke his own record, purchasing another Basquiat – *Untitled* (1982) – for $110 million including the buyer's premium. Fair warning… fair warning, rang out twice, at Sotheby's New York, before the gavel came down and his telephone bid was secured. The hope was that this piece would travel here, to the Lorken gallery to take pride of place at what was considered to be the most comprehensive collection of Basquiat's work ever.

To see one or two – Ever had been fortunate enough to have seen ten in a previous exhibition at the Gagosian – was an extraordinary experience. But he was trepidatious at seeing this many, the emotional overload that possibly upwards of eighty pieces, almost two thirds of his catalogue, would carry.

At first there were drinks, Krug of course, served by an identically-dressed team of men and women with perfect diversity, in the lobby of this architectural monument that had a cold but dramatic metallic feel, softened by giant curls of shining steel. Natural materials represented by wood and grey slate, slate that glistened, as if permanently wet and continually moving. The whole space had the feel of an endless churn of energy on the move; though it was obviously going nowhere.

Ever could see Miss Money-Root, who was far too busy to make any efforts at communication at this stage, dealing, most likely, with those who had donated their works. There were also, apparently, a few pieces that were available for sale, but with a history of his works not dropping below the 30 million mark, Ever didn't anticipate too much movement in that area this evening. Lomita attracted an enormous amount of attention that went beyond the conscious, sentimental sympathy usually afforded to the wheelchair-bound: she was truly breathtaking. Ever felt it a privilege to be associated with her, albeit in his capacity this evening as Mr Jacob. He should think up a first name, he thought, as her supposed business representative, then dismissed the distraction. She was in conversation, displaying her surprising knowledge, with three people, already reflecting on the validity of Basquiat as a graffiti artist, on his collaboration with Warhol and his addiction, his statement of his desire to be a star. He certainly was burnt and gone before attention was fully paid. So there was no personality to confuse the issue, he was purely a commodity, he had become what he never wanted to be – a gallery mascot.

He would probably have hated this evening.

Then the man of the moment, Ingmar Lorken, Ever prayed that a moment was all the time he was going to command, stepped onto the platform at the end of the lobby. The platform looked like a piece of curved aluminium foil. It was the approach to the gallery holding the paintings. He made a brief, eloquent speech thanking all who had enabled this exhibition, to those who had travelled far and wide to be here: Madonna, John McEnroe, Leonardo DiCaprio, Jay-Z and Beyoncé. It was Madonna who had been there at the beginning, before the fire had truly became an inferno, even though the paintings he gave her were destroyed after their break-up. Suzanne Mallouk was there but no Alexis Adler. Debbie Harry was there, and a special reference was made to her contribution to the exhibition – the first painting that Basquiat ever sold.

Ever was humming the telephone hanging song and staring. It was a memory plucked from his childhood. It carried a little sadness.

There was no more speech for him, only Blondie. His father had loved Blondie.

The time arrived for the doors to be opened, the aluminium stage moved aside unaided, and there was a reverent silence of anticipation. Lomita requested not to rush, or push, or to go in early, stating she was happy to sit, observe and engage in conversation with whoever was passing and seemed of interest to her – they were on her terms, these conversations.

She was, quite simply, charismatic. Ever felt comfortably insignificant in her presence. She was shining – she had been polished to a brilliance like the diamonds around her neck and the ones dropping from her ears like a goddess's tears. The diamond, clear, pure, with nothing to hide: transparent, adored by all. The honest jewel. No flies to be found on a diamond.

Ever could never have anticipated what was about to happen to him. They were amongst the last to enter, but the crowd was not too large – select, he thought, so that it would not inhibit an intimate and individual appreciation of the works.

He wheeled Lomita into the centre of the marble cavern, white-floored, white-walled, white-ceilinged; it had an unusual lack of complication for Gehry, with lighting that had a focus, but was invisible.

There she sat and he stood.

The mental disturbance from the paintings went straight into his cerebrum.

The distortion of image and the misrepresentation or reinterpretation of natural images felt like they were coming from his own head. He had no distance from them, no objectivity. No clarity, no separation, they became one mass of pain and chaos and his brain told him he looked like the faces, that it was his way of seeing the world, that he had had a hand in these creations. That he was responsible for the distortion, the ugliness, it had become revolting to him, what everyone else was interpreting as having captured a magical beauty and magnificence and a fresh view of the world. For Ever, it was like he had always lived like this, there were too many in the one space, as big as it was, he felt the sweat soak the back of his shirt, hoping it didn't pierce through his jacket, he was glad to have the wheelchair to support him, he searched for Lomita's hand, she had already sensed his turbulence, transferring comfort with both hands. He wanted to rip all the shit off the walls. How could anyone else see the world like he did? He understood the artist should be dead, you couldn't paint like this and be alive, you couldn't come this close to infantilising the world into sub-primitive form and get away with it. It was genius all wrong, they shouldn't be here, these people, he shouldn't be here, this was wrong. He left Lomita and went outside to breathe the air, look at the normal, and make sure his brain hadn't left him for good. He wanted the world back, not the one according to Basquiat, but according to God, or to anyone who didn't see it as he knew it to be, like this man had shown it. This was insane, hell on a wall. He knew, in that moment, as yet more vomit left his mouth and hit the pavement, missing his aim for the gutter, that there had been something seriously wrong with this man, that no one should paint like that, and if they did they should keep it to themselves. He was gone to the best place, this artist, the only place he could be in comfort, the only place anyone who saw the world like that could be. They had to be dead.

That was it.

Death.

And Ever, in his subsequent thought, understood he saw the world like that too.

Ever was, of course, being taken for a stupid idiot who had

pigged himself on the free champagne and was having a chunder.

The security guards were casting a disdainful glance and obviously his return was going to be tricky. A very considerate valet attendant came over with a bottle of water, which was used in a semi-successful attempt to get the rest of the vomit that hadn't made it into the gutter slushed off the pavement. He was grateful for some compassion, even if directed towards the pavement.

On his way past the glare of the security guards, he muttered the words bad and fish in vague connection, a weak attempt in paranoid thought to dispel their conviction that it was the alcohol. He was allowed back in, his exit having been well noticed; he saw Lomita, now outside the gallery space in the slowly-emptying lobby, talking to Miss Money-Root and Mr Lorken.

Obviously the ever-professional Miss Money-Root had made the introduction and he could already read on his approach that Lomita had charmed her two companions.

'Hello. Mr Jacob.'

Ever said by way of introduction, and in a spur-of-the-moment thought that would avoid any online checking:

'But everyone just calls me Jacob. I guess I have the status of a one-name guy. Or Just Jacob, if you must.'

His attempt at the icebreaker joke, always a risky strategy, fell slowly to the floor and no attempt was made to salvage the minimal mess.

'Of course, you know Mr Lorken.'

A calmly cruel Miss Money-Root, putting air back into the vacuum.

'And you remember, of course—'

These 'of courses' almost presupposed he was incapable of compiling thought and putting it into the form of memory. She continued:

'Our meeting, when you came with your initial inquiry.'

That word pronounced again with the American intonation.

'Pleased to meet you.'

No handshake was offered by Mr Lorken, and Ever returned his wandering hand to his side.

'I am so delighted to have had the opportunity of talking to Lomita, if I may be so bold as to call you that?'

Everybody had that reaction to Lomita, the asking of permission to be intimate with her name. At least, Ever remembered having the same experience.

Mr Lorken continued:

'We were talking about her desire to review some pieces we have housed in our collection.'

Miss Money-Root saved him.

'John Everett Millen.'

He had obviously completely forgotten the name in the brief time since it had originally hit the air.

'Of course, yes, and we would be delighted to organise that for you. I will leave all the details to Miss Money-Root.'

He clearly enjoyed saying the name, and Ever wondered if that is how she got the job, it was his work represented by a name. Money is the root.

'I must take my leave, but as we are near neighbours...'

A conversation missed by Ever, but a question that would have been asked as a way to establish socio-economic status: to get a fix on Lomita.

'I would also like to extend a dinner invitation, at my house, to you, Lomita. Details will be supplied through the same channel.'

Pointing to his black-suited assistant, a suit that was clinging with perfect tightness, not too much, not too little.

'I do hope you will accept, and once again, thank you for

gracing us with your presence. I look forward to our next meeting, when I will be a little less distracted.'

And with a final,

'Excuse me.'

With no acknowledgement of the minion – Ever – Mr Lorken took his leave, planting the most delicate of near-miss kisses on Lomita's right hand, which she had extended in expectation of some regal signing off. My God, she could perform, our Lomita.

'I will be in touch.'

Miss Money-Root wrapping up, having directed the small stuff to Ever. She too took her leave, again with an understandable excess of attention to Lomita and the minimal requirement of effort directed towards Ever. The way it should be, he thought, as she, in their eyes, and indeed in his, was the money. In more ways than one. Money on the table. Lomita, who was well into her role, handed Ever the phone, having dialled, and asked him to summon Manita. An interesting choice of word, he thought; the phone was ringing by the time he put it to his ear.

Within five minutes they were back on the 10 – this triumvirate – heading back to Oakhurst Drive, with a sense of mission accomplished. Lomita said she was truly exhausted, looked drained and very pale. With some concern, she told Manita that she had forgotten to take her medication before she left. But nevertheless gave her summary of the evening.

'I liked Mr Lorken, I think, yes I did, very charming, and Basquiat was not a well man, although his spirit fired out of his work and had he been helped, I suppose, we wouldn't have witnessed that manic genius. Although do all artists operate, or rather create, in an altered state? I always hesitate to use that word, genius, and so I retract it. But he was close. Wasn't he?'

Lomita was indeed very weak, helping her out of the car to

her bedroom was more effort than normal. In the event, Ever took her all the way into the bedroom, not stopping at the door.

'Don't worry, my sweet, Manita will put me to bed. I feel that was all a little much, but I had the most wonderful time. Tell me about your escapades in the morning.'

A pause. Lomita held his look.

'Did you think I was unaware? Would I be that naive?'

He smiled.

'But may I suggest you take a diazepam and calm yourself.'

That had been her first reference to his dramatic exit; he was relieved he didn't have to go into it now.

It was a pill and the shopping channel for him.

And maybe if he felt together enough, a call to Clarissa.

He didn't feel together enough, realised he had eaten nothing, and what he did have in his stomach was now in a gutter downtown. He went into the kitchen, made some toast and a cup of tea, but could find no marmalade, so just settled for hot toast and melted butter, and a cup of tea. Comfort food at its finest.

He took it back to his room and devoured it while watching a woman having her hair curled with a brush that heated and had an option to blow hot air at the same time. He had the sound down but enjoyed the company of inanity as opposed to insanity. He wondered why there was only one letter difference in the two polar opposite words. That must have caused some errors in the past with the slip of a finger.

This man is inane.

Would let you off the hook far better than the pronouncement –

This man is insane.

Big difference. A life could be changed by that. And with that thought, inanely rolling around his insanely fuzzing brain, he drifted for a couple of hours into the sleep of the fortunate.

Dreamless.

He woke, two hours later, and watched the shopping channel with the joy of brain removed from thought.

A lipstick that stayed on through whatever you did to it, then a tray of sparkling gems was rotating under the bright studio lights to make them twinkle.

Twinkle, twinkle little star how I love you what you are. No, those aren't the right words. He couldn't remember and turned off the television.

The remote felt uncomfortable in his hand, he had pressed the off button with an incorrect feeling that remained in his fingers. He switched it back on in an attempt to get the right feeling and turned it off again, keeping a hold on the button, hoping the feeling would change and result in a comforting feeling that would enable him to release, but he couldn't feel the comfort and his finger squirmed on the remote; he started to sweat and forced the button down to turn it off. The feeling crawled through his body, spurring a growing mental discomfort.

He switched it back on and there was a relief as the television shone its colour, then the desire to turn it off and be left with the correct feelings returned. He was nervous that his finger, a different finger this time, would leave him with satisfaction; he pressed and maintained a pressure on the button, waiting for the permission that he would grant himself, that he hoped would come, so he could remove his finger. It didn't come, he was rolling now on the bed, fired with heat and a panic that he would never be able to release the button and gain the satisfaction required for him not to turn it on again. Then the thought that if the correct feeling didn't happen, a terrible thing would happen to who? To whom? He was confused as he resisted the mind-squeeze that pressured him – to Jacob. Get it right. Please. He pressed it off and on again, and off and on again, each time holding the finger to relieve the curse that had now transferred to Clarissa, then after seventeen attempts, odd number is good, he took his finger off the button, and waited, until the compulsion to do it again had been satisfied. It wasn't, then it was, after twenty-seven times.

Twenty-seven times, then, with the relief of a faint, he experienced the correct feeling in his finger. Nothing bad was going to happen to anyone, he was OK, Jacob was going to be OK, Clarissa was going to be OK, the television was off, all was right in the world.

He was wet and his sheet, as he threw it off himself, was clinging and showed dark over his body. That was an obsessive-compulsive act, and he hadn't had them since they medicated him in the institution, but now they were back. It was all coming back.

God, to God he prayed getting out of bed, like a seven-year-old, kneeling and praying for the safety of those he loved, and for the preservation of his brain. He was praying to God to keep him sane long enough to commit an act of insanity. A murder. Did God know? Ever swore he wouldn't tell him. And craved for half a bottle of tequila to be downed in one effective and all-consuming effort.

Ever didn't have that long now, the ball was starting to roll; the hill was getting increasingly steep.

# *Chapter Twenty-four*

The dawning day would bring the meeting with Bruce Wong.

A car he didn't care anything for, so long as it could go forward when engaged in a gear. He wasn't fussy about which gear. The first trip was to La Cienega. A trip he had taken for granted, but Lomita was not really prepared for his departure anywhere. She stated clearly that he was not fit. Could she tell? Could she sense that there had been a further collapse in the night? Paranoia and an inability had descended on him, he seemed to have forgotten how to act to show that he was normal, fit for purpose. He was behaving awkwardly, was he? He had no idea. How do you behave, when you are telling someone that you are going to return your rental car? Negotiation, you negotiate, you convince, you do normal things like say—

'Oh, I would love a cup of coffee.'

Which he said, not wanting one.

'I'll pick one up from—'

Not completing the sentence as he couldn't think of a coffee place; Starbucks wasn't exactly a memory tester, really. Trust, he had to build trust.

'I'll be fine, back in a couple of hours.'

Not even beginning to explain the piece of crap that he

would be returning with, that was going to be parked on her elegant driveway. No, it could go in the garage. It was a four-car garage. No problem. Straight in there, really.

He hadn't got back to sleep since his remote episode and felt nervous at touching or leaving or inhabiting any space, or light switching, or door closing, or any action that might involve the cold creeping horror of repetition. It was in this state that he felt the respectful need to convince Lomita that he was safe to go and purchase this car on his own and return his Discovery to Sixt on La Cienega. It was a matter of economising.

She was not convinced he was in any state to do anything, sensing the edge that a lack of sleep gives to a person. She could tell, God, she could tell. That feeling of alienation, of not being in the game. Not playing. Being inanely insane.

Manita was to accompany him.

'I really don't want to put Manita through this – it'll just be boring.'

'Then company will relieve the boredom.'

This was a really bad idea. For all the reasons that anybody could immediately think of.

Including Ever, who was way ahead on these reasons, also realising he had to take a trip to the ATM; in his head he started to panic again; the not getting his own way; the knowing it was wrong but not wanting to be told he was wrong.

He was getting a little cross. Like a child, not being allowed out to play. They had a disagreement, he kept it polite, he promised, vowed that he would be fine. It would take him two hours and he would be back, she had his number, he had his phone, they were connected. He was, inside himself, so grateful and full of a soft emotion, that she cared.

She cared more than he did, he was just compulsed, on a railway line, stuck with a magnetic force that wouldn't let him off, but that was starting to eat him from the inside. It didn't like him being stuck, his psyche, it was giving him things that were breaking down his confidence, his control over his obsessive compulsion. He was being devoured. That way, maybe he could, without knowing it himself, be released. He was being split from the inside. And it was beginning to hurt.

He left anyway, with Lomita pleading the opposite, though with no bad feeling. He started the engine on his Discovery and couldn't let go of the key. Three times he went through the process of turning it on and off, until it felt right.

Inside.

What was Mr Wong going to think?

The car was deposited at the rental company with the minimum of fuss, which involved a routine check for damage. He never understood this process, as he was fully insured. The check revealed nothing that he could be accused of, be hauled before the rental company and put on trial for unintentional, or was it wilful damage, to the vehicle. But the smell of vomit, lingering, caused a glance, disturbed, from the inspecting man.

What can you say about vomit?

'A friend's dog,'

Mumbled Ever, following the inspecting man round the car.

Had that helped?

It's not damage – fact – an act of life, a natural event. An act of God. He always felt he was in the wrong.

Wherever.

Whatever.

He was on his cell, ordering a cab from the Beverly Hills Cab Company to take him to Chinatown; on completion of the call Clarissa's name was illuminating the screen. The ringing barely had a chance to tone itself before he had pressed the button to accept, resisting, with an agony, the urge to cancel the call.

Had his dealing with the remote last night caused a problem? To Jacob?

He spurted.

'Everything is all right isn't it?'

It came out with such an urgency that it surprised Clarissa.

'And with you?'

'Yes fine.'

Was his reply. Not definitive.

'Why are you still there? What are you doing?'

'I'll be back soon.'

He lied.

'I want you to come back, it's all shit. I'm an idiot, I'm sorry Ever. I don't know what I want. Sorry, I've had a few drinks. Jacob's good. He's asleep.'

'Does he ask after me?'

Weedy thought, Ever.

'Yes, he does, of course he does, he knows fuck all, he misses you, you are his father for fuck's sake, nothing is going to change that, in his head, it's in his head, at least not until he's older and he can understand and asks and we will explain. Won't we? Will we? Ever?'

What was in Jacob's head was Jacob's truth. The facts didn't change that because he didn't know. Jacob didn't know. Ever's father didn't know. Ever was lost.

'Hello, Ever, can you hear me? Hello?'

He found himself.

'Yes.'

'Did you hear what I said about the father thing?'

Why did she have to continue with that thought, and why couldn't she have just left it without it having the explaining problem attached? That had now presented another situation, another issue to be addressed.

'Yes.'

Was all he could summon.

'We'll just explain one day, won't we?'

'But yes, yes of course.'

He didn't know why he began those words with a But.

But the cab was arriving.

'Hang on, I'm just getting into a cab... I'm going to Bunker Hill Avenue, Chinatown.'

He said addressing the driver. Clarissa shouted.

'Why the fuck are you going there? Bit early for spare bibs.'

'You mean ribs?'

She laughed, he liked to hear her laugh. He liked people laughing.

'Too much kid stuff. Kid stuff all the time.'

'I'm going to meet someone to do with my father's will. I still have things to wrap up, you know, I'm not just pissing around.'

That wasn't all a lie.

'Love you both, and miss you, I'll be back in about a week.'

That was a lie. Though not all of it.

'I'll let you know what I'm doing.'

That was also a lie.

'Are you OK?'

He wanted to pass the focus over.

'Yes, but I am just a fucking mess Ever. My life just feels a mess. I'm sorry to call. I'm drunk and I'm an idiot and I should never have done... one day you will understand.'

'I do understand, already I do. I know why you did what you did.'

His hand was rubbing his thigh back and forth in a pattern that he had to keep up till the phone call ended. He tried to end it.

'I'll call tomorrow. I do try, you know, and you don't pick up.'

'Sometimes I turn my phone off, I just can't face shit. Not all the time, I am in a different space than I was, you know, where I was.'

He was not concentrating now. Only on his leg.

'I love you babes.'

Oh fuck, don't call me that. Did he say that or think it?

He could hear the noise of liquid falling down her throat, swallowed in large intakes, large breaths in between, she was giving it some.

'Got to go. Nearly there.'

'Love you babes.'

He obviously hadn't said it.

'Love you too.'

He didn't think that was a lie.

'Kiss to Jacob.'

'Kiss to you. Big fucking kiss, I want that. Can you talk to me Ever?'

'How do you mean?'

'You know, make me come.'

'I'm in a taxi.'

'Please.'

'I can't.'

'I'm doing it anyway, I'm going to come.'

'Got to go.'

He could hear her breathing and he knew what was about to happen.

His leg could now stop being rubbed; he turned off the phone with one hand and exhaled a breath of relief that she was still with him, Jacob was all right, and that he could stop rubbing his leg. Knowing she would still be rubbing herself; well probably just about coming to a stop.

'Which number, you want?'

'It's at the cross with Cesar Chavez Avenue, 1402. Building on the corner.'

'Where you from?'

'Originally here, then the UK.'

Here we go again.

'And where's the trouble coming from?'

'The what?'

'On the other end of the phone, forgive me asking, just messing with you.'

'Yeah, a lot of people do that. That's my wife. She's OK, just misses me.'

'Yeah, right, and they always have a funny way of showing it.'

The journey then continued in silence, filled for Ever with a visual image of Clarissa. Step by step. And then a little post-masturbatory doze.

'This good for you, my friend?'

Back to it.

'Yeah that's good.'

'That's going to cost you the best part of fifty-five bucks.'

'OK, that's…'

Before Ever could continue.

'That's a thirty-minute ride. That, per hour, is not a big rate. I'm not totally unskilled labour, you know, I'm responsible for your life, for those minutes, my friend.'

'Yes, no, I'm grateful, thank you.'

The English in the Englishman kicking in. What he really wanted to say was fuck you, big fucking deal. Go fuck your sister.

No he didn't really, not all that, just the first part.

He gave him sixty; the cab driver counted and gave a reluctant,

'You take care now.'

As if still assessing the questionable generosity of the tip.

Tip culture, this America. Everybody expects, and gets, a fucking tip.

He wasn't going to tip Mr Wong, no, me old China, he was going to bargain.

Fuck – the ATM.

He was at Mr Wong's address at the right time, but now he needed a bank. His cab was still there, hadn't moved, as the driver was putting his counted cash into a pouch. A leather pouch that he must have had his whole cab driving career. Probably his wife's gift on day one.

'Excuse me, I'm sorry, but I need a bank.'

'Oh, you finally realised you didn't give me enough tip.'

A laugh, as it was, he thought, a joke.

'No.'

Said Ever, taken aback, a little.

'Just messing with you, my friend.'

Fuck the 'my friend' bit. He didn't say that did he?

'Get in, we'll have a look round.'

The look around was going to be an obvious one, back to the main drag, Broadway. At the corner of Cesar E. Chavez Avenue – he wondered what this Latino had done to deserve immortalisation in a Chinese neighbourhood – a left turn took them underneath the two curling dragons that formed an arch over the road at the start of Broadway, proper, full-on Chinatown. Pagodas with triple tiers of cake, one on top of the other, diminishing in size at every level, smallest at the top, marked the entrances to the shopping streets. These were adorned with hundreds of red lanterns, strung across and blowing and swaying with every gust of wind. On the other side of the street, the density of market stalls forced the pedestrians off the sidewalk. They were selling everything from shoes and hats to kitchen utensils and pots and pans. And, of course, woks.

And as for banks.

The street displayed an embarrassment of banks. The Cathay Bank, Far East National Bank, East West Bank. On and on, true Left and Right Bank zone. He plumped for the East West Bank, the mention of his side of the world gave him the vaguest hope of it having an ATM that would recognise his bank in the Old Country.

It was situated right by the Mandarin Plaza. All that was needed now was the good fortune of a cookie to be able to get the money out in $500 tranches. Would luck hold out? Don't get compulsive. Just do it. No touching. His brow felt a drip run down into his right eye, he was keying in the pin, resisting the temptation to restart every time. Got it, done it all, as the third drip ran its same course, into the same eye. A channel must have been grooved. Back to the waiting cab. Well done, me old China. That was it, his father's expression, Ever wondered why he was saying it: china plate/mate. Me old China. Another pinch of sadness.

The Opium Wars were forgiven at this bank, at least.

The smell of food at the endless restaurants and food stalls made his mouth fill with the craving for something to eat. Would they put in MSG here, he wondered, in the real thing? He was tempted. But then you'd have to have a beer or two and then. No. His phone bird chirped. It was a text from Clarissa, it simply said.

'Mean bastard.'

That took her longer than he'd thought.

'From whence we came. Please.'

'You mean back?'

'Yes.'

He said to relieve the need for explanation; puzzled that he had used the word in the first place.

'Back, thanks.'

'Give me a ten, we'll call it quits.'

It wasn't a deal.

But Ever didn't argue. He parted with a twenty-dollar bill

and received a ten in return. Did he detect a pause in the passing? Not another tip surely? Forget it, my friend: just a thought.

He was standing at the foot of what looked like a slice of communist architecture.

Imposing itself a few hundred yards off the main drag, on the appropriately named Bunker Hill Avenue. The apartment building, built in the last ten years he imagined, with less imagination than Ever had just used to guess the age. It looked like a bunker, maybe that was the architect's brief. Which came first? The building to appear appropriate in the street of that name; or had they given up on seeing the building and thought fuck it, let's make it look intentional and rename the street? The bottom two floors were encased by metal railings behind which cars were parked.

Ever supposed this was where they would be ending up for the viewing.

He pressed the bell, having with some difficulty accessed the entrance. The bell with the name, Wong, written on a piece of paper, in capitals, inserted behind a blurred plastic holder, was followed by the Chinese version. He presumed. Calligraphy. He guessed that the 8b against the name suggested the eighth floor. There was an 8a, an 8c, an 8d, an 8e, he was counting, thinking they must be small apartments as the block was not that big, then a voice came through the intercom.

'Hello?'

'It's Mr Smith. About the car.'

He was now Mr Smith, and his thoughts and actions would be as Mr Smith: that was Mr Smith's decision.

'Stay there. Come down.'

He stayed there, for what seemed like a long time; it

occurred to Mr Smith that maybe there was no elevator. Then the door opened.

'Mr Smith.'

A statement.

'Yes.'

'Mr Wong.'

A man of about fifty, fit-looking, save for a literal pot of a belly, otherwise slim. Long black hair, slightly greying in a ponytail that, as he turned to close the door, he could see was not far short of his waist. And a goatee beard, a long goatee beard, again greying.

'Round the back, we need to go.'

Obediently, Mr Smith followed and not a word was spoken during the walk round to the back of the building.

'In lowest level. But ground level, not a problem.'

For who and why? Thought Mr Smith. From this different street the building looked exactly the same. So back and front were interesting definitions. Conformity, yes, but not a conformity with style. On purpose? Why was Mr Smith so fixed on his disappointment with the building? He cleared the thought. Could Mr Smith do that?

They arrived at an unimpressive vehicle, amongst a selection of unimpressive vehicles. Mr Wong had stopped in front of the unimpressive vehicle. It was truly the dullest, most anonymous car Mr Smith had ever seen. Ever thought so too. Perfect.

'You want to hear it? Please take a seat, inside, sit down in it.'

He sat in the car and was handed the keys, and an invitation to turn over the engine. Twice he had to turn the key and on the second attempt the tired old horses came to life, resenting every second. They had nothing left in them that could be defined as horsepower.

'It works, see, you want me to come with you, we drive. Around?'

Mr Wong circled his hand.

Mr Smith seriously thought about this, and was not sure he was prepared to accept the effort of social proximity that the drive would demand.

'OK.'

Was Mr Smith's reticent response.

Mr Wong climbed in beside him. Conversation, or rather lack of it, was not something that bothered Mr Wong one bit. They exited across a metal ramp, strips of metal with gaps, usually in place to prevent cows from crossing, who knows, with a judder and a shudder. And then the car was on the open road. Back onto the big straight Roman Caesar road, over the hill the other way into a less residential area. Open her up, let her go.

All the tired horses in the sun, watch this old car run.

Just a noisy chug, the exhausted exhaust had a hole and he could sense that fumes would be clouding out of it. But it went forward through all the gears. Automatic transmission. He tried reverse, and then thought he should show dissatisfaction at this awful car that was just perfect.

They returned the car to the cow-proof parking area.

'OK, few problems, I'll give you seventeen-fifty.'

Said with the toughest of voices.

'The price is nineteen-hundred dollars, you don't want it, you don't take it. It has a few problems, that why nineteen-hundred dollars.'

That was it for Mr Smith, he was out of ruthless bargaining technique. For the second time in the space of an hour he felt his money-dealing skills were poor to say the least. He had no ruthlessness. No killer instinct. Well, wait a second, that was questionable, most certainly up for debate. In relation to Ever at least.

'OK. I'll take it.'

'Good. All the paperwork is here in the car. I just need to fill in your name for the vehicle's title, we both need to sign, and I put price sold. Odometer statement as the car is over ten years old, you don't really need. But I give you anyway. 176,042 miles. Here is the current smog certificate. And I will need to go and draw up a bill of sale that will help you show proof of ownership to the DMV. Then you know you have ten days to register. You from here?'

'Originally, yes.'

'So you know what to do at DMV to make it your car?'

The thought of it being his car was crippling.

'You know, you don't need to bother with that. It will be fine. It's OK.'

Ever wasn't sure what Mr Wong didn't need to bother with, he just wanted to get it all over with. Quickly.

'OK, sign here.'

Said Mr Wong producing the title deed exchange. Mr Smith was about to sign and remembered, as the ballpoint went to the paper, to sign J. Smith. He adopted a rather creative squirl, over curly writing style.

'Wait, first the money?'

Mr Wong said, too late to stop the signature, Mr Smith thought briefly of kicking him out of the car – no he didn't – stupid thought. Charm was not Mr Wong's need in life, but never having had it he wouldn't be aware of it not being there. Or even probably that it was a commodity that some people traded in.

Mr Smith handed over $1,900 for this four-speed 2.3-litre engine in a V6 pattern, naturally aspirated, no sunroof, tan interior, that he suspected might be leather but was so close to vinyl plastic it was a difficult call; it had power windows, and was about seventeen years old.

The offside front wing had been sprayed, presumably as a result of an accident, he wondered how many collisions this car had had, it was a different shade of red than the rest of the car panels which, through the sun, had lost forever their ability to produce a shine.

This car would be forever dull.

The deal was done and it was impossible to tell if Mr Wong was pleased or not, as his face had not changed expression from the moment they had met.

'Do you like Bruce Lee?'

Mr Wong said, the first piece of unnecessary conversation.

'Yes.'

Said Mr Smith, devoid of a committed opinion, but surprised into an immediate response.

'He taught by my father. And they killed him you know.'

'Bruce Lee?'

Wondering for a second if he meant his father.

'Yes, disclosing secrets of Wing Chun to the world.'

He wasn't picking up Mr Smith's obvious lack of enthusiasm.

'You want me to show you pictures of my father with Bruce Lee, training, very small group, with Yip Man in Kowloon. With me also, when I was young. My name is Bruce.'

And really the next sentence was understood and digested before Mr Wong continued.

'I am named after Bruce Lee. Bruce Wong.'

This animated Mr Wong was really having quite a transformative experience.

Mr Smith wanted to go but Mr Wong said,

'We take car, your car now, round to the front, give me ten minutes, I show you pictures. I will come down. No elevator. It is broken.'

Suddenly this man was a conversationalist supreme.

There was no choice as Mr Wong shut the door. Mr Smith

had a moment of further disappointment in the architect, as he had failed to give access from the garage to the apartments. You parked your car and then were forced to go around to the front entrance. Who was he?

The thought that this might have been the only building he designed in his entire life shadowed Mr Smith's rapidly developing off-kilter brain. He felt a moment of compassion: compassion for the mediocrity of the architect's talent.

And a little concern at the thoughts and persona belonging to Mr Smith.

'Come we go. You will enjoy. Wonderful man Bruce Lee, had a whole philosophy of life, I try to follow. I still train.'

When was this going to stop? It was like being herded into a sheep pen by a pack of dogs: there appeared to be no escape. If there was an invitation to go up however many flights to the eighth floor he was convinced he would decline. They arrived at the front of the building, where there was no parking allowed.

'No parking, you stay with the car, your car now.'

As if Mr Smith was the most gullible idiot ever.

He was thinking of just leaving, letting Mr Wong show his pictures to the air, but he waited, and down came Mr Wong with a book. A published book. Not what was expected, and there, sure enough, was a picture on page sixty-five, well marked, of Bruce Lee and a man standing in the Shaolin White Crane pose, opposite each other, and along with the pose description underneath the photograph, were the names – Bruce Lee and Wang Bo Wong. Bruce Wong's father, he assumed, and then Mr Wong confirmed the assumption.

'My father. And there is me with Bruce Lee.'

Turning another page.

'Let me show you girl I was boyfriend with.'

Strange phrasing thought Mr Smith; he turned the pages to

reveal a beautiful girl in, as was described, a Gong Fu stance, the name below, Diana Lee Incosanto.

'Bruce Lee was her godfather. My good friend. She and me are still good friends. You see he was a great man, Bruce Lee.'

This was most unexpected in the purchase of a Honda Accord EX V6 sedan with power windows; but it was so human, and obviously Mr Wong was a very lonely man.

'You enjoy the car. Good to see you. I must go.'

As if Mr Smith had been detaining him.

'I still train.'

'Yes, you told me that.'

'I will go for that now. Here is the bill of sale. Thank you, Mr Smith.'

Then Mr Wong was keying his way into his building and Mr Smith, the proud new owner of a dull red car, chugged down the street.

To block out the noise of the engine he put his earphones in and played Lana Del Rey; now, she didn't wail, but she could have a moan; he was now Ever again, reverting back to type, out of his adopted character; relieved – Mr Smith was beginning to bother him.

He enjoyed being absorbed in Lana's misery.

'The Blackest Day' was playing and he found his way west. No Kate this time, to help.

Never sure if Lana was singing about sex or just life; just life, well well, life. Depth and darkness and enduring pain. Anyway, he empathised with it, in the way he wanted to. Take it as you sense it. That's the point, there is no right way.

What in the name of God does 'Purple Rain' mean? He knew for him what he wanted it to mean and that was enough and he wasn't telling. Anyone.

On the journey back, he was looking for another piece to add to his plan. He wanted a piece of wasteland where he could dump and possibly destroy this beauty and attract minimum attention in the middle of an afternoon. There was more than one option, he catalogued them in a brain which didn't have a lot of space. But he could remember the key things. The compulsive satisfier things. He drove onto one empty, disregarded piece of land backing onto the high and windowless wall of a warehouse – an industrial-type building – to see what the movement was like around it; he parked the car and sat.

It saw no persons walk across its potholed earth and the worn-out, given-up attempts at a gravelled surface. The patch of land was almost underneath the 110 Freeway and couldn't have been more than a quarter of a mile from the gallery area. Looming over the land was an isolated tower with the words 'Ritz Carlton' blazing out at the top; from where he was standing it was an incongruous sight of poverty swamped by wealth.

The street adjacent to this piece of land was homeless central, plastic housing, in sheets of blue and occasional yellow, one after the other, their sounds drowned by the cars' endless journeys overhead on the freeway, their dreams spilt on the side of the road, and they had the agony, now, he supposed, but with a developed immunity, of being dwarfed by the mega millions of the buildings of the downtown areas. In particular the Ritz Carlton.

Ever always had these moments of reflection at the absurdity of the world.

He then got out, walked around, noticing an alley to the left of the building; through that to the street on the other side were a couple of cafés and a Milagro's Market, the Chinese influence giving way to Mexico; but there was a final Eastern attempt at territorial dominance in the form of a functional, plastic-seat, red-and-white-check-tablecloth Chinese restaurant.

The description 'authentic' fitted all these places perfectly.

But what really captured Ever's eye was a hotel; five floors high; two-room width; with a fire escape zigzagging its way up the front of the building.

It was called Isis Adelphia.

The sign worn, the bead curtain that represented the front door had had a thousand rippling noises declare arrival into this miniature, decayed palace. The name when built, Isis, goddess of the sky, must have carried a romance; now it had whole different connotation and he supposed this was the reason for there having been no attempt to revitalise the sign. Or did they even care? Adelphia was, he seemed to remember, just the name of a town in ancient Greece, and could give it no significance beyond that. Or was it Delphi?

The road he had turned off was a constantly flowing two-lane road and the chain link fence was partly broken down, with just the one entrance, the one he had used. Piles of non-disposable trash had amassed, over what looked like a long, long time; vegetation had grown through the tyres, there were smashed concrete blocks, an old fridge, and sofas with visible springs that even the homeless had disregarded. No residential life around, it just felt lonely. The land was not going to be used for parking, save for the one truck that was there, he was sure of that.

There was the heartening sight of a car, completely stripped of all inside that was ever of value, standing as a shell. A pale blue shell. His new car fitted in perfectly. A good sign. This was somewhere he could melt into insignificance after the act.

And he appreciated the irony of its location.

He never thought a piece of nondescript neglect could give him a feeling of such satisfaction. He climbed back into the car, his car, that was a hard concept to grasp; without a thrill, and not feeling like himself, he drove out.

Was he then, the thought passed through, defined by what

he owned in terms of quality? Did this car make him feel less of a person? Of course, what a stupid question, it made him feel like a loser: but what he was going to use it for made him feel full of achievement.

Did Mr Lorken's car – his intention took him there – make him feel something, or did he have so much that to him it was the equivalent of this Honda Accord? That was a depressing thought, that riches took away appreciation of things. They took away decency, he knew that, but did they also take away the excitement of acquisition? Where did the pleasure come from? Power then – power – over all around. Power over people. Taking away the power of the people: that was what had happened: more people, fewer with power. Where would that end up? An elite of, say, five, dominating eight billion – distillation. It was not a new thought to him: it was one of his nightmares.

He pulled onto the road and continued west. On 8th Street the car needed gas, Mr Wong was not a generous car trader: Ever should have stuck on seventeen-fifty. He pulled into a 76 with the intention of buying a can for extra fuel. He filled the car and the gas can, but only after a struggle to find where the release button for the filler cap was.

He had asked no questions about the car's functions. Why would he? He couldn't care less. Paid in cash for the gas, and drove slowly; that was what Ms Del Rey dictated. A compelling drone. He felt sorry that she wasn't singing in a better car, she deserved more; he decided to switch her off and unplug his ears, and listen to the car to make sure it didn't have noises it shouldn't. Mr Wong, for all his training, it appeared, was a smoker: he hadn't even bothered to empty the ashtray. He wondered how Bruce managed his climb to the eighth floor.

Should have stuck on seventeen-fifty. Erase the Mr Smith

email account; he hoped Mr Smith would disappear into Chinese thin air.

The thing about buying a car from a Chinese man is you want to do it again in couple of hours.

Nearly worked, chuckled Ever, appalled at his cheapness, but liberated to be able to tread on that territory. He always considered himself respectful; maybe he was drying out like a piece of clay; his conscience slowly crumbling away.

He would soon be uncontactable and as unmemorable as the car.

His potential anonymity brought him only a temporary comfort.

He was starting to feel that everybody was noticing him in this car. He had stayed off the freeway, not trusting the lump in relentless traffic, taking in Little Mexico, turning down through parts of Koreatown, with its endless medical buildings, to get onto Olympic and continue west before making a right and getting up to Santa Monica Boulevard. He was approaching the more sophisticated parts of Santa Monica Boulevard; he could feel people looking at him, couldn't he? Questioning why he was driving that car. Why was he in that car? Why was he? He was now, one part of him at least, demanding an explanation, from the other part, as to what he thought he was doing.

Rational thought scared this brain, a brain that was being exhausted by its focus on this obsessive journey; a commitment to this journey which required abandonment of sense, the health food for the brain. He couldn't take this conversation, no – discussion, no – argument, no – it was a fight. He pressed the Thin White Duke into his ears for comfort. He'd got his car, he'd got his gun. He hummed a song, not the one he was listening to, so it riffed in counterpoint to what was pumping into his head.

The thought of the police came in and wouldn't leave. He plucked out the buds and voiced a God Bless to Bowie. What would he say if he was stopped?

'Yes, I have just bought this car.'

'Documents? Name doesn't match ID.'

A panic poured over him in liquid form.

He got wet. And cold. There was only one word for it and he knew it; he couldn't face that word, because it was irreversible, you can never come back when you have crossed over, it was – madness.

Madness that is coupled with an action while in that state allows no control. He was in the middle of an episode; of indeterminate length; of obsessively committed insanity.

He needed desperately to be in the cool darkness and protection of Lomita's garage.

His idea of a paradise was to sit there and hide: no one would ever be able to find him. He started to feel the strangeness of the steering wheel, uncomfortable in his hands, he was forced to stroke it to find the comfort area of the wheel. His hands were perspiring; the cheap plastic of the steering wheel, with the worn construct of finger indentation, mass-produced several million times, only made the attempt at smooth contact worse.

He wanted to rub the wheel to erase, until a flatness was there; until the finger bumps were gone, the plastic levelled. His hands were hurting as he fought to keep the car on the road.

He was in Beverly Hills now, turning up Doheny – he was nearly there. He had remembered to do what no one remembers to do when they return a rental: they always leave the garage remote in the rental. He had remembered it, and he felt proud that he was functioning at that level of detail; it gave him confidence. He pressed it with a shaking, wet hand, it opened and he entered; he felt the cold darkness cover him with a safety, then he re-pressed the remote, the darkness increased and then the comfort of the sound of door into frame, completing its descent, hit his ears. He was swamped with relief.

Then came the fight – the compulsion to re-press – to continue to go over the process again, and again; he threw the remote into the back of the car – out of reach.

They couldn't find him now.

He was safe.

Safe, and he wanted to talk to Lomita; but not for another hour.

He wanted to sit for an hour and try to smooth out this fucking steering wheel. He stroked and stroked it, until the desire left him and he was able to calm, just calm.

He had a full minute of consideration as to whether to turn off the engine or let it run in the dark enclosed space. He guided his hand to the ignition and killed the horses, breathless and spuming, in the engine.

He slept for a dreamless ten minutes.

At least, he thought he slept, but had no way of knowing because no dream came to mind; no other world that would confirm he had left this one. After what he decided was a wake-up, he accepted a peace. He stopped sweating. He had to force memory back into his head; what had passed that day. Force hard, his brain not going there, or wanting to go there, and accept what he had done.

He had only bought a car. No biggie. Jesus Christ, come on.

What was going to happen? When?

Crumbling conscience.

## *Chapter Twenty-five*

Ever slept with his mother until he was thirteen.

Meaning in the same bed; and it didn't happen every night. The reason for leaving his solitary bed was the dream of the pale blue hand and he would invariably, on opening his eyes from the waking nightmare, leave his room and go into his parents' room, in the middle of the night, and climb into their bed. Then as he got older, and bigger, his father would reluctantly, to create space, leave the bed and climb into the vacated one, in the next room.

It was interesting to Ever that his room was always known as the guest bedroom; he was never allowed to put up posters or anything to stake his claim, show any evidence, a physically imposed kind of evidence, that this was his own personal space. It had another single bed alongside his. So it was a twin-bedded room, the bed covers, or eiderdowns, as they were known, were in the same shade of lilac as those that were in his mother's bedroom. It was never referred to as his father's bedroom, although he'd inherited the house, or his parents' bedroom, always his mother's bedroom. The wallpaper also made no concession to the fact that a boy slept there. It had a green background, with flowers and tree branches, factory rolled out and printed in pale colours; only after a long study – he was probably the only person who had bothered to give it that length of study – when in the summer he lay awake, the light fading, staring and staring, squinting his eyes, screwing them up to extract some definition, did he find something in its purposeful blandness. Ever questioned the pattern's integrity, the reason to make it: a sort of a garden feel, with a Chinese influence. But why put the outside on the inside? He was six.

His conclusion, from these times of pondering, was that it was a really anonymous wallpaper and he hated it.

He never felt he belonged in his room: the room that was kept for guests. There was a much smaller room, attic-style, that he would go to on the occasion that guests came to stay. That only happened once, that he could remember, when his aunt and uncle came to stay for one night. His father was hated by his mother's brother so it was not pleasant and that was probably the explanation for the single stay.

But the room remained in name terms – the guest room.

Not Ever's room.

Ever.

Even though it was in this bed that he was visited in the winter, when he would fall ill with bronchitis that would then develop into pneumonia, to be given daily penicillin injections by a Scottish doctor by the name of Dr Triptle.

The injections were delivered into his buttock, a slow and increasingly agonising pain, that built and built during the release of the fluid: so he knew that at the insertion of the thick needle there was nothing to look forward to as this was only the beginning of the increasing pain cycle while the serum journeyed into Ever's system.

Ever was relieved that when he was ten he was put into Wildwood School in Los Angeles for a year. A bold move and a good one, during another period of success for his father. Ever loved it as the primary consideration was not education: but for the children to be happy. But the most exciting thing for him was that he didn't get bronchitis. It was his mother who always battled to spend Christmas in England. Both Ever and his father could see the sense of staying in the comparative warmth of Santa Monica but his mother didn't really care. Her way was the way.

She was a short woman, quite plump but with a pretty pre-war type face, although she was born five years after the end of the Second World War; her face always maintained an out-of-date traditionalism in its looks. Her name was Dorothy, no middle name, just the one, his mother often stated a resentment towards her parents for their lack of effort, in that they never came up with two names, at least the gift of a middle name.

'That's all you want in life is choice.'

That's what she said, it was a kind of her mantra, she applied it to a lot of things. She hated the name Dorothy. Ever agreed that it never seemed to represent her, or suit her; she was more contemporary than the name implied. But she drank a lot, which she did in front of him and his father; there was never any one else around. There was what she thought to be secret drinking going on, a bottle of gin, kept under the bed, but Ever knew and his father had always known, she probably knew they knew and just didn't care. The mornings would find her in the kitchen, grumpy, with a hangover, then around midday it was time for a 'little drinky', spoken with her welsh lilt in the hope that it would provide a distracting charm. Then in the evening she would state she would 'only have the one'. But in fact, she had kept herself topped up from under the bed during the course of the afternoon. Anyway she never just stuck to 'the one'.

Ever always felt a sadness for his mother, she never appeared, unless drinking, to extract any happiness from life.

He was seven years old when she sat him on her lap and said that he was the only reason she was staying alive, that she didn't kill herself.

From that moment he felt a two-fold duty to keep her alive and to keep her happy. To ease the complications of their transatlantic existence, education-wise, at least, Ever was eventually put into a boarding school in England. The shock was made even greater when a postcard arrived for him, after only a couple of weeks at the school, saying that she was having a wonderful time in Los Angeles. This compounded his feeling of rejection, and confusion, in that she had always been the one wanting to go back to England. It also made him worry that he wasn't there to help her. His thoughts were not about himself, in those early years of his life, never, they were concern for her.

The letters which followed from his mother, which he dutifully replied to, were always signed off: Yours affec. Mum. No kisses. He had no idea what this meant, he would ask the other boys what was written at the end of their letters, how their mothers signed off: without exception, they divulged, lots of love, all my love, I love you, one of the three, or one of the first two – then an I love you as well. And followed with lots of kisses. He asked his mother, in a letter, what it meant, she explained – Yours Affectionately.

His immediate thought was, couldn't she be bothered to write the whole word? He never suggested she change her sign-off, though, so he continued to receive letters ending with those three words, Yours affec. Mum. And no kisses.

He got his first mobile phone when he was fifteen, probably as a result of his near death experience, rather than any attempt at technological advancement, just to be able to keep in touch; her emails or texts still ended with the same remote formality.

There was an event that left Ever with an ineradicable feeling of both guilt and horror.

When he asked, at the age of thirteen, if he could spend a night in his mother's bed. He felt frightened at the anticipation of the pale blue hand.

This, by now, was making his father's anger grow at every request, he repeatedly stated the boy was too old for this now, and, as if to lighten the complaint, always added that he didn't want to spend the night on his own.

He got lonely too.

The he's-away-at-school-it's-a-treat argument came up, in a defence from his mother, and his father was forced to acquiesce. Ever got his way, on this particular night, which is written in indelible ink. During the course of the night, he remembers his mother's nightdress riding up, and for the first time he wanted to see her body, naked; he lifted the sheets but could see nothing in the darkness, and sense only the smell of Chanel No 5, his mother, he supposed in her sleep, seemed to push her bottom in his direction, he, to his horror, realised he had an erection and immediately turned his back on her and lay there, starting to gently masturbate; but he aroused himself more, and in the weakness of single sexual focus he turned back towards his mother, with his erect penis he pushed tentatively and slowly towards her, his heart made his whole body pound and he realised he was shaking, there was no resistance from his mother, he pushed his penis further to what he could only describe as her bottom; there was a definite feel of wetness on the end of his penis but he knew nothing about what he was doing, or the consequences of what he was doing, he pushed a little more and there still was no resistance, he felt he had entered something that was containing him; and it was, his first image and an obvious one; that it was dark.

A dark place with a comfort like nothing he had ever sensed from anything in his life.

That is all he could think, he continued to go further inside this darkness and his mother didn't move.

He pulled out a little, just once, and pushed back inside; then in a panic that he was going to orgasm, he pulled out and rubbed his penis and, for the first time, with his ejaculation, a substantial amount of semen shot out; he felt covered in his own guilty product.

He lay there, still, with heart pounding, no longer shaking and waiting to sense any sound or movement from his mother. He listened hard to her breathing to hear if there was the slightest change in rhythm, or depth of intake of breath. But nothing.

He lay there, without moving, until dawn. In an awareness of having done something terrible but not knowing if his mother had any knowledge of what had happened and would he, or she, say anything about it. For the hour after his ejaculation he kept his hand that had been around his penis to his nose and inhaled the smell of the place he had lived and entered the world through.

He felt a shame, the greatest feeling of shame he had ever felt: a guilt about his father crawled over him like ants, always waiting for more pain, from more bites. His father wouldn't have any ability or place to go to find an understanding of this act, as he remained in what for once could be honestly referred to as blissful ignorance. How could Ever eradicate this from his brain or deal with the relationship he now had with his unknowing father?

It had all changed, his life, his relationship with his mother and father, in the space of a single minute. A single minute that would make the years, however many he lived, never be the same again. How could he make it up to his father, to get his forgiveness, apologise, for an act he assumed he would never know had been committed? All the words, forgiveness, apology, were feeble in comparison to what he had done. He had committed an act that would haunt him: and it did every day of his life.

That morning, the morning after the night, and throughout the day, nothing was said. He said nothing, his mother behaved in her usual grumpy way; the result of the previous night's alcohol consumption.

The problem was cemented in time for Ever, because it was a year later that his parents split up and ultimately divorced. His father moved permanently to Los Angeles; Ever was left with his mother during school time; during the holidays, he would divide the time and fly to see his father.

He never slept in his mother's bed again.

But the guilt that lay inside him was so profound, his agony was increased by the fact that it could never be discussed or addressed; it existed at a level that was really beyond the acceptable bounds of conversation. But he blamed himself, he always believed that in this incestuous Oedipal act, the desire came from him and was the cause of the break-up of his parents' marriage.

He has never, to this day, had any idea what his mother's awareness, if any, was of the situation; it has never been referred to.

Ever is trapped in his own deviant and perverted world of blame.

Ever and his mother rarely communicate: but he puts it down to the alcohol.

Not the fact that he fucked her.

# *Chapter Twenty-six*

After his sojourn in the garage.

He walked back into the house through the door that Manita always used. He had received an email from Miss Money-Root. The email account he had opened specifically for Miss Money-Root, at the same time as becoming Mr Smith for Mr Wong, was in the name of n.investjacob@gmail.com: he had introduced himself to her through that guise. Clever name he thought.

With the Lorken gallery logo, her email read:

THE LORKEN GALLERY

*From the office of Peony Money-Root.*

*Dear Mr Jacob*

*I wonder if you would be kind enough to pass on an invitation to Miss Lomita Nairn from Mr Lorken, inviting her to dinner at home, on Friday night. The details are in the attachment below.*

*I do hope I have gone through the correct channel in approaching you: I am unable to access a direct communication with Miss*

*Nairn. Of course, if the date does not suit, please inform and we can accommodate.*

*I do not wish to presume an intrusion.*

*With reference to John Everett Millen: we are in the process of arranging the transportation of these works to our private viewing room at the beginning of next week – hopefully Monday.*

*I would be grateful if you could confirm a suitable day for Miss Nairn's appraisal of these works thereafter, if that proves convenient.*

*Please excuse the demand for two confirmations in one communication.*

*If there is anything else I can help you with, please do not hesitate to contact me.*

*Many thanks.*

*Yours*

*Peony Money-Root.*

*Gallery Development Executive.*

pdf

invitation.pdf

2.4 MB

Ever sensed a suggestion of humour towards the end of the email, but he couldn't visualise her face in response to that humour: he had never seen her smile.

And, of course, he was the minion and was not invited. A fly on the wall: he wished to be.

The house was quiet, it was always quiet; but it seemed to have the sound of sleep hanging in the air on his return. Manita did not appear to be around.

After a brief lie-down on his bed, and a difficult time with the remote, trying, without panic, to access the shopping channel, he felt the need for some calming medication.

This could only be administered by his resident physician Miss Lomita Nairn.

He walked out of his room, stood outside her door, listening for any sound and taking in the sun. Always the sun, playing with the trees: he was glad of the air conditioning that brought a cool to the world inside. It made looking outside at the warmth like a visit to a planetarium or an aquarium, where the observer is placed in a different environment. Complete separation. He was living in a different climate: he was in a different world. He knocked quietly on her door.

'Hello?'

Was the surprise response. Mainly because the knock was so quiet: good hearing, he thought.

'What do you want?'

A warm tone to the question.

'It's me, Ever.'

'Come in, my sweet. Come in.'

He opened the door; she was fully in bed, looking pale and tired, but not unhappy to see him. She patted the bed and invited him to sit. It was usually the other way round, with her showing the concern, and sitting, like the doctor, on the bed.

'I have just overdone it a bit, my sweet. I've missed you. Did everything go all right?'

'Yes.'

He said simply. He did not want to invite questions.

'No problems, I now have a car that is cheaper than a month's rental.'

A stretch, but not far off the truth. Right area, thereabouts, anyway.

'You have an invitation from Mr Lorken for dinner at his home.'

'Oh my. Show me.'

She said, with an obvious pleasure at her social calendar opening up.

He passed his phone and showed her the attached invitation.

'Very formal. Dietary requirements? Alcohol.'

Was her sole rider and there was a gurgle of laughter.

'On Friday? My, a couple of days to recover. I will look forward to that. At least it's early.'

Noting the 6.30 arrival time.

'I can't go. I'm not invited.'

'Of course you're not. You work for me.'

He was a little taken aback, expecting – 'I can't go without you.' But no, she was straight into—

'I'll wear my kingfisher blue dress. That'll knock them dead. Valentino. My favourite, I think. Made for me.'

Ever didn't doubt it.

'And I will not go in my goddam wheelchair.'

'My arm won't be there.'

'I will take my fist cane.'

The puzzled look spurred her explanation.

'I use it, a silver carved fist turned with fingers up. That's the handle. So hand can grip hand – it's made from ebony. I had to put a bit of ugly rubber on the bottom, it was slipping everywhere, but it does not, I assure you, detract from the overall picture of elegance.'

Again, Ever didn't doubt it.

'I am doing all this for you, you know, my sweet. Peck my cheek. Both of them.'

He obeyed.

'Thank you. What is it about you Ever? That I want. That I want to help?'

She seemed to correct herself, in case it had the suggestion of where they never go now.

He mused, though, that they both wanted to: and wondered why they didn't. But he had felt the invader the last and only time, and was not about to repeat that unpleasantness, that feeling.

Lomita and Ever ate an omelette.

Prepared by Manita, they sat in silence in the brown of the dining room. They drank sparkling water, followed by camomile tea.

The garden lights shone bright, the sun was switched off and the last of the hummingbirds had gone to bed. Lomita was in her wheelchair and her Pucci wrap. Exhaustion was on her face like make-up, and Ever, always one to go for guilt, felt it was because of him; it prompted his question.

'Should I leave? Would it make it easier for you?'

'I don't know why you came into my life, Ever, but it was too quiet before.'

A smile. He did not understand her change in tone.

'What am I doing, Ever? What are you really going to do, and do you think I am going to condone it? You are not well. Don't you see that? Why don't you see that?'

Ever's world took a gravity drop in terms of shock, a bump

on the ground of understanding – he thought he was there – that she was with him. Did he really, when had she ever said that?

'I won't do this anymore. What can I do? Call your doctor, tell him what you are going to do? I don't even know that you have clearly expressed what the hell you are going to do.'

A long exhalation that left no breath in her lungs, and a pause for the refill.

'You are seriously going to kill a man who thwarted your father's creativity?'

'Yes.'

There was a pause filled with her amazement.

'I think so, yes.'

'On the basis that your father was what? Exposed as a no-talent, a commercially non-viable artist?'

Ever had never entertained these kinds of words with these kinds of sounds and formations.

'My father is—'

Was all he found himself saying.

'You are blaming a man for your father's death.'

'No, for the death of my father's life. You don't understand the concept, a physical death is one thing, but to kill the spirit is another.'

'Why do you believe that? Have you not understood what I have done to try to discourage this belief in you?'

'I was just an entertainment, you thought my belief in revenge would pass. Is that it? Well it hasn't, and I understand you want nothing to do with me anymore.'

'I can't do this, if that is what you continue to believe. I have to remove myself from this, my sweet, as much as I care for you. I can't be party to a murder. I thought that with help and a little bit of love, a relationship, you would realise, change, come through, but you are still fixated. I don't think you are being honest with me. I am going to my bed. And I think you should do the same, and tomorrow we must address this.'

'And you want me to go?'

'What I want is to see this through, help you. Get rid of your pain. I recognise pain, I understand it, and maybe we are both not being honest with each other. You can't live like you live. I know that feeling. When you can't live with something.'

You don't.

Ever kept his disagreement to himself: it never developed beyond a thought.

'I won't feed or enable your madness, my sweet, I thought I could calm it and make reason come into that brain of yours.'

He was angry, but continued to keep quiet. He couldn't understand, they had met and he believed she understood the predicament, the development toward a solution, the tragedy of what happened, the needing to be rid.

Ever's internal jousting stopped. He turned into himself. Did she see through him and his gestures of anger? Was he being honest? Could he ever be truly honest? Did he not recognise in himself there were other, or there was one other reason for this execution?

She wheeled herself back towards the bedroom, he asked for something to help him sleep. It seemed with a sadness she gave him a diazepam and a zolpidem.

'My sweet, sweet dreams. It will be all right.'

She at that moment ceased to be just another human for him; he sensed that she was the first person to understand what it was he wanted to do for his father. Not to know the detail but to understand the depth of there being another reason kicking in his being.

The love he never knew if he had lost from his father.

A way to make it all up.

And with that plague in his head.

Wednesday turned into Thursday with the shopping channel and no volume accompanying Ever through his wakeful sleep. Never really sure, as always was the case, whether he was asleep or not.

# *Chapter Twenty-seven*

Thursday was warmer.

The leaves from the pool had been cleared by the weekly spruce-up, and he decided, as Lomita was still in bed, to swim.

In his underpants, he had no swimming costume, that had never been in his plan, to end up in a pool. Unheated. It was March, and the desert night had instilled a chill in the pool: the cold wrapped itself around his brain and hurt a little. A little like a brain-freeze, and then he wished his brain would freeze. Just freeze over and not operate.

He swam under the water, the sounds all around him were silenced and he felt that if he could hold his breath forever – this is where he would like to be. Brain numbed into silence. Surrounded by pale blue tiles, some cracked; he found that a little disconcerting, the colour that is, not the cracking.

Was it possible to think the same thoughts while holding your breath? As his breath was running out underwater his thoughts went to instinct – the instinct to survive. He liked that, only one thought – survival. Yet he was preparing more agony for himself, underwater he stayed, thinking hard about his father who ended his life floating and bloating in water.

The reason he had lost the will to live. Ever still had a will to live, because he wanted to come up for air.

He wondered then which happened first, his father's decision not to fight for survival, or death without thought. The choice taken away. He would never know. He broke the surface, pulled in air; he felt the pool water and his tears combine.

The afternoon brought a request from Lomita, for him to push her round the block in her wheelchair. But Ever, as she was preparing for this event, was gone.

Gone to the house his father had lived in.

Rented low down on Chautauqua Boulevard. He was on his way in a taxi, courtesy of the Beverly Hills Cab Company, and wondered why he had never gone there before; to where he used to stay whenever he visited.

The taxi pulled up three quarters of the way down Chautauqua, on the left towards the ocean. He stood outside looking at the remembered horrible paint colour. A painful yellow: it did cause genuine peeper pain. A colour that didn't offer an acceptable position on the colour spectrum. Then, nearly tripping, he looked down at the curbside; smothered with rubber scuffs from wayward tyres was the number of the house. He had not made the connection, not retained the memory: 2027 Chautauqua Boulevard. 2027. 2-0-2-7.

He sat on the wall. Where the front door had been was now boarded up with nailed pieces of wood in a diagonal cross adding the final statement to its closure. He opened the gate, he was only going to look through the windows. There was no furniture left in the house, as far as he could see. The memories in the spaces of the rooms existed: where he painted; where he slept. The curtains were ripped and faded and non-existent in most places, he could see the water stains two feet from the wooden floor which was now twisted and buckled from the flood.

Was it Ever with his mother that had destroyed his father? Is that what he wanted to kill? The me in him, the him in me.

The me in her.

The umbrella still stood in the garden – down – but not tied tight against the wind, frayed with holes visible where the sun would sheer through at certain periods of the day, spotting the table, shafting the table, with hot burning light that his father in his later years stayed out of, having at one time lived in the sun all day long.

What has happened, Dad? Please can you tell me? Talk to me. What do you want? He thought this was taking place in his own silence, with the noise in his head, then he realised he was talking out loud, in the belief that his father could hear.

Why couldn't he?

He could not turn it off. The same circle of thought. And he repeated the questions again, out loud, in an attempt to get a response.

None came; he felt a disappointment that he had not crossed the spiritual barrier. Incapable of transcending.

He slumped into the belief that Lomita had just given up on the idea of viewing his father's paintings and didn't have it in her heart to tell him. No, she said she would. He wanted his father's work to be a wonder, so he could see that he hadn't been destroyed. Lost his spirit: destroyed by his son. He sat on the stone paving at the back, by the rolled umbrella in a concrete stand. Was he blaming the wrong man?

After a long and numbing sit, he left the house with a vocalised goodbye, sending it to his father; he walked the length of Ocean Avenue, heading for Chez Jay's, the bar where his father spent hour after hour and where Ever felt so grown up whenever he joined him. He thought it was the most beautiful walk.

He remembered that when he first got to the top of the hill and saw the palm trees, tall and tropical growing out of their grass surround, he thought the beach, the sand, was just the other side.

His father took him to the edge and, as Ever repeated the move now, that feeling, of immense disappointment, that there was a long drop down to a busy road, Pacific Coast Highway, then some houses and then the beach, hit him afresh.

At the bar he ordered a beer with a tequila chaser and decided to drink.

Maybe a lucidity would appear through the haze of alcohol. After three more beers and the equal amount of tequila, life had taken a propeller turn, a full turn to the other end of the spectrum.

People were filling up the bar as late afternoon set in.

Ever, now, at 4.15, this minute, hated the world and all that was in it.

The complicated artistry of the outside of the bar was pure 1950s architecture: the horizontal yellow neon Chez, the vertical and larger turquoise neon of Jay, iconic enough to survive when the rest of the old buildings had been razed to the ground and new development had erupted. An anonymous development. The brutality inside of the crude wooden tables was too much of a conflict with the outside and anyway the people were horrible.

What was going on with these people in the bar? Maybe they could solve his problem once and for all.

He looked too long once, once too long, with a longing to look for the solution, and received a straight punch in the face from a thickset trucker he didn't know was a trucker, why would he, he just didn't respond in the correct way he supposed, but he responded in the way he wanted to respond. He was mopping his nose with a piece of old tissue from his pocket that was not enough to cope with the steady flow of the red stuff. It didn't hurt and his reply to the question, 'what do you think you're looking at?' came, without pause, from his mouth.

'Your cunt of a face.'

An understandable reaction: trucker or no trucker. He had no memory of why, but he was lying, with disappointment, on the concrete sidewalk outside, shaking his head to clear the stars, to bring back function, a function to which he had no desire to return.

Is this how he might feel after putting a bullet in the head of the man who stole his father's spirit? Who did steal his father's spirit? Who was it? He shook his head again to clear the thoughts.

Here he could say sorry, sorry cunt face, and move on: but with a gun there was no need for the word. The word 'sorry' would be redundant. It was not changeable, he would have committed an irreversible act.

All acts are irreversible. That's the problem.

Now thrown out and on the ground, he desperately tried to hold onto the thought of what it would be like after the shot.

Would his father feel better?

Would his work be better after the disposal of the man who got it wrong?

Would Ever be better?

Would Ever be forgiven?

By whom and for what?

Everyone would know. Everyone would know. Everyone would know.

He rolled on the pavement, to get more comfortable, and

was happy to stay rolling. There was a man asking him for money, with the flap of a piece of paper.

The check. The twenty-five-dollar check.

'Fuck you.'

A kick.

'Fuck off.'

Another kick.

'Here's forty.'

'Fuck off, jerk.'

The man said taking the dollars.

Ever's dad could never go there again.

It was a shame; he enjoyed having a drink with his dad in Chez Jay's. He started the walk to the pier, the Santa Monica Pier, not just any old pier, virtually opposite. The sun was down and at the end of the pier he looked at the water. The water, the ocean that contained his father's ashes. He threw his bloodied tissue into the sea as a kind of communion with his father: pointless but with the right sentiment. Blood and burnt body mix.

Alive and dead.

Crumbling and crumbled.

He could not let go of the handrail, was touching over and over again the metal rail that ran horizontally one below the other, bottom, second and top, bottom, second, third, top. He was on a roll, just a bad one. He was stuck. Stuck and truly fucked, but determined.

It was his life he wanted over.

His own. Life.

# *Chapter Twenty-eight*

He was about to ask when; when as had happened before between them – she just said.

'Wednesday. I should, or we should, go on Wednesday.'

'Fine. I will let them know.'

There was no mention of his disappearance or the swelling around his right eye or the gash across the top of his nose.

She was out of the picture, Lomita, she wanted no part; she thought he would change; she hadn't realised the possibility of this persistence. Going to see the paintings would sort it out. Would it though, Lomita?

The evening meal was a replica of the previous night.

They were like the military: waiting for a mission to be called. There was an air of suspense; the night's business took the same pattern. Two pills for him and a goodnight with no physical touch from her.

Friday brought a different Lomita.

She woke with a determination. Manita was in preparation mode, he could hear the sound of a hair dryer, clothes were brought out and steamed in the laundry room. Lomita took all afternoon to get ready, metamorphosing at six o'clock.

She looked to Ever the quintessence of perfection, the smell that qualified his appreciation wafted across as he was sitting at the piano, making no attempt at playing, he couldn't – a tune anyway – she bravely walked with her sliver fist-handled cane to the door.

'Bring the Suburban round.'

She ordered, politely. Still having made no reference to his absence and his mess of a face. He had thought that she had given up. His time was up, come in. Time up. Roll back a few weeks. You're on your own.

Tolerance over.

Lomita Nairn arrived at North Crescent Drive with Ever driving the black Suburban.

Ever helped her out of the car to the front door where a member of staff, outfitted in black, was already waiting, having buzzed them in at the gate. The two iron gates had moved with the majesty of a liner across the granite-paved driveway.

Ever wanted so much to be present at the dinner, wanted to hear the conversation, grasp the attitude of this man, to be that fly. But Lomita in her role, playing it to perfection, instructed him, with a please, to stay with the car.

'Do you see, then I won't have to call when I am ready to leave.'

And with the support of her stick taking over from Ever's arm she walked with confidence across the hallway, following another member of staff, into the nothing-less-than-expected grandeur of the living room, where guests were already gathered.

Versailles came to mind, Lomita thought to herself – why would a man who had hired Frank Gehry to build a gallery live in a house that was paying tribute to the past?

It looked like a French chateau, not really a small version: it was an enormous property. Why the hell wouldn't it be?

The walk past the exquisite organisation of plants had been illuminated by soft and invisible light leading to the twenty-foot-high wrought iron and glass double doors.

On entering, the first visual intake was the art. This presented an anomaly, a man known for his comprehensive collection of post-war contemporary art and all the art that she could see on the walls, appeared, as far as she could tell, to be old masters. Well, old anyway, the masters tag just seemed to trip into her thoughts as appropriate in this environment.

Lomita always arrived ten minutes after the stated time on the invitation, she liked an entrance.

She was making one.

She was wearing the kingfisher blue Valentino, in silk, with chiffon sleeves cuffed at the wrist; a large bow was tied in the blue silk at her neck; the skirt was in soft pleats ending at mid-calf; with the bow occupying her neck, she wore a diamond bracelet that sat on top of the cuff and grasped her wrist with a tightness that allowed the minimum of movement, just the softness of an occasional flop, a little rattle and roll. Her soft greying hair was in a french pleat. A pin with a diamond, like a chopstick, was randomly but perfectly placed in her hair. Every inch was refinement and beauty: a beauty that might be fading but still had sufficient dazzle to wash over the guests as the introductions were taking place.

She was nervous, this was not familiar territory for Lomita, not for many years, and she had the desire to pee, to use the bathroom, but thought how odd that would appear on arrival. How old and incontinent. Maybe she just wanted to pee and claim some territory. She was first greeted by Dinah Lorken, who introduced herself, understandably, as Ingmar Lorken's wife; she walked Lomita across the marble floor, at a considerate pace, acknowledging the need for the use of the cane, to be introduced to a Japanese gentleman, elegantly dressed in all black Yohji Yamamoto.

'Madam.'

He bowed as he spoke and stopped his head inches from the back of Lomita's hand, which he had taken in offer of a formal handshake.

'Daizō Mori. I suppose I am acting as a kind of cultural attaché, on behalf of Japan, obviously.'

This was followed by a smile, and in the style of an intimate confession, he leaned closer:

'I think I am here as an extremely inadequate replacement, in the absence of Yusaku Maezawa.'

This time the smile was accompanied by a laugh as he enjoyed his moment of self-deprecation.

His accent was impeccably English. Lomita felt a bond with this fellow outsider.

'I'm sure you'll prove to be far more than adequate.'

She said regaining possession of her hand and smoothing the side of her dress. It was, she sensed, a nervous reaction.

Then there came Arnott and Abby Pascal; he was introduced as the CEO of a hedge fund that specialised in art acquisitions. ArtAQ. She of course, Abby, was introduced as, simply, his wife.

Lomita felt achievement of some sort after these introductions that she wasn't presented as a wife to someone or other. She could see through to the dining room which revealed two sets of candles, three candles in each candelabra, on the table; she realised this would be a Shabbat dinner. Friday.

They were all escorted, without the offer of an arrival drink – the sun was going down – into the dinng room. Against the far wall were pinned two members of staff, not against their will, dressed in black with white linen napkins draped over their right arms; the placements dictated position. Lomita was opposite Daizō Mori, she was sitting on Mr Lorken's right, who was at the head of the table; on her right was Arnott Pascal; Dinah Lorken was sitting at the other head; on her right sat Abby Pascal.

The challah was brought in, the braided bread: Lomita hoped the blessing would be brief, that not too much singing would take place. This was not by any means her first experience of what was usually a joyous occasion, as long as the prayers were kept to a minimum. Mr Lorken was very brief, blessing the bread, made by Dinah herself, Lomita somehow doubted this; the wine was also blessed along with the guests, then the gratitude at the delight of life and the ability that God had given them to enjoy that life. And that was that: clear, concise and most welcome, thought Lomita. The tough bit was having to eat a piece of the bread, she hated bread. There was an olive tapenade, fortunately, with which she could smother the bread.

Ever was outside playing minion.

And thought he should stand by the car and have a cigarette, like the other driver of a Cadillac Escalade, which was all black and cleaner than his teeth.

He so wanted to hear what was being said and paced, imagining. His frustration led him through the endless question of his life, the thing that went around. The stuck record.

Ever took a cigarette from the other driver, who was called Rigo. It turned out Rigo was a lot more than just a driver, he had been a Marine, then had left to go into private security and now worked full time for Arnott Pascal – Ever was guessing on a big wage increase from the military.

Ever felt rather inadequate as stories of fitness and endurance and Rigo's regular training regime were discussed; although enjoying the tobacco even without marijuana, he wanted the time on his own and brought the conversation to a polite conclusion at the first I've-listened-enough-this-is-a-polite-moment-to-leave moment. Which coincided with the finished cigarette going to ground to be crushed underfoot.

Rigo looked at him, hard, he had most certainly broken a rule, and he bent down and picked up the butt just as one of the staff came forward with a dustpan and brush contraption, both with long handles that negated the need for bending; the remaining ash was swept up and the dustpan offered as a receptacle for Ever's crunched cigarette. No class, thought Ever, he had no class. He wandered back to his own shiny black mass and transferred his guilt from father to wife. The tennis game of guilt.

He sat in the car with the door open to receive the night air, he was sure running the engine would also be a rule broken, and plugged his ears to listen to Lana.

If there was a person to go back into one's life with a burden of doubt it was Lana Del Rey.

He had graduated from Sussex University in economics; then did a year at law school in London; and was now working at a hedge fund company at their legal offices which were in Chandos Street, just by the Langham Hotel where he often went in for a cocktail after a day at work. Work that he was finding increasingly unrewarding. He had a good income and after two years had been able to purchase a mews house in Bayswater, London W2.

Although politically opposed, the physical attraction was there and it was not long before items of Clarissa's were spending more time in Ever's mews house than they did in Oxford Gardens, which she was still sharing with Amy.

Along with the chronic sleep disorder diagnosis, she had

started to explore, much to his annoyance, the confusion of his body ownership, mainly because Ever had always put forward the alien theory: that he was an alien. She explored the possibility, he always assumed in a sense of joking, that if an anterior portion of his temporal lobes had been removed as a treatment for his early onset epilepsy, a *petit mal*, that had been associated with developing adolescence, this could then explain his mental state, his alien, outside feeling. His own personal depersonalisation-derealisation syndrome. But he hadn't had the invasive procedure of a temporal lobectomy; at least he didn't think he had; at least he hoped he hadn't; but he supposed if he had then it was possible that the ownership and control of his body was not his own. That would have been a result.

But he had no scar on his head, well, only the one he got playing rugby from a kick in the head that produced a concussion, and he couldn't remember anything for a few days afterwards.

Oh God no, come on. Ridiculous. Agency and ownership.

Ever was not the best to contradict this argument as he never really thought he inhabited his own body and was not in control of it. An excuse, oh Ever, as ever.

Ever had explored this phenomenon with the use of ketamine, for a short time: a drug that really induces the idea of one's limbs not being one's own. But that had never produced a surprise in Ever. He felt completely at home with that feeling, it wasn't alien to him, just normal. Ketamine ultimately altered no state of his: it was a short-lived experiment.

It was a pretty good reason for the mood swings, though, the chronic sleep thing and the question of ownership due to possible interference of the temporal lobes. But it was something he refused to consider; in the daylight hours anyway.

The creeping obsessive compulsive disorder, however, he

kept to himself, the whole time, no one has ever known; therapist; psychiatrist; any of the jumble. No one was any the wiser as to how many times he had to turn lights off or open and close doors or touch things to the count of whatever was comfortable, which would then would allow the release of the touch.

Of course, there was no point, beyond earning money, in his world; maybe he just knew that and it was as simple as that. Maybe he had given up. She tried to educate him in sleep discipline, even sent him for three days to a sleep clinic, but he just kept taking the pills, to force himself through the night to enable getting up early to be at work by 7.30 – when the first deals that he would be overseeing would come through.

Deals from the far east, Tokyo: he would always contact his father at this time, in Los Angeles, and they would chat or email, his father being a night owl, or just a non-sleeper. He always felt the need to communicate with him, every day. The closeness he felt towards his father was unlike anything else he felt, or anything he had felt with anyone else. As the time zone swept west and made the London hours appropriate, he dealt with Russia and Africa. Acquisitions that he had to go through in exhausting detail to make sure no illegalities were taking place. Ruthless business practice did not count as an illegality, and the job wore down even his limited social conscience.

He had his first bout of serious depression and anxiety after they had been together for only six months, Clarissa was able to help him through that. They had been together for twelve months when they went to the registry office, with Amy as the witness, and got married, not bothering to tell his mother – she was living in her own oblivion in Birmingham – but telling his father, who was living in his own private hell in Los Angeles. A hell that at that time Ever was unaware of in its full context, thinking his father was painting and still able to live off the amount, he had understood to be substantial, which had been paid for his catalogue of work by the art collector Ingmar Lorken.

But he had sensed a break in the man: broken by Lorken.

Something that had gone from him; his need to tell Ever the details of his days had gone. The closeness was breaking apart. More crumbling.

Clarissa's parents had come down from Liverpool for the wedding. They were as fun and charming and easy-going as always and they expected nothing from life. Ever was a little jealous of the bond that Clarissa had with her parents; the pride that they showed in her achievements. They seemed to be just happy, as everything that happened they took with gratitude, turned the bad around into good, one way or another.

That was something else Ever envied; he felt a stranger wherever he was: home was a place he had never had the comfort of recognising.

He reflected, looking along the perfect line of cypress trees, that it was because he never told anyone about his actions or his thoughts, mostly because he felt they were his business, but partly because he was genuinely ashamed. He felt that this contributed to the lack, of whatever it was in his relationship, but it was a lack, because he could never truly be known for who he really was. After all, he didn't know who to present as himself.

Who was he?

In a way Clarissa really had married an ethereal alien being.

That made him smile.

He lived a series of secrets.

He even lied to his therapist and found out early on that he could really say anything he wanted; the therapist, when he suggested to her that he could just talk rubbish, said that they were trained to see through that, but he knew she wasn't. He could project a mood or a state that she would entirely believe, not that it was helping him, but he liked the idea of being able to manipulate people who thought they were manipulating him. Cleverer than him: like his wife.

Ever was convinced he would be the one to struggle first in both his job and his marriage; his increasing bouts of depression made both become harder and he developed a disenchantment.

But it was not him: it was Clarissa who became disillusioned. She started an open criticism of the ethics, the morality of his work, the social irresponsibility of it all, and spent time returning to see her parents in Liverpool, eventually leaving her job as an in-house counsellor and working as a freelance to individual private patients. But she found the work demoralising; her patients would fall off the wagon and return to their habit, or transfer to another addiction, sometimes after years of being clean.

Ever was unaware initially that she had made contact with Adam again, the violinist, although she claimed when she went to see him, she was always open about it, that it was merely a friendship; they had history and they enjoyed the discussions of the past and of their failed dreams and ambitions: he felt there was something more. This and his work led to his major collapse – the Big One – when he ended up being institutionalised. By this point his relationship with Clarissa had moments of punishing cruelty. He witnessed in her a temper and an anger that he had never been aware of before.

Passion – yes, and fury – yes: but never at him.

Never truly, horribly because of him, because of situations, yes, but he always felt not as a result of what he had done. He had always been a part of the wholeness of them both; but when he was in the hospital being pumped with medication he felt it probably was the end of his life, his marriage, of everything. He understood it was his mental state that must have caused an enormous disappointment for Clarissa; a tragedy in her mind that she was married to someone, who – she had enough knowledge of the brain to know – would never be the same person again, never be who he was for her when they met: never again. The medication had taken away his desire for her, he supposed she felt unloved – though she wasn't, and unwanted – which she wasn't.

But for a woman, well anyone really, who was losing faith in the world, not to be desired is an event of profound proportion. He somehow did not blame her for what she had done. But he knew that she blamed herself and this is what had caused the breakdown in her ability to behave with any love and compassion; everywhere she turned she was reminded of the betrayal of her life, of her guilt, that had resulted in the creation of another life.

A boy.

Jacob.

And on that Wednesday evening, she could hold that in her system no longer.

Guilt, the two of them destroying their lives through guilt.

Ever stood wishing he had another cigarette.

He counted twenty-seven cypress trees, twenty-seven, Jesus, yes, for sure, immaculately identical in shape and height, lining the driveway. Twenty-seven on each side. Fifty-four in total, adds up to nine, divisible by three. Holy Trinity. This informed his return to the present: everything has a point.

After the blessing the two chandeliers over the dining table dimmed.

To allow the candlelight to gain its authority. Lomita was unsure how to address the company, basically insecure because she didn't know anyone. This was confirmed by Mr Lorken's icebreaker statement.

'Lomita and I have only recently met, at my Basquiat exhibition, whereas I have known Arnott and Abby for a long, long time and Mr Mori not so long.'

There was little ripple of ironic laughter that he was the new boy on the scene; certainly a pause had been left for some response, which Daizō wasted no time in filling.

'Please let's not be so formal…'

Mr Mori wasn't allowed to continue. Mr Lorken interrupted.

'But I am sure Lomita will very soon become a dear friend.'

'And please call me Daizō.'

Daizō Mori was not going to be defeated.

'Of course.'

Acknowledged Mr Lorken, closing the subject, with an extravagant unfolding of his napkin.

There was murmuring from the two wives that was inaudible to Lomita; the table, although only seating six, was capable of at least twelve, and Lomita was sure, judging by the size of the room, that forty could be accommodated without any effort; just a few more black-suited waiters. So conversation had to be directed with the precision of a stage performer.

'Thank you.'

Lomita found herself centre stage, and needed a few lines.

'It's a real pleasure to be here on your Shabbat dinner, I so appreciate being invited to share it with you.'

And then her focus went to the Japanese gentleman, with a stare, mainly because he was straight in front of her, and his smile invited conversation.

'So, I am fascinated as to why Mr Maezawa's Basquiat never made an appearance, Daizō.'

His pause at letting the words reach him across the linen tablecloth was brief. But somehow felt.

'I hope that's not a criticism.'

Lomita now squirmed in her chair; she really wanted to pee, perhaps because her opening had been a little strong, nerves were setting in.

'Not at all. Sorry, I just would have, and I'm sure everyone else would have, just loved to have seen it.'

To excuse her directness, and having a vague recollection about Japan and politeness, she added as a diplomatic calmer,

' Sorry, I hope, I mean, I, in no way, meant to cause offence.'

'And of course, none taken.'

Daizō said and she felt sad that she might have muted his ebullience. Move on. He had an earnest quality, but she found him endearing. But potentially sticky? No, it was her.

'It was, I am afraid, already committed, it had been announced at the museum in Chiba, just outside Tokyo, so the efforts to extricate it from that arrangement were just too complicated. But come to Japan and see it, I would be delighted to escort you. Chiba is where my parents live.'

The possibility of that happening, she wanted to say, would be less likely than – she couldn't think long enough as Dinah, maybe the sensitive one, but probably just the hostess, sensed the delay in reply, and came in with the obvious.

'I so love your dress, may I say the colour matches your eyes. You look gorgeous. Who is it by?'

This was her reply in the Palace of Versailles. It would hold up.

'Valentino. He picked the colour to match my eyes.'

At this point the salmon salad on a bed of lettuce was served by the immaculately-clad and remarkably similar-looking waiters. Lomita thought up until now she was performing satisfactorily. The wine was offered, red or white. A Puligny-Montrachet. Don't pronounce the g in the middle, she wanted to say, too late, and a Château Lynch-Bages, Pauillac region, Grand Cru Classé. No contest, thought Lomita, pour it, but only when I want it poured. Lomita wanted to voice her opinion to the waiter on pouring, but thought it too early to be dictating. Give it time. Everyone chose the red.

Then in came Arnott. Tall and tanned and bald and hunky, the man from Montecito starts talking.

'So, you were at the preview night?'

The only reply that made sense, as it had already been clarified, produced a polite but firm confirmation.

'Yes.'

'So, are you a collector?'

The only reply that made sense was, what has it got to do with you, don't suss me out. Lomita was feeling defensive, a little on trial, but instead, as the polite guest that she was not used to being, not impolite, just not a guest these days, responded with a non-committal shrug. Lomita had a history to protect.

'Well I have one or two pieces. My first husband had a valuable collection.'

She knew he was not going to give up, leave me alone, talk to the other people. Lomita was so used in company, to being evasive. She did not like to be questioned or indeed to question.

'May I ask the content?'

Saved by Abby, this time, female support, that is what she felt she needed in the male zone. She wished she could move seats.

'Oh come on now, not business tonight.'

But Mr Lorken was not to be dictated to in his own house.

'No, let me explain the connections and if you like, the questions. Lomita first expressed an interest in an artist I didn't even know I had.'

Lomita experienced a gripe in her stomach. It was a sadness for Ever.

'Who is that?'

The on-the-button Daizō. But an age moment, she sensed, a senior moment, had hit Mr Lorken.

'My goodness I can't remember his name now.'

No such senility for Lomita.

'John Everett Millen.'

'Millen or Millais?'

Interjected Arnott, rather casually, considering the content of his question.

'God not Millais, wouldn't have forgotten that name. Unfortunately, Millen.'

The first put-down of the night. The lack of respect for Ever's father was going to build, she was sure. She was glad Ever wasn't present. Lomita steeled herself.

'I remember having a portrait of his, about twenty years ago, and wondered what had happened to him, so I employed my dealer, well researcher really, to check around. He traced a collection that Mr Lorken—'

'Please, Ingmar.'

'Of course, Ingmar, had purchased some time ago.'

Never to be told; Mr Lorken had to be in control it seemed; take the higher ground; always accustomed to flying higher in the sky.

'Well not me exactly. That was at a time, before I had built my gallery, to house my collection of established post-fifties art...'

Lomita was amazed he felt the need to explain. A very important man still feeling small, could be the only reason. Is a plateau of content never reached? They have never been humiliated, thought Lomita. These people didn't know that one.

'...that I thought I should be adventurous.'

Mr Lorken continued.

' I bought three small galleries, two in Venice, here, and one in Santa Barbara, on a limited budget of twenty million dollars.'

A pause for that amount to hit the table.

'I employed, along with the gallerists, two dealers to get out there and see if they could come up with any original, outstanding talent.'

'And did they?'

Of course not, Lomita was way ahead here, otherwise what's the point of the story? Speed up Daizō: although he could just have been bored.

'Not one. So, you can understand my interest in Lomita, when she asks to view this man's remaining works. Which, of course, I am happy to facilitate.'

The chicken, cooked in lemon and herbs with onion roasted potatoes and spring beans, was being served. More food filled Lomita with dread; the bread turned out to be just an amusing mouth experience; the first course plates were now being removed by the waiters, she couldn't tell who was who. That's money, she supposed, when you can hire twins.

'I think tastes might be different, I might appreciate some of his work.'

'I doubt that very much.'

I won't have that, Lomita rose, not up, but to the occasion. In silence.

'Well let's see, shall we?'

'It depends whether you want to waste your money on something that will never appreciate, or just buy something, which I have never understood, that you like.'

The last word was extended and dismissed in condemnation. And followed by a loud, short mocking laugh.

Abby and Dinah were talking away together: Lomita wished she wasn't penned in by the men, so she could talk about something maybe a little delicate, abstruse even.

'I have always collected major, already established artists. Koons, de Kooning, Pollock, Clyfford Still, Warhol, never really got Rothko, and I did buy my first Warhol when I was quite young. I went for what I considered to be the easiest market. Ideally the dead white male. Pre-Basquiat, of course.'

A statement of power.

A silence.

'I love Diego Rivera.'

Lomita loved Mexico basically. This remark was ignored by Mr Lorken, now growing, Lomita thought, with self-importance between the mouthfuls of chicken and potatoes. Nevertheless, he continued, food in mouth, with that annoying habit that was supposed to make it acceptable, of covering the mouth with the hand while talking.

'Then in the nineties, I decided to retire from my businesses in manufacturing, and really concentrate on what was essentially my hobby, expanding my collection of established artists.'

A grab for the napkin.

'It was around this time that I made my miscalculation of trying to find the new, bright thing. I mean people have done it, Saatchi, for one, but it is not for me: he's smarter than me anyway.'

A wave of laughter, relief, perhaps, at his first hint of self-deprecation.

'Art is dictated by money not the artist *per se*. I don't buy art to ingratiate myself with the artist, to nurture. Who are the people who are truly important in the art world? The people who establish the price and control the market. Is Schnabel a lesser painter than Basquiat? Probably not, but Yusaku Maezawa put Basquiat on the map, or rather confirmed his place on the map by his money. His money. People who have bought Schnabel don't sell him at auction. They keep him. They like him, so he has barely become a million-dollar artist. You see, going back to the Medicis, the bankers, yes, we need the artist to create the work in the first place, but they are nothing without people like me, us. They come, are born and die and are replaced. Hence History of Art.'

Another snap of laughter.

Ever was outside looking at the stars with his usual observations.

They come, are born and die and are replaced. Universal law.

Lomita was displaced by this, by what she interpreted as blind arrogance.

This discomfiture enabled him to continue speaking, she sensed she was not perhaps alone in her assessment; the arrogance of the money putting itself before the talent; the chef before the product; the baby before the sperm; the chicken before the egg.

She was losing focus: lost in Lynch-Bages.

'But they will always be around, we just have to exploit that talent.'

Lomita had looked around during what was essentially a monologue; the waiters were unusually not pouring at her pace, even they had stopped; she caught a waiter's eye just as she caught the word exploit. And felt comfortable and becalmed enough to repeat.

'Exploit?'

But it was taken as a feed; a support, not the start of criticism.

'Yes, but, of course, I am in it for the beauty and the process of education, educating the world through art. Blah, blah, blah.'

That is an annoying speech-affected habit. That blah, blah, blah thing. Like manual quotation marks. Lomita wanted to put voice to her thoughts but didn't, of course, in deference to her host.

'But mainly for its value.'

His words were not being received in sequential flow now by Lomita, but as intermittent punctuations amidst the general babble.

'Does that mean I am going to bid for a pool of boiling snot?'

Is there such a thing? Lomita hesitated, about to ask, but the acceptance from Abby and Dinah precluded the doubt that there was indeed an artwork that contained boiling snot. She took a mouthful of her onion potato, it was delicious, even though the texture of the onion was questionable in the light of the topic.

'No, let a Saatchi do that. I want the solid bets. I don't want to house a crash, as fashion changes; but there are some artists, I think, who are beyond fashion.'

Maybe they should all lighten up. But no, not the players, pondered a slightly wobbly Lomita.

'Well this is a fine Shabbat dinner: we are, and you can't deny it, Ingmar, we are talking business.'

God bless Dinah. And do it now please, God. Lomita had had enough of the justification of their existence. But don't we all do that? It's just that these people have so much to go on about. She was in conversation with herself, there could be no argument there.

Let's just deal with Millen. But it was carrying on.

'Not business, Dinah-pie, there are no deals, it's the philosophy of business. I really don't care about the artist, in fact if they die, it is often better.'

You are going to have to try harder Dinah. Don't give up. She was so glad Ever was not witness to this: if what she could sense was on its way, he wouldn't be wielding a Glock 17. It would be a Kalashnikov.

'Ingmar, really.'

Come on Lomita. She was bringing herself round. Why am I here?

'May I just go back a little?'

She had succeeded in gaining Mr Lorken's attention.

'What about Millen?'

'I couldn't remember a thing about him. Anyway I asked my marketing director to give me an update which I can give you now, or have it written out for you when you view.'

'Horse's mouth.'

She said. Let's not mess about, she thought.

'Well, he had about thirty pieces and my curators liked his stuff; we offered to buy his whole collection. Now that's a gift for any artist. We gave him sixty per cent, up front, of what they thought he would sell for. That's why they don't work for me any longer.'

A laugh from the court of Mr Lorken. But numbers: she has always thought numbers sounded impressive. She believed a number.

'And what happened? Did you not like them?'

Exactly, my Japanese friend, I am with you. A diplomat.

'I didn't have an opinion, I never even saw them, but he got greedy by all accounts, and said he had more that he could get ready, so they said – fine – and he painted, too many, too quick. They were not good, but we took them anyway, lucky guy, at a cheaper rate, I'm relieved to say. Exhibited him in Venice. Here not Italy. Sold nothing. Bang, it was a case of –

luzzem gone. To the warehouse. I was beginning to feel like a shlemiel in this enterprise. Not just with him, but the whole searching process.'

Lomita was weary, at least weary of the thoughts that surrounded Mr Lorken.

She desperately wanted to pee.

'Well he's dead now, so maybe it's the perfect opportunity for you to re-evaluate.'

Lomita was astounded by the directness he had brought out in her.

'Wait till you see them.'

Another laughter snap.

'Half were sold off to a friend of mine, Mr Chang, who's in the hotel business, for some place in San Diego, apparently.'

Oh God. Lomita's heart sank. To the bottom of the well, drowning.

Mr Lorken continued hammering in the nail.

'You know the sort of art you walk past without noticing in the lobby, but it puts out a pleasant enough colour into the environment. It's wallpaper.'

So that is what happened to the twenty-seven, in that moment Lomita had a profound sympathy for Ever's father. Even though he had been unaware, his assumption had been accurate: his work, his talent had been treated with derision.

'I hate San Diego,'

Abby interrupted.

And now the lightweight repartee. It didn't lighten Lomita.

'Once – you've been.'

Suggested her husband, Arnott. Tentatively.

'Enough.'

'Perfect place for them, by the sounds.'

Tall and tanned interjected again.

Mr Lorken remained unphased.

'I am not being a zhlub, but his value is in the toilet.'

That word got Lomita going.

'May I be directed to the restroom?'

She asked the approaching waiter.

As she was leaving the conversation died down, just from the carrying of voices aspect. She got to the end of the dining room on her stick, no mean feat, this was a large room; she could just about detect a tonal change that suggested a mild scolding of Ingmar that was obviously acceptable among old friends.

The restroom was of course enormous, catering for multiple use, four washbasins and three toilets, nice balance, with dark brown marble, shocked with grey lightning strikes, chandeliers, taps the shape of spouting fish and towels vomiting out of cherubs' mouths. There was, remarkably, an attendant waiting to clear up. A probability that this would only happen three, four times tonight. Did the woman leave when the men went in? Then the second part of the thought led her to the possibility of a separate gentlemen's restroom. Surely not? That was something in a home; but it wasn't really a home: it was an example in physical terms of extreme wealth.

She arrived at the table after the long walk back, enjoyed the courtesy of the pulled-out chair, although she did also appreciate the man from Japan, the diplomatic Daizō, standing up on her return.

Mr Lorken was off again, in more ways than one.

'I don't know why you are bothering. I wouldn't even know what to sell them for. Give them to you probably. Rather than return them all the way to San Bernadino.'

'OK, I'll take them if that's how you feel. Sell them to a hotel in San Diego.'

This time Lomita's thought was voiced, she managed to extract a tense ejection of laughter from the two women.

'Please, this is very unlike you Ingmar, this really is. I told you, come on darling.'

Lomita could guess what he had been told during her bathroom trip—

Shut it.

The softening of Mr Lorken came in the form of a presentation of how to make money. Always a good one, appreciated by all.

'This is the man you should talk to, if you seriously want to invest. Arnott. Give him half a million dollars and he'll put it into an art fund, and you'll get a good return on your money. And now, Dinah, this is business on the Sabbath.'

The Bordeaux had released the beast.

Dinah looked down in exasperation. Her napkin hit the table.

'Come on – talk about how much it cost to build our home, landscape our garden. How many seats you wanted in our screening room. The two kitchens, anything. It takes what we are talking about. I could go on.'

Please don't, thought Lomita. Where did all that come from? Out of the apparent blue in the ceiling fresco. Her look returned to the table. Dinah now raised her head with a fixed glare, that indicated a row later.

'Yes, always a percentage of the money in reserve.'

Tall and tanned was away answering an unasked question.

At least Lomita hadn't heard the question, she was drifting a little, her concentration wavering with tiredness.

'We sell at auction and with the right hype and the wind behind us we make some massive profits.'

'What do you take?'

Lomita asked, back on track.

'From the transaction, you mean?'

'Yes.'

'Twenty per cent.'

Numbers again, she loved them: they were irrefutable.

'I mean really Lomita, I think you are wasting your time.'

Mr Lorken's summation was founded, Lomita wished, out of ignorance, but somehow she doubted that.

You don't know why I am here, I am trying to bring about a series of events that might save your life, save you from being killed by a man who believes you are responsible for all the pain his father lived and died with.

But she could never have said it.

A good killing might be just what you need.

She certainly couldn't have said that.

She idled the wine glass below her chin, suggesting an attention to the liquid while the thoughts unfolded.

'I don't think he painted anything after you bought all his work. I mean we failed to find any more recent works.'

She spoke without lifting her look.

'When did he die?'

'Very recently.'

'And that's my fault, that he painted no more, I mean?'

'I never implied that.'

Defended Lomita.

'Well his work is as dead as he is. Particularly if he's hanging in a hotel.'

That seemed to supply a full stop from Mr Lorken.

But Daizō intervened.

'I have been listening to this, and I would just like to say that I sense a certain unhappiness in the treatment of this artist, but I want to say that Mr Lorken cannot be expected to have responsibility for the welfare of an artist.'

And Lomita thought he was going to be sympathetic.

'Only that, if they are successful, access needs to be maintained to their works. That is, brutal or not, the prime consideration.'

This was Arnott's contribution.

Lomita was alone here.

The women had given up, engrossed in their own conversation. But they were laughing: it was Shabbat after all. So that was something, and the candles were still burning bright.

'Yes, and if one fails or drops in value. Do I care? Do I feel guilty? Do I feel I didn't do enough? No, of course not.'

That didn't need to be said, it was a given, Mr Lorken.

Lomita folding her napkin, secreted her thought inside.

'It was his fault anyway, in this particular case, he couldn't survive through the tough times, he produced shit in an attempt to get more money. To exploit the market, if you like.'

He exploited a market that you have already claimed as your own and declared is totally controlled by you: more of Lomita's thoughts gifted to the napkin.

'You've got to be able to survive. Do you think everyone liked Warhol at the time? Van Gogh? No.'

'We have all had to survive, it's just that a little help is what being human is about.'

Lomita said, discarding the now triangular folded napkin.

'The point is, and I believe you mentioned that this artist, whatever he's called, knocked out some abstract expressionist work. That particular movement peaked in the post-war fifties in New York. You have to be original. That is what we are paying for.'

'Not skill?'

As Lomita spoke, questioning Arnott, she could see her words balloon their irrelevance into the air.

'Skill means shit. Excuse me, but it makes something with skill alone, worth shit. The never-seen-before. Unless you sense a gimmick, and even then, in this reduced-attention-span era, it could pass. Soundbite art.'

Lomita had no reply for Arnott, her attention was wavering, she didn't have the energy to argue.

Mr Lorken took a sip of wine and spoke through the swallow.

'I think the man who paid thirty million dollars for *Apocalypse Now*, you know, by Christopher Wool, must be feeling an idiot. It won't hold.'

'It has held.'

Obviously it was now in Arnott's art fund.

Disagreement at the top level. A fundamental flaw in the argument from two knowledgeable opinions: the experts disagree. How would that develop?

Defused by Abby, bless her, just as Lomita's interest was reviving.

'What about Howard Hodgkin? He was an abstract expressionist and maintained a price.'

Abby bringing in the sentiment of the recently deceased. An appreciated attempt at humanising.

'He was a colourist, and there was no one like him.'

Said Daizō.

'I would never buy him.'

Interjected Mr Lorken.

'Once you've had the energy of Jackson Pollock. Why recreate it? You're forty years too late.'

Said Arnott.

'I'll say it again.'

Please don't, Lomita nearly said.

'I am not in the business of supporting artists; some people are, of nurturing and watching them grow. I thought at one time I was, but I am not. I am in the business of having the most valuable collection of contemporary art in the world. But

I won't stop the nurturers. I will just buy the artists when they are nurtured.'

Lomita suspected that Mr Lorken was stuck on his own train of thought. Maybe a touch intoxicated.

'Come and talk to me, Lomita, about investing.'

Arnott was not giving up.

Lomita would rather bathe in the boiling snot exhibit. She had stopped playing head tennis: the words just dropped into the air, from where she ceased to care.

'Now this is business. You should all be ashamed.'

Finalised Dinah.

'Mediocrity is what you are going to see, Lomita.'

Mr Lorken was back.

'When?'

'Maybe. Wednesday?'

'I won't be there. Only Mondays and Fridays.'

'Well, would you take me to lunch on Friday; I will give you my honest opinion. And we can go from there? I would like you to hear, one on one, what I really think.'

'Love a challenge, Lomita. I will check my diary and be in touch. I will of course move heaven and earth.'

Just the earth, thought Lomita, heaven won't listen.

'It's always the bottom line.'

Where did that come from?

Arnott was speaking.

'The bottom line is that Ingmar and about fifty other people in the world, they are the only ones that can compete in the over-fifty-million market. They are really more important than the artist. I think Ingmar's earlier example of Schnabel and Basquiat shows exactly what I mean.'

The chocolate mousse now just left tracks on the plates. Lomita had declined the desert: she perused the calligraphic menus lying by the placements, elaborately twirled by hand with pen and ink.

Lomita's disengagement, she thought, might bring about that lull that often inspired a change of direction.

'My son now runs my online business.'

A sugar-revived Mr Lorken started up.

'I think art online is for decorators.'

A little contentious from Daizō.

'Yes, it's low price. Cheap end, limited market. But a market. He would have looked, Jonathan, my son, through our warehouse stock, thousands of works, and he didn't even bother to put this man Millen's work online.'

'And what about the demoralisation of the artist?'

'The what? You are asking me what? About the feeling of the artist if his work doesn't sell?'

A stupid question, Lomita realised before the breath had left her mouth.

'I think we've been here.'

More Eastern diplomacy.

'Could I give a damn?'

Less Western diplomacy.

'Excuse me. Ladies, shall we move to the drawing room for coffee and chocolate truffles? Arnott? Daizō?'

'Thank you, Dinah.'

Said a relieved Lomita.

With that there was the Exodus: though not of Biblical proportions.

But with a sense of relief from certain parties. Abby and Dinah linked arms and made an empathetic attempt to rescue Lomita from what they realised to have been a bit of a celebration of power.

Moving from the table gave change in perspective, it made Lomita look at all these privileged people with a familiar feeling. It took her back, to a world of not caring. A time when no one had cared for her. A time when the extreme of not caring had run into abuse.

She sat for the coffee only briefly, she was exhausted.

She asked if she could take her leave: they all stood up and were beyond polite in their partings. Daizō Mori once more bowed. Lomita expressed her genuine gratitude at their hospitality; even if the sentiment of the conversation had been disturbing to say the least. Mr Lorken escorted her to the door.

'I hope for Friday.'

Then as a postscript, thrown in with the faint quality of a pencil inclusion.

'Did you not tell me, at my gallery that you had a Metzinger in your collection?'

'Did I?'

Wondering why she had, if she had.

'Which one?'

'I do not think I am obliged to tell you that, Ingmar.'

There was a pause, where she felt true guilt. An outsider in a world of constant awareness of persecution. A plunderer of Jewish art.

'Are you suggesting I might be in possession of a stolen painting?'

Not sure why she said that, either. Other than she was not a fool.

'Of course not. I admire his work, that's all.'

A pause and a stare; the stare not returned by Lomita.

'I am of course interested in any pieces in a collection – the motive behind the collection.'

She parted with the unbearable taunt.

'My first husband had a Caravaggio.'

And on the slow walk, the tap of her cane punctuated the wind-blown silence as she approached the waiting Ever, what to tell him she knew not. Yes, she smiled in her heart, privately down in there, at the fuck you of her thought: the Caravaggio was stolen: so was the Metzinger: but not by her.

She climbed into the Suburban.

She expressed a tiredness that prevented words and dwelt on having been sussed by Mr Lorken.

'I agree with you, Ever,'

She said.

'I think we have a problem.'

The decision was made that the debrief of the evening would take place at breakfast.

Lomita was truly exhausted and could hardly afford the turn of her head to say goodnight. She almost felt she had stooped to a crawl on her way to bed.

Valentino would have to spend the night on the floor.

Her hair was lowered and her lipstick and eyes were removed; she could not wait for the lying down to begin; the heaviness of body was out of proportion to its size and her head had started its stress pain. She fingertipped the scar on the right side of her head, now long since covered by her lush hair, and she remembered her pain.

The opening of her head to the elements.

## *Chapter Twenty-nine*

Baja California is the twelfth largest state, by area, in Mexico.

It hangs like an undernourished limb on the map; Baja translates as lower, Baja California Sur is the southern portion of this land mass. Its capital, La Paz, lies a thousand miles south of the border town of Tijuana. The southernmost tip rounds into the East Cape, its shore is washed by the Sea of Cortez, the Vermilion Sea, so named as the reflected sunset for brief moments in its daily death paints the resplendent colour across the sea.

This is where Lomita had found a sanctuary, a peace, an avoidance of the questioning of life and the exposure of her history.

In the early eighties she travelled to this part of the world and came upon the town of San José del Cabo, a quiet, locally populated town forty-five minutes' drive to the east of the familiar destination of Cabo San Lucas.

She wanted more isolation than the golden corridor could provide. On arriving at San José she wanted even more isolation.

She drove towards Los Barriles, leaving San José, crossing the large arroyo that housed a temporary bridge. Temporary for the reason that it was washed away every year as the river torrent took its place during hurricane season in September and October.

But this was late November.

She drove, leaving the barely paved roads of the town to travel across the rutted dust tracks that entered the desert landscape. The cacti lined her route, cardon – the giants, mesquite, chirinola, lechuguilla, nopal – a flat paddle-like growth, barrel cactus, chollas, the jumping cactus – it will always manage to spike – a pitaya, the blossoming elephant trees – the torote, the agave plants, the aloe vera with their stem ending in a spear of yellow flower, and the brilliant red flowers of the fishhook cactus, nestled like a fruit. It was a colourful desert.

The rancheros allowed, encouraged even, their donkeys and cattle to roam free across land and track. The track represented no barrier for them: it was all just land to the animals.

The expanse of the mountain range, in the distance, and the desert were endless during her drive towards the coastal track alongside the Sea of Cortez.

The turkey vultures hovered waiting for a kill, the ospreys doing their own work for food.

After a seventeen-mile drive, the sea, straight ahead, appeared to roll onto a shore where the pelicans were the only life. She followed the coastal track to the north at the ocean, for a short distance; one or two settlement areas started to appear on the desert side of the track.

Then the epiphany. She drove down a narrow arroyo, the volume of the ocean increased in this high-sided ravine, she could hear the angels singing. And there it was, relentlessly rolling in front of her, for her alone.

She got out of her truck, walked barefoot along the softness of the sand which stretched as far as her eyes could take her, left and right. Whales were breaching, their water blows sprayed into the blue, blue everywhere. This was pure: this was pure essence.

She wanted to live here. She would spend the winter months in the perfect climate of this deserted, desert Eden.

Live with the turtles and the whales and the birds and the manta ray and the skipjacks and the sierra; with a wind that seemed to blow all that wasn't needed away.

She built her house on the dunes above this stretch of beach which was called Shipwrecks. It was 1985.

Her house she named Casa Lomita.

It was just twenty-four steps down to the beach and the ocean.

It was nearly ten years later that she was driving into the town of San José.

With the sun lying low in the west, burning out her drive in an overexposure of light, the dust billowing around her truck, on a track where rain hadn't fallen for months. She suddenly, but too late, blinded by the dropping sun, her hand across her face behaving like a shield, collided with some cattle that had wandered unconcernedly into the road. It was not a full-on collision but enough for her truck to jackknife and roll to its right, hitting the high wall of compacted sand that stood as a carving by the side of the road. Her head smashed against the pillar on the right side of the windscreen; she fell instantly unconscious.

Rarely did traffic go along this road; the population was sparse, the dusk was descending and most of this area's inhabitants were in bed by eight o' clock.

Known as Baja midnight.

The blood poured out of her head wound. She was crumpled in a protective curl, nearer to the end by the minute as the red continued to leave her. After a time had passed, she was unaware of its passing, or that there was such a thing as time or breath, a man called Jeff Murphy was returning from San José back to his camp which he set up in the winter months; he was an Alaskan snowbird. He lived there between November and April, as everyone seemed to do, he knew the truck and Lomita well.

He carried her from the wreck, feeling life in her, but fearing she wouldn't survive the thirty-minute drive. He lay her across the back seat of his truck, and turned it round to head back into San José and the one hospital.

She was put into intensive care, barely holding on to her life, a blood transfusion was needed if survival was at all a possibility.

Jeff stayed through the night as they transfused someone else's donated blood to revitalise her depleted stock of liquid life.

Manita arrived, the process of communication in the Cape in those days, and even now, is slow. There was no phone service and physical message or radio was the only way.

She held Lomita's hand, spoke to her as if she wasn't in a coma, discussing the day's events, not that there were many, and the weather, not that it ever changed, and what would she like to eat, her diet was consistently the same.

It was just Manita's refusal to believe she would not be around anymore. She couldn't go. And after prayer after prayer she didn't.

*Gracias a Dios.*

After forty-eight hours of blackness – a mind travelling to a place of no memory or light – Lomita opened her eyes.

She remembered nothing of what happened and at first asked if Manita was all right, as if she was the one with the problem. She couldn't move, the stitches and brace that held her head in place, to protect her brain, was to provide a long, slow recovery. She had fractured her skull, allowed light into a place that was always in the dark. She wondered, through that crack where the light shone in, whether it had changed her perception of life and her feeling towards the things that had happened in her life. It made her give a thank you every day; she had never felt the need before, in a way it made her brighter, that light. It brightened up her life.

Lomita had survived, but the blood transfusion was to carry another story.

*Nativity with St Francis and St Lawrence* by Caravaggio was painted in 1609.

It was stolen from the Oratorio di San Lorenzo in Palermo, Sicily on 18 October 1969. So there you have it. By the Mafia. Roberto dePirizone was owed a massive payment for work executed in Los Angeles and there was no way of paying him. This was used as collateral; pledged as security for the payment that would eventually come. On the black market the painting would fetch only a tenth of its market value, which was estimated at $25 million. But if all else failed this was a good fallback. So, for a time Roberto and Lomita, though in intense privacy, and not benefitting from it on their wall, were the proud owners of a Caravaggio.

Jean Metzinger painted *En Canot* in 1914.

It had been missing since 1938.

After the Degenerate Art Exhibition, it had been supposedly pillaged by the Nazi regime. Which indeed it was, but was traded in a transaction in the 1950s from an about-to-be-publicly-embarrassed German family to the Mafia in Naples. It then, through an amicable interfamilial negotiation, found its way to Roberto, again as payment for work achieved and underpaid: he had no particular affection for cubism, just liked the idea that it was valuable and celebrated.

This time it did get across to Los Angeles and it did hang on his wall. His security only allowed selected visitors and, in their world, there was an understanding that you did not ask questions. It lived happily with them both, Lomita being oblivious to its dubious history until the unravelling of her dead husband's estate revealed its provenance.

She immediately asked her second husband to dispose of it. To where she never asked, nor expressed concern.

She just wanted no part of the involvement in that kind of world. That world died, and with great relief, with Roberto dePirizone.

Did Ingmar Lorken know about all that?

Her history would be accessible to anyone who put in the effort to unravel it: as far as the law was concerned, she had paid her penance and was in the clear. Well almost. But for the art world that would be a new revelation, perhaps. She still thought it would be impossible to trace. And even if the trace was achieved, she had no responsibility for either acquisition.

Did she?

The light comes in, and it brings a joy to help others.

That is what she wanted to do with Ever; it made her feel good to be able to do that. Enlightened, you could say.

But in doing so, it had, in this case, thrown the light onto herself.

She had craved anonymity and had succeeded in hiding her past for nearly forty years, but had now exposed herself to a person who was interested in re-evaluating her position in the world.

She woke feeling as though the restorative process of sleep had not taken place.

She also realised she had failed to take her medication the night before.

If you miss a dose do not double up: imprinted on her memory for years. But the evening had drained her, she felt unable to move and was equally unenthusiastic about discussing the previous night with Ever. How could she possibly begin? With a lie, of course.

She called through to Manita and asked for her coffee. A large espresso to start her up. For years she had ground her own beans, made the coffee as a ritual, now it took twenty-four seconds with a Nespresso machine; Arpeggio, in purple, was her favourite flavour. She felt embarrassed to be such a coffee purist traitor. But it did the trick. One minute later, allowing for the walk across the big brown room, Manita presented her with her coffee and plumped up her pillows, understanding these days of exhaustion that periodically arrived.

No breakfast was required; Lomita asked if Ever had made an appearance. She hadn't seen him and was now wondering what to suggest.

The blinds were drawn back, the Los Angeles desert morning started its gradual simmer to full spring temperature. Manita returned from the medicine cabinet with the pharmaceutical cocktail, and a lavender bed jacket, in colour not scent; the smell of lavender reminded Lomita of old ladies. She hated it. She would just have to hope she stayed strong; that her immune system would hold up. When she first started on these drugs the side effects caused intense nausea that was as incapacitating as the illness. But her body adjusted during the time it took to interpret the pharmaceutical invasion; those effects faded.

Maybe Ever could join her for coffee, she thought, and he could be relieved of the suspense of finding out what happened. Not that he would be finding out the truth: just get it over with.

Was she transferring her tension to Ever?

He might be fine.

That was answered in a second: Ever was knocking on her door.

From outside he started and never entered the room, or even cracked the door.

Even a little bit. He spoke to the closed door.

'I am not coming in. I know it all went like shit, because if it didn't you would have told me it all went well, last night. I know, so you don't have to protect me. Did they really not like his work? I don't want to know, we're still seeing it right, on Wednesday, I mean, who cares what they think? What did they think? Don't tell me if it's bad. I don't want to know. How did you bring it up? Or did they? I mean who spoke first? You don't have to tell me, if you don't want to. I know they hated it right. I'm going out anyway. I don't want to know. You'd have told me last night, not let me spend a night awake. I'm sorry, are you feeling OK? Did you sleep all right? Do you feel better? I don't want to know about my Dad, just you, OK? How are you?'

Better than you by the sounds of things, thought Lomita, and then summoning her inner calm, she managed.

'Come in.'

The door opened.

'Would you like some coffee?'

He walked into the room, Lomita and Manita stared with apprehension, a little bit of tension, even.

'Yes, I would love some coffee.'

'Sit down.'

She said pointing to the chair by the window. Manita left to make some coffee, knowing how he liked it, same as Lomita, but longer. The thirty-two-second version.

'It was fine, the subject didn't really come up until the end, and that was more of a confirmation of the viewing. It was a Shabbat dinner, so business was avoided, it was delicious food and joyous conversation about houses and decorating and favourite places to eat, and where to go on vacation. You know rich stuff. Spoilt behaviour stuff. Sort of very splendid. And terribly grand, unbelievably so.'

Ever didn't know what to think.

To be a believer or not. To trust in God or be an atheist or an agnostic. He hadn't slept, and was most likely not looking at his best. Unbrushed in the hair area, unshaved in the face area and he stank in the underarm area.

In his underpants and a T-shirt, he felt disrespectful, Manita brought in his coffee that was probably cold, his was the longer version, but even allowing for the walk across the room, unless the delay happened at the beginning, this coffee was not going to be piping hot. It wasn't and Ever knew what Manita thought of him today. It happened, some good days and some not so good.

'Thank you Manita.'

Cup to lip revealed the tepidity. No need for a cooling blow.

'How do I know if you are telling me the truth?'

'You don't. What would you like to hear? That they thought his paintings were wonderful. Then why were they in a warehouse?'

She felt severe, but he couldn't be expecting the genius revelation.

'I suppose I hoped they might have acknowledged making a mistake.'

'They don't make mistakes. If they do, they don't recognise them.'

'OK. Thank you for going. I appreciate it enormously and I'm glad you had a good time and I'm sorry it has knackered you.'

'Done what to me?'

'You know, I mean, tired you out.'

A censorious pause.

'I am doing this for you, you know, Ever.'

'Then why did you say we had a problem?'

'Did I?'

'You did, you know you did. Last night, first thing you said, why do you think I didn't sleep?'

'I think in a strange way Ever, I am joining you on your journey. It seems to be determining its own destination.'

'I need a shower.'

It seemed too much for Ever to handle. Too hot. Too fucking obtuse. Too much for Ever.

Myalgic encephalomyelitis, ME, chronic fatigue syndrome, CFS, or Epstein–Barr.

All provide symptoms of intense and chronic fatigue; she had days when her physical condition could have indeed indicated all of these as possible diagnoses. Initially her exhaustion was put down to the contraction of Epstein–Barr, human herpesvirus 4.

It took two years for her blood to reveal the presence of the Human Immunodeficiency Virus. HIV.

This could only be traced back to the blood transfusion and the use of unscreened blood. She was taking antiretrovirals to boost her immune system and keep her CD4 T blood count at acceptable levels to avoid the collapse of her system into Acquired Immune Deficiency Syndrome. AIDS. But stress and exhaustion put her immune system under pressure; the concern was for her not to contract tuberculosis or develop lymphoma or any of the other essentially fatal conditions associated with the syndrome.

Ever appeared washed: to have brushed up well; the face damage looked less dramatic and he was dressed in non-smelling clothes.

Black T-shirt and a pair of blue jeans and sneakers. He was not as sartorially exciting as Lomita. But he had the devastating effect of youth on his side.

'Would you like me to wheel you round the block?'

He said from outside the door.

Not one of the most exciting offers she'd ever had, but it was from Ever and that made it one of the most special.

'That would be lovely, my sweet. Give me thirty minutes.'

He could have joined in as a chorus from the 'give me' stage. Always waiting for Lomita.

# *Chapter Thirty*

He didn't exactly know if he was trying to kill his mother.

There was a garage, an air raid shelter and a coal hole. The first two had a relevance, the coal hole didn't. The air raid shelter was too scary to go down into and always struck Ever as an extraordinary thing to have in a suburban garden.

No one moved the leaves that were waist high; a mixture of rotted and fresh that collected at the door at the bottom of the steps. On his only trip down there, which he was forced to make or have his pants taken down by the girls next door, a concrete bunker room was revealed.

That was it.

That was it, against a bomb.

Maybe it was having this continual presence of something that protected you from bombs that gave Ever the idea to make one.

The coal hole, well, that kept coal, not used anymore and, every New Year's Eve, Ever would have coal dust smeared on his face, then have to knock on the front door to be let in as a good luck charm. To bring good fortune to the coming year. This superstition was to do with his Welsh mother being the daughter of a coal miner. Although the need to have an abundance of coal in the mines the following year was lost on Ever, even as a child,

Then there was the garage where he found some old fireworks, bangers, whose sole purpose was to make a bang, probably too damp on bonfire night but now, months later, dried out. The fourth prompter into action was as non-sequential as the other three. There was a soda syphon, red, with the press down arm, and the place where the sparklet of gas was inserted was in chrome. Plastic chrome. When the gas had gone into the water and had been shaken for ten minutes or so, you got the miracle of soda. Leaving an empty mini torpedo of metal with a pierced hole at the top. It was an ancient contraption. It was obvious really: fill an empty sparklet with the gunpowder from the fireworks. Compress it in tight, pack it. Create a pressure. There was a bomb, that would explode and send the metal, shrapnel-like, everywhere.

After this preparation he took the bomb into the garden, laid a long trail of gunpowder that he could light and that would travel up to the bomb.

And.

He laid it on the bit of terrace that dropped down two steps by the fence and the posts that held the washing line. He spread the trail of gunpowder, the fuse, up the path away from the washing line until the gunpowder ran out. Quite a way up the path. He wanted to be safe. He lit it.

Then his mother came out with a pile of washing in a pale blue plastic version of a latticed basket, with a cigarette in her mouth. And he shouted.

'Hang on Mum.'

And repeated the shout.

Did he shout loud enough?

She ignored him as was her way, or didn't hear him, and

the crackling trail of flame was heading towards the loaded sparklet.

His mother put the basket down; she had pulled the first sheet out of it to hang on the line when the explosion happened.

Explosion was the word.

The noise was deafening, the metal did indeed shatter and fly everywhere, most of it towards the sheet, but some buried into his mother's leg. Neither of them could hear anything as the noise had left them in a ringing mime show. Completely deafened ears. His mother, he could tell was screaming, by the shape of her mouth and body; he was in shock. About, he thought, to cry but was not sure what the appropriate emotion or action was when you have nearly blown up your mother.

The first thing was to see the extent of the damage to her leg. She was hopping on the other leg. As far as he could see, there were several pieces of sparklet embedded in her flesh, and blood; there was bleeding; he hoped, in a moment of startling banality, that tweezers could purpose the extraction.

At least that was his thinking.

The silence was still deafening, the ears continued to scream with a sound generated only by them: but his mother was calmer, assessing the extent of her damage, still not knowing what had caused it. He was fourteen; the divorce was in process; his father had already moved permanently to Los Angeles.

That night between him and his mother had taken place over a year previously.

He sat with ringing ears and wondered if he had really tried to kill his mother.

No of course not, she wasn't there when he lit the fuse.

But had he not waited until he saw her carrying the washing in the basket from the house and then put the match to the gunpowder?

No, he had not done that.

No, for sure, in the name of Our Lord Jesus Christ he was not crazy. Where did that religious fervour come from?

He was beaten by his mother with a wooden spoon.

Three dining chairs were piled onto him as he sat in the green and brown striped Parker Knoll chair; then these were tied down with string. He had no desire to move even if he could because he would be beaten again.

Ever was still smallish and was yet to experience the viral pneumonia that would nearly kill him and keep him bedridden for months. It was during this illness, an illness that hit him when he was fifteen, that he grew.

Not in proportion, as his body grew but his legs stayed short. He emerged months later from his bed six inches taller; six inches taller in his body. His legs later caught up by a couple of inches but he looked a weird one for a while.

A scrawny, out-of-proportion weird one.

His mother was still alive, though.

Next time.

Eh?

He was telling this story to Lomita.

He was pushing her around the indefectibly groomed sidewalks of Beverly Hills, where the grass seemed to know that it is not allowed to grow over onto the sidewalk and where women, mostly women, walked with sun-visors at a quick pace wearing trainers and tracksuits. This was the activity of the streets, the prolonging of life through the speed walk. He wanted so much to unload the burden of his Oedipal experience on Lomita but felt that it threw an obvious question mark over their relationship.

Although he didn't think in any way he was looking for a relationship with a mother figure. Lomita was more intent on discussing how they, or how Ever, was going to deal with the showing of his father's paintings on Wednesday. How would he deal with whatever they revealed themselves to be?

The Good the Bad or the Ugly.

Even the Mediocre. Which would it be?

Lomita was thinking this through; she couldn't believe that she was being pushed through these empty streets by a man who was contemplating murder. On every other level he was a sensitive, caring human being but this madness had blocked his life and she was surmising, being pushed, that this wasn't the whole story: the whole reason for seeking this retribution for his father.

And now there was the complication of revelation in her life.

Did she also have the desire before, before Ever, to know the truth about herself, to analyse what she had lived through?

Is this what these two people recognised in each other: the desire to unload the truth?

To find it. To be honest, to unburden; did it not make the world they lived in start on an unfair level every day? Did the accumulation of these events in their lives cause a twist and a discomfiture in the brain that built up and made it an impossible place to inhabit?

Is this what bonded them without them knowing?

She could see the help that she could give to ease the accumulation of pain that builds through wrongdoing. The difference between them was that he had the misconception that by the destruction of a life and the destruction of his own, he could right whatever he felt was wrong. And she had holed up, and was now extending a hand, as a lifeline to care for someone, after a life of hiding her own pain and lying to all around, including herself, that everything was all right.

Would it help if she showed him what she had been through?

Lomita had interpreted the attempt at matricide without any judgement; the random behaviour of a bored, early-teenaged boy.

Ever had not included the bits about when he had actually lit the fuse.

And did he shout?

# *Chapter Thirty-one*

The day came.

The Wednesday. The nervous pair were driven to the gallery by Manita in the black Suburban. All felt dark, as if an enormous gulf had opened up between them in the aftermath of a row, a serious disagreement, but there had been no such thing.

Silence accompanied them on the drive.

The drive downtown: the journey to the viewing of John Everett Millen's work. They were deposited by the car at the entrance with no need to valet as Manita was in charge of the black mass. They got out, the wheelchair was pulled from the back, Ever took her arm and walked her to the ease of her chair. They then adopted the familiar position of pushed and pusher and entered the gallery.

They walked to the section with the hermetically sealed glass doors, which opened without any effort from either of them, and towards the desk, millennia of metamorphic rock beneath their feet, to the waiting Miss Money-Root.

'Good morning. Are we ready?'

'Yes.'

Was all Ever could produce, he thought that charm and the attempt at conversation were over as she was needed no more.

They were escorted to a small gallery at the back of the building with a stone column carved with Private No Entry, vertically. It stood by the twenty-foot-high door, which Miss Money-Root opened with the minimum of effort despite its size. What was it with these doors? Ever brought his head back to an upright position, having read the sign.

'I will leave you to it.'

Was her exit line.

Ever was in one of his sweats. And a panic, of course, and the shakes. He was about to see the reality of what he had kept inside him, of his father as a painter with a stymied talent, a genius cut off in his prime.

Lomita wheeled herself to the centre of the gallery, which was comparatively small by the standards of the rest of the building. She sat without a word.

There were twenty paintings: ten each on opposite walls and none on the other two. That was the first thing that struck Ever about the curating: why hadn't they spread them evenly around the room?

The canvases were a blur, his nerves were making his eyes lose focus, this gave him time to make a prayer for them to be everything he wanted them to be. He prayed till the focus returned, for the lens, like a camera to pull to the point of precision.

And then.

Some of the paintings he recognised; his head swept across them all, fast, wanting to take them all in at once. He had seen some of them before, had spoken to his father about them.

There was the giant abstract of *The Wave* and *The People on a Bright Day*, contorted figures blasted by a yellow smear across their faces. A series of paintings of a woman walking away in a swirl of colour around her, as she, painting by painting, disappeared further into the distance. A series of five. There were explosions of colour thrown onto the canvas in enthusiasm, anger, or despair; some return to figurative pieces, the face of an old hobo, his face engraved with deep grooves, grotesque, like fissures in stone, starting to ooze the first signs of blood, such was their depth.

But there was one he had never seen before.

It stopped all awareness of nerves and shaking and rendered him in a suspended state of a past and drowning life: it framed itself in front of his eyes in a jumping, inconstant rhythm that through four words made him believe and disbelieve all in one moment; he would have been granted a blessing if he was removed from the world in this second of seeing.

It was a graphic piece, in that it was on a background of white: large black lettering spilling over at the sides spelling out.

WELL, DID YOU EVER?

After the initial time-freeze, the song from *High Society* played as a pacifier in his mind – he remembered listening to it on the radio on his drive back from Palm Springs. But that thought could only provide a millisecond of avoidance.

He knew that spelling to be WELL, DID YOU EVAH? It was A-H, A-H for God's sake.

What next offered itself as a diversion, was to scrutinise. He was walking towards it, staring at the brush strokes that made up the lettering, looking for the emotion in the stroke, the shake, the bend, the curve, the deviation from an exact calligraphic replication of the letters. Looking for a deviation from precision. It was done by hand as opposed to print or stencil. But it was calm, it had been pondered on till the emotion in the execution was gone. The emotion, all connection with the words had passed. It was unavoidable.

He sat in front of this piece on one of the benches covered in black studded leather that were centred in the room.

Ever wondered, no he just feared, with no more distracting thoughts, that the agony was – is – that he will never know. For as long as he was, in that moment, unfortunate to live.

'What do you think?'

Said Lomita.

'What do *you* think?'

Was sent straight back after two more prompts of the question.

'I feel that he ran out of himself, he had nothing left and these were… I don't know if they were the last things he ever did.'

'Amongst them.'

Replied Ever.

'But they don't seem to have any passionate content. Or seem to have taken a lot of time.'

'Is that a criterion – the time?'

'I don't know, I mean commitment.'

'What the fuck do you mean?'

Came from the contortion that had shaped Ever's mouth; he was still seated and still staring. He was not with Lomita's attempts at encouraging an analytical discussion.

Lomita's head turned in a questioning movement, at both his tone and choice of word.

'I mean. There is nothing that hasn't been said before and probably by him. If every spark has a life and every star burns out, it looks like he was on the way to burning.'

Lomita knew she was on dangerous ground, but she had to express what she felt to be her honest opinion. This man had harboured the belief his father was wronged and maybe he wasn't.

'I love them.'

Said Ever, unconvincingly, still staring at the lettering.

There was nothing left for Ever at that moment. No life. No future. Nothing. He felt as if all had left him, that he was responsible: had broken the spirit of his father and mother. That he was all that was wrong. He just wanted to sit. He could do nothing. He never wanted to leave this room because if he did he would have to face it all.

Didn't anybody understand this?

'Don't you understand this?'

He said as if he had been having the conversation with Lomita.

'Yes.'

She replied, because he had.

'Do you like any of them?'

Ever said, after a while.

'Do you mean enough to buy? To live with?'

'I don't know, let's just start with like. At all. Shall we?'

'I like *The Wave*. I like the first image of the disappearing woman. I don't understand writing paintings. Never have.'

'I do.'

Offered Ever.

'I think.'

More time passed in a silence; then Ever said,

'Do you want to go?'

'If you like?'

Ever was tempted to photograph the exhibition on his phone, but that would encapsulate, what? A memory of sadness, regret – negativity.

Will I never see them again? Are they gone now? Is that it? Back to a warehouse.

Tears were pouring down his face but there was no noise coming from the face. Did no one understand what it was like to be trapped in perpetual doubt and sadness and regret? For even breathing.

Lomita sat and watched and knew.

She knew.

This was the moment.

Did those paintings deserve to have never seen the light of day after one exhibition?

This was the question Lomita felt propelled to answer and would it make any difference whatever she said: where did she begin? She could most definitely see talent, she could see why the artist had attracted attention in the first place. But did he meet the wrong people when he came into town? Did he not meet his Tarantino? Was he like her? He didn't make the right person sit in wonder and awe. Is that because he never met them, or because his work was not good enough to demand that response? Would anyone ever know the answer to the question of luck, good fortune and synchronicity. Being in the right place, to meet the right people, at the right time?

Was it just that?

Lomita wheeled herself towards the door.

'Please stay. Tell me all that you were just thinking.'

'I think he was alone.'

Lomita delicately suggested.

'And if you don't have a spiritual guide, you need a human one, I don't think he had that. He was good Ever, he was.'

'But not brilliant, genius?'

'You know the answer to that. How many are in a century? Or not necessarily even every century. But it doesn't change anything. What we make, do, create, are.'

'Of course it does. It defines us.'

'Then no, he wasn't a genius. Is that what you want to hear? Does it make it better if I say he was?'

'Why do we make such a lot of fuss about being on this

planet, why do we put ourselves through such pain? Is it to be immortal? Why are we so driven to be successful?'

'Not everyone is.'

'He wanted to be. He thought he deserved to be.'

'How do you calculate that?'

'What?'

Said Ever.

'Deserving? Through the agony you put yourself or others through? That doesn't make you better.'

Ever opened the door, with no effort; they passed Miss Money-Root at her marble slice of a desk.

'Would you ask Mr Lorken if indeed he is free for lunch on Friday, as it was suggested he might be?'

'Of course, Miss Nairn. His only two days at the gallery here are Monday and Friday, so he does get extremely busy, but if he suggested Friday then I am sure it is in his diary. I will email Mr Jacob to confirm.'

'Would you please bring the car round.'

Ever was told directly, and oddly, as he wasn't driving, but correctly sensing the suggestion of dismissal, he obeyed and went to inform Manita. Lomita stayed with Miss Money-Root with the intention of purpose; and Miss Money-Root, in anticipation of purpose, paid attention.

Lomita followed in due course, wheeling with an energy, but making a slow and proud exit. Ever stood waiting with the door open to the car, on the street outside the gallery.

John Everett Millen had got his showing in the Gehry building after all.

A posthumous exhibition.

Aren't they meant to be the best?

Carry the most romantic concept of a lost talent, bringing more value and appreciation to the remaining works?

Ever received an email alert.

This interrupted his reflection on Monday and Friday being Mr Lorken's only days at the gallery. That information had been imparted with ease, accessed without effort.

The email was from Dr Aran, telling him the initial blood tests were clear of any viral infection. But he would need another after a six-week period from the date of intercourse.

Thanks: his flippancy towards the information reflected the fact that he couldn't have cared less, either way.

He couldn't speak in the car, he was drained: an empty sink but full of residue.

It was as if he had just witnessed the death of his father all over again.

He was bleeding for his father; for what this son had done to him. When emotion turned in on itself: it was directed at the easiest target, after all, and it was always a bullseye.

## *Chapter Thirty-two*

They arrived back at Oakhurst Drive.

In what had seemed a much quicker time than their trip had taken to the gallery. The usual procedure took place and Lomita even asked, in an almost exact replica of his very first time there, if they could please have some tea. Ever took her arm and Manita took the car.

Lomita could only think of showing him something that was as shocking to her as she felt the truth of his father's work or the burial of his father's work was to him. When they got inside she asked Ever to follow her to the screening room.

She laced up the projector, pulled the blinds down and waited for the tea to arrive. This would not shock or upset Lomita anymore, but she was interested in what it would do to Ever.

The tea arrived in silence and the exquisite movement followed, with her pouring. After they had had a couple of sips she quite calmly asked,

'Are you ready now, my sweet?'

For what, he had no idea.

'Yes.'

He stuttered anyway.

The lights were dimmed and the whirr of the projector began to throw its flicker on the screen. The one thing Lomita could not bear was the sound, so that was down. The images started to appear on the screen and the discomfort was instant; not from the content initially, but from the bad quality of the acting. The preambling set-up. The 8 mm celluloid spooling its way through the light of the projector added a vulgarity of colour to the image. It gave it an instant feeling of authenticity, of stark reality, of it happening now, the handheld inexactitude giving it the sense of capturing a real event. Unrehearsed and captured as a once-only. A do or die: now or never.

The first physical onslaught of this beautiful girl took place and then the unquestionable reality hit. Hard and relentless. Ever could instantly recognise it to be Lomita, she was so innocently breathtaking in her beauty. The events that followed he could barely watch, he kept looking at Lomita in an unspoken demand for it to stop. She returned, by gesture, his eyes to the screen.

It was sick-making.

Truly sick-making and Ever wanted to complete the physical act of vomiting. He was prone to a chunder. He kept his face turned to the screen, but Lomita was unable to see his eyes close at the parts that were unbearable to watch. Eventually the rape came to an end and Lomita stood, to put the lights on, and turn off the projector.

'That was my film debut.'

She said.

And realised that she had never watched the film with anyone before and now it had reached her; because she had viewed it through the eyes of someone else, she had experienced someone else's shock; she started to cry and all the pain that had never come out seemed to come in one torrent of tears. In the presence of Ever: the only person who had sat and watched the film with her.

Even though she was unaware that he had at moments been forced to close his eyes, unprepared to be an audience to the degradation. He didn't want to carry those images in his head forever. Not in his head.

Afterwards he did not know what to do but sit and be a witness to this pain, this realised pain. She spoke through her sobs.

'Do you think I was good? Should I have gone on to great things?'

Ever was white, at least he felt white, pallid, the blood had gone from him.

He got up to leave.

'Please don't go, my sweet.'

'I'll get you some tissues.'

He returned with a box from his bedroom, giving himself at least some oxygen to breathe, out of the airless confine of the screening room.

And to receive some different images on his retinas.

They sat and he wanted to hold her but felt that a physical action, even one of tenderness, would have no place, having seen what he had just seen.

He would have killed for her. He would have done that. He could understand what had been done. It made sense to him, but then that was the concern: his understanding.

She went through the process of a gentle blowing of the nose and a careful mopping of the eyes. He thought of the waterproof mascara on the shopping channel and wondered if that was what she was wearing.

There was no run.

After a time, she composed herself: they left to go and sit in the garden, catching something positive and natural from the sun.

The sun was a good idea, her idea, it has life and brilliance and health and warmth. All the things missing in those fifteen minutes.

Ever was still fixed on the resulting aftermath.

That revenge was taken. That murder happened after that. And maiming.

It worried him that he condoned that aftermath.

'Why show me that?'

'I don't know. No one has ever watched it with me.'

She was scraping, with her thumbnail, some candle wax off the white marble table. Removing the red dried spill, cleaning and cleansing.

Ever thought the wax shape resembled India or Africa. They always to him looked like they had run out of energy as they thinned towards their southern tail, run out of spill.

'Just bad things happen, things that shouldn't.'

Said Lomita.

'Did you feel better when what happened to them happened? To those people?'

'Yes, I did. But eventually it was worse, because I had joined them. And then you are finished. Polluted.'

'Would you mind if I had a drink?'

Said Ever.

'I will join you. Martinis?'

'In or out?'

'Out, I think, don't you?'

Said Lomita.

Ever knew what was coming next.

'I'll give you fifteen minutes.'

The length of the 8 mm agony. He was shaking as he waited; he wanted to ask for a diazepam to calm down.

It had been a day.

My God, if you are listening, what a day.

WELL, DID YOU EVER?

That was never going to leave him. He had never seen that one before. Did it mean what he thought it meant, were those his final words to his son? The fifteen minutes he was glad of, but he didn't need to change, he was already at his sartorial peak.

Armani outlet and a shirt. It gets no better than that for Ever. The truth, here, was a one-sided affair. Lomita had revealed her truth but Ever was incapable of revealing his truth. The imbalance provided yet another area for guilt to build, to persecute and prosecute his mind.

## *Chapter Thirty-three*

Ever was swimming in the ocean alone.

He swam alone, there was no one else to swim with, he floated in the water watching the whales with their leap of child-joy out of the water. The triggerfish and the skipjacks swimming around him, right by his feet, happy at his being there, and as happy as he could be, being there.

He kept his eyes open while swimming, knowing the redness would stay with him but he needed an awareness of jellyfish which sometimes bred in the Sea of Cortez, and this was the time for the Portuguese man-of-war, from whose sting it would be a relief to be released into death. He watched for the purple strands that drift in the water without any apparent purpose other than to cause intense pain. He heeded Pedro's advice to the letter. The pelicans in their radar-like flight, feet off the ocean surface; the ospreys with their talons ready to scoop the catch. The falcons and hawks circling for movement on the ground, ready for their dive.

The beach was always deserted and the blue took over his world, the blue and the sand. The pink and grey of the shells interrupted his walk across every step of the spread of beige, the only time the colour has a true majesty.

Beige – on a beach.

He walked tentatively around the old rusted shipwreck, half buried in the sand, fearing the snag of metal on his feet, and climbed the twenty-four steps to return him to the house.

An art deco house, that from the beach belied its depth and size. The curved terrace with seven circular columns supporting the roof overhang, protecting the glass of the doors, that opened into the house, from the sun. The floor inside was of marble and the curved multi-layered ceiling rose to a central dome that outside continued its journey skywards in the shape of a lighthouse, atop of which was perched an osprey; Ever's constant companion with its high-pitched whistle that would greet him on his return. Inside the house dropped a large art-deco chandelier-type light from the interior of the fifteen feet of rising column.

He never liked to wash the salt off his body after he'd been bathed by the ocean and put on his recently acquired grey T-shirt and navy shorts and his flip-flops, ready for his journey into town. He left his bedroom and stared, as he had grown accustomed to doing in the last few days, at the paintings that surrounded him. Some were in his bedroom and some in the guest house and the screening room.

Pedro, the caretaker, had spent the last days putting the paintings in position. A position decided by the curator of his father's final exhibition. Ever. *The Wave* graced the wall opposite the ocean-facing glass and WELL, DID YOU EVER? asked its perpetual question, hanging by the counter that curved as a separation between the living area and the kitchen. From the four expanses of glass, all the beauty of the ocean was revealed, as if on a series of cinema screens; two of the glass expanses could be slid back to introduce the breeze into the house and carry the ozone and soft smell of the sea.

He walked to the car, closing behind him the front doors,

cast in concrete, with the indentation of the handles providing a smile and the two glass portholes – the eyes – completing the image of a smiling face. He walked through the first courtyard which housed the outdoor kitchen and fireplace and agave and cactus and aloe vera and the elephant tree with its dying-looking bark, all its health lying like a lie beneath the surface. A duplicitous tree.

All were shielded from the wind by the circular walls that encased the house, allowing the bougainvillea the protection to bloom in stillness.

In the outer courtyard was the guest house and the parking, as was tradition in Baja, reserved exclusively for the residents' cars. The screening room was housed in an oval building on the left and then, through another set of gates to the further courtyard, was the caretaker's casita. In effect the property was protected by three sets of gates. At the final gate was, a practical inclusion this time, a cattlegrid, to prevent the horned Criollo cows from meandering as slowly as they could onto the property, and eating bushes that looked to be dead – the forbs – before continuing their aimless trek.

This was the magnificence that was Casa Lomita.

He was on his way to see Lomita, who was in the newly built hospital in San José del Cabo behind the gathering of food stalls that were known under the collective title of the Mercado. Ever climbed into the Toyota F J Cruiser, sand-coloured and sand-covered, and left the area through the gates to the outside, the perimeter of the property dipping down onto the dust road, checking left and right before the drop and the two mile trip that led to the newly paved road.

The fifteen-mile journey to the edge of the town lay ahead: he played Lana Del Rey and found 'The Blackest Day' to be a repeat that he didn't acknowledge as repetition but as necessity. The necessity of comfort with the lyrical clarification of his destiny. Deep, dark, and getting harder.

The mimosas, the ironwood and the cacti living for hundreds of years, placed the relevance of his short history into perspective. The same cacti would see generations pass from their same position without a change of opinion or condition during their life. A constancy of which the human has no comprehension. We, who wander, change and spill our lives in front of ourselves like vomit. It had been a long journey, literally, the events that unfolded; but now he was dealing with a deep and new sadness. He drove off the paved road into the newly developed outskirts of San José funded by Mr Navarro, the Corona Beer owner, over the newly constructed bridge, took a left turn to the Hotel Zoneria and then up along to the start of the Golden Corridor with the five-star deluxe hotels in the monolithic style of contemporary Mexican architecture.

He was on his own again, and Lana seemed to agree.

The hospital appeared on the right. New and modest in comparison to the hotels, although a comfort to the potential guests with its clean presence. It was at least there. Access to healthcare is an important American tourist consideration.

He sat by the bed, he was now truly the doctor attending the patient, he could not hold back the tears. Lomita had contracted pneumocystis pneumonia, PCP. She was critically ill.

It was critical. He was critical of her being critical: the word had started to lose meaning.

Manita was allowed to be a constant presence by her bedside but Lomita had expressly given Ever visiting hours, hence his solitary journey; she found the emotion of seeing him too much and he had to be limited. The prognosis was not good, but she was content to be in Mexico, the country that had offered her salvation through her difficult years and now ultimately was responsible for the taking of her life. She had physically wasted away so much, her long journey from Los Angeles way down south had done her no good, it was necessary, but it had not helped her condition.

Their journey down had taken place five days earlier and had taken them three days.

It should under normal circumstances have been a pleasure. Manita and Ever shared the driving. They had crossed the border at Tecate, east of Tijuana, a much gentler border to cross, no hassle, it takes you through the wine country and it's a four-hour drive to San Quintín on the Pacific coast. Ever was the only one who needed to fill in a visa document – there were no lines – it took minutes. Manita travelled on a Mexican passport and Lomita had Mexican residency. Their first stop, at the Jardines Hotel, at the end of a long dirt road, gave them a feeling of being able to breathe new air. It was quiet, being nearly midnight, with few people around. Lomita started to wake on their arrival and witnessed the beautiful driveway lined with palm trees that took them to the main building, where they were met by Carlos, who went to get Esmerelda from her bed: they were the owners and knew Lomita well.

They were escorted to the basic casitas but on their way passed the bar; it was Lomita who asked Carlos if he could make one of his margaritas and maybe prepare some food. She turned to Manita to assess her response and fell to the ground. She had fainted, passed out: out cold. Was this the heart condition, or just sheer exhaustion? Two hours after the tablets had been consumed, just before they reached Tecate, she had said her heart was getting better. Ever looked at her, fragile as the skin that surrounded her, picked her up in his arms, her head fell back and he whispered softly that it was going to be all right and no one was going to leave her. They took her straight to lie down, sensing the fever in her as she fell restlessly into a sleep.

Ever was exhausted from the day and took a bottle of tequila from the bar to sit and watch the stars.

Manita bedded down next to Lomita, making sure she took all her medication, including another beta blocker in case it was the heart; it was impossible to get any coherence out of Lomita. She was in and out of feverish sleep.

Ever tried to get some kind of perspective on the turn their lives had taken in the last twelve hours. The stars in the heavens were in their same constellations but for him and for Lomita, their constellations were irreversibly altered. He drank the Don Julio añejo tequila and wondered what he had brought about in the placidity of these peoples' lives. He was, had always been, a force of destruction, a breaker of comfort, a black hole in the middle of a white light. Why was Orion unperturbed by him? Because they had gone, the stars, a long time before all this happened, and they were now in a state of the past – non-existence. He felt his love for Lomita, sat with it like it was an animal, allowed it to comfort him; he prayed that she felt it too.

In the morning she was no better. The drive through the desert, the boulders and cerrito trees was overlooked: it seemed just more relentless beauty in the agony that was connected with the concern for Lomita, who lay on the back seat in a state of sleep and startled wakes.

They had to get to San Ignacio Springs on this day, a mile for every day of the year. A 365-mile journey, they could do the year in a day. But the feeling in the car was strange as Manita did not know what had happened, she was only concerned with the rapidly decreasing health of Lomita. Lomita who was in shock and decay, her immune system disintegrating by the minute, exacerbated by the intensity of what had taken place. The desert landscape and its simplicity, its basic function of primal reptile life and cacti and circling birds drove a confusion, an embarrassment, into Ever's brain; he was now realising in his conscience the reality of what had been done.

The World Heritage Site of San Ignacio with its churches and endless religious artefacts became an annoying contrast to the position that Ever and his travelling companions were in. It was like hell driving through heaven.

The beauty and the incorruptibility shouted out loud.

He couldn't wait for the neutrality of the open road. A cactus to breathe with, not a church, not a spectre of all that was good. They decided that they could not move Lomita and stayed in the car for the night, going out to get bottled water. She wanted no food; both he and Manita were content to grab a few hours' sleep, carry on to Loreto and then move into a hotel on their night-time arrival. They had woken early to start their drive, stopping off at a roadside food stall for a breakfast burrito. Lomita only took in the water. Although wrapped up against the cold, the damp from the night air had in no way helped Lomita's condition and Ever felt that a big mistake had been made in their decision.

They pulled into the roadside for a stop to urinate and whatever else. Manita carried Lomita out of the car for that purpose. There was nothing else in her but water.

They took a left turn out of San Ignacio heading to Santa Rosalía and continued the drive to Loreto down the coast of the Sea of Cortez.

It was difficult to take any of it in with Lomita in the back of the car appearing unmoving, in a state of catatonia. The radio, with its threat of connection to reality, was switched off. San Bruno and Punta Chivato were passed through and by. Eventually they arrived at Loreto.

A most beautiful town but with more churches: the reminder, the continual reminder. Ever was amazed he could consume diazepam and still drive with enough focus, it just kept the edge of panic from his brain.

They took two rooms at the Oasis Hotel on the beach, it was the perfect place to get Lomita out of the car and into a room with an overhead fan. She could be cared for.

Ever needed to collapse and close down.

To save his mind; to conserve as much rational thought that he was finding an increasing struggle to summon.

The roads south of Loreto were rough.

The washing away from the rains had caused cracks and potholes, the journey slowed.

Then it slowed to a stop as they were pulled over at a military-style checkpoint.

On top of a jeep was a mounted machine gun behind which a masked man stood with intention while on the ground several other military personnel, similarly masked and also with intention, stood, rifles at the hip, in silence; there was one man doing the talking. He moved into view and stood beside the jeep.

*'Bájense del coche. Manos en la cabeza. Abran el maletero.'*

His voice was far older than his face, almost an aged larynx growl: Ever did as he was told, he guessed, aided by gesticulations. He opened the trunk, just keeping the one hand on his head. His legs were shaking, he felt there was a line of sweat oozing from his crack. Manita was arguing, Ever wanted her to shut up. He was a shining beacon of guilt.

*'Ella no puede bajarse. Ella es muy vieja y tiene dolor del estómago. Mucho dolor.'*

Pleaded Manita.

*'Déja la viejita. ¡Ahorita!'*

The man said from a throat lined with gravel, followed by a hawk and a spit.

To Ever's relief Manita finally calmed down and obeyed, leaving Lomita silent in the back of the Suburban.

The Mexican Federal Police were looking for drugs, fighting against the drug cartel takeover in the area.

Ever stood, a sweltering bag of nerves; Manita marble cool; they were waved on with another growl from the unmasked man, hinting a smile as he did so. Ever climbed back in and started up his lungs again along with the Suburban.

The cows and burros, the little donkeys, wandered onto the road and at every corner it was necessary to slow down and be prepared.

Manita didn't speak to Ever, her position when not driving was in the back with Lomita's reclined head on her lap.

When they reached La Paz, it felt like the world had arrived to hit them: it appeared busy and informed; Ever did not enjoy the sense of connection with an informed world. From La Paz they, it was actually Manita's choice, decided to cross to Todos Santos so that they could access the new toll road and avoid the coastal track through Los Barriles, which was more direct but rough. They would then head on the smoother road into San José.

The hospital would be their first port of call, in what had certainly been a storm.

Now the journey had an increased desperation: Lomita had slipped into a permanent state of sleep and Manita was unable, for the first time, to control her emotion.

Ever had not witnessed this before; Manita sat in the back sobbing her heart out. Six hours later with his eyes like pins, small, clenching and unclenching to keep awake, determined and focused to get to the hospital, with instructions from Manita; just before dusk, they pulled into the forecourt. Manita, only a notch below hysterical, demanded a gurney and the attention of anyone who was prepared to listen.

Lomita was taken in, after endless form-filling by Manita, to a private room, and the first thing was the insertion of an IV line to give her fluids and nutrition.

This had taken over from the events of three days ago, the concern for Lomita, Ever had not listened to the news, or wanted to, or taken in any of the outside world. It was all about Lomita and only Lomita. After a couple of hours, bloods had been taken from her and Manita suggested to the now slumped Ever, who had been sat in the same seat in the corridor, drifting in and out of somewhere, that they go to the house and return early in the morning to start the next day's vigil.

She kindly felt, Ever interpreted it as a kindness anyway, that he needed to know where the house was and from there he got the sense it would be up to him. He was not a priority; he agreed, he wasn't.

They drove from the hospital, leaving San José to the north along a paved road and then a dirt track, driving slowly, as a precaution against wandering animals; the temptation to put it to the floor and get there and breathe was almost irresistible.

On the instruction to turn right up a sandy bank they entered the first set of gates of Casa Lomita. Pedro came out of the caretaker's casita and opened up the house with a warm greeting for Manita.

Ever walked into this world of its own.

With the only sound being the sea and the whistling osprey, which Manita pointed out, settled on top of the lighthouse, lit by the light beneath. Ever looked up and then he saw the stars.

Clear, close, and talking. They parked the Suburban next to a sand-coloured Toyota F J Cruiser, and walked through the house; Pedro opened the doors, Ever stepped out onto the terrace and the moon, not full but waning, still had the strength to throw light across the ocean, enabling him to see a world with no problems and no relation or connection to anything. It was a dream that could never be dreamt, spread before you in reality better than any fantastical construction could ever be. Pedro, as is the traditional hospitality of Baja, produced a bottle of tequila and a small shot glass and placed them on the marble-topped table on the terrace.

'Welcome to Casa Lomita, señor. Tomorrow I start early with the delivery. I wish you to sleep well. *Buenas noches*.'

Ever returned the courtesy of a goodnight, not attempting Spanish to Pedro's near perfect English.

Ever did not question the delivery of what, he just wanted to sit and drink and get lost in the haze of the distilled agave, the beauty of the sky, the sound of the sea and the smell. He realised it was the same feeling that he got from Lomita, that smell of confidence of being at one. It was nature, pure and simple. Manita came to say goodnight and told him to lock the terrace door when he went to his bed, which was to his left at the end of the living room. He wasn't sure whether lying down with his thoughts on his own would be possible tonight or indeed ever again. The chill of the wind made him aware he had nothing with him, just what he sat with, there had been no preparation, no thought put into this adventure. It was a strange turn of events that had brought them here. Nothing would ever be the same again.

How long would it take?

The next morning after a sleepless night.

But one that had taken him inside when the damp from the ocean presented a chill to his bones, too tired to resist its invasion. And then there came the sound of engines. His first fear quickly evaporated. The reality of the noise became apparent. Pedro arrived in a convoy of four pickup trucks as the sun was rising over the ocean. Manita handed Ever a cup of coffee: life started early here. He was standing outside with a stare, he could see uncovered *The Wave*. Pedro handed him a piece of paper: the delivery logistics and timeframe. The trucks contained his father's paintings and had been picked up from a storage facility at the back of the old town in San José, next to the church, according to the instruction, where they had been delivered, driven straight down from the gallery in downtown Los Angeles.

A world away now and Lomita had known when he had asked if he would ever see them again that he would. But what else she knew then he had no idea. He, with a surprisingly relaxed feel, wandered around the trucks and counted twenty paintings. He sank to his knees, his head dropped to his chest and he prayed; the four Mexicans didn't seem too concerned, and even seemed to accept that the act had a normality, a place. He prayed to his God, he prayed for Lomita and gave her the biggest thank you he had the power to give in his soul. He stood up and walked away into his own world and wept. Wept for them both.

What had he done?

He recognised the imbalance that he always knew was in him.

Now the gyroscope had levelled.

There was no more he could do.

He was done.

The viral pneumonia didn't respond to antibiotic treatment, understandably.

But they had to try everything, and steroidal antiviral treatment did not prevent Ever from slipping into a coma brought about by an ever-decreasing weakness in his immune system and his soul having decided finally to go. It thought, his soul, that it should never really have come back. Ten days he lay in this condition, his mother, in a rare display of emotion, unbeknown to Ever, was dragged away from his bedside, screaming, when she was told to prepare for the worst. Ever's fading memory, as he drifted, was of the deep-voiced consultant in his pinstripe suit looking at him with that look of concern reserved for the truly sick. Ever knew he was truly sick because a smell emanated from him that he had never smelt before or since. It was a heavy, overpowering smell, stale – yes, putrid – not quite. It just hung and it came from deep in his body, his body that was fighting at a cellular level where the rot was being forced out. He was fifteen.

# *Chapter Thirty-four*

'I can't believe you bought them and gave me way more than I would have asked. Or, to be honest, even expected, so I will most definitely adjust your payment. They are well on their way.'

Mr Lorken was sitting opposite Lomita at their Friday lunch appointment. They were dining at Atalam, a restaurant afforded its celebrity by the owner chef, Transient Dillane. Lomita had ordered a kale salad and Mr Lorken had the squid ink bucatini.

A dish Lomita never understood, turning your mouth a dark colour with the dubious over-intensity of fishy taste. And you ended up looking like a schoolkid who'd sucked his pen. She was happy she would be able to push around a few walnuts and some quinoa, another food she failed to understand.

'And Mexico, you have a house there.'

'No, it's a gallery. I am sending them to a gallery. I have faith Ingmar, you see, they will have a life.'

'Well I admire your faith, but I think in this case it's misplaced. Certainly not a safe bet. Not like a Metzinger.'

'Oh, you mentioned this before.'

Lomita was feeling her fears were about to be justified.

'You never told me which one, and you see, Lomita, I can account for ownership of every single one, either in personal collections or museums. Except for one.'

'I didn't say I still had it.'

'No, that is true. So which one was it?'

'I told you. I don't feel obliged to tell you.'

'You do not have a completely anonymous past. I mean it is possible to find out who you were connected to.'

'And you obviously have.'

Said a resigned Lomita.

'Yes. It was your quip about the Caravaggio that gave me the clue. I mean those Masters have an easy-to-trace provenance. And it only left one. And that was stolen by the same group of people that your husband was in business with.'

'My goodness Ingmar, you have been busy.'

'I have done nothing. I pay people who are in positions to gain access to information on anyone. You are not really that difficult to unearth.'

The stress gave the word – unearth – the weight of discovering an Egyptian relic.

'All the way back to Pittsburgh in fact.'

'So what.'

Suddenly a toughness appeared to come out of a past Lomita.

'What are you going to do about it. I am in the clear.'

'Are you? Neither of those paintings have been recovered. I am sure there are people who would like to talk to you.'

Lomita felt the secluded bubble of her world disintegrate. The privacy she craved caved in. By this little fuck.

'I suppose I would be more than happy to talk to whoever, to help clarify a situation I know nothing about.'

Said Lomita.

'Perhaps you're right, maybe I am being a little… I don't know.'

He was doing that annoying hand over mouth thing again, covering his eating, while his mouth turned black-blue. A quite revolting sight.

Lomita had pushed around enough food and was now sipping her sparkling water.

'How does it help, Ingmar? I don't know a thing, he has been dead for thirty-five years.'

This time she resisted the reference to Roberto dePirizone by the title of husband. Well, ex-husband, in fact dead husband. Why was this man bothering to persecute her in this way?

'It's just that the Metzinger I feel strongly about, it was a Nazi confiscation, put in the Degenerate Art Exhibition and then—'

He paused.

'Gone. But then you.'

He hadn't really made sense of these non sequiturs and she knew that it was because he was deeply angry, understandably deeply angry as a Jew, that this work by a Jewish artist had been treated with such disrespect by the Nazis and then, she presumed he thought, by her husband, who in some way had collaborated post war with their sympathisers. Totally understandable. She was with him. She just didn't want to be part of this, dragged into an investigation of how this painting had landed in her possession. The annoying part was that she didn't really like it anyway. He could stuff his Metzinger.

They finished eating. They were keeping a surprising civility, mostly due to her, and ordered coffee.

'And you will continue with this?'

Tendered Lomita, after the plates had been cleared.

'I don't feel I have any choice not to continue. To uncover what happened and to bring about some form of, hopefully, of conclusion, closure if you like, to a much-maligned artist. Who I do think was touched with that word.'

'Genius?'

Questioned Lomita; he was not an obtuse man.

'Of course.'

'Are you going back to Beverly Hills after lunch?'

Lomita asked.

'If not don't worry, I just need to call my driver.'

'No, please don't, I would be delighted to drop you off. It is not a problem, no effort at all.'

'Thank you so much.'

'Would you like a chocolate truffle?'

He asked, after much appraisal of room and people.

'They keep them for me. I love them.'

'Not for me, thanks very much.'

And she sat and watched him munch his truffle and reflected on how trying to help someone gets you into a fine fucking mess. At that moment, as another truffle was being bitten in two, she hated the fucking sight of this pompous, rich, self-important fuck.

'Delicious lunch, thank you.'

She proffered.

He remained oblivious to her feeling, her strength of feeling.

'We don't have to wait for the check.'

Of course you don't, she thought, I'm sure you own the place.

They were standing on the sidewalk.

He very graciously had lent his arm as an additional support to her cane. He was waving his twenty-dollar bill and then escorted her to the opening door of his electric blue Dawn; top down; the piece of substantial flash. She made no comment about his car on purpose, knowing that this was the only reason he had bought it. She was climbing in, sit first, legs swing in later, when she noticed a dull red Honda, a car she would never have paid any attention to had it not been for the fact that Ever was sitting behind the wheel: directly facing the Rolls.

Mr Lorken climbed in to the driver's side and purred the engine. No Ever, please God, no. This was surely not the ordained day, the day that after all the talking, the communication, the outpouring of love and the giving of time, and the realisation that this man had ultimately done no wrong to John Everett Millen, that Ever was still intent on seeing through his obsessive action, the consummation of his act. No, please God.

The Rolls moved away from the kerb and followed its well-worn route towards Beverly Hills; Lomita had no idea if Ever was following. Mr Lorken started on his Metzinger conversation again.

'It's not a personal attack, you must understand that. I like you, Lomita.'

There was no response from Lomita.

'It is the righting of a wrong. Returning what belongs to a nation, a state, if you like. A justice. I would be seriously remiss if I ignored the situation. Don't you think?'

The last words spoken with a turn of his head in the direction of his unresponsive passenger.

She sat in silence clutching her thick fake fur, leopard skin, Fendi bag. The righting of goddam wrongs again, what is it with this attempt at the impossible. Clutching at her clutch, with damp seeping from her pores, thickening the fur and matting its sheen.

Did he not think what it would do to her life? Did he care? She asked him directly.

'It would affect the privacy of my life enormously, I mean, disrupt my life entirely, even if there was no criminality involved.'

'I don't suppose there is criminality involved directly with you Lomita, but yes I can't deny that your life, for a time anyway, would be turned upside down. I suppose it's about whether you benefitted from the theft of stolen artefacts in any way.'

'That's difficult to prove. Is it not? I mean whether I actually benefitted?'

He expressed a sound that could be confirmed as a questioning –

'Mmmm.'

She felt upside down now, dizzy and very weak. Unwell would be a reasonable description. This was going to make her unwell, this could kill her. I don't suppose he had thought of that.

'I am not a well woman, Ingmar.'

She offered by way of a plea.

'But it is really about the art, not you.'

Of course the man had no heart, why would he? You can't appeal to someone who puts objects, however beautiful, before people.

'Then you wouldn't care what happened to me?'

'I would care, but I wouldn't necessarily anticipate a negative outcome. In other words, it wouldn't stop me.'

'My health then, would not be important to you?'

'It would not be the prime consideration. No. If I am being totally honest.'

And why would you be anything else, when it suits you? Unvoiced.

Does this man have no feeling? Unvoiced.

What a man, she thought, how extraordinary to be involved with a man like that. She was seething and sarcasm offered her an immediate vent. They had turned up La Cienega, taking a left on Burton Way.

'Would you mind, the sun is making me quite dizzy. Do you think you could put the top up on the car?'

'Of course, sorry, yes, I should have asked earlier. I think I'm made of leather.'

So true, you certainly are. Unvoiced.

He slowed down by the Hermitage Hotel.

The valet parking attendants experienced a momentary excitement at the prospect of taking the car. He didn't need to stop: in twenty seconds the top was secured. One more piece of protection from Ever, thought Lomita. Please Ever, see some sense. Please.

She believed her silent pleas of please would get out there; connect in the ether. She closed her eyes to concentrate the effort: she felt like a witch.

They gathered speed towards Crescent Drive and the turn north. She had managed to turn around and take a look as the top was going up; an acceptably unsuspicious thing to do, with all that activity, not that Mr Lorken was anticipating any kind of problem. But she could see no Ever. They crossed Santa Monica Boulevard: she wondered what Ever would be doing now. Where was he? She was sweating and felt the world leaving her; her heart was double timing and it was causing a lightheadedness, she pressured down to keep from fainting. Like taking a crap with a push. They were approaching the stop sign at Carmelita, she opened her Fendi bag and exclaimed in a panic,

'Oh my God! My phone! I've left my phone!'

His instinctive reaction betrayed an audible groan of annoyance. He slowed to a stop, fifteen yards from the four-way stop at Carmelita, suggesting he call the restaurant. At that moment she saw Ever's car emerge from the east onto Carmelita, and drive into the middle of the road, past the stop sign: she knew, although she couldn't see, that he would be staring at the Rolls. The Honda turned left onto the other side of the road while Mr Lorken was calling the restaurant. Ever pulled up and got out of the car, nothing suspicious in that for Mr Lorken, who didn't even notice. Ever had the look of purpose but she couldn't see a gun. What else was he going to do? He wasn't coming to say hello.

'You know where we were sitting, where I always sit, just look at your seating chart, for Christ's sake!'

The voice continued on the phone. Ever was now virtually upon the car and Mr Lorken turned in reaction to the approaching 6' 2".

'What the fuck!'

It was flat aggression from Mr Lorken.

Lomita almost at a scream.

'Found it! Got it here!'

He turned back to Lomita, distracted, with an exhale.

'Thank God.'

They were just completed, those two words. Her hand went inside the Fendi bag, feeling for the grip and grasping the handle of a Beretta 70. She released two bullets into Mr Lorken's chest: they managed over the short distance to revolve inside the body, increasing the damage, the bag was pressed tight to his body, muffling the sound, the impact was instant, unmissable and fatal.

The thick leather seat took the rest of the hit as one of the bullets passed through. The other was lodged in the spine, having made contact on the vertical moment of its revolution.

The last word he had spoken was 'God'.

Let's hope he heard.

Lomita's heart literally skipped a beat but did not go back to its sinus rhythm, it was constantly skipping, a supraventricular tachycardia kind of attack; her atrial fibrillation had kicked in. And with this misbehaving heart she scrambled for the door, reached the handle and cracked the door open. Ever rushed round to her side of the car, completed the opening of the door and helped her out, carrying her, off the ground, to his waiting Honda. A woman speed-walked past with a sun visor, headphones, track suit and trainers, apparently oblivious to what was going on. Without a second to calculate the situation he turned the car around and went east on Carmelita; without thought but instinctive panic got the hell out of town as fast as grabbing no attention would take him. Up Oakhurst Drive, with the briefest of a split second that registered the possibility of going to her home for tablets: ignoring her plea, he went south on Doheny, all the way down to Olympic, travelling east towards Koreatown.

Lomita was in a state of hysterics, sobbing, shouting and screaming: it was all incoherent and his ears weren't tuned to hear. Or tuned to her.

Lomita had been a long-term sufferer of atrial fibrillation.

Controlling the condition with flecainide tablets on a daily basis to regulate the rhythm, keep it in sinus rhythm: but this trauma had overridden the control that the tablets gave, resulting in a non-sinus rhythm phase. Lomita was panicked and breathless. The blood was not being pumped out of the atria and could pool there, just sit there, given up, relieved of responsibility, making its statement that its job was done. The downside of this non-emptying atria, at least its irregularity, was the potential for clotting and therefore a stroke. Thus things were not at this moment going well for Lomita. She hadn't had an AF attack for a number of years and its return produced its own shock. She needed some tablets. Beta blockers or more flecainide.

'Why did you do that?'

'You made me. I did it for you. You don't, you understand, kill me now, kill me please. I can't live with it. I don't want to anymore. Ever please.'

What she wanted him to do with her cries, he had no idea; he was too isolated in his own emotion to take time to wonder.

This continued all the way through the Mid-City and started to die, the noise, from pure exhaustion, as they were crossing Western; he took a left up on to 8th Street in an attempt to find his patch of anonymous land.

Had he made Lomita do this?

Ever the bringer of all that is bad and negative into people's lives. The soulless one. Ever. Forever doing the same thing: consistent in the wrong.

Ever had had no gun with him – he hadn't been carrying a gun – what had been his intention towards Mr Lorken? He was unable to think in straight coherent logic as Lomita was mixing her thoughts with his, he couldn't work out which were his and which were hers, so long had the idea of this kill been in his mind. But he had been walking towards Mr Lorken in his car without his Glock 17. No gun.

She was now slumped, the hysterics had calmed but the emotion had the same power, it was just the machinery that pumped out the expression was weakening, stumbling, breaking down, running out of gas.

He got to 8th Street where the 110 appeared up on its stilts, took a right down South Union Street and then he remembered the left that should bring him to his haven; his piece of peace and solitude. The isolation patch. He stopped the car in an attempt to gather his bearings.

He could see the tower of the Ritz Carlton, it should be directly beneath, just this side of the 110; he started to move forward and there it was on his left behind the wire, he had turned down a street, but one street too early, unable to access the entrance.

He doubled back and went one beyond, there he was: there were the blue tarpaulins of the homeless camps and there was his gate to solitude. The same as it was on his last trip; minus the truck.

No one cared about this patch, no one looked after this patch, even the birds looked disillusioned, wandering with no real attempt at finding any sustenance, a bird boredom had taken wing. Flying seemed a waste, they hopped a few feet at a time in a vague attempt at escape, probably thinking death to be an acceptable alternative to this existence. Ever was transferring; he stopped.

He parked in the middle of the wasteland as accurately as he could assess. He blanked his mental process and breathed deep. Five times until he started to feel a dizziness.

Had he made Lomita do this?

Her sobs were now pathetic whimpers; he got her out of the car, found the alley at the side of the land, he knew that through to the other side was the Isis Adelphia and Milagro's Market. He picked her up, one arm under her legs another round her back, cupping his hand under her arm, she struggled to keep her head up. She was aware of what was happening, making noises that he couldn't determine as words.

'We need to get Manita down here.'

Ever was saying on repeat, waiting for acknowledgement of reception of the message. Then she formulated words.

'Where are we?'

'Have you got your phone?'

'No, I left it in the restaurant. I told him.'

What the fuck. Her bag was back in the car. Not in the restaurant, please.

'I told him.'

She repeated, fixated on the false truth.

They turned, rather he did, she had no choice but to follow the motion of his arms, and then back to the car with the hope of the Fendi bag within.

The bag was burnt through with a hole and no blood. Browned at the edges. It occurred even at that moment that that was a strange thing. Perhaps the brown was dried blood.

He opened it and there was her phone, positioned alongside her gun. Both were inert and incapable. Dependant on operation: the constitutional defence.

'It's here, thank God, it's here.'

'No, but I told him I had left it.'

There was confusion, he just felt relief.

'We have it. We've got it.'

He was now, at as fast a pace as he could manage, heading back to the Isis.

'We need to phone Manita.'

'Where are we?'

'Manita.'

The conversation was bullet point, appropriate term, just the words that needed to go in. Like the bullet.

'I will.'

They burst through the confines of the alley and emerged facing the Isis Adelphia Hotel. On the other side of the street. They went through the beaded curtains, he had now released her from his grip and was supporting her with his arm around her waist. The beads made their xylophonic ripple of warning and a lady came out from behind another set of multi-coloured beads to take up position behind a desk. She was Chinese. So was the desk, with the ornate carving of dragons forming the base.

'Do you have room?'

'A room?'

'Yes.'

'One or two?'

She said taking in Lomita.

'One is fine.'

'How many night?'

'Wait a second please.'

Lomita was now sitting on the one chair in the lobby. A bamboo rocker. He presumed unless there was interest in a room she would not be allowed to continue this small luxury. He spoke close to her ear.

'Call Manita and tell her to come and get us.'

'And we'll go to Mexico.'

Added Lomita. She took out her phone and dialled Manita; she could see the face of the Chinese woman looking at her, waiting for the answer of how many nights.

She couldn't think.

'Just the one room. One night.'

Confirmed Ever.

He passed a hundred-dollar bill across the desk.

'A hundred-twenty-five dollar.'

Came the response, he dug for further money, hearing the muffled sound of a phone ringing and being answered.

'*Hola Manita, escucha atentamente y cuidadosamente. Vamos a México. Solo empaca las cosas médicas y ven a recogernos. Ever está conmigo. Ven rápido por favor.* Where are we?'

She put her hand over the phone to speak to Ever, although it wasn't a secret. Ever lent into her ear and told her.

*'En la esquina de 8th Street y South Union Street. El hotel se llama la Isis de Adelphia. ¿Adelphia con 'ph'?'*

'Yes.'

Said Ever, surprised at his subliminal understanding of the language.

*'Lleva los pasaportes.'*

'Where is yours?'

'US and UK, bedside drawer.'

*'Los dos están en el cajón al lado de la cama. Y las pastillas, Manita, para mi corazón. Pon la dirección del hotel en el GPS. Llámame con cualquier problema. Ven tan rápido como puedas. Gracias. Nos vemos pronto.'*

The Chinese woman was no wiser: Ever was only a bit more so.

He now addressed the Chinese lady.

'I'm going to get the luggage while my friend here can just get her breath back. It'll take me a few minutes, do you have some water perhaps for her?'

'I can take her to the room.'

Oh God is nothing simple?

'No, won't be long.'

Working out that Manita would be at least forty minutes. Maybe that wasn't such a bad idea.

'OK, to the room. And some water. Please.'

Ever and Lomita and the Chinese lady walked to the tiny collapsible metal-gated door of the elevator that did not look capable of carrying its ambitious load. It was, according to the notice inside, a four-person maximum. What size people crossed one of Ever's lobes, not sinking too deep as a thought. There was no room in brain or elevator.

Only one floor.

Fine.

It clanked and groaned with complaint to the one floor. God help the trip to the second. Ever made a note to walk down. And directly opposite was the room.

One bed, one window, one chair and a bathroom down the hall. Chinese scroll calligraphy hung on the walls. Twice.

'Thank you. Perfect.'

Confirmed Ever.

Lomita was reluctant for him to go; the Chinese lady exited, giving him the key.

'Ten minutes. I'll be back in ten minutes.'

Lomita clutched him and he could feel the tremor that wasn't essential. At this point he was proud of his composure. But it was superficial as his bowels gurgled and his head pained. Lomita sat struggling with her heart that was not telling her the beat of life was inevitable and straightforward. It wasn't her drum she was beating to.

He ran down the stairs and out of the Isis Hotel, going immediately into the Milagro's store. Purchasing calm from the universe.

'A box of matches please.'

He handed over a dollar bill.

'Oh and a bottle of water.'

'Still?'

'Yes.'

'In the refrigerator behind you.'

'Thank you.'

'Three fifty-five.'

He pulled out a five-dollar bill.

Another thanks, and left.

Now he was running towards the car.

On entering the haven, it was there, anonymously, he

looked around for any old dry material. Other than plastic, concrete and metal he could find nothing that would absorb. He thought of the bomb and his mother, he remembered laying the trail that had been so effective. No gunpowder.

He drank the water and took off his socks. He opened the trunk of the car and pulled out the can of petrol. And poured it on the seats and floor of the car, then onto a sock and into the water bottle. The seats were vinyl and wouldn't absorb so he opened the petrol cap and poured some petrol all around the opening, and with shaking hands opened the matchbox, most of the matches fell out; he rammed the end of the soaked sock into the bottle and lit it. And then, when convinced it wasn't going to go out, threw it into the open back door of the car.

And ran.

Waiting for the boom.

He thought, there would be a boom, wouldn't there? He turned, hearing no boom. Twenty feet away and nobody around, nobody carrying their washing, he could see the haze of heat as the inside of the car was on fire, the petrol cap was open and the fire was grasping at the fumes outside on the paint work. Then came the boom. The petrol tank released its pressure, like the sparklet, the car became a burning furnace; he was running like a madman for the alley exit.

He stopped and turned for one last look, his Honda EX V6 sedan in dull red was being destroyed before his eyes. A magnificent sight. Fuzzy with the shimmering, adding to the heat of the day. The squealing noise as the metal contorted in pain, the plastic loving and lapping up the flames with a fizz. Burning in a frenzy. It was going to be a shell and become even less memorable than it was before.

He could have cooked some potatoes there.

It was sad that it was burning on gravel and caked mud.

Nothing to spread the fire.

Lomita – ten maybe fifteen minutes must have gone.

What had Lomita done? He had made her, hadn't he?

It was his fault again. He imagined himself sitting in the front of the burning Honda with the flames caressing him, paining and searing at his flesh. Would he burn in an explosive way or just cook slowly like a piece of pork? Nearest thing to human flesh isn't? He should have done that, he should have sat in the front seat of the car while it was burning and joined it in the smoke.

The meat and no potato.

He ran back the long way around, looking to see if anyone was paying any attention to him, or following him.

The Isis Adelphia's beads rippled again and he didn't wait for the Chinese lady.

Double-stepping the stairs, he stopped on the fourth step and returned to the lobby. The television hanging to the right of the Chinese desk was showing pictures, with the sound down, of an electric blue Rolls-Royce Dawn Drophead coupé, parked on a street in Beverly Hills, swarming with police and forensic-suited investigators. He turned around, put his head through the beads and threw up. Breathed in, escaped the trailing beads and ran past the now emerged Chinese lady, double-stepped again and opened the door to the room.

Lomita was sitting in the chair looking like death. Well she was the bringer of death. The harbinger, the grim reaper, she did it. He didn't want to enter into any discussion about what had happened: keep it simple.

'Where's Manita?'

Lomita without expression went to the bag and picked up her phone; had a freeze moment as the sight of the gun took her back; she pressed the name Manita on the recent call page.

'*¿Cuánto tiempo hasta que llegues?*'

She pressed the red button.

'Thirty minutes.'

Exhaled Lomita.

'She'll be another thirty minutes.'

Another thirty minutes. Had all communication broken down, what do you say now? Did either of them want to speak? Could Lomita speak? She looked like she had lived every second of her seventy-six years, the poor soul. What could he possibly say to her?

'Did you get your water?'

Was the best.

'Yes, thank you. What do we do with the gun?'

She asked and it had to be said.

'In the bag. It's still in the bag.'

'Leave it in the bag.'

Ever said for no reason other than he had no idea what to do with it. But it sounded authoritative. And then after the longest exhalation that her tiny lungs could expel, she replenished with some innocent air.

'What have I done to us Ever? What have I done?'

This, thought Ever in a moment of intense cruelty, could be the record that played around and around forever. The stuck record. At least for the next thirty minutes.

'Let's get on the road and we can talk.'

'In front of Manita? I don't think so.'

'Talk now, is that what we should do? What do we do then?'

'We go to Mexico and wait. They will find me. They have connections to me. I was the last person seen with him. I had lunch with him. They will at least find me, to ask me questions. At the very least.'

Ever couldn't begin to comprehend life now.

Certainly a massive traumatic situation does wonders for brain focus and gyroscopic balancing. Survival becomes different, it means different things. It's not about being happy or sad, it's about survival. It's how he supposed you would feel in a war zone. You know you're not happy, so you go beyond that, to just surviving; there are no demands on the brain other than to stay clear enough to fend off the beast. To live. He thought they should call Manita again or go and wait in the lobby. Lomita suggested the latter, give it five, and go down. The phone rang it was Manita.

Lomita answered and ended the brief call.

'Five minutes according to the GPS.'

She said, followed by,

'Please would you hold me tight, my sweet. Please.'

She didn't need the second please, he was on his feet and swept her out of the chair and held her for all he was worth. At that moment she did receive all the love he had left in the world. He wanted it to flood into her body so that she would know.

He also carried all the guilt in the world; that he wasn't sure if she should know. They broke apart and without words to speak they went downstairs: he carried her weight down the stairs and in perfect timing, they arrived at the lobby; through the multi-coloured hanging trails of beading the black mass of the Suburban pulled up outside the Isis Adelphia Hotel.

'Back after we've had something to eat.'

Said Ever to the Chinese lady, with an impressive throw-away casualness.

'Yes OK. And then you sign register, we forget to do the signing.'

'Of course, that won't be a problem.'

The beads parted for the last time.

And rippled back into place. As he hit the sidewalk he could see some wafts of smoke across the street behind the warehouse wall, and he smelt for a second, either from memory or from the now, the smell of the powerful dark of the smoke from fire.

Manita, as was expected, asked no questions.

Other than to express concern over the welfare of Lomita. Lomita was eased into the back seat by Ever and she immediately asked for the flecainade and a beta blocker: Ever, unusually for him, had no knowledge of this medication, but responding to Lomita's desperation, gave her the tablets with some water; she would now wait for her heart to see sense and get back into a sinus rhythm.

It was an unnerving feeling, atrial fibrillation, delivering intense anxiety, disorientation, a suspension of confidence in the continuation of your life. Ever sat in the back of the black mass and nestled her in his arms.

The trip was to take them to the easiest border to negotiate, Tecate, Tijuana being the more direct but busier, with its concerns over drug cartels and the delays caused by a car search. Ever presumed Manita was more than familiar with the route but he felt a nostalgia for the Englishness of Kate on Waze. He programmed the route in, was comforted by her words, always calm and consistent in emotion, or lack of, giving him the feeling of isolation in his own private space that nothing could invade, guiding them on their way. He spoke to her once or twice, bringing no response from his fellow passengers. Whether Manita listened to Kate's advice was really irrelevant to Ever, he just wanted her to talk to him in an English accent and make him feel that nothing had changed in his world.

That it was all the same.

Simple, it was the only thing that connected him to a place before, where nothing had yet gone wrong. Kate was ignorant of their situation, and he liked that.

A hundred and sixty miles and a two-and-a-half-hour journey. Down the I-5 and then a little kick east to Tecate, avoiding Tijuana, and then Mexico. Ever took over the driving an hour across the border, and felt no tiredness at all. He supposed adrenaline-fuelled anxiety conquered all. They were heading towards their first stop, San Quintín, hoping to get there before midnight.

Was he ever going to tell Lomita he wasn't carrying a gun?

# *Chapter Thirty-five*

A morning that had started, as all seemed to in Baja, with the rise of the shining sun.

Across the ocean flashing the room with a brightness that could only come from a divine source: Ever was still not recovered from the emotional onslaught of his father's paintings.

He was now driving with Manita back into San José to the hospital to see how Lomita had fared through the night. Ever needed something to help him calm down, and asked Manita if by any chance she had any medication on her. She said that she didn't but that wasn't a problem as they could stop at a pharmacy in San José, where there was a large selection of pharmacies, some generous, some more particular. Ever was confused by Manita's lack of questioning, he wanted to unload all that had happened, to get a reaction, to disturb her composure, but she just drove and all she had asked, albeit with concern was,

'How are you today, Señor Ever?'

It was the first time she had directly used his name, he was convinced he had never heard it before, he would have remembered the strange inflection, making it sound circular not direct, and certainly the first time it had been coupled with the dignity of a Señor.

'Well I feel I need a little something to calm my nerves.'

On their arrival in the town she directed him to a pharmacy by the church, which she described as a generous one.

*'Con dinero, baila el perro.'*

She said rubbing forefinger and thumb together. A gesture his father used to make when he wanted a roll-up. He got the idea about money, but making your dog dance was lost on him.

Ever walked into his idea of retail heaven. Signs were displayed on the shelves in capital letter handwriting with a felt tip pen; the names of medication for sale. No prescription was needed: everything a boy could ever want.

A benzo paradise.

Lorazepam, diazepam, Valium, the Z family, Ambien, no Zimovane, those were truly his bag, his soul food, alongside Vicodin and painkillers of every name, tramadol, dihydrocodeine, and even, oh heaven, diamorphine, what a country, and the full range of erectile dysfunction pills, Viagra, Cialis, Levitra. It was endless. It was his toy shop.

He left with some diazepam and Ambien, and some Vicodin for those special little moments of pain.

He now felt medically self-sufficient; he should, he had enough diazepam, one hundred tablets, to finish himself off in one sleepy go. He popped a diazepam, the full 10 mg, as soon as got into the car.

Thrilled that he had ninety-nine more.

Other than that highlight, on his return to earth, there was a feeling of a mutual tension in the car. What condition Lomita would be in on their arrival?

'Thank you, Manita, thank you for your help and everything.'

His wandering gratitude brought about no response, but he did feel grateful that she had taken him to the pharmacy, so made no demand for a reply. The practicalities of what had happened could not be faced by Ever, who had placed the survival of Lomita above all, but there was so much more than her health and he just couldn't, or wouldn't, he wasn't sure which, be able to face the reality. It was all over, he supposed, when his brain alighted on the subject, with the momentary perch of a bird on a branch before it swoops off to new territories. A new focus was needed, one which carried a future, that was the problem he could not get beyond: there was no future. He could not perch on anything but the question of Lomita's survival; not what would happen if she did survive.

The hospital corridor was surprisingly cheery for a hospital corridor.

There was a sense of life not death in the place. That was probably due to the Mexican music piped into the veins of the corridor.

They opened the door to the same room that they had left her in the previous night.

There was a nurse who was happy to leave after a few words from Manita.

Lomita's hair was down now, lying with an independence on the pillow, not washed, she was obviously not strong enough for water to be applied too heavily to her body.

Manita was first to hold her hand.

'*Siento que ya no estoy aquí Manita—*'

She stopped and started again in English as she registered Ever's presence.

'I feel like I am not here anymore.'

Then adding the question.

'Am I?'

'Of course you are, it will all be fine.'

Manita was able to say that at least; unaware as she was of the truth.

What else can you say? This is a fucking huge, big, massive mess that will crash around us and change us all forever?

And that was with 10 mg of diazepam refusing the brain its full swirl of neurosis.

'Can you leave me with Ever a while please Manita?'

She left, presumably to sit outside, and Ever took up a position by the bed and extended his hand towards hers.

They held.

Her eyes closed and she started to exhale with the faintest noise of congestion.

'Hello Ever. How are you my sweet?'

She closed her eyes as if she was preventing more pain from coming in that could be received through the windows of sight and light.

'I am OK. And you?'

'I don't know Ever, but will you at this point in my life, in our life, where all this has brought us – be true with me?'

A strange expression he thought; as strange as the first time she had used it. Truly. Do we like each other truly? He remembered.

'Be true, yes I will. Of course I will.'

'Tell me please Ever, what you feel about me.'

Ever did not know what to say.

'In the way of my emotions?'

'Yes.'

Said Lomita.

The banal directness of his own question embarrassed him but appeared to have flown over the frailty of Lomita.

'I want to hear from you what you feel about me. After what I have done.'

Ever didn't expect that coda to the question. He rethought his route through the unexpected turn in the conversation.

'I don't feel anything has changed in me, about you, with what has happened.'

'It has for me. I can't and don't want to live with what I have done; the excuse that I didn't mean to, or want to, would not even be true. That's what I mean about true. Be true. I did what I did because of you Ever. So be true to me.'

'You did what you did because of me, to stop me doing what you knew I would do.'

He wasn't sure if that carried a question in its inflection, it was a repeat to allow his brain time. He needed some time. Diazepam did that. He couldn't tell her he had no gun. He had no gun. He couldn't do that. He made the decision then that he would never tell her that. He would not tell her that.

'I did it for you Ever because of how I feel about you.'

There was a silence between them.

'I love you.'

There was another silence.

One that he could not fill with the expected response, not because he didn't feel anything, it was just rare that people said that to him. And he felt its rarity: its sinking in to his core.

'I love you Ever. That is all that matters to me and I will take with me, to my God, the horror of what I did and I will face that and take full responsibility for that. I did it because I love you.'

That time of saying, her eyes had opened and the blue from them spread into the room and into his eyes; tears appeared from his ducts at the corner of his eyes, but did not run down his face; he said what he truly felt from the bottom of his heart, and maybe his soul had arrived to lend support.

'I love you.'

Then the tears ran, at a pace, to escape his eyes: find a freedom in a world that was less painful.

They looked at each other, a smile did not physicalise, it did not need to. It lived deep inside, in another time and place; in a realm of feeling that took them away from the limitations of this existence.

These walls, the building, the town, the desert and the world.

She was on a silver screen with him and they were both in the sky with the stars.

The silence went on without effort, their hands joined with their hearts and their eyes. A tear moved tentatively out of Lomita's right eye, shyly making its way down her face as if it were the first time it had ever left home.

It was a tear she expelled with a different feeling from all the other tears that had rolled on the same journey.

It was a slow and contemplative tear.

And they sat and sat, they had sat and sat so many times in their lives in modes of contemplation, isolated and alone; now in harmony in the same thought, with contentment and purity of love.

Ever wished their relationship had remained pure and had not been consummated; but then their physical connection had made them one in their understanding of how their lives could have been, it had shaped them to meet and end their days together.

Because that is what they're facing: this is the end of it all.

Two hours passed in this state of connection, nurses put their heads around the door and had their own interpretation of what they saw; Lomita and Ever cared not for the world and its opinions, they existed only for each other.

And would for all time.

'I want you to know this Ever, you are the only person who I have ever wanted inside me. Physically and in my heart.'

There was a knock followed by a doctor.

Dr Jose Serrano, according to his introduction; Lomita thought he was familiar but Ever had not seen him before. He took the chart from the end of her bed and studied it in preparation for asking some questions.

Lomita suggested that Ever should leave the room.

'I am happy to stay.'

'No, my sweet, please leave, just for a few minutes.'

The door closed.

'*¿Ingles o Español?*'

She obviously hadn't seen him before.

'I don't mind.'

Replied Lomita.

'How long have you been taking the antiretroviral medication for your condition at this dose?'

The doctor had made his own decision.

'About three years. When my CD4 cells fell below the accepted level of stability and I got repeated bouts of pneumonia. I have my cell count checked on a regular basis but it has proved difficult for me to get the cell count back up.'

He was studying the clipboarded chart.

'It is below the level now and the X-rays reveal the presence of pulminory infiltrates. You have a very low arterial oxygen level that leads to the diagnosis of pneumocystis pneumonia, PCP.'

Lomita was hearing and that was about all.

'We will need to put you on a course of steroids and a combination of trimetrexate and primaquine.'

'Please slow down, even in my first language. Slower.'

'Or, and I will be consulting the specialist on his arrival, trimethoprim and sulfamethoxazole.'

'I don't really care.'

'These are extremely powerful drugs and the question of using the second combination is based on whether your body can take them.'

Dr Jose Serrano revelled in the verbiage of his job.

'That it has the strength to deal with the side effects. So—'

He was not giving up although his audience had.

'We need to boost your immune system. You are on—'

More consulting of the clipboard.

'Additional intravenous vitamin pushes and, yes, we are regulating immunoglobulin intake. I must explain.'

Lomita hadn't asked.

'There is a controversial aspect to the intensification of the treatment, as sometimes reduction is what can enable a boost to the system. But it can take about four days for that increase to appear. And—'

She didn't want to, or care to, acknowledge his fading and.

'You speak very good English.'

'It's my first language. Born in New Mexico. Moved to San Lucas after graduation.'

'I understand that this puts enormous pressure on my system to fight this off, I probably don't have the immune power, if that's the right way of putting it, to do that, then. Do I?'

'That we would have to see. You will be closely monitored, of course, but I have to tell you it is a tough infection and usually only gets those whose immune system has been compromised. We will wait for the specialist and we will consult and then we can start the appropriate course of medication. OK? That will be today, in about an hour.'

'I feel I have very little choice. But please don't worry about me, I am fine.'

She moved her head to the side, away from his focus and smiled to herself.

Jose Serrano went for the door and invited Ever to return; deferring as he did so to Lomita.

'Could you ask Manita to come in, my sweet.'

Lomita informed them of the severity of her condition. The details of the PCP infection, as a result of the weakening of her immune system due to the failure of the antiretrovral medication. It took her much less time than Dr Serrano. It wasn't a surprise to Manita, and she didn't register it as such. She had already anticipated a diagnosis that carried a fatal consequence.

Ever however could say nothing, he was physically incapable of speaking.

'You understand now, I think, don't you, my sweet.'

A world contained in one sentence.

Ever could only nod.

'About everything.'

Ever nodded again.

'Can you get in touch with Guillermo for me please; ask him to come in tomorrow. And now I do need to rest; Ever must go, it is too much for me, but please come tomorrow with Guillermo. He's my lawyer.'

She said by way of explanation to Ever.

'I need to rest now.'

The yeast-like fungus inhabited Lomita's lungs.

It continued to do its worst; although there is very little coughing with this condition, the sputum being too viscous to move, the weight loss, shortness of breath and night sweats debilitate at a rapid pace.

Ever asked Manita to drop him off in San José.

He said he could get a taxi back later. He went to the old part of the town, sat in the church, knelt and prayed to God for help – advice – just asking and thinking what to do. He prayed for Lomita. Talking to God or anybody who would listen out there. A lost soul who had always floated in and out of a body was now a soul floating in a mess.

The church inside was basic, but he presumed it was the same God, not a more basic version with less influence, that would be a blow. It was a Missionary Church painted creamy white with benches, a central aisle with brass chandeliers, three running up the centre hanging over the green and cream tiled floor. Quite ordinary, thought Ever, a spectacularly ordinary place to be praying about a very extraordinary event.

A once in a lifetime, life-ending event.

He felt the need for a drink and said his goodbye to God, wondering if it would be his last goodbye inside a church.

When he returned tomorrow would Lomita be alive? Should he go back?

What had he made Lomita do?

What had Lomita done to him?

He didn't care.

Have a diazepam.

He took a right out of the church and walked down the opposite side of the road to a bar called the Retro Bar. It was one flight up, hulked above a respectable, touristy restaurant called the Tropicana. The Retro Bar advertised television. Bare wood on the floors, and a little higher up on the benches: same wood, in fact, and the same wood on the table. Same tree?

He ordered guacamole, totopos, beer and tequila – Patrón Silver: taking him back to the comparatively innocent days at Gil Turner's before he met the woman who changed his world.

Televisions.

There were four televisions around the bar playing sports. He asked if one could be put to the news on an American channel; it was only him and five other people; this was not an outlandish request.

He was afforded his own television and sat watching the news on the Fox channel which was starting its predictable roll. All blonde, the women, all handsome with parted hair, the men, all Republican, and all aliens. Humiens.

He had to face the music, so to speak, beyond Lana Del Rey.

The main story was the assassination, as they called it, of one of the world's most celebrated art collectors, leaving the legacy of his gallery behind, having been tragically taken from this world in a motiveless killing, and so it went on. There were respects paid by the great and the questionable: his wife, tearful, ran an interview about the purposelessness of it all.

Even as someone who was once fixated on the death of this man, Ever couldn't disagree; there was a definite pointlessness to the event; once again he was covered in the slime of guilt, this time with the additional coating of being pursued.

Not by a pale blue hand, but by the world.

For justice.

But he hadn't been carrying a gun.

He had not been intending to kill Mr Lorken.

There were no leads, no witnesses, no motive. Ever found it difficult to analyse his feelings, watching this outpouring of grief and concern and recognition of injustice. He experimented with a few different emotional concepts.

Fuck him; sorry for him; laughter; comeuppance; hatred; compassion; relief; a strike for the people; sorry for the wife; for the family; joy; celebration; achievement; success.

The last two would have at one time carried the most connection for him, the appreciation of a job done, but now, he felt the foulnesss of having polluted himself with his thoughts, thoughts that had permeated into another person's brain.

A parasitical involvement.

That's what he had wanted.

Osmotic dependency.

And now. Now he had infested Lomita's brain and those parasites had multiplied to the point of total colonisation.

Ever felt at this moment in a bar in San José that he should not be alive.

He tried to fix on his obsessional hatred for the man who initiated his father's collapse toward death, for some respite at least; but felt only the guilt oozing through the cracks. He didn't attempt to wipe it away.

This was going to cause the death of Lomita: he would be the cause of the death of Lomita.

He downed the shot of tequila.

Eventually the police would make their way down here to check out where the paintings were ordered to be delivered by the woman who was the last to have lunch with Mr Lorken. Lomita Nairn.

He drank the Corona in one sustained hold of breath.

Days. Hours. Minutes. A lifetime of seconds.

He ordered a second round.

He thought of Clarissa and Jacob and envied their ignorance of the circumstance.

But he was completely unable to communicate in any form.

He wondered if he ever could, or would, again.

His night came to an early end.

He walked down to the taxi rank by the Pemex gas station and the start of the bridge across to the East Cape; he took a taxi to the waiting osprey. Thirty-five minutes later he was paying the man, walking towards the house with the intention of sitting by the ocean and having a final tequila for the night. The osprey whistled and flapped its wings; Ever attempted a whistle back but the dryness on his lips made it sound feeble and ungenerous. A sad musical call, a failed response to the clear warmth of the bird. He was dried up and at the end.

He sat on the terrace with his drink; his head fell back at an angle, facilitating his look at the stars.

The moonlight takes 1.3 seconds to reach us, some of the stars are still there and burning, but some died when Ancient Rome was in its heyday – their light is only reaching us now. Ever could never grasp this, his mind would not take it in; like infinity, it was a concept that defeated his already defeated brain.

But he had to count a hundred stars before he could go to bed.

A hundred stars a hundred times. It got worse the longer he sat. The stars would have a problem with this concept.

It works both ways.

Star fuckers.

Lomita was lying in bed in a state of fear.

Abject fear: she felt she wanted to take her own life although the disease inside her gave her the comfort that was not going to be necessary. That was going to be done for her: she was going to be taken care of.

God was looking after her, and preparing to welcome her. She stopped with the horror that what if he wasn't. What if he was not going to welcome her. She had committed a murder; a cold-blooded, unpremeditated act, but an impulsive act to save the life of another.

Her sweat was soaking the sheets, she reached to press the

bell for some water and to be made dry: the sweat was making her shiver.

She was cold.

She didn't press the bell.

She fell asleep, then woke and slept and woke. No pleasure in either state, she was always waiting for the knock on the door. How long would it be? How long would she be alive and have to wait?

She was starting to hallucinate in her fever.

A companion, a lover, wearing a white dress, walking down an aisle, with somebody wanting her through love, doing the things she had never done as a woman, as a human being, having a child, carrying it in her arms, breastfeeding. Loving with physical pleasure the body of Ever, enjoying all the things that happened to a man and a woman that she never enjoyed. The physical pleasure that only came to exist for a passing minute in an entire lifetime, once, in a passing minute, in a shower.

Sharing a life free of guilt about her past; just an emotional relaxed freedom. No abuse.

But never was she infused with any ingratitude or regret.

To her it was always the way it had been, the no-alternative never permitted a regret, because like Ever there was nothing to compare the journey of her soul with anything.

These were objective hallucinations: her in positions of life she had never been in.

It was like viewing another person on a screen.

A silver one.

This was her state as Ever walked into the room.

The next morning. He had changed into his newly acquired forty-eight pesos T-shirt from La Comer Supermarket in a dark shade of grey, depositing the Toyota F J in the parking lot, carrying a little bunch of red fishhook cactus flowers, picked from the roadside, with a smile creasing his face out of a love that he beamed into the room. Manita was already there; Guillermo was due in one hour. They sat passing the idle time of day with talk of weather and whales but nothing medical, nothing about her condition. No questions were asked: it was an inevitability.

Ever could smell that smell that he had only smelt once before: not her unique smell, but the one he had smelt on himself.

When he was near to dying, when he was fifteen.

Guillermo Gonzales, a long-time acquaintance, knocked and entered with a tentative respect.

Small and neatly combed, late fifties, besuited in an almost well-fitting suit in dark grey with a white shirt, and, rather ominously, a black tie.

Lomita spoke weakly and economically.

'This is simple and I want no contradictions or objections. I do not have the energy. Manita gets my house in Beverly Hills and fifty per cent of all my monies. The tax, Guillermo, you have to work that out, but we are well prepared in all that for Manita. Manita we have already taken care of. The only change is regarding Ever, who gets Casa Lomita and money to live and look after it. It is in my Mexican company's name so I do not anticipate a tax problem, as you are also a director of the company, Guillermo.

'That is all, and would you please execute this as my full and final will.

'Palm Springs would you sell and divide the revenue between the three of you, so we include Ever. That is a thank you Guillermo, for your work and loyalty to me, and

Guillermo, if there are any issues of any sort regarding Ever bring in adoption papers for me to sign, later, and I will adopt him as my son and therefore he will be my heir. If that makes life more straightforward. There are no other beneficiaries. And I would like to be cremated, but I guess burial is fine. What do I care? My death, as was my life, towards the end, is in Ever's hands.'

Ever sat silently in thought, questioning the adoption section. Acquiring a new mother was an interesting concept, but it complicated things for him: he would then have had two mothers and would have fucked them both.

That put him in the realm of being a true Motherfucker.

Lomita, breathing from just the top of her lungs, in shallow gasps, continued.

'And I would like to take full responsibility, this is going to shock two of you in the room, for the death of Ingmar Lorken. I would like, Guillermo, for you to arrange the police to come in so I can make a full confession. Do you think I should do that?'

There was an expected silence, no one confident as to who she was asking.

'The murder weapon is in the house. It is in my Fendi bag, Manita.'

Not a hair turned on Manita's head.

Guillermo had shut down into a frozen pose.

Still not a word was spoken; Lomita closed her eyes.

'Just for a little rest.'

She said.

Guillermo who had been typing all this on his laptop had long since stopped. He looked at the instrument as if it had told him to go fuck himself. He was pallid and red at the same time in different parts of his face. After a struggle that was apparent with the sweat that oozed out of his forehead, Guillermo spoke with a higher voice than before.

'I will need your full name and the address of your permanent residence for my paperwork, Señor Ever.'

It was duly offered; a thank you was returned.

'I need to find a printer.'

He said exiting with the relief of a sickly bowel movement.

The two of them sat.

Not a word was spoken until Guillermo returned with forms for Lomita to sign, which she duly did. There were then copies handed to both Manita and Ever.

They studied what she had dictated. It started with the name at the top of the document.

*I, Lomita Tracy Nairn, have dictated this as my full and final settlement.*

It went on but Ever was incapable of reading the rest: he reread the first sentence, then again, and then again.

The Tracy who had HIV/AIDS: this person would change his life.

It carried no concern for him, it was his ultimate gamble, the reason for his life.

The journey.

The arrival.

The final destination.

There was no panic, no nausea, no shaking, it had a beautiful justice, the most perfect eventuality.

This was his Tracy, it was now revealed, the weakness, the illness, the tiredness, the medication, the wasting, the wheelchair: it was all clear, beautifully, star-gazingly clear; as clear as the universe in its ultimate justice; the perfect sky; the rounding of all in life; the returning of the soul; the reason for existence.

She was his Tracy.

His very own.

She had led to him the clearest picture of life that he could ever have contemplated, imagined or constructed.

She had given him his reason for life, she had rounded and completed the circle.

The purpose and reason to stop it all.

The madness.

His destiny.

His fate.

Lomita spoke.

'Is everyone happy? Oh, and Guillermo, if there is a civil action brought against me after my death, I am sure you will be able to make any financial compensation that is pursued impossible with the complex structure of my offshore companies. What I am basically saying is, and it may seem ungracious, but I do not want a billionaire's wife, even though I killed her husband, benefitting in any way from my estate. Do I make myself clear?'

Lomita smiled in the face of the bluntness of her statement.

'Yes.'

Was all Guillermo could muster. No one else spoke a word; not even a thank you.

This seemed to have a finality, an end. A full stop.

For Ever it had produced a gurgle of laughter at the back of his throat, a result of excitement.

He swallowed hard.

Recognising a remnant of the gangster's moll.

Dr Serrano came in; again, following a knock.

He wanted to discuss her medication and state. This time, again, they were asked to leave but Lomita requested Ever to remain. The doctor started the way doctors do, with the assessment of a situation that was not good.

'Owing to your immune system being so debilitated with Acquired Immune Deficiency...'

Ever took in the medical diagnosis, but it was characterless, like hearing the weather. He had already felt the rain. He breathed deeply, this moment did not belong to him.

'Your blood count has revealed the CD4 cells are not picking up beyond the two hundred mark. Unfortunately the prognosis is therefore not positive; we are not having any luck combatting the fungus.'

It's not really about luck though is it doctor? It's not cards.

Ever, always critical of the medical profession, gave no voice to his thoughts, but that didn't stop them coming.

'You don't put luck into the equation in the world of medical science.'

This last part he apparently had voiced as the reply was coming from Dr Serrano.

'Well, shall we say the body has its own form of fortune and sometimes rallies to the cause with less medication than might have been felt to be necessary, but in this case the body has not had good fortune on its side. The unknown quantities, the unexpected and unexplained turns of nature have not been playing on our side. Does that clarify the position a little better?'

No not really, it was just annoying to introduce a sports analogy.

More thoughts: this time private.

'There is now the issue of oxygen starvation at tissue level that is becoming apparent, hypoxia; this will facilitate the eventuality of a high arterial carbon dioxide presence in your lungs.'

'I do not care now. And I do not understand or want to understand anyway.'

Said Lomita.

'I have one request please, to stop my medication, all of it, and leave me with Ever here, and I would like a bed for him to stay next to me.'

Dr Serrano did not look like he had an ounce of agreement in relation to her request. The bed maybe.

'It is your choice to not take medication, though it will be presented, and our advice of course will be to take it: and we will attempt for that to be enforced.'

Yeah, thought Ever, empathising with Lomita's request, what are you going to do, hold her nose?

The bed arrived and was put alongside Lomita's.

In anticipation that her death was imminent; that was unspoken but accepted. They could lie as they had done in their familiar position, side by side. His tiredness hit him in the middle of the afternoon, while she was in a permanent state of drifting in and out of a fevered sleep; his extended hand reached for hers and in silence, as one, they held each other's hands and drifted to meet in their sleep.

After a time that had not defined itself, there was a knock at the door, a knock that carried with it a knocking unlike other knocks and he knew it was the knock.

Ever said:

'Come in.'

The need for the command indicated it was not hospital staff and before him in his vulnerable lying position stood two members of what looked like the police.

Was this the result of Guillermo's summoning?

Ever scrambled like an egg to his feet, a mush. Lomita was not capable of taking in any of this, she attempted to awake from a deep sleep. The nurse who was hovering in the background came forward to continue the waking up process, propping up Lomita on some pillows.

Death waits for no man: neither do the police.

Lomita drooped her eyes open, smiled and explained unnecessarily to the gentlemen that she was not well.

They introduced themselves as members of the Baja California Police fugitive squad who had been contacted by the US Marshals Service and were acting as liaison officers for the LAPD.

This was not Guillermo's summoning.

They knew they were the wrong men for the job the minute they walked in: the second officer stood with an FX-05 assault rifle blushing, even through his weather-trashed skin, with the absurdity of the overkill.

They were following up on the person who was last seen with Mr Lorken, also the tracking of the paintings that were sent in that person's name to a warehouse in San José del Cabo.

Lomita Nairn was the name appropriate to both circumstances.

From the warehouse to Casa Lomita and Pedro's information had then led them to the hospital.

Dr Jose Serrano made his entrance, and in a protective manner toward his patient stood between the two officers and Lomita.

This was not a typical assignment for the Baja State Police, they normally dealt with fugitive criminals who had set themselves up in Baja California with their illegal monies and, after sometimes years of tracking, were then extradited by his team: his team of seven men.

Señor Delgado stood in silence for a time before coming out

with the admission that he was indeed the wrong man for the job.

*'Esta es la responsabilidad de la Policía Federal no de mis hombres. Perdón por molestarte.'*

He said to Dr Serrano, his native tongue letting him off the formal hook.

Confronted by a frail and dying old lady in a hospital bed, he was uncomfortable. There was a laugh followed by the statement.

*'Es como usar un martillo para quebrar un huevo.'*

'Hammer to crack an egg, I don't know if you have that saying?'

Señor Delgado dropped in his own translation, effortlessly and not without irony.

It had got a gurgle going in Lomita, just the slightest one.

Señor Delgado was now enjoying his audience; he continued in his humorous vein, saying he would spare her his customary opening line.

'Now you don't have the right to remain silent, you only have the right to tell me everything I ask you.'

Señor Delgado loved that one too, he relaxed onto his left leg in an on-the-spot swagger.

Lomita took control of the situation even though she was the weakest person in the room.

'I am Lomita Tracy Nairn,'

The second confirmation of her name.

'You might want to take this down. English or Spanish?'

Señor Delgado shrugged at the same time as a nod, not answering but conveying a confidence in either.

The confession came out of her, explaining time, place, exact details, and the only lie was in the way she got home.

'I shot Ingmar Lorken twice in the chest with my Beretta 70, the gun was in my bag which I pressed to his chest, I have told my housekeeper where to locate it. It is in my Fendi bag, a fake leopard skin print fur bag, and you will see the burn marks from the exiting bullets, shot at point blank range against his chest.'

She repeated herself as if she didn't want to forget.

'Two bullets. I left the car and walked home and neither my friend here nor Manita, my housekeeper, knew anything about it. I suggested we drive to my house here in Mexico. Nothing unusual, we do it often. The reason I killed him?'

It seemed both a question and a statement.

She stopped, breath was hard to come by and her eyes closed, she put out her hand to Ever, not wanting to suffer the indignity of death in front of these men, should it come, alone.

'I killed him because he was threatening to expose my past, and the illegalities of my past regarding—'

Again she stopped, this was a feeling, that Ever was so familiar with as a child, of not being able to access any air, just no breath. She continued.

'Some valuable pieces of art, obtained unlawfully, that I was in possession of through my late husband. Nobody else had any knowledge of my action. I was alone in my action.'

Again a blackout pause.

'Completely alone.'

Señor Delgado, who had been ready to leave had now been prompted into action, had started, on her command, to record the statement and at the same time was writing down on an old-fashioned pad. Lomita completed with the finality of—

'That is my statement.'

Señor Delgado, after several studious minutes, thanked her for her clarity. He would place the case in a more appropriate department, the bag and gun, fingerprinting and a DNA swab would all be requested. He then sincerely apologised for taking up her time, in acknowledgement of her physical condition.

He confirmed that a report, not by him, would be sent to the US authorities and then the Mexican courts would be presented with all the information, in Spanish, as was the legal requirement, and the extradition process would commence. The major concern being the death penalty in the state of California, as the Mexican courts were not in agreement with extradition that would lead to execution. Although that was usually only applicable to Mexican nationals, which he assumed she wasn't.

The last part was spoken with the hope of a question.

Her US citizenship was confirmed.

Señor Delgado stood to attention, lowered his head and turned to the door. Dr Serrano followed him and quietly explained that Lomita would not be leaving this hospital. Señor Delgado returned from the doorway with the concern of putting Lomita's mind at rest, stating that nothing would be happening in the near future. He left with the words,

'*Siento estar aquí en este momento, Señorita Nairn. Vaya con Dios.*'

Señor Delgado had the air of a revolutionary.

He crossed himself as he left the room.

'What a charming man.'

Was Lomita's response to the event and his departure.

Ever wondered if there was just a hint of sarcasm, a beautifully dignified go fuck yourself, an anarchism that went all the way back to the sixties. Pigs.

It had a nostalgia that Ever was capable of appreciating.

When they were once again on their own, Lomita whispered, more through lack of breath than secrecy,

'Did I do enough to keep you in the clear?'

She tried to laugh at the back of her throat but the viscosity of the phlegm prevented it, producing a gag. Ever prayed she wasn't going to throw up. He would have behaved appallingly in that circumstance.

A nurse came in, understandably flustered. Manita followed and Ever took it upon himself to ask her to call Guillermo. The nurse gave Lomita three cups containing her pills and she requested they be left on her bedside table. They were never going to see the back of her throat. She had already unplugged the IV medications that were pumping into her system; when the nurse reconnected them, she did the same thing.

She was dying.

Ever talked to the oblivious nurse in a confused panic, explaining the requirement for her to spend her last nights here in the hospital and for her burial, or cremation, as was in her will, to happen on Mexican soil. He was talking to the nurse, the wrong person; as he did so he realised she didn't understand but more depressingly was not interested.

That was Guillermo's job. To organise the cremation. Lomita did not want her body taken back to the United States. That was Guillermo's job: he would call Guillermo.

Then all was quiet, the night turned down the light and people after the panic seemed to fade away. Except for the Policía Federal guard who had turned up and stood outside the door. Yes, she was of course going to make a run for it.

He imagined Señor Delgado, on the end of a cigarillo, now passing the paperwork over to a more appropriate police department to start the process of getting a terminally ill seventy-six-year-old back to the United States to stand trial, and stripping someone of their skin for putting him in this position in the first place.

It seemed as though they would be left in peace.

But more medication was brought in and handed to Lomita who left it on her bedside table. It would take a while, extradition. Death, probably not so long.

Lomita's breathing was effortful and minimal, he lay holding her hand, the hypoxia had caused a reddening, the oxygen being deprived of its flow through the blood. Dry was her hand but still he felt the slightest of grip and he put all his being into his grip, with a gentleness; sensing and waiting for any change. The breathing became more audible, the effort was increasing in relation to the amount of air that was inhaled.

He moved onto his left elbow, still holding her hand, so that he could look at her face; she registered his move and he could see the effort around her eyes being made to open them, the muscles working with determination and the blue did appear, the smile came, she absorbed him with her eyes, sucking him into her soul.

'I love you Ever forever.'

'And I love you forever.'

He moved closer, his lips lay upon hers and they kissed with only the slightest movement in his mouth, her mouth registering a stillness apart from a minute smile, a corner to corner movement.

Her eyes closed, the smile stayed, the breathing was gone.

The last exhalation of the breath that passed around the body of Lomita was gifted back to the world.

Lomita had died.

Ever put his head next to hers and cried the silent cry that was for him alone. All alone now. There was no one to hear. He stayed with her until the dawn shone a perspective into his life, he used a cramped hand to reach for the button and called the nurse to explain the eventuality had happened.

There was nothing more.

Guillermo Gonzales was now her representative on earth.

And he had supported under oath her confession and put forward the request for the cremation to be performed here in Mexico. She was dead after all, but the concern from Guillermo was the possible requirement for her body to be returned to the United States. He had no real foundation for this but put it forward, Lomita's request being to remain in Mexico, they should take the matter into their own hands and do it fast. Did extradition pertain to the dead where a will was involved?

Lomita had to be cremated within forty-eight hours under Mexican law; Ever was in no state to be able to deal with anything; Manita had come in and prayed on her knees next to Lomita; in anticipation of the inevitable she had arrived with clothes to prepare Lomita for the coffin.

Manita insisted she take the responsibility for the preparation alone.

Guillermo Gonzales addressed Ever, now in his normal deeper voice.

'I have contacted the US Consular Agency in San José. I know the man there, we have a history, and I have the death certificate from the hospital. I have made copies and will send them to the relevant authorities of course. So Señor Ever—'

There was a pause, it had emotional content; he was preparing to advise about the cremation.

'La Paz is the nearest crematorium. About two hundred kilometres. You need a permit to transport a—'

He paused again, before the word.

'Corpse more than one hundred kilometres. But that is just – I don't know – I am sorry.'

He searched for a handkerchief. He didn't have one. Ever was transfixed and unintentionally unhelpful.

'I would ignore the ruling, anyway, and let's hope the crematorium will accommodate you. You know with money.'

He made the same gesture as Manita, of rubbing forefinger and thumb together, and again Ever felt his father wanted a roll-up.

Guillermo Gonzales turned on his heel with his head down, having thought about a handshake but something in him just couldn't do it. Ever stared at the back of the departing rumpled suit.

Ever looked down at the death certificate: Lomita's death was timed at 4.05am.

Ever had informed them of this fact. They had argued that it should be the time of medical confirmation. Ever, releasing his pain, screamed and screamed in anger until they acquiesced.

It was his own personal witching hour. 4.05am.

The digital image in red, by the bed, remained in clear imprint in his head.

Manita had decided to use the Pucci wrap for the occasion, birds and flowers – life.

Ever could not watch, nor was he invited, she took her to the bathroom to prepare her, the hypoxia had made the skin too delicate to bathe, but she was going to wash her hair to make her look like she knew she would want to look on her final entrance towards her exit.

A gurney was bought in and a nurse aided in the body transfer from bed to bathroom. Lomita had not worn the official hospital gown, in a bleached-out green, but her own nightdress in the palest of pinks and the softest of cottons.

Of course.

Ever intended to wait outside for the arrival of the coffin. He went back into the room. He wanted to return the gesture, to go in and help with the washing of her hair, physically recalling the sensation of her washing his hair. He went back into the room and heard the running water inside the bathroom, he stepped to the closed door, he couldn't do it and knew anyway he would not be welcome.

Then Ever heard a hair dryer. He left and walked outside.

The cremation would be private and have its own practicality.

There was no celebration in this death.

Two black-suited men arrived, from the funeral parlour, the coffin was not to be brought into the hospital but Lomita was be taken out on a gurney to be put into the coffin outside.

Ever directed the men and they returned pushing a covered-up body on a gurney to the waiting black hearse, then opened the massive black block to the rear of the other car, it was of course the Suburban. The first observation Ever had made about it was exactly that, that it looked like a big black hearse: now it was truly that. They removed the coffin from their vehicle. The wood was plain and unfinished, nothing grand; this is what you burn in Mexico.

Ever stood looking at Manita as the body was transferred from gurney to coffin, which was then lifted into its final position in the trunk of the Suburban.

'I will drive Señor Ever.'

Ever nodded in response and climbed into the black mass.

The cremation was to be at 5.00pm. That gave them four hours to do the two-and-a-half-hour journey. Cross over to

Todos Santos and take Highway 19 into La Paz. Kate would help them find the crematorium.

Ever, at the start of the journey, couldn't remember why they had hurried the process, he couldn't take in the events, he had forgotten the details of the why and the when in a brain blank. He forced himself to go through everything; the shock had removed him from the present.

On his own he would have been frozen. Then it started to piece together: the possible police intervention, the length of journey and extradition.

I am getting there, he consoled himself, I am catching up.

Manita pulled over and turned off the engine, just before the pay booths on the toll road.

'We have no priest.'

She just stopped, had seemed to give up. Ever was the first to turn his head and Manita's head mirrored his movement.

'We can do it, can't we?'

She said.

'We can do it ourselves. I will call the local priest, Francisco Modalo, we can do it on the beach.'

Ever took not a second to disagree, but wondered what law they would be breaking.

Slight in the light of murder one.

Lomita would be able to stay with them, be with them, be close, till the very very end.

Manita didn't hesitate, started up and U-turned round across four lanes and headed back to the East Cape. Before turning into Casa Lomita she went to visit Jeff Murphy, the man who had rescued Lomita after her accident. She explained their idea, to make a funeral pyre. 8.00pm that night was the set time. They pulled into the second courtyard in the house, the three of them rested in the car, two of them to reflect on their decision.

Ever couldn't deal with the coffin and went down in the late afternoon sun to the beach; the fire would not burn the bones through, he thought, not in a bonfire, not if it only turns a potato black. Ever could see his burnt black lump of potato: there would be a skull and the bones, even if the fire burnt for days.

A burial at sea.

Rocks in the coffin and a burial at sea. He ran back to the house, avoiding the rusty wreck, and two-stepped the stairs. Manita understood immediately and left with one word – 'Jeff.'

Ever returned to the beach, searching for rocks to pile up on the edge of the hard sand. He found two rocks and sat down on the sand.

What had he made Lomita do?

He turned to the west, hearing an outboard engine, and witnessed the arrival of Pedro with a boat. A GMC pickup truck driven by a shock of blond hair came along the hard sand carrying rocks and fishing nets and chains, and piles of wood, underneath which Ever could see the pale wood of the coffin. Jeff had needed no persuasion, the inadequacy of a fire had hit him too. A large tarpaulin would go around the body with chains to secure, then the rocks were to go inside the net with more chains wrapped around to make sure the body stayed down. It was then placed inside the coffin.

The body would be released from the coffin when out at sea.

Cumbersome and heavy but Jeff, an experienced fisherman in the East Cape winter, in construction in the Alaskan summer, was convinced it would work and secure Lomita Nairn to the depths of the ocean.

'Hey buddy. Take it easy.'

Seeing Ever's disturbance at the plan.

Strong handshake. No sentiment. All function.

'I'll do the tarp, you build the fire. It'll work. Trust me. Trust me.'

It was Jeff's mantra. He produced a bottle of port, offered it to Ever, who declined.

'Keeps me warm.'

He said, putting the neck to his lips.

Odd, thought Ever, in this climate.

'Trust me, trust me.'

Was chanted in Ever's direction intermittently to ease any doubts.

Jeff was the man to have on the front line. I've got your back would mean a lot. Ever turned away as the tarpaulin was being wrapped and the chains were secured around the body.

He returned to the house and sat in the main room.

Listening to Lana and staring at WELL, DID YOU EVER?

The fire would burn on the beach during the journey out to sea and, because of the weight, only Jeff, Manita and Ever would be in the boat. The priest, Francisco, would say his prayer and final blessing on land; Lomita wasn't even a Catholic, Ever thought, but this was Manita's wish. The ceremony should be kept low-key and essentially a secret.

The sun was going down and the sea, in reflected sunset, turned a vermilion red.

The Vermilion Sea.

The moon would be in its second night of fullness and a bottle of tequila was brought down in preparation to toast Lomita's departure. It was now a celebration. A private celebration of a private life. The priest started his prayers.

*Dios te salve, María;*
*llena eres de gracia;*
*el Señor es contigo;*
*bendita Tú eres entre todas las mujeres, y bendito es el fruto de Tui vientre, Jesús.*
*Santa Maria, Madre de Dios,*
*ruega por nosotros pecadores,*
*ahora y en la hora de nuestra muerte.*
*Amén.*

With the Ave Maria completed, the four of them struggled to lift the coffin into the boat, which was floating in the shallows, buffeted by the waves that rolled in. They waited for a lull in the set, the engine motored to keep the boat steady as possible. The coffin was lifted aboard.

They would wait for moonrise. Manita and Ever climbed on, drenched to the skin waist down. With practicality taking over from emotion the boat motored out to meet the whales, the priest making the sign of the cross in the distance lit up by the flames.

There was silence during the journey out, the boat travelled slowly, the moon started its rise over the horizon, a red-painted giant; they headed towards it to the east and a straight beam of moonlight shone directly across the boat. They followed its reflection on the water like a calling. The moment came for the drop of the body into the sea, having sailed beyond the current line. Jeff and Ever lifted the end of the coffin to the edge of the boat, the boat leaned with its weight, countered by Manita on the opposite side of the boat, the balance of the coffin continued to tilt the boat seaward, washing water onto the boat. The lid was removed, the coffin turned and the tarpaulin-covered body started its slide into the dark blue.

There was a sense of presence and the noise of some motors.

They, on the boat, turned around towards the shore and saw about twenty fishing boats, paddle boards and kayaks, with candles burning on the windless night and the boats lit up, keeping the distance of respect and paying a silent tribute. The illumination backdropped by the rocks and the beach, a silent moment of adoration for Lomita Tracy Nairn.

A silent goodbye.

The love sent, the body disappeared to join the Sea of Cortez and the humpback whales.

At the moment of submersion two whales breached within feet of the boat.

The world was in tune with a divine spirit and moved with it.

A trio of whales slapped their tails on the surface of the water, sending an echo rebounding back from the shore.

Ever looked back to the beach and saw the fire burning on the beach, beyond the floating tribute, beyond, to the lights of the house where he would live.

He marked the burial spot in his mind for all time. Lomita would forever be close, be seen, be there.

Manita crossed herself, the moment was over, and again in silence the boat made its way back to shore.

Goodbye.

Each of them whispered in their own way.

On their return Jeff deposited the coffin onto the fire and took his leave, climbing into his truck. The priest departed with a wave, leaving Manita and Ever, who with the intimacy of a hug sent Pedro on his way back up the twenty-four steps to the house, the boat having been beached to be dealt with on a new day.

Ever took a shot of tequila.

He lay back on the sand feeling the fire and watching the coffin burn, lose its shape and take away its association with death. He was feeling the moon and feeling the stars. He was a wound feeling everything. He didn't want to leave the beach; he didn't want to break the connection with the sea and where she was.

He pondered with his God on whether a person who had done what she had done, and what he had done in thought, could ever consider themselves not to be evil.

Then why was there a divinity at her death?

'Well done.'

He said to Manita when she wished him goodnight. After what had seemed an age sitting on the beach together. They had had a long journey of it all and he still had no idea what Manita felt about the whole thing. He supposed he would never know; their lives would no longer be forced together.

They would live apart having experienced so much together.

That night went with diazepam and tequila into a dream of haze, part spent on the beach and part in the bamboo rocker outside his room and then his phone rang.

Again.

A FaceTime ring.

A serious ring. It was Clarissa. It was the fourth time she had called him and he was unable to bring himself to pick up.

He couldn't deal with his reality now. He let it ring out.

He went to his bed, there was a letter addressed to him, placed on his pillow.

The handwriting he didn't recognise, it simply said Ever on the envelope.

*Ever, my sweet,*

*You are lost now, I know you are, I am in the easier place. I am gone although we will always meet whenever you want, I want you to know you have a wonderful heart that is punished by your head. Let it all go, follow your heart and all will be well. You won't be lost. This is short and true because I could go on and on about what you mean to me. But you know that, ask your heart.*

*See you soon, my sweet,*

*Lomita for Ever.*

There was nothing to say to that, other than a feeling that he had met who he was meant to meet. He felt worryingly bereft of emotion, wrung out, a little dry, if he was honest, which was what he intended to be now. Honest that is.

That his life, for the first time, had in it some kind of honesty and revelation: the finding out the truth about a secret, the opening, the cataract removal, the glasses on, the sight restored, the engine started, the road opened, the trains running, the race won, the exam finished, the bike ridden for the first time, balance, the learning to swim, the understanding of the alphabet, the first spoken word, the triumph of walking, the eating on your own, the co-ordination of limbs, the principle of life, the geometric understanding, the arithmetic formula, the tying of a shoelace. One foot in front of another, the forward process.

The handwriting was as elegant as the writer.

With a curl and an impracticality of line, not functional; not there for the reason of placing one letter after another; it showed a lifetime of trying and wanting to express; but being held back by behaviour, process, event, an effort to hold it all together.

An avalanche of movement on the page, waiting to be unleashed.

A thunderstorm that never rained.

Never got there.

Almost, but not quite.

It took a long time to get there but he imagined the phone call with Clarissa.

Version 1:

*Your four weeks are way up, what's going on?*

*I am going to quit my job. Are you both well?*

*What do you mean? How are you going to live?*

*I've sorted it, and you will always have money, I will send you an allowance. It's just that you can't be with me. You can't be with me. It is not good.*

*What the fuck are you talking about?*

*What I have just said is how it stands. I love you both, but I will finish with you both. Please understand, and in a few months maybe you can come and see me but right now you cannot.*

*Where the fuck are you?*

*Mexico.*

*That's great. That's just great. Ever, you are a shit.*

*So are you. I love Jacob and I will see him but you I'm not too bothered about.*

*Is that all you can say? Does it not go any deeper than that?*

*No, I don't think so, fuck you.*

Version 2:

*Where are you?*

*I'm in Mexico, it's really hard to explain but the man who bought my father's paintings and who basically fucked his life has been shot. You might have heard about it, Ingmar Lorken.*

*Yes I have, that's you, you're connected with that, what the hell have you been doing?*

*No, well yes, but the old lady I was staying with, she shot him.*

*What the fuck! Have you lost it again Ever? Have you? Oh, please God no.*

*Listen, I want you to come to the house she gave me.*

*She what, why, why would she do that, were you fucking her? Ever this is sick.*

Neither was what he wanted: both were ridiculous realities.

Ever couldn't even complete this conversation, as the details would take a lifetime to explain and a phone call would be impossible. Was his life with them? Follow your heart. Not your fucking crazy head.

He wanted Jacob, he wanted to see Clarissa. He wanted life with a family, he wanted children and love and sharing. Not isolation, like his parents, like Lomita. He wanted to belong to the human race for the first time. He was a human. With a thousand to one chance of a healthy life.

A thousand to one.

Good odds.

He'd take them.

But to be honest, he didn't really care. Because it had been well worth it.

And death had never appeared to be that tough an option.

A situation that hadn't been anticipated.

Was the press attention that the killer of Ingmar Lorken would receive.

Two days after the burial there were photographers taking pictures of the outside of Casa Lomita, an investigative reporter who asked for an interview regarding the final works that Lomita Nairn had bought from the man she killed.

The work of John Everett Millen.

Ever did not give an interview but became aware of the notoriety that his father's work had achieved.

Mr Chang, the hotel owner in San Diego, who had picked up the work for a pittance, now claimed, in an interview, that he had commissioned the work from this outstanding artist.

Ever had the idea of sending two paintings to an auction house in Los Angeles in the wake of the scandal. The association of horror and murder with an artist is the stuff of Caravaggio.

It was with a perversity that he asked Guillermo Gonzales, as an executor of the Nairn Estate, if he would be so kind as to call the newly opened Los Angeles branch of Christie's and ask if they would be interested in auctioning two paintings recently bought by the woman who shot Ingmar Lorken. That they were being sold as part of her estate.

Their response was typically dismissive at the opportunism of the inquiry.

Mr Gonzales left his contact information. Days later he

received an email, stating that they would be prepared to include them in their July catalogue. He thought, what the fuck. Divine justice?

*The Wave* and *The People on a Bright Day* were transported back to Los Angeles. Ever, of course, valued the paintings and put an excessive reserve of $250,000 on each painting.

He waited.

Clarissa and Jacob exited the terminal at San José del Cabo airport.

Small, neat, completed and then rebuilt after Hurricane Odile in 2014 decided she didn't like it.

Heat that hits, both of them standing with four suitcases, three for Clarissa and just the one for Jacob. They stood with a letter, Fedexed from Guillermo Gonzales containing an address and a request not to contact Ever in advance, he was in a bit of trouble. The inference was emotional turmoil.

They had no idea how long they would stay or whether they wanted to stay, just the arrival occupied their thoughts.

They had made the trip.

She was aware that the person who had killed Mr Lorken had also purchased John Everett Millen's work. She had called Ever but there was no response. But there had been no specific information about him on the news, just the passing reference to the last works this woman had purchased.

She supposed she was looking for a taxi but they were both fazed out, having flown in to Los Angeles and then taken a connecting Alaskan Airways flight down. They wandered to the rank and handed the address over to a short heavyset man with no English: they don't often get those rides so there was a mild, surprised joy at the prospect.

Big trip.

For all of them.

Ever was having an afternoon swim after a couple of calming beers at lunch.

He'd had a nap and was using the ocean to wake. To clear the dull head. He always swam out towards where Lomita had been buried, not that far, just in the direction, and always at the same distance out came the moment in his head, the decision to just carry on swimming to solve all the doubt and effort and worry and anger that he had towards the world and himself.

His father's ashes had ended up in the sea and Lomita was in the sea; it seemed an understandable place to be.

He supposed that every day, on his swim, he was contemplating the simplicity that suicide would bring. When would the balance swing, was it just a question of time, before he would keep swimming, the weakness would take over, three times going under, life flashing before your eyes, who knows that one? And then, problem solved.

The puzzle of it all.

This was a routine; he never quite understood what it was that made him turn around and return to the shore. Maybe one day he would have the courage, no it wasn't courage it would be what, weakness, no, not a direct opposite, it would be what, it would be being alone. That's what would do it for him.

Being on his own forevermore, having lost the confidence in his ability to form, construct a life with someone.

He let the wave bring him onto the sand and he stumbled, he was on all fours, clumsily returning to the beach. The adoring sun dried his back in seconds and allowed the heat to warm him after the wet had gone. The sun had moved to the west, it was behind him as he walked past the jagged rusted remains of the shipwreck and it followed him up the twenty-four steps to the house where he hosed the sand off his feet and left the rest of his body salt-covered. Standing with the hose, experiencing his daily realisation that he was doing this action, again, that he was still here.

That he had swum back.

This time.

Pedro opened the smile of a front door and ushered two people inside.

They stood on the marble floor looking towards the ocean and the man who had just slid back the glass door to make his entrance. There was not a beat to count in the moment before the word bounced around the room.

'Dada!'

Jacob ran, in bumpy, wobbly fashion, towards his father, who picked up his bundle of joy and hugged him to the salt on his body. There had been no time between them, it was all carrying on as if there had been no gap, no space, no physical separation. It was completely normal.

Clarissa stood motionless and could understand nothing.

She took in the world around her and it was beyond a word, a question, there was nothing she could say. Hello even refused to come out of her mouth. She stood, Pedro came in for the second time to complete the four-bag line-up inside the door; he understood the moment had stopped in time and that it was his moment to leave.

Clarissa would be waiting for an explanation and it would take a long time. Time to explain and time to understand, Ever sensed all this from Clarissa while she stood, emotionally in collapse at the door, which smiled behind her.

But they would have a long time.

Ever thought, and, in his own moment, he hoped it would be a lifetime. Outside, the osprey's whistled notes could just be heard, but only recognised by Ever. The welcome was just beginning.

'Water, Dada? Please? Carry me. Now.'

Clarissa, Jacob and Ever in the same room; but all in a different place.

# *Chapter Thirty-six*

The epilogue or the afterword.

The pale blue hand finally has reason for Ever.

It has become an understandable reality to Ever after all these years.

While he sleeps, the pale blue hand, now welcomed, comes to guide his astral body, shrouding the soul, into a higher realm.

There on the astral plane, Ever and Lomita come together in a non-corporeal world where time and space are of no consequence, in endless process.

Lomita, a true ethereal beauty, united with Ever through the depth of their love, his soul now filled with contentment.

In death there is no judgement.

At last he has become a soulful human being.

Ever's journey through life will always hold confusion.

But now, at least, he is not alone, his soul travels with him.

The final word.

John Everett Millen's paintings, *The Wave* and *The People on a Bright Day,* sold at Christie's for $450,000 and $500,000 respectively.

Ever's father's work was finally celebrated. The money was put into Jacob's bank account.

Minus twenty per cent, of course, transportation fees and a little bit of commission for Señor Gonzales.

There is one particular thing that is nothing whatsoever, in any way shape or form like any other, there is nothing like some fame.

There is nothing you can name that is anything like some fame.

THE END

Unbound is the world's first crowdfunding publisher, established in 2011.

We believe that wonderful things can happen when you clear a path for people who share a passion. That's why we've built a platform that brings together readers and authors to crowdfund books they believe in – and give fresh ideas that don't fit the traditional mould the chance they deserve.

This book is in your hands because readers made it possible. Everyone who pledged their support is listed at the front of the book and below. Join them by visiting unbound.com and supporting a book today.

Charlie Beaumont
Ali Burns
GMark Cole
Carlo Navato
Siobhan Taylor
Laura Thompson
Sheila Tindal
Andrew Weaver